Also by Tod Wodicka

All Shall Be Well; and All Shall Be Well; and
All Manner of Things Shall Be Well

The Household Spirit

The Household Spirit

Tod Wodicka

Pantheon Books

NEW YORK

All rights reserved. Published in the United States by Pantheon Books, a division of Random House LLC, New York, and in Canada by Random House of Canada Limited, Toronto, Penguin Random House companies.

Pantheon Books and colophon are registered trademarks of Random House LLC.

Library of Congress Cataloging-in-Publication Data
Wodicka, Tod, [date]
The household spirit / Tod Wodicka.
pages ; cm
ISBN 978-0-307-37705-0 (hardcover : acid-free paper). ISBN 978-1-101-87029-7 (eBook).
1. Introverts—Fiction.   2. Friendship—Fiction.   I. Title.
PS3623.O43H68 2015   813'.6—dc23   2014018990

www.pantheonbooks.com

Jacket images: (face) Mercy, private collection, © Look and Learn/ Bridgeman Images; (fern) bilwissedition/akg-images
Jacket design by Joan Wong

Printed in the United States of America

First Edition

2 4 6 8 9 7 5 3 1

For Charly

During sleep we enter a strange, mysterious realm which science has thus far not explored. Beyond the border-line of slumber the investigator may not pass with his common-sense rule and test. Sleep with softest touch locks all the gates of our physical senses and lulls to rest the conscious will—the disciplinarian of our waking thoughts. Then the spirit wrenches itself free from the sinewy arms of reason and like a winged courser spurns the firm green earth and speeds away upon wind and cloud, leaving neither trace nor footprint by which science may track its flight and bring us knowledge of the distant, shadowy country that we nightly visit. When we come back from the dream-realm, we can give no reasonable report of what we met there. But once across the border, we feel at home as if we had always lived there and had never made any excursions into this rational daylight world.

—Helen Keller, *The World I Live In*

Don't go to sleep, so many people die there.

—Mark Twain

part one

———————

the Creep

1
—

Ever since Howie Jeffries could remember, people had been asking him if anything was wrong. It was his face, mostly. The last face on earth. First, as a small boy, he assumed that something must be wrong and this frightened him. Later, realizing that maybe he himself was wrong, Howie would say that he guessed he was just having a bad day. Weeks, months, then years of bad days. Finally, he gave up and when called to account for his woeful demeanor, merely shrugged. "Cheer up," people told him, "it'll never happen."

But Howie's face was always happening. Even now, at fifty. There, he thought, staring into the bathroom mirror. Still happening.

He washed his hands.

The last face on earth was how his ex-wife had once described the gaunt, arboreal lonesomeness of his features. "I love it to bits," she assured him. Probably he was supposed to be alone.

Howie dried his hands.

This was still his family's house in the same way a story still belongs to its characters even if most of them are dead by the end. Howie Jeffries's wife and his daughter were not dead, they just lived elsewhere and with other people. Sometimes, when falling asleep, he still heard the clattering, indigestive sounds the kitchen made when his wife cooked. Or, getting dressed, he'd recall how his wife rolled his socks into tight, tiny animals. Open the sock drawer and there they were, waiting. Howie once had a drawer devoted entirely to socks. He'd remember their wall calendar, how they'd present themselves before it, peer into it together, his wife writing in her red and green and black markers, commanding Howie to watch—*participate*—as she explained the future. Generally speaking, the future was Howie's fault.

She left him for a man who knew how to talk about her feelings and who, moreover, was named Timmy, not Tim or Timothy. Timmy had introduced notions like potential. Timmy wasn't content to sit and grow old and potentially die of freaking boredom night after night, now was he? Timmy was knowledgeable about things that happened in other languages. He was a painter of houses, landscapes. He was eight years younger than Howie and his wife.

The divorce was a swift, anesthetized procedure. Three lawyers, his and hers. His wife had a new signature to go along with her new dress, her bright, naked fingers. Signing here and here and, right, good, and just there too, please. OK. Howie writing his name slowly, meticulously, as if there might yet be a reprieve, an *on second thought,* going so far as to include his neglected middle name for those three extra marital seconds. Victor. His great-grandfather's name, his uncle's too, stalling there between the Howard and the Jeffries. VICTOR.

Howie had been thirty, his daughter, nearly five. Twenty years later and none of them had died, not of freaking boredom or otherwise. They were all OK now.

Howie and his daughter, were friends on the internet computer. He loved Harriet but was unsure as to whether he knew her, and he wondered if this made a difference. But good for her, he often thought, unable to attach any weight to the locution as he slid down through Harri's Facebook life in New York City. Good for you. Sounding, he knew, not unlike his own father and the bloodless there-you-go's the old man reserved for the people who had disappointed him most.

Because, really, why impose? Why say anything at all?

Howie brushed his teeth. Four in the morning and he'd forgotten the toothpaste again. He smiled as if someone were standing behind him, a woman in the mirror, a wife who appreciated this small, endearing hiccup in his hygienic routine. Howie, you goofball. Her arms around his waist.

Some years ago at the GE company picnic, Howie had been drinking beer with his co-workers and their spouses, one of whom had been holding a little boy. Ever attuned to such things, Howie had tried to minimize his face. The boy stared. Nothing wrong, Howie wanted to explain. It's just me. This is what I look like. Then someone had said something funny and Howie, trying not to laugh, couldn't help smiling. The kid, a toddler, had recoiled as if slapped. Everyone pretended to get a kick out of this, even Howie. Later, the boy's mother pulled Howie aside. "*Kids*," she said. "Howie, sweetie, I'm so embarrassed. I guess your smile just rattled him." Like this was an obvious thing, something long accepted, past the point of discussion. Howie Jeffries had a rattling smile.

Still, small children generally liked him, dogs and elderly women, too. Folks with disabilities. His daughter once said that he had a distinguished face. Try and remember that. But just the fact that Harri had told him this out of the blue, as if in conclusion to some long-running internal debate—*yeah, distinguished, actually*—well, why even say it?

Howie flossed.

He was not, he knew, an unhappy man. What had he ever done with these hands that he should be ashamed of? Things needed doing, you do them. You treat folks like you expect to be treated back. Howie had never found a good or bad reason to believe in God and believed only that things were getting too noisy and that most people were insane.

He had only just returned from his night shift at the General Electric Waste Water Treatment Plant in Schenectady, New York. He enjoyed the forty-five-minute commute. The road at night was where Howie made the most sense to himself. In fact, had he put more stock in self-determination or the pursuit of happiness, he surely would have been a long-haul truck driver. Instead, he'd been with GE for exactly thirty years, something he knew only because his co-workers had recently started teasing him with the possibility of an anniversary party.

"Just when you least expect it," Steve Dube had said. "Jeffries, you do know we're going to party the shit out of you this time, right? Thirty years, champ. Shit is for real. This time we mean it."

They didn't, of course. The guys just really liked threatening Howie with large social events. Each year as his birthday approached, he'd be put on warning. Shit could be lurking behind any door. Threatening to celebrate Howie was their way of celebrating Howie. There were worse things, he supposed, than being misidentified as someone who might be killed by a surprise party.

Howie had been working two weeks of day shifts followed by two weeks of night shifts for thirty years. His ex-wife had insisted that this was part of his problem, by which she meant her problem with him. The way he willfully curled his life around a different clock than everyone else.

Howie recoiled at the intimacy of his own blood. He'd gotten carried away with the flossing again.

Howie spit.

Howie turned off the bathroom light but continued to stand at the sink. Darkness emboldened the sound of his breathing, his heart. Would you listen to that. Crickets and a far-off dog. Dogs? Owls.

Howie approached the bathroom window. He allowed his eyes time to adjust. The treetops moved as if the air had slowed and thickened into water. Pines, mostly, but some elm. There was no moon. Then there was: hard, white, and rolling from behind a bank of silver clouds. He focused on his neighbor's house, its weak glow. Beyond this, the dark.

And he saw her. She was moving along the edge of the woods like you might pace beside a pool you're not quite ready to jump into.

Then, just when Howie began to think that maybe she wouldn't tonight, she did. She was gone, into the forest, leaving only the slightest splash of night behind her. That and Howie, his face against the bathroom window.

Howie Jeffries and his only neighbor, Emily Phane, lived way out on Route 29, a twisted old country road that followed the Kayaderosseras Creek. (*Kayaderosseras* was an Iroquois word, but it might as well have been a hieroglyph, since, when written in cursive, the word resembled the squiggle of the actual creek as represented on most maps of the county.) Howie's and Emily's houses were twins. Once identical, now fraternal. Both had been built in 1860 as dormitories for immigrant paper mill workers, some of whose names you could still find carved, umlauts and all, onto doors and the inside of cupboards. Howie's place still had its original wood siding, but Emily's was aluminum now, painted yellow, as if it were getting ready to go for a jog.

He still expected to come home one day and find it gone. What else had managed to stick around on Route 29? Not a whole lot. The paper mills had fallen into ruin decades before Howie was born and most of the colonial farmhouses had disappeared, too, their fields rented out for billboard space. Huge spotlighted headstones to fast food, Lutheranism, and debt management, apparently aimed at the truck drivers whose ceaseless attentions sometimes seemed like the only thing keeping Route 29 from slithering off into the hills. For miles and miles, Howie and Emily were it.

He had known Emily since she was a baby, and though they'd hardly ever spoken, the young woman was dear to him. He considered himself her friend. She was twenty-four, the same age as Howie's daughter. Harriet and Emily had gone to different schools but were friendly, or at least Howie had once liked to think that they were. Harri had been a wary, angry teenager. Perhaps she was angry still, or perhaps it wasn't anger anymore or never had been, what did Howie know? Their relationship was exactly what it was supposed to be. You take a certain solace in rejection, in their independence. Howie assumed that she loved him as he had truly loved his own father, a man he never managed to feel entirely whole around. Why force a thing?

Time he thought about hitting the hay. Leave the bathroom window, leave Emily Phane. But he couldn't, knew he wouldn't, and his waiting continued. He yawned.

Fool.

Because Howie couldn't go to sleep until he saw her safely back inside her own house or at least out of the forest. There: she was on her knees, Howie saw her. Right there. She was a shape near the fuzziest edge of woods, not so far from where she'd entered a good few minutes back. Emily was digging. He'd been watching her do this and activities very much like this for a month or so now. Far as he could tell, she was uprooting a shrub. He'd seen her with saplings, pussy willows, adolescent trees, wild flowers, and, once, with what looked like wheat, an armful of wheat, but was probably only a heap of mown lawn or twigs or corn.

Emily stood.

He wished she'd just go inside now and be normal. We both need our sleep.

He lost her again.

Refocus.

There. She had circled around the dark side of the shrub and was lifting it, holding it before her like some fresh kill or offering. Finally, she began to walk toward her house, shrubbery cradled in her arms. The closer she got to her house the clearer Howie could see her face, a bubble approaching the surface of a pond: round, paler than usual.

Emily stopped; she'd heard him. She heard. Howie knew that she had, though he hadn't made a noise.

Crap.

He was the only fellow about, the only man for miles, so of course she could hear him. Though that didn't make one lick of sense.

Yet there it was. Emily standing in her backyard, in the middle of her moon-crisped lawn, staring straight up at Howie, a man she shouldn't under any circumstances have been able to see.

Howie got into bed. He placed his *Fishing the Adirondacks* book on his lap, more an anchor to his worries than something he had any intention of rereading. It was a good, heavy friend.

Emily Phane was in trouble.

What more proof did he need exactly? What was Howie waiting for?

She hadn't been the same since her grandfather died. But this was more than that now, wasn't it?

Howie had assumed that after the funeral she would return to college in Boston, but months became a year, then almost another year and, far as Howie could tell, she barely left the house for groceries now. First there had been visitors, a few, probably old friends from Queens Falls High, but they'd long since stopped coming, and Howie had begun to see less and less of Emily herself, especially during the day. Besides her grandfather, she'd had no family that he knew of. Was she eating the underbrush? Was she addicted to illegal drugs? No, no, no—well, maybe? It just didn't seem like something Emily would do, and even if she was doing illegal drugs, from where exactly would she be procuring the stuff? You don't forage for crack cocaine among the pines at night. No. On TV, Howie knew, you purchased illegal drugs from black children in the ghetto.

Howie looked at photographs of fish. *Land Locked Atlantic Salmon. Trout. Perch. Smallmouth Bass. Largemouth Bass. Northern Pike . . .*

Could blacks be sending Emily drugs by mail?

Howie shut the book.

They were a community, the two of them. Emily and Howie alone on Route 29. This was something that had to be taken seriously. You took care of your own.

But how? He couldn't go lumbering across the lawn, Howie to

the rescue. Not in the dark. Not with that face. Then there was the fact that he'd hardly said boo to her in the nearly twenty-five years she'd lived next door. Twenty-five years. There's that, Howie, isn't there? You going to ruin that, you really want to tear your safe and ordered community apart by finally stepping out from behind how you seem—and how exactly do you think you *do* seem to this young woman? Who are you to her?

Howie got out of bed and went back to the bathroom. He drank a glass of water. He had long ago adjusted his life in order to protect himself and others from how he seemed. Sure, most people were insane. But Emily? There was no longer any question: He would find out what was wrong. He would help. If not him, then who?

Whom?

Howie looked at himself in the mirror and rattled. Distinguished, huh? But it wasn't just his face. He examined it: You're fifty years old and you gonna blame all your problems on *that*?

Howie returned to bed.

Cheer up, he thought. It might never happen. He stared at the crystal chandelier his ex-wife had inherited from her grandmother's dining room and, in her grief, insisted on hanging in their bedroom above the bed. Then insisted, also in her grief, on leaving it behind because, *Gran always liked you.* It was like having the old woman's skeleton knocking about up there. Gran hadn't liked anyone. The flame-shaped bulbs had extinguished themselves some fifteen years earlier, but OK. Howie let it alone. It represented a kind of stability to him now. Everyone needs something in his life that he can safely despise.

He clicked off the bedside lamp.

Everyone knew. The book on his lap knew. His father had made no bones about knowing. His fishing buddies and the guys at work and their happy families and even this room, his ex-wife's room, which would never warm to him: they all knew and it was OK. Howie Jeffries was a man distorted by timidity. Howie was only shy.

He clicked the lamp back on.

But you take care of your own. You got to. What are you if you can't take care of your own? Howie opened his book and turned the pages, kept turning, turning, and not for the first time wished himself beneath the surface with all the wise, thoughtless fish.

2

In the beginning, Howie's wife liked to pretend that Peter and Gillian Phane were cute. Living next door to them was going to be like having their very own pet grandparents.

"They don't want to know us," Howie said. "Take my word."

"They don't want to know us, Howard, because they don't know us yet."

Gillian, in particular, made Howie uneasy. She resembled a bat without looking anything like an actual bat. He watched her toil daily in a garden from which she never picked a single vegetable.

"She's just a little old lady, Howard. C'mon, *get*." Howie's wife shooed him away from the window. "And since when exactly are you this expert on vegetables?"

Toil was exactly the word you'd use to describe it, too. Gillian sacrificing herself and her vegetables to some higher good that was supposed to feel bad. He decided that she was growing them vindictively, raising them for the pleasure of getting to watch them rot. She had a way of stabbing dirt.

If Howie waved, she waved back. Might even smile. But he thought that she made a point of waving or smiling far to the left or right of where he was actually standing, as if that's where he *ought* to be, way over there engaged in something more productive, like digging a hole to die in. Gillian's husband, Peter, was retired but it was impossible to guess from what. From everything. Howie thought that he understood the man's reticence.

"I don't care, Howard, I'm going to bring them brownies."

"I wouldn't."

Exactly. His wife wouldn't have wanted to either if Howie hadn't been so vocal about leaving well enough alone. This was twenty-seven years ago, that first summer on Route 29. Howie began to worry that her efforts weren't directed at the Phanes so much as they were a sideways assault on her new husband, that baked inside his wife's campaign of cookies and casseroles and unaccepted luncheon invitations was a slowly congealing reproach and rejection of his nature. Howie's shy, comfortable disengagement. It was like they were living next door to a premonition. She had to prove to herself that the Phanes were all right so that someday she and Howie would be all right, too.

The Jeffrieses had moved to Route 29, a fifteen-minute drive from the relative civilization of Queens Falls, New York, because it was the biggest house they could afford. It was never meant to be permanent; it was a first home, a starter, which they hoped to move at a profit, what with the renovations Howie had begun and the fact that it really was a gorgeous old heap. It had character, as they say. Howie had saved up from his first few years at GE, and his wife had just graduated from SUNY Albany and taken a position teaching earth science at Queens Falls Middle School. They'd been sweethearts since Mr. Roske's seventh-grade homeroom in that very same school, only two rooms over from her very own classroom. That was part of it, probably. It felt to his wife as if she'd both never left school and already retired.

It wasn't a street or a road, she'd complain. It was a *route*. Normal people didn't live on routes, they drove through them on their way to normal streets named after people or places or trees, to neighborhoods with normal neighbors who, unlike her husband and these Phanes, appreciated small talk and luncheons and, like, basic human decency? For freaking starters. The Phanes were pets like mongooses are pets, like ghosts or ferrets or bacteria are pets.

Some friends of theirs hadn't even finished college yet and here they were, Howie and his wife, already in their dotage, living way up the ass end of nowhere watching a horror-movie version of their future unfold next door. What had happened and why had it happened so quickly?

The closest she got to winning over the Phanes was a typewritten note that Peter Phane affixed to the Jeffrieses' front screen door.

Thank you for the thoughtful pastries, it began.

The note went on to explain that Mrs. Phane hadn't been able to enjoy them because of a preexisting condition. They would not be requiring any more. It didn't exactly welcome the Jeffrieses to the neighborhood because Route 29 wasn't exactly a neighborhood, but it was enough for Howie's wife. The victory all the more sweet for being both comical—from then on, Rice Krispies Treats were *thoughtful pastries*—and for not in any way leading to further interaction with the starchy, unbearable pair next door. Clearly, the Phanes weren't like them at all. One of them had a condition.

Peter and Gillian Phane had probably always been too old to have kids. Their house just didn't seem to be one that had ever bent itself to anything so base as the noise or needs of child rearing. It was too dry. Nothing was missing, nothing had ever escaped. Condition or no, it was difficult to imagine either of them preexisting.

They never had visitors, mistaken or otherwise. NO SOLICITORS was written larger than PHANE on their utilitarian tin mailbox. NO FRIENDS OR FAMILY, it should have read. NO HOPE. NO POINT WHATSOEVER.

However, Howie's wife learned from QF Middle School records that they'd had one child, a daughter, Nancy, apparently a talented singer who hadn't been seen in decades. Rumor was she'd gone out west, possibly New Mexico.

Nancy returned to Route 29 a month before Howie's daughter, Harriet, was born. Howie and his wife knew it was her, their lost Phane, almost as soon as Nancy pulled her small, heavily bumper-stickered Oldsmobile into the driveway. It wasn't only the New Mexican plates. The woman was a mess. They'd long since decided that if Nancy Phane still existed, she would have to be a total mess.

"There's just no way," Howie had said, watching from the window.

His wife agreed. "Impossible!"

But they knew and they were thrilled. Nancy was heavily set, probably in her early forties. She matched her car's tantrum of bumper stickers with her own tattoos. The skin on her arms looked as if it had been wrapped in the pages of a comic book. Her boots were black, her hair was black. Everything on her face was pierced, punctuated by metallic commas, periods, quotation marks: a word-less, jumbled grammar of egregious self-expression that Howie didn't like one bit. But she was pretty. Howie's wife thought so, anyway. Sassy. Cute under all that. Howie, who feared extroverts, wasn't so sure.

"That's their *kid*?" Howie's wife rubbed her unborn belly. *That can happen to someone's kid?*

There was something mysterious and proprietary in the way Nancy waited, smoking, standing next to her car and staring down the old house. It was as if the house had finally come to her. Big whoop, you found me. Here I am. So fucking *what*?

Gillian Phane emerged. Howie thought that the old woman was laughing. She was not laughing. Three months later they would both be dead, mother and daughter, but at the time it was refresh-ing, almost silly, watching Gillian swatting at the air, trying to hoot her daughter back into the car or the woods, the Kayaderosseras, New Mexico, however far the momentum of her displeasure would extend. Everything made more complex by the revelation that Nancy wasn't merely overweight.

"Howard, oh my God. She's not." Gasp. "She *is*."

The way she held her middle while trying to calm her mother. Gillian saw it, too. And promptly marched herself back inside.

Minutes later, Peter Phane appeared on the driveway with a glass of milk. His daughter laughed at it, or him, and then he laughed too. But she accepted the milk, slowly drank, and in handing the empty glass back to her father, began to sob. Peter placed the glass on the roof of the car and helped his daughter up the driveway, into their house.

The glass would stay atop the Oldsmobile for four days. "It's still there," Howie's wife said. "Howie, I'm serious, do you think I should go over and say something?"

"About what?"

"I don't like it."

"OK."

"No, it is not OK!"

Then, on the evening of the fourth day, Howie's wife got up in the middle of Johnny Carson, went upstairs, took a shower, and returned fully dressed. Howie's heart flinched; he was instantly standing, grinning. The baby was officially due in a few weeks, but they were told to be ready for anything. "It's time?"

"No, Howard," she said. She laughed. Then her face closed. It was nearly midnight. "I'm going for a walk," she said.

Howie's wife had never once gone for a walk during the *day*.

But first she went to the window. The lights were off at the Phane house. "Honey?" Howie said.

"It's none of your business," she snapped. She exited through the front door.

Howie watched her stroll down their driveway—she was *strolling*, even with her pregnancy—turn left on Route 29, then another left directly up Peter and Gillian Phane's driveway. She removed the empty glass from the top of Nancy's car. She carried it to the Phanes' front porch, left it there, paused, and turned back the way she came. Driveway, Route 29, driveway. There was something in the fact that she hadn't simply walked across the lawn.

Though his instinct was to sit this one out in the kitchen, Howie waited for her at the door. She entered, oddly startled to see her husband.

"There," she said.

"It's OK," Howie told her. "You're just tired."

"*You're* tired," she said.

Six days after becoming parents again, Peter and Gillian Phane were grandparents. Howie rarely saw Nancy with her baby. Mostly, he saw her alone, sitting in a lawn chair on the driveway, never on the lawn, right next to her getaway car, that Oldsmobile, smoking and reading magazines. She rarely went into the backyard. The backyard was Gillianland. From Howie's house, from the upstairs bathroom window, you could watch the goings on in the Phanes' back- and front yards simultaneously. Sometimes their movements would mimic each other: when one sat, the other sat. If Gillian began a spat of furious gardening, Nancy would become agitated and start pacing, absently plucking at shrubbery, bark, the heads of flowers. It was uncanny. If Gillian went to the corner of their property where a sharp slice of the Kayaderosseras Creek nearly elbowed through the forest and onto their lawn, Nancy would be standing right up against the shore of Route 29, staring down into it.

Their obituaries, some three months later, left few clues. Not to what Gillian and Nancy's problems had been, or who the infant's father was. There was a twenty-year hole in Nancy's life. She had a degree in music and theater from a college in Philadelphia. She had been promising. The obituary said she had lived most of her adult life in California, despite the New Mexican Oldsmobile that killed her. She had been loved, survived by a father, Peter, and a daughter, Emily Margaret Phane. This is the way in which Howie and his wife learned the child's name.

The accompanying photograph of Nancy was from the Queens Falls High yearbook, the car crash enabling her to revert to who she was before she became what she would be, returning the promising Nancy back from wherever the troubled, tattooed woman had stashed her away. The only new information in Gillian's obituary was that she had grown up in New York City, in Queens, and that her maiden name had been Wolf.

Harriet was born a week and a day after Howie's wife removed the empty glass from Nancy's Oldsmobile.

Fatherhood was confounding. It felt like Howie had been debunked. Found out. The *preexisting* him, that old condition of Howie Jeffries he'd worked out for himself? Gone. He understood happiness, he thought, suddenly, and this left him exposed and giddy in a way that ashamed him. Was this normal? Didn't feel normal. But it felt good, trying and failing to subsume the swooning fear he'd get while holding his little Harri. ("Howard, stop calling her that this instant!" Laughing. "I'm warning you!") Her impossible toes. Her eyes were just about the cleanest things that he had ever seen.

In the beginning, Howie would rather have his daughter screaming than unconscious. He didn't trust sleep. "Let's wake her up," he'd suggest.

"Shhhh." The slow, mammal weirdness of motherhood. Whispering: "Silly, silly. You have got to be kidding me. Your silly daddy has simply got to be kidding me."

"But it's the middle of the afternoon."

"Howard, she's a *baby*." A finger to Howie's lips. "Shhhh."

Mostly, his wife seemed tired, and she hardened. It soon became important for her to pretend that it was no big deal and that nothing had changed, but this stance required a lot of energy and changed her. She became flippant, almost blowzy. She snorted instead of laughed; she swore more, abstracting objects as *shit* and swapping *freaking* for *fucking* in a way that turned Howie's stomach. She began playing the Top 40 at all hours and drinking through dinners she stopped apologizing for the meagerness of. Meatloaf again? *Meatloaf forever.* Howie sometimes caught her looking at Harriet in the same way she looked at the ingredients of a meal she'd laid out but suddenly didn't feel like preparing.

But there was contentment, too. In islands that Howie learned to appreciate and maneuver, hopping from one to another, trying not to think about how small they were getting, and rare, or how choppy the sea that surrounded them had become. Tuesday was good, the following Wednesday OK, then what about the way he awoke the following Friday to find his wife's hand on his penis, her lips at his neck? In such a manner did Howie start stringing together the narrative of his new, archipelagoed life. His wife suddenly present again, coming to him naked with their daughter, curling into him on the sofa, removing the television remote from his hand and killing *Wheel of Fortune.* In that silence, breathing. Beings being tired together. Shush. The invigorations of a washing machine through a wall. Their arms holding each other, so many arms—are these all for us?—and Howie would experience that happiness again, the kind that troubled him.

They saw little of Peter and Gillian's granddaughter in the months before the accident. Howie's wife, in a flurry of postnatal superstition, decided that "that shit" next door was contagious, and, for a time, they stopped discussing the Phanes. They didn't stop watching.

It should have been strange that the two new mothers hadn't once visited, communicated, or acknowledged their common providence. Nary a nod or a tray of thoughtful pastries passed between them. It did not feel strange. This was, after all, a route, not a neighborhood. Meanwhile, the Phane household continued to purge itself daily. The old woman out back, the younger one out front. And would you look at that: both smoking now. When Howie did see the baby, she was with her grandfather. The tall old man contained such stillness, never rocking the baby, only looking off into the forest while he whispered or quietly sang. Catching Peter Phane lullaby Emily alone in the backyard was similar to the way time stopped when, as a teenager, alone in the mountains, he would realize that within some ordinary patch of forest he had been watching there had been, all that time, a deer, stone still, watching him back. Then, like that, another deer. And another. The real world gone otherworldly. Howie imagined one day stepping out of time, joining Peter, the two of them holding their babies, singing.

Howie had been in his backyard the September afternoon that Emily's mother and grandmother were killed in a head-on collision with a car that Howie always imagined as a Saab.

Howie's wife had taken the baby shopping. Then they'd be stopping by her parents' house for dinner and, if he knew his mother-in-law, a few hours of the sloppy, gin-garbled mayhem she considered advice. Howie had decided on a headache, and he took the opportunity to clear a path through the woods to the Kayaderosseras Creek. Someday he would build a small dock and a bench for his family here. He loved the creek's cold hum. He loved the Indian summer smell of the forest bed, the Halloween mess of pine needles and orange and yellow and red leaves. The buggy shafts of light hanging from the treetops. Foxes quiet as fish. The semiotic squabble of deer prints in the mud by the bank of the creek. Chipmunks, wasps, squirrels, birds. This is my spot. This is where I make our home. He would fish here someday, sitting on his dock, and when Harriet was old enough he'd build her a boat, asking what color she wanted Daddy to paint it. Every color, she would say, all of them. But let's paint it together.

His wife, of course, still bristled at any project that implied permanence. Let her. Because someday they would sit out here and sip iced tea, maybe even wine, the pink kind she liked, watching the water move the dusk into evening. Howie would get candles; she'd like that. Candles that smell like purple or apple pie. Put some there maybe, fix them to that tree. He would get a dog, a kindly one that ate snakes.

Thing was, you had to be delicate. His wife didn't enjoy watching him labor intensively on anything suggesting that their world couldn't change tomorrow at the drop of a hat. It was probably a phase but boy was he getting sick of explaining the differences between the construction of a prison and a family. Couldn't she at least try and be happy?

Exiting the woods that day, Howie turned to the Phane house. Peter stood facing him.

Their eyes met.

Peter was by the back screen door and he was holding Harri.

Howie's first thought: *He's kidnapped my baby.* His second thought as well, and his third, as if Harriet, his little Harri, were the only one of her kind. Not a human infant, a species unto herself.

The sudden realization that his happiness was ordinary, shared, and based on a common enough prop, that all of it amounted to nothing much at all. That from a short distance, yards, mere yards, he couldn't even tell the difference between the thing he loved the most in the world and something he didn't yet know the name or gender of . . .

Peter Phane's face mimicked the way he wore his pants high up over his belly. Chin and bottom lip up: preposterous, formidable. Handsome as an old barn, or at least Howie's wife had once said so.

Their eyes held.

Howie's face stiffened, then snapped shut. He felt it happen. Couldn't help it. Maybe if he'd been holding Harri it would have been better, but Howie held nothing.

Peter Phane grinned. It was as intimate and unexpected as if he'd actually dropped his trousers. Then he held his grandchild up in the air, actually lifted her over his head for Howie to see. Would you look at *this*? Such a smile.

Howie shook his head no.

He didn't realize what he was doing; then he'd done it. No. Shaking his head as if to say, Shame on you, old man. Why, you oughta be ashamed.

Peter Phane nodded plainly, and, pulling the infant down to his chest, he walked back into his house.

Thirty minutes later the police arrived with the news of Nancy's and Gillian's deaths. They arrived at Howie's house first, dreamlike, mistaken, two uniformed men hand-delivering their blue hats.

3

—

Marty, a colleague from work, had given him the internet computer, an old one, apparently, though all computers looked inherently new to Howie. He frequented websites and forums dedicated to fish. He enjoyed photographs of boats. For over twenty years, ever since his wife and daughter left Route 29, Howie had been saving up to purchase a sailboat. Nobody knew this. He had not meant for this to become a secret, but the opportunity to inform someone had never presented itself and now, Howie felt, it was too late and probably too weird to suddenly tell someone, his daughter, for example, that, oh by the way, for twenty-some years I've been stashing away money for a giant wooden boat that I will someday live on. His dream was a 1971 Catalina 27. In good condition, one might put him back anywhere from twenty to thirty thousand dollars. Depending on how much more he had to subsidize Harri in New York City—she was out of work again—he hoped to be able to purchase this two-bedroom sailboat by the time he was retired in ten years. (Two bedrooms had always been the plan, just in case Harri ever wanted to visit him—and though she never visited him now, he did not want to assume that this would always be the case, especially if he had a boat. Even though she hated boats.) Howie knew a fellow, a hushed old coot, Earl Stolaroff, who might even let him dock the boat at his summer cottage on Lake Jogues. Once, while ice fishing, they'd talked around the issue. Stolaroff took snapshots of Lake Jogues and posted them for people to see on Facebook. Howie liked these immensely.

He had initially misunderstood the internet computer. Harri insisted that he sign on to the Facebook, and so he did and became, once again, her Father, officially listed now, Howard V. Jeffries, right there above Mother, his grainy face grimacing from an old photograph that Daughter had e-mailed him while helping register his account. Being Family on the computer meant that they didn't need to talk on the telephone so much anymore.

He had started by writing Harri letters on her wall. "Dear Harriet," these would begin. Minutes later, they'd be gone. This happened over a dozen times. Perhaps he'd misclicked? He consulted the Facebook troubleshoot, Howard V. Jeffries troubleshot, but still couldn't quite figure it. Well, huh. Concerned, finally, he posted a final letter on Harri's wall asking why none of his previous letters had been delivered. This too disappeared.

Shortly after, he received a private e-mail.

love you to death dad but please enough with the graffiti? :)

He'd thought that was the point, why she'd asked him to join, but OK. He apologized.

: (

Howie was friends with his ex-wife now, on and off the internet computer. (There was no official Ex-husband status on Facebook.) In fact, months after joining he had forty-three friends. Pressing the Confirm button had not been easy. It was as bad as a doorbell—an announcement of engagement, presence. They now know exactly where I am. They know I am here. Howie was someone who knocked, always, and the obtrusive clicking, pinging sounds by which the computer marked his movement through its world embarrassed him. Shhhhh. Most of these friends were unrecognizably aged men and women whom he may have known from high school, and after Howie's initial confirmation of friendship no other communication was ever forthcoming or apparently deemed necessary. Often they hid their years behind profile photographs of their grandchildren or pets. He was friends with GE employees, past and present, and some of their spouses who remembered him fondly from picnics, Secret Santa, potluck Super Bowl fiascos. He was friends with Ken Tapper's wife's dog. But it was not helpful, almost an affront, having different shifts of his life coexist at the same time inside the internet computer. The machine made it harder to punch out or move forward cleanly.

Harri had 453 friends. Howie would sometimes look through them, vacillating between pride and incredulity. In high school, Harri hadn't had more than 3 friends that Howie knew of. His ex-wife had 249 friends now, and his ex-wife's latest husband, Drew Sullivan, had even more. Deservedly, Howie thought. He'd met Drew on numerous occasions and genuinely liked the man and his relaxed, attractive intelligence. He was older than Howie, a retired high school English teacher from downstate, and he sometimes called wanting to know whether Howie'd like to go out with him for a brew, he'd say, maybe catch the game at Sandy's Clam Bar. Howie never accepted but often wished that he had. Drew posted poems and links to articles about how Republicans were berserk onto Harri's wall. She would often comment on these—OMFG! LOL! NSFW!—and her stepfather would comment back, others also chiming in, Liking, and Howie enjoyed keeping up with their easy, winking repartee. Last May, Drew had been the only one to call Howie on his fiftieth birthday. Everyone, meanwhile, remembered on Facebook.

:)

Emily Margaret Phane was not Howard Jeffries's Facebook friend. Still, he'd spent a fair amount of time monitoring her profile. That is, until it disappeared shortly after she returned from Boston to nurse her dying grandfather.

Before that, Howie had been able to keep track of her at Boston

University. She made 72 new friends. She was even "in a relationship with" what appeared to be an Oriental young man. In photographs she appeared happy, if overworked. Howie sometimes
lingered over the doorbell of her Add Friend button, swirling his
arrow, thinking, Why not?

Thinking: Because you are a ridiculous man.

His intentions, he knew, were chaste. Protective but not prohibitive. His interest in his neighbor no more inappropriate than that
of an elderly female relative who cared from afar: Howie desired
nothing more from Emily than the knowledge that she was doing
OK. Even though she was closer now, no longer in Boston, right
next door in fact, yards away, snug inside her house doing God
knew what, Emily felt farther away than she ever had. She had
deleted herself. He would plug her name into the internet computer search: emily phane. But there was no longer any active
emily phane, or EMILY PHANE or Emily M. Phane or emily margaret phane, or any of the variations Howie tried. None of them was
now doing OK.

If most adults are failed children, as Howie vaguely assumed, then
Emily had been a rare success. She was first-rate. Year by year
she didn't grow out of or actively debase her girlhood but grew
gracefully into the peculiar child that she had been. That was his
take, anyway. Her presence next door enlightened him—made his
days and thoughts *lighter*—especially after his own daughter had
begun to become something he adored but could no longer entirely
comprehend.

Emily never smiled while waving hello to Howie. She got him.
She did not smile so that he would not have to smile back. Because
she sure smiled at everything else. She was made of nimbler stuff,
maybe, more refined matter than the everyday heaviness Howie
pushed through. Like everything was absurd, a joke, and watching her you felt in on that joke, aligned with the bright, mocking interrogatory light she shone on everything. Some people, no

matter what, when they start laughing, you can't help but laugh along, even if you have absolutely no idea what's so funny. Even if it's abundantly clear that nothing ever really is. Not that Howie ever actually joined in laughing, alone, at his house, at his window. Because that would have been nuts.

Her face was round but not chubby, not quite. Her hair was black, shoulder length, with bangs that drew a line above her dark eyebrows and grey eyes. Then her freckles. Rare on someone with her coloring, they looked as if they'd been painted on her high, wide cheeks—a light brown, almost tribal smear of them. If Howie had to guess, he would say that the girl's father might have been an Eskimo. Though, from a distance—a next-door neighbor's upstairs bathroom window, say—it looked like her father might just as well have been a panda bear. She had looked that way since she was five.

The first years after the death of her mother and grandmother, Emily didn't lack for feminine care. Old women abounded. Five or six of them took turns stopping by, badly parking their cars— sometimes in Howie's driveway by mistake—bringing Tupper- wared meals, pink baby supplies, cardboard boxes of used toys. One of the women stayed overnight occasionally, and Howie's wife claimed to have seen this one holding hands with Peter out in the backyard, smoothing his eyebrows. Peter was to have many such friends in the years that followed, but never for longer than a few months. Howie couldn't figure out where they came from, or why they left. He assumed they'd known Peter from before, must have, and that they'd long been kept at bay. Tellingly, the NO SOLICITORS sign disappeared a month after Gillian's death. Later, when Emily began to walk, the old women came less and less, though they never entirely stopped. One theory is that they'd begun dying off. More likely is that they were unnerved.

Howie's wife called her the Little Biddy. Emily adopted the old man's walk, even the manner in which he puckered his pock- ets with his hands, and the part ministerial, part astonished way his head tilted when he spoke. Little Emily chugging around the lawn, wearing grown-up sweaters and blouses as dresses. Gillian's clothes, most likely. Howie would watch the two of them tending the garden, or sitting together in the backyard, conversing—the six-year-old girl, her hand on her chin, hmmmming and nodding in time with her grandfather. *Yes, yes, but of course.* Timeless old friends comfy inside a total lack of necessity. Harriet wouldn't ever sit still and talk to Howie, not like that. He tried. His wife said that this was because Harriet was healthy and not a freaking freak, actually, and, Jesus, what the hell did Howie think that they were supposed to talk about, anyway? *Fishing?*

For starters, Howie thought. Sure, maybe fishing.

Harriet and Emily parallel played. Together, yards away. Tiny Harriet in their living room with her books and remarkable drawings, her paintings; Emily in her backyard and garden. Howie's wife and Harriet shared and magnified each other's suspicion of everything outside their house—meaning everything Howie most loved and wanted to share with them. He'd try to get his daughter to come outside with him, let's go see the baby ducks at the creek, let's name them, feed them bread, but the girl would look at her mother and begin to cry. Mommy, don't make me. Route 29 and its psycho trucks were too close to their house. Drowning in the Kayaderosseras was too close to their house. Rabies was too close. Bees and skunks. Peter Phane and his unnerving granddaughter were far, far too close. There were clouds that spat lightning and giant trees that dropped branches the size of small trees and deer carrying ticks carrying Lyme disease and God knows what kind of other crap. Bears. Everything was too close to their house that was far away from everything. Harriet was in agreement with her mother: they were surrounded.

The toddler spent most of her days "with other children" at day care, or at her grandmother's house or one of Harri's new, honorary aunts' houses.

But Howie knew that Harri watched Emily, sometimes, particularly when her mother wasn't around. Once he caught his four-year-old daughter at the living room window, watching Emily and Peter in their backyard. Harri was whispering, giggling, as if talking along with them. Emily saw Harri, waved. Peter waved, too. Harri made a thump of a sound, quickly turned, saw Howie watching her, and burst into tears.

Howie's wife had been trying the best she could. She loved him, she said, and every so often he knew that this was true. But it wasn't enough, not for either of them. They had reached adulthood at different times, he with her, before they even married, whereas she was struggling into hers before his eyes. She was helpless inside herself. She felt smothered and afraid of her feral discontentment and the direction she could not stop growing in. He figured this out later. She did not want to hurt anyone, Howie especially, him most of all, but she could not remain as she had been or where she was. She no longer fit. She wore herself badly. It made Howie love her more, and sometimes the pain she felt at not being able to reciprocate her husband's love, or the life he tried so hard to create, actually made her love him more, too. But this was a love that fed on self-hate, on the guilt for a wrongness she couldn't help throwing around her in destructive desperation.

Peter and Emily Phane vexed her. Their garden particularly. Whereas Gillian's garden had had all the regulation and rot of a vegetable concentration camp, after Emily and Peter's liberation, it grew effusive, ramshackle, and right out onto their lawn and toward their home. Its fecundity spoke of something unwholesome, depraved. Those two, that house.

"It's not normal," Howie's wife would say. "Do not even tell me that that is a normal thing!"

The years passed, his family departed, and Howie was left with Emily and old man Phane. He knew her shifts as well as his own. He knew when she was home sick from school, and at night he could follow her from room to room in her house, and through that make guesses at what she was doing—when she did her homework, ate her supper, watched the TV, when she was talking on the tele-phone upstairs while Peter thought she was doing her homework. He didn't stare or obsess; Howie would just glance from a window now and again, unthinkingly, as one checks a clock for the time or the sky for weather.

Unlike Harri, Emily appeared to have a lot of friends. Boy-friends, too. Howie followed her academic achievements in the local paper—a solid student, Emily M. Phane always made the honor roll, and once or twice the principal's list—and then what characters she played in the Adirondack Children's Troupe produc-tions that it didn't feel proper to attend, though he wanted to, and even waited up after the first night of *Free to Be . . . You and Me*, trying to gauge by her expression how it had gone. It went great! Likewise her roles in *A Light in the Attic* and *Charlotte's Web*. To earn money for college, she worked for a few years as a waitress at Davidson Brothers. Howie never visited during her shifts. He did, however, go when he knew she wasn't working, and he'd imagine the honorable manner in which she served people who couldn't possibly have appreciated her. He felt bittersweet on her seven-teenth birthday when Peter bought her the used Mazda.

Howie and Peter began to nod more meaningfully at each other once Howie's wife and daughter left, but that was about it. They never spoke. Sometimes, in the winter, after returning from a night shift at GE, Howie would clear the Phanes' driveway of snow before they awoke. He generally mowed their lawn after he finished his. The community was comfortable within itself.

Sometime after Emily received her Mazda, Howie and Harri ran into her at the Aviation Road mall.

Howie had been called in last minute for a quick shift of quality time. His ex-wife had to work late grading standardized tests and needed him to pick their daughter up from an after-school advanced oil painting class she was taking at Adirondack Community College. Though still a senior in high school, due to her past achievements, Harri had more than qualified for the class and would even be earning transferrable credits. He was proud of her.

They were at the mall because she needed some art supplies. For Harri, this meant cheap, spangled "Bingo Night" clothing from Sears, kitten-festooned junk from the Dollar Store ("you know, to *melt*"), and even some actual paint—though this was house paint, Sears again, not oil or acrylic. Well, OK. Howie thought that maybe she'd want some new clothing for herself, too, maybe something less black? She did not. Countess Dracula, his ex-wife had begun calling the talented young woman she still refused to call Harri.

Since Harri rarely came up to Route 29 and since she professed—maybe too strongly—a distaste for motherfucking nature, your so-called natural world, most of the time that Howie and his daughter spent together over the last few years had been walking around this mall or at the movies. They showed old foreign films at the Queens Falls Library most Thursdays and Harri liked having her father take her to these.

"I can't watch films with Mom," Harri once told him. "She makes, like, Mom noises. She's got to be present in whatever's going on, you know, letting the characters know whether she agrees or disagrees with their decisions. I think she's scared of the dark, actually. Scared of letting go. But you disappear, Dad. Disappearing is the whole point. You get it."

Howie rarely got it. Those movies. He was just good at being quiet, at watching, waiting, fishing, that's all—and he was happy to spend any amount of time sitting next to his daughter. Sometimes, afterward, they'd go out to dinner—"creepy date night," Harri called it—and she'd talk about the film, never *movie*, with a glimmering, awed openness that she never showed him on any other subject. Howie came to know his daughter best through the Swedish or Soviet movies she enthused about.

Lately, Howie's ex-wife felt Harriet had been spending too much time painting in the basement. Her weight had been fluctuating. She was smoking, probably. Her grades were high but she'd stopped listening to the angry music that Howie's ex-wife had disliked but understood and started playing old, creakingly sad-sounding stuff that just made no sense whatsoever. Gothic music, apparently, like moaning, low-hanging clouds, or slow, endless single-note piano songs. Ding. Ding. Ding. Ding. Suicidal doorbell music, she called it. Hearing it come up from the basement at all hours was unnerving. "Your daughter's turning the house into Transyl-freaking-vania, Howard. Talk to her."

They—meaning Howie, mostly—were paying for the ACC oil painting class because if Harri was going to spend all her after-school time painting, she could at least do so above ground.

Some years ago Harri's paintings had been extraordinary. Everyone said so. Harri, before turning on the concept of competition and, seemingly, her own talent, had won a number of contests and awards and even had her work shown for a month in the New York State Children's Museum in Albany, and then another place up in Plattsburgh.

It hadn't been until Harriet was four that Howie realized how tiny his daughter was. True, she was smaller than Emily Phane, herself a small girl, but until he saw Harriet up close among the other children on her first day of preschool it hadn't occurred to him. These others were all at least a head taller. Howie had assumed that all children tended to be the same size until they hit puberty. But then there was Harri, instantly diminished, holding his leg, weeping in that soundless, unobtrusive way she had when strangers were around, not wanting to be left alone among the big boys, the big girls. How could he do a thing like that? Howie told the teacher that there must be some mistake here. Had he misunderstood his wife and taken Harriet to the wrong room or preschool? Must have. These freakishly plus-size kids were six or seven, at least, and his daughter, she wasn't even five yet. The teacher had laughed, scooping little Harriet into her arms. "They're all four or five, Mr. Jeffries," she'd said. "But none of them are as sweet and cute as *you*," she told Harriet. Though Harriet continued to cry, she didn't reach out or appear to expect any deliverance from her father.

That night, when Howie told his wife how tiny their daughter was and asked if she had known this, his wife bristled, like what the fuck are you even talking about? "She's perfectly normal. What is wrong with you?"

Harriet had been self-contained, morbidly sensitive, occasionally nasty, intermittently enthusiastic and joyful, but mostly all alone. Just her on the floor with her drawings and her storybooks. But until that first day of preschool, she, like Howie, hadn't known that there was anything physically unusual about her. She really hadn't known how small she was either. This changed her, almost overnight, and she grew smaller. Internally now, and how could Howie not see himself in this, how over the years he had become how he appeared? To Howie and his wife's surprise, Harriet began taping her construction paper together, making giant mosaics, needing her art to be bigger than she was now, always, as big as she could make it. Table sized, mommy sized. She'd make drawings the size of the living room floor. They got her giant sheets of white drawing paper. This was something that wouldn't change. She rarely drew or painted something smaller than her body. It was as if her art had demonstrably grown in importance to her and now had to be big enough to both contain her physical body and be someplace that she could imagine herself walking off into.

Several months after Harriet started preschool and began supersizing her art, Howie's wife fell in love with Timmy, or started sleeping with Timmy, anyway, and finally realized how unhealthy her husband and Route 29 were for her and her daughter, how they had been stunting their growth in every way possible.

By the time Harriet was a teenager her giant paintings were lovely. Strange, oddly colored landscapes. Still lifes—toys and household appliances—and self-portraits where she only managed to capture the positive, the unseen magic of whatever was around her, even or especially if it was only a toaster or pink Barbie hair dryer. But by her senior year at Saratoga High, something was missing. She still wanted to show Howie her work back then, trusting his silence in the same way she came to distrust her mother's cloying, effusive praise or, more lately, her frustrated bafflement. Howie would go down to her basement studio and feel oppressed. It looked like she was purposely draining her paintings of life. Countess Dracula indeed. What was she even painting now? Howie sure didn't know. Obsessively detailed decay? Mucus? Why would anyone want to look at such hostile, unhappy paintings? Moreover, the idea of little Harriet walking into one of these and disappearing seemed both too horrible and too real.

"What do you think?" she'd ask.

"I like them."

Howie wanted to destroy them. Painting used to bring her joy, recognition. But this was art that had turned in on itself. It was compulsive: the gabbling demands of a monster.

Howie tried to think back to when he was her age. He and Harri's mother had spent their time necking, riding bikes, swimming in Lake Jogues, occasionally sneaking boxes of Franzia white zinfandel from Howie's cousin with the water bed, watching lots of TV and speaking with authority about the future, happy in that animal, anticipatory manner specific to virgins in love. Well, Howie thought, at least his daughter wasn't going to be crippled by disillusionment! Unlike her mother, Harri seemed to have been spared a sense of direct ownership of the future . . .

Now, the day they met Emily in the mall, Harri was in a pretty good mood. She had just been told by her ACC art instructor that her latest painting was distressing.

"Distressing?" Howie asked.

"The class is kind of a joke," Harri said. "Distressing and offensive, she actually said. Them her words. They want me to paint, like, trees and mountains. Bad enough I have to live up here, but paint it, too? Marlene—we have to call her Marlene—she's always trying to explain to us the difference between her so-called natural world and everything that Marlene hates. Plastic and ringtones and cigarettes, for example. I told her that everything in existence is just as natural as everything else in existence. I'm sorry, but a Taco Bell is *just* as natural as a waterfall, you know?"

"You used to paint trees and mountains."

"What?" Harri said. "That's never what I was actually painting, Dad."

Well, that's what they'd looked like to Howie. He asked, "Well, are you learning anything?"

"Doing my best not to," Harri said. "I don't know. I guess I like a few of the other students. They're cool, they get my stuff. It's better than high school. It's just Marlene—she's a marshmallow. The way she talks. Like her mouth is full of marshmallows. She's totally insane, actually. By painting a lake over and over again she thinks she'll be able to understand a lake."

Howie said, "Which lake?"

"You're incredible. *Which lake.*"

Lakes were Howie's favorite thing. Ten or so years ago, Harriet had painted Howie a pond-sized painting of Lake Jogues for his birthday. It took up an entire wall and, without exaggerating, had been among the things on earth that made Howie the most happy. But Harri had recently taken it from his living room wall, telling him it was an embarrassing piece of shit, juvenilia, she'd said, and she seriously couldn't stomach it up there another single fucking second. Made her want to puke. Howie didn't complain. He said he understood and helped cut it in two and drive it back to her mother's house so she could take it to the basement and further desecrate its corpse. He asked Harri for another painting, a replacement, maybe a less juvenile lake? Eventually she brought him a large canvas that looked like rust and spleen.

Howie wasn't hungry but hoped that Harri was. He liked taking her to dinner, something they hadn't done in months. In fact, as was typical, they hadn't seen or spoken to each other in four weeks. "Would you like to get some dinner before I take you home?"

Sometimes Harri was a vegetarian, but usually she wasn't. It wasn't that she liked animals, she once told him, it was more that she was sick to fucking death of plants. There were way too many in her opinion. "Could we go to Bellaggio's?"

"Yes."

The little things, like his daughter asking him if they could do something and Howie being able to answer in the affirmative. Here, for you, a *yes*. Bellaggio's, an apparently authentic downstate Italian place marooned inside an upstate strip mall between the Radio Shack and Feigenbaum Cleaners, was a favorite of theirs. The owner and chef, Roger Bellaggio, was married to the daughter of one of Howie's co-workers and always served seventeen-year-old Harri a red plastic Coca-Cola glass a quarter full of their house red wine. "And one Italian soda for the young lady," he'd say, and wink. Howie liked how Roger Bellaggio, a father of three girls himself, regarded them. Howie always felt more like a real father in that restaurant, like a whole damn family, sitting there, eating sausage pizza or pasta and sharing the Coca-Cola transgression with his wonderful daughter, being recognized by big Roger Bellaggio as the kind of man who both had a wonderful daughter and didn't balk at breaking laws that infringed upon her happiness. He was *that* guy. So he let Harri have a little wine with dinner, so what? You got a problem with that? Harri got endless enjoyment from Roger Bellaggio's dozens of framed photographs of a spry, mustached version of himself on the set of *Rocky IV,* a movie his brother had done the catering for. She loved that the massive Italian's name was *Roger.* Harri would get him to tell different variations of the same tales of Dolph Lundgren and Carl Weathers. Roger Bellaggio never mentioned Sylvester Stallone. Harri invented dark, complex reasons for the omission.

Howie and Harri were on their way out of the mall, passing through the food court when Harri's walking stiffened.

Emily Phane alone, standing by the door. She spotted them, waved. Harri pretended not to notice, then, embarrassed that she had so obviously pretended not to notice, reciprocated the wave, and then, inhaling, went over, leaving Howie behind, a can of Sears house paint in each of his hands. Brown and slightly less brown.

It looked like Emily, who was at least two heads taller than Harri, was sucking Howie's daughter into her. The way they stood. Like Emily was one of Harri's earlier, more beautiful paintings, a fantasy self-portrait she wanted to disappear into. They spoke.

Probably.

But Howie could also imagine them just standing there, silently. Staring.

It was intrusive, meeting Emily here like this. His tiny, aggrieved Harriet poking out from one of her black tents, ripped stockings, hair nearly shaved from her childlike head, and then Emily Phane with the smiling. It was illusory, unpleasant, the two of them together. Like two different species. Their childhood parallel play had continued through their lives: always aware of each other, always watching, but never exactly friends. Harri was too quiet, too antisocial—and, on top of that, the two of them went to different schools, Emily to Queens Falls High and Harri to Saratoga. Emily, though eccentric, was effortless. She dressed normally. Prettily, Howie supposed. Or, you never really noticed how she dressed. Harri, on the other hand, made a great effort to assure that you noticed. Emily was quick to laugh. Harri quick to close in on herself. Howie felt a strong, unfeasible bond with the girl next door, but seeing Emily's open energy diminish his daughter, he wished that he could just turn Emily down a smidgeon. Please, leave my little girl alone.

Howie imagined his daughter walking straight up into Emily

and disappearing, as if that's where she belonged anyway, who she actually was, or who she could have been if Howie hadn't failed so spectacularly. Emily and Harriet living next door as one.

"God, Dad," Harri said, returning to him. She lifted her eyebrows. One of them pierced with a metal beetle.

Emily was gone.

"That," she continued, "was your next-door neighbor. By the way. Maybe you've seen her around once or twice in the past seventeen years?"

"I'm sorry," Howie said. He tried to fix his face.

"Don't be," she said. "I love how you don't even pretend to give a shit. You're an inspiration. But did you see how wasted Emily looked?"

Howie had seen nothing of the sort. "She has a lot of freckles," he said.

"Observant," Harri said. "No, I mean, it looks like she hasn't slept in years. I feel bad for her. There are all these bitchy rumors now, you know? These slut rumors. I fucking hate high school."

Harri liked testing her father with new words and concepts. He said, "She was probably up late studying."

"Probably not, Dad."

Harri took out her phone, began tapping.

Howie said, "The freckles make her look strange."

Silence. Had he gone too far, defending Emily? He felt guilty—as if he'd just been caught cheating on his daughter with another daughter. He said, "You're much prettier."

"Jesus." Harri made a face. "What are you even talking about?"

"I'm sure she gets enough sleep," Howie continued.

"What the hell, Dad."

"OK."

"You are so weird. I don't think she's ever really liked me. I don't know," and Harri turned around, back to where Emily had been standing. She watched that spot.

Moments later, Harri's phone beeped. "Uh-oh," she said. "It's Mom. She says you promised to buy me a new jacket."

"OK."

"Not OK. I don't need a new jacket. I could use some new boots though, actually. Maybe before Bellaggio's?"

"That sounds nice."

"*Nice?*" Harri laughed. "You're a maniac."

Howie liked Harri best when they were shopping. She became younger, more possible, and so they went back, deeper back into the Aviation Road mall, Harri pulling him toward a not inexpensive pair of Frankensteins she promised he'd be in a holy shitload of trouble for getting her. "Mom'll manslaughter you!" How could he resist?

They put the shopping bags and cans of paint into the backseat of Howie's car. They got in the front. Howie put his seat belt on. Harri, of course, did not. She'd grown unwieldy again.

"Bellaggio's?" he said.

"I don't know, maybe just take me home."

Howie said, "OK."

He started the car.

"Yeah, take me home."

"OK."

"I *know* it is, Dad."

They drove in silence. Howie, at a loss, asked a question about Emily, wondered what they'd talked about at the mall, if Emily was applying to any of the same colleges as Harri.

"Seriously?" Harri said.

She didn't wear seat belts because of the way they fell across her neck: she was just way too small. They left marks. Her skin irritated easily. "The worst thing is, I'm small but I'm not *cute*," she once told him. "I'm small the way bugs are small."

Other children had been cruel to her. Likely they still were. But even she wouldn't let that take the blame for the inscrutable, constant costume changes of her moods. "Hey," she said, finally, as they approached her mother's house. "Hey." She squeezed Howie's arm. "I'm sorry, Dad. I love you."

Pulling his car out of his ex-wife's driveway, Howie honked three times, something he only ever did with her and only because when his daughter was little she'd absolutely insisted on it. Three honks.

Dad!

Dad!

Dad!

His daughter was still little. She waved good-bye, playful now, happy, a brand-new boot comically gloving each of her hands. She raised them above her head and waggled them, then bent them slowly, back and forth, like the antennae of an insect someone had just stepped on.

4

—

M essage. One," said the telephone robot. "Friday. Eleven. Four. Tee. One. P. M."

BEEEEP!

"Hi, this is Emily Phane from next door. Peter's granddaughter. Mr. Jeffries, I'm really sorry to bother you, but I'm calling because—*no I'm calling him now, I'm actually on the phone right now, I'm* [mostly unintelligible]—"

BEEEEP!

"Message. Two. Friday. Eleven. Four. Tee. Four. P.M."

BEEEEP!

"Sorry. Emily Phane again, from next door. From Boston. I know this is unusual but could you please call me back as soon as you get this? It's an emergency. I mean, I hope it's not an emergency, but— here, my number is six one seven, eight three eight, five five six one. Please call. Even the middle of the night, whenever you get this message. That's area code six one seven, five five five, five five six one. Thanks so much. Thank you. Thanks. Bye!"

BEEEEP!

"Message. Three. Friday. Eleven. Four. Tee. Nine. P. M."

". . ."

BEEEEP.

"End. Of. Messages."

. . .

Nearly three years ago, on a Friday at 11:58 p.m., Howie stood waiting for his telephone to ring again. He had been sitting down but that began to feel inappropriate. The phone was more likely to cooperate if he was standing.

It would ring on Saturday, he thought. In two minutes. He was in his kitchen and had been all evening, through all nine unanswered phone calls and two messages. In the same way one might obsessively peel back a bandage and poke a wound, Howie wanted badly for the phone to ring again. He knew what he was when the phone was ringing. He was a coward. When it wasn't, he actually entertained the idea of answering it were it to ring again. Why not? Then it would ring again and he would remember. He was paralyzed. He could not answer, just as he knew that he would never be able to call Emily Phane back, knew it even as he was writing down her number in his address book, circling it in red marker, twice, as if to differentiate it from all the other less important numbers he also was not ever going to call.

EMILY EMERGENCY 617-555-5561.

Or, as she said, perhaps there wasn't an emergency. What then? Why had she been calling? How did she even have his number? He was confounded.

Message one was the first time that he had ever heard Emily's voice up close, certainly the first time she had ever been in his house. His kitchen. *His kitchen table.* Emily, for the most part, sounded like she was supposed to.

Telephones that you expect to ring look markedly different from telephones you do not ever expect to ring. Howie played the messages again. BEEEEP! Then once again.

The unintelligible part on the first message concerned him. There was someone there with Emily, a male someone. Was he the emergency? That did not make sense. If not an emergency, the male was certainly an asshole, possibly even a *fucking* asshole, this much

Howie gathered because he thought that he could hear Emily, her hand momentarily over the receiver, calling him exactly that. Back in Howie's day, that kind of language certainly would have constituted a low-level emergency, but a call to your next-door neighbor hundreds of miles away? Doubtful.

Howie sat down and looked into the internet computer.

On Facebook, Emily Phane was currently in a relationship with a young man named Ethan Caldwell. Ethan Caldwell's profile was private, but his photograph revealed an Oriental man in a robe. Twenty-six years old and standing on a hilltop with a sword. The male someone Howie heard during the muffled portion of the recorded message did not sound characteristically Oriental, but huh. Really, what did Howie know? The sword was, potentially, a problem.

It was morning now. Past midnight, anyway. Howie watched the phone and the bossy old clock above the stove. It clicked 12:17. Then, in what seemed like significantly more than sixty seconds, another click. A clunk.

12:18.

Howie yawned.

He had put that clock up there after his wife left. The louder the time, the better. Once, this kitchen had been a place for mornings. That was before his family fled, and long before Marty's internet computer had installed itself on the round oak table. There between the toaster, microwave, radio, telephone, and the answering machine. Ex-husbandhood meant he could do this, crowd his antique kitchen table with machines. Because why not make toast or reheat Bellaggio's pizza where you're going to actually eat Bellaggio's pizza? The resulting spaghetti of wires extending through the air from the kitchen table to the kitchen counter didn't bug Howie in the least and, in fact, the limits they imposed upon kitchen mobility were satisfying. There were already too many ways one could do things. Howie rarely thought of his wife preparing breakfast anymore.

The computer crackled with exertion. He watched a pop-up ad for heartburn relief. Indigestion as poignant blobs of red light. Howie had pulled a night shift yesterday and then, before dawn, on a whim, drove straight from the GE Waste Water Treatment Plant to East Caroga Lake, where he'd spent the majority of the day fishing.

The phone rang.

His first reaction was that it was an alarm, and that it was time to wake up, go to work. He reached for it, instinctually, as if to hit snooze.

The red blobs on the screen yo-yoed from stomach to neck and back again. Caressingly, almost. They looked like something you might enjoy having inside you. Why fight it?

Howie was exhausted.

The phone kept ringing, so Howie kept his right hand on the receiver, feeling a ticklish electric purr, holding the receiver down, shhhhhhhhhh, as if there were a genuine possibility of it leaping up and answering itself or Howie's left hand going rogue and finding out why Emily Phane had been calling all night.

It stopped ringing.

Harri, age sixteen, spoke from the table: "My technophobic dad's not home right now. Or, who knows, actually. He probably totally is. Either way, leave a message after the—"

BEEEEP!

Then, Emily: "I'm sorry, Mr. Jeffries, I'm sure you're at work or out night fishing but . . ." Howie yanked his hand off the phone as if it had actually become the top of his neighbor's head. Emily paused then, as if in confused reaction to the removal of Howie's hand. Like they were both listening for the other now through the static snow of distance. Boston and Route 29. Breathing. Both of them waiting for the other to make a move. Then, "Well, so, I've been calling my grandfather since yesterday and he hasn't picked up. If you're listening to this, could you look and see if his car's there? If it is, please go and see if he's OK, Mr. Jeffries. It's probably nothing. I'm sure it's nothing. It's usually nothing. His phone is probably unplugged or the TV's too loud or something. But please. I'm worried. I'll try calling again in the morning."

BEEEEP!

From the kitchen window, Howie could see the Phane house. The lights were on downstairs, all of them, and Peter's car, a sable black Cadillac DeVille, was in the driveway.

The disappointment lasted only a moment. It was replaced by incredulity. What else did he possibly think she could have been calling for? She was not his daughter. She had not been calling him for *money*—nor was she calling because she was inebriated, alone, momentarily sloppy hearted . . .

He looked out at the Cadillac again. Now that Emily was at college, Peter Phane was lights out by nine. It was well past midnight now. The windows had the cold, empty light of a refrigerator opened at 2:00 a.m.

Emily knew that Howie liked to fish.

He went upstairs. He tucked in his shirt, combed his grey hair back; he brushed his teeth, shaved, and put on his good shoes. He brushed his teeth again. Then he took off his good shoes and put on his sneakers. This could be an emergency.

And, well, sure she knew that he fished. They had lived next door to each other for twenty years.

Downstairs, back in the kitchen, the so-called screen saver had snapped on. It bubbled. Cartoon fish. Shortly after Harriet's birth, Howie had stopped killing them. Fish. If he could help it, and he mostly could, he'd chuck them back into the lake, only once in a while making a trophy of one, like the twenty-four-pound muskellunge pike he caught seven years ago ice fishing on Lake Champlain. He rarely thought of fish as something that could also be food.

Howie walked down his driveway. Reaching Route 29, he turned left. Then another left up the Phanes' driveway. Do this proper. No sudden movements. His hands were in his pockets. This, he realized, probably made him look shifty. He removed his hands from his pockets. He wished he had brought his book because nobody would be afraid of someone walking up a driveway with a book. Howie wanted the house to know that he was approaching it with only helpful, neighborly intentions. He'd briefly considered driving over.

Howie had never stood on the Phanes' front porch before. It was his house, but wrong—and yellow.

Howie knocked on the door.

He could hear the TV.

Knock, knock.

He could hear a ringing telephone. Fine. Howie found the doorbell. Fool thing, he thought. It ding-donged joyfully.

He did not expect an answer. If he had, would he have even come over? Probably he would not have.

He stepped off the porch and approached the living room window, standing among waist-high shrubs. The mulch felt queasy underfoot. Howie saw Peter Phane on a rug, TV light flickering over him. He was not wearing trousers. His eyes were open.

Howie found himself trying to open the front door.

Locked.

He hurried around the back, on the grass now. The back door was unlocked.

The kitchen was a crime-scene reenactment of his own kitchen. Dishes everywhere; a broken glass on the table. Flies and candy wrappings and slices of bread hardened into mossy stone; unopened mail, opened mail, and sticky dried beige stains on the linoleum. Lots of newspapers from New York City. The refrigerator was open.

Then down a hallway decorated with framed photographs.

Howie had the same hallway, of course, but his was barren but for the twenty-four-pound muskellunge pike on the wall across from the bathroom door, so whenever you exited the downstairs bathroom: *remarkably big fish.* ("Dad, whoa, that is the single weirdest place to put a fish. Is that even a fish? You're so awesome. You're art. What is *wrong* with you?")

What was wrong here?

The living room was humid and bad. Howie smelled something chalky, rotten, medicinal. His feet crunched through a spill of unexpectedly cheerful breakfast cereal—Peter Phane ate Lucky Charms? *Froot Loops?* Pills, too. There were bloody tissues, a splayed *Sports Illustrated* magazine, orange peels. The TV applauded. Two black women began to sing. The phone began ringing. It was there next to the TV. The black women on the TV seemed annoyed by this. Peter was too, each ring registering on his face like a slap.

"Em," he said. "Em, em, em."

Howie waited for the phone to stop ringing. This was just as natural as a waterfall, a Taco Bell, a tree. Once it stopped ringing, he picked it up. He dialed 911 and requested an ambulance.

"Route Twenty-Nine. Yes. Route Two Nine. That's correct."

Howie would not look directly at Peter Phane. Even when he had to look, he tried, for propriety's sake, not to see. Peter Phane was like something without a shell. Howie found a quilt and covered the lower half of his body. He maneuvered a segment of sofa under Peter's oddly weightless head and, like that, the TV stopped singing.

The phone again.

Howie got down, told Peter that everything was fine. Peter tried to disagree, tried to get Howie to answer the phone. Tried to say the name of his granddaughter. But Howie only stood, stared out the window at his own house, and when he finally heard the ambulance he turned off the TV, unlocked the front door, and left out the back.

. . .

Emily was home the next day. A week later, Howie received a tray of Rice Krispies Treats with a note.

You saved his life. Thank you, Mr. Jeffries. —E.

It could not have been a coincidence. Howie wanted to call his ex-wife, tell her the thoughtful pastries had come full circle, but he lacked the wherewithal and the implications troubled him. Emily was, after all, about the age his wife had been when she'd begun her futile cookie-based courtship of Gillian and Peter Phane.

"I've lived a lot of life since then, Howard," his ex-wife had said the last time he had tried to share an old Route 29 memory with her. "That was so long ago. I guess I remember."

No, no. The implications were clear.

Emily would not return to Boston, and one year later, Peter Phane was gone. He had been ninety-four years old.

Her nocturnal ambles began soon afterward. Well, what else could you call them? Sleepwalkings? Excursions? They weren't quite walks. Howie did not understand them. When he first saw her out back after midnight he assumed that she was looking for a dog, though he knew that she didn't have a dog. Someone else's dog? That made less sense. She would hurry out, her movement tripping the motion sensor spotlights, a fluorescent blight that turned the grass into a ghostly *lawn* and the dark that surrounded her property into pure absence. Which is where Howie would be, watching. In a window, normally the upstairs bathroom window, but sometimes the kitchen window, sunken back in that deeper night she had created. She would poke around the corners of her property. Something was missing. But what? True, she spent a lot of this time just sitting out there in a lawn chair, sipping something. Milk? Tea? Looking normal, more or less, except it was 3:00 a.m. and it was about the creepiest thing that Howie had ever seen. Sometimes she would busy herself with night gardening, vegetable picking.

They were a community though. You saw things. You see things and you worry. There were wild dogs in the area, packs of them, apparently, and every few years a bear would waddle down from the mountains. Foxes didn't bite but they might, Howie supposed. They sure might.

Things got worse. Emily's garden was nothing but soil and lack now. There was an emptying going on next door. She had begun pulling it all up: shrubs, small trees, ferns. The vegetables and the flowers had gone first, almost overnight. Then the entire garden. She razed anything the spotlights touched, like clearing her yard of plaque. Then she started off into the darkness beyond, back where Howie could not follow. He nearly expected to return from work one night and hear her out back felling pines with a chain saw.

She was in trouble. She was only separated from Howie by a wall and several yards of lawn.

Howie had not saved Peter Phane's life, merely prolonged it by a year. Eleven months. Most of which Peter wasn't even exactly present for, or so Howie had to assume. He should not have meddled. If he had not gone over then Emily would not have dropped out of college to move back in and nurse him to death. She, at least, would have been spared. Howie was responsible. The future was all his fault.

He stood at a kitchen cupboard.

There, in an old green Folgers decaf can, he put two one-hundred-dollar bills. This month's boat savings. He hadn't been able to save for the past half year because Harri had needed a little support in New York City. Why? Wasn't his place to ask. Howie had half his boat money in the Trustco Savings Bank and half here, in the Folgers decaf can. It was childish, but so was thinking that he could someday sail away from himself on a wooden boat. The physicality of the money inspired him. The paper was more likely to become a boat if he could keep an occasional, encouraging eye on it. You can do it.

Howie hadn't seen a light on upstairs at Emily's house in over a year. Only the living room and the kitchen, and those were hardly ever off. The living room windows were now completely obscured by plants. They hummed green.

Tomorrow, he thought.

But *tomorrow* was still the extent of Howie's plan to save Emily Phane. Today, of course, was yesterday's tomorrow, and yesterday had been the day before that's tomorrow. There'd been weeks of that. Months? Sure. OK. But tomorrow was coming, Howie knew, and here was a Folgers decaf can full of more than a hundred hundred-dollar bills to prove it. He shook it.

Back when his wife had been trying to conceive, she had gone on about how caffeine capsized estrogen levels, caused bladder cancer, irritability, muscle tremors. She cut strident, coupon-sized articles from health magazines and stuck them to the refrigerator, obituaries for this or that formerly enjoyable food product.

"Why don't we just get one big sign for the refrigerator that says 'Eating may cause disease'?"

A kiss on the cheek. "You may cause disease, Howard Jeffries."

He never went back to caffeinated coffee. First because Howie wanted to prove his ex-wife wrong by drinking a pot of decaf every day for the rest of his life and coming down with bladder cancer anyway, ha ha ha, and then, now, seriously, because that's where his money lived. His boat, his silly, secret future. Howie liked to drink the stuff and think about his Folgers decaf bank account in the kitchen cupboard and how maybe, just maybe, there was some surprise left in him yet.

part two

———

Emily,
without Eyelids

5

—

Meanwhile, next door, Emily Phane was losing her mind. She stood on a mattress in the center of the living room. She bounced. Or maybe I'm just tired, she thought. This was her pet debate, the conclusion pretty much foregone: Emily was tired *and* insane.

The plants were closing in.

Puckered-up flowers, vines, ferns, saplings. They were vibratory now. And they reached for her.

The room was padded. Everything insulated, top to bottom, and you couldn't even see out the windows anymore. Not like there was really anything going on out there, just more plants.

Emily passed her days in a state of besieged wakelessness. Kind of like dreaming and kind of like hiding—but without the inherent safety of either. The plants protected her, if not from totally losing it, then from total inactivity. There was a continuum that she tapped into while silently, thoughtlessly tending them. Since Peppy died, this was the only safe place that she knew.

She hadn't slept in two, maybe three days.

She rarely ventured upstairs. The doors to the bedrooms might as well be wall. Everything huddled here in the living room, safe, or relatively safe, waiting it out. It'd been almost two years and what had once seemed like an only slightly batty and temporary and understandable spatial adjustment to loss now risked approaching the territory of someone who, years after the death of a baby, refused to remove the half-consumed container of Gerber's from the fridge. Emily knew that this was not normal.

Emily was bouncing on a mattress.

More than she slept on it, she stood on it, stepped on it, desultorily bounced on it. Like right now. The mattress was a slab in the center of the room. She rarely thought of it as a bed.

She stopped.

Sleep, when it happened, happened like a cough. Her body suddenly too huge and heavy to feel, her vision muffled, squirrely, her brain just totally shot and then *cough*, like that but bigger— COUGH!—and she'd either fall where she stood or make it to a chair, or a nice spot on the floor.

The mattress was surrounded by potted shrubs and buckets of wildflowers.

These came from out back, some of them. There was a dreamy, wholly unexamined system here. Others Emily adopted from the hills and trails around Queens Falls: strays surreptitiously dug up from the littery banks of the roads she found herself walking some nights. She'd even gone out behind Mr. Jeffries's place the other night. Not like he'd notice. The guy was a tree. Emily thought that maybe someday she'd take him in, too, plant him over by the fireplace, water him until he sprouted a smile, a pulse, anything.

Emily laughed.

The TV was company.

She changed the channel.

Emily wasn't particular but she especially loved documentaries about anything that had happened in black and white. Musicals as well; they reminded her of Peppy and Peppy's version of her mother, Nancy. *Anything Goes. My Fair Lady. Seven Brides for Seven Brothers.* Emily loved baseball. Baseball was a log in the fireplace. But not watching, only listening. Peppy'd watch the game on his radio out in the backyard, and it wasn't until Emily was six that she finally saw the game on TV. It looked nothing like it was supposed to. They were playing it all wrong. Real world baseball was stodgy, inexplicable. But weren't most things, actually, if you opened your eyes and bothered?

The bathroom was off the hall that led from the living room to the kitchen. Only door on the right.

She walked by it.

Emily Phane was walking.

The hall itself was longer than you'd think, especially at night. It was a tunnel lined with the dead. Emily's grandparents, great-grandparents, great-uncles in great, awesome hats. Nancy, age seven, on stage in dancing duck costume. The NDE Emily had called it: their hallway as a near death experience. "Go toward the light, Peppy," she'd joke when he got up for a snack during a commercial. They used to joke about everything.

Compared to the plant-choked living room, the kitchen was a sky. Four uncovered windows. Everything washed out by a hundred years of direct sunlight: pale wooden cupboards, a steel marshmallow of a fridge, a microwave and a toaster and ostensibly brown wallpaper that had long since camouflaged itself into the exact color of the light that struck it. The linoleum was permanently clammy and nice underfoot.

In the kitchen there were doors. Laundry room door. Door to the backyard. Door to Peppy's office.

It was past midnight.

Emily refilled the yellow ceramic jug at the sink. Then back to the living room to water the plants.

They thickened and hushed expectantly. Stupid things. Stupid me. Emily's eyes wanted to sleep, but her head, she knew, was no mattress. Who said that? Sometimes she'd close only one eye, as if this would be enough, tricking herself, giving half her head relief. Keep busier than time and time goes away. That was also a trick. Because it wouldn't be past midnight forever; soon, once again, it'd be before midnight. Meaning what? Meaning Emily didn't know, just do something before you fucking fall asleep. Not fall, she thought. Plummet.

She watered a particularly sullen tree. Its tilt and sag worried her. Then a shrub, a matriarch, Emily decided, with a sudden gust of goodwill toward her own peculiarities. You're a good old girl, aren't you? Look at you. You're a grandmamma.

Then on to the spider-eyed berry thing. Then the one with the pointy clown wings. She watered a palm that reminded her of a blind hunting dog.

Emily's old professor reprimanding her again: enough with the animism, Ms. Phane!

Was that all she was doing?

Back before all this, at Boston University, she'd made motions toward a study of botany, plant biology, environmental science. That kind of thing. In the end, she'd felt too drowsily bemused to adapt herself to another view of reality. Science seemed fussy, insincere. Biometrics had made her sad. She had, however, become loosely interested in the more esoteric end of so-called plant neuro-biology, specifically in long-dismissed studies of CIA agents who'd hooked up houseplants to galvanometers. It made sense to her that lie detector machines could pick up the electrical stress of plants when you thought about eating them or setting them ablaze. Emily couldn't quite believe in the line that separated plants from animals, or, for that matter, sleep from the waking world. Plants dominated the world. That was a fact. They ate light and invented aspirin and talked to one another via chemical signaling. They learned. They gossiped with one another over great distances. In a sense, they were time machines. Plants existed in a different, slower dimension.

They were kind of terrifying, actually.

Look at one under a microscope and try not to freak out.

Start small. Baby steps. Snap out of it. Emily could still maybe go back to before all this, couldn't she? She could! She wasn't one of those women who later found themselves half eaten by cats, or mummified in a room wallpapered in aluminum foil. No way. She'd always been the cutup, the class clown. This was like that. This was *quirky*. Seriously, what could be funnier than a room full of sentient, stolen plants?

Tomorrow she could jump in her Mazda and drive down to the Aviation Road mall. Buy a new smartphone. Clothes, shoes: new things for a brand-new you. She could even hit up Burger King and buy back some of the weight she'd lost.

The mouth of the fireplace was fanged with cacti. Urgh. You guys. Emily did not like them one bit. She poured water over their heads.

You're quirky, all right, she thought.

She laughed.

Quirky as a crippling bone disease.

They were zombies, these cacti. Part here, part irretrievably elsewhere. They reminded Emily of Peppy's last months on the sofa. The hospice nurses in their Honda Civics coming by to water him. The way his beard continued to grow, eyes bald and calked over. How inappropriate TV was, but how terrified Emily'd been to click it off. The glaucoma of TV light further draining her grandfather's face of color, as if he were entering a horrific version of one of those Turner Classic Movies he so loved. Caterpillar whorls of hair growing from his ears, and oh my God did that mean he'd always trimmed his ear hair before? Should Emily have? How? With what? She wished she could have joked with him about that too, about all that fuzziness filling up his ear—Can you hear it growing, Peppy? *There's more hair inside your ear now than on the top of your head!* The two of them laughing instead of sitting there watching those plastic tubes pump him full of absence.

She'd plugged the cacti into the fireplace partly as a warning and partly as proof that her sense of humor was intact. Best of both worlds. She'd gotten to threaten houseplants with fiery death, safe in the knowledge that threatening houseplants was also, obviously, kind of hilarious. Oh it was satisfying. The only question being, at what point does having a sense of humor about your own eccentricities cross over into the lane with the people who wander around laughing at everything for no apparent reason? Because maybe insane laughing people are only laughing in order to prove to themselves that they are self-aware and not, in fact, insane. They get it; they're totally in on the joke. They're still fucking insane.

6

—

She was everybody's second-best friend. Growing up, Emily wasn't lonely or necessarily unpopular, but something was missing.

She'd watch other girls being best friends. She'd fixate, zone in on it, couldn't help it. She measured best friends against her own limper friendships, sometimes jealously, always inquisitively. Studying how they'd entangle their laughter, perfumes, ringtones, slang, blouses (the word itself, *blouse*, was, to Emily, a best friend word, a mom word, something Emily wanted to discuss, *what do you think of this blouse*, but didn't know how or with whom). The way they did their hair, seemingly *shared* their hair; best friends applying cosmetics together, using each other as mirrors, finishing their eyes with the precision of synchronized swimmers. Their high-pitched hallway hugs and the giggly, locker-side huddles. The way best friends rode through hallways as if they were in the back of invisible taxis, discussing what and who they saw from the windows as if nobody could see or hear them, nobody important, anyway. Nobody that mattered. Emily had wanted to have that too, to feel like she was in the back of a cab with another girl, awesome and mattering. Instead, she'd begun to feel as if her very girlhood was unrequited.

You saw them everywhere. Texting each other. Confiding. Best buds bitching on TV, solving crimes, sharing rapturous advice about home equity insurance and butter substitutes. Best friends talking about boys—freaking *dwelling* on the retarded conversational minutia of boys, as if what happened when Tucker e-mailed Caite was some kind of a Buddhist koan. Even in the pages of Emily's Spanish exercise book. Repeat after me: *"Eres una amiga maravillosa . . ."* It was a conspiracy! Like something from a new Richard Scarry children's book. *Best Friends Come in All Shapes and Sizes.* Because they did! But not in Emily's shape, or size, and she didn't want to feel sorry for herself but at that age, at twelve, thirteen, fourteen, whatever, sometimes feeling sorry for yourself can be indistinguishable from feeling anything at all.

Did they sense her neediness? Was need always the same thing as desperation? Can there be something so wrong with you that people pick up on it on some other level, a level they don't even consciously know they're picking up on? Because even weirdos, as far as Emily could tell, found best friends. Even jerks. There was this shy girl, also named Emily, Emily Hecker, and she didn't seem to have any friends, like, ever, and seemed as if she couldn't even raise her voice to normal talking levels. Kids called her Meep. Then, one day, Meep had a best friend too. Two of them meeping obliviously down the hall. How? Were Meep's parents loaded? Was it because Emily Hecker *had* parents? Emily Phane couldn't talk to her grandfather about this. Peppy was the best but not at being a girl; if she tried then he would probably only wonder why she cared so much about pleasing idiots anyway and then she'd have to talk herself blue explaining that she *didn't* and that they *weren't*. Don't worry, he'd say. You work yourself up, he'd say. Can't force that kind of thing.

Fine.

Probably he was right, she'd concede. Though, of course, the conversation hadn't even actually happened, so *who* was right? Concede to *whom*? Emily would, for a time, try to stop pleasing the idiots, pleasing anyone, but then she'd realize that in doing this she was only trying to please Peppy, and, worse, she was trying to please a Peppy that she'd made up in her head! Her grandfather hadn't said a word about not forcing something or Annie Sweeney being an idiot, though he was right, Annie Sweeney totally was.

Emily'd suss out a room for potential best friend material; it was second nature. She did this scan. Like, who was unattached? Were there weak links, current best friendships on the waver, going stale? She looked for small, potentially exploitable stylistic divergences that maybe portended some kind of greater rift on the horizon—a girl experimenting with Hot Topic goth, suddenly, and directly in the confused face of her Old Navy BFF . . . Emily knew best friend-hood was coming, must be, like losing her virginity, graduating from high school, learning to drive. Have a little faith. Everyone gets a best friend. Emily wasn't shy. People liked her. Her wavy anti-seriousness drew people in, but it was becoming clear that Emily was attractive to other girls in the same way that the poison-ous, toothy things are the most attractive things at an aquarium or zoo. It was like they knew what happened to her at night, like she was contagious. Knew without knowing. Press your palms to the glass, get close, but not best friend forever close. You best-friend one of those fish, girl, and you're done for.

It was different with the guys. The skaters, burgeoning potheads, and the sarcastic, unhappy brainiacs. Emily didn't like the jocks as much, but even some of them, the cute ones, whatever, they could be fun to hang with too. They had a bovine niceness that could be hypnotizing. But boys didn't count. That kind of buddyhood was way too easy: all braying loud surfaces, body humor, *dude*. Dude, check this out. Emily needed someone to hold on to through the storm of puberty—though, of course, that wasn't at all how she thought about it back then.

Basically, middle school sucked. That's when the second-best-friend thing started. That *sobriquet*, as Peppy would say. Seven girls over a period of three, four years. Oh, it was like they *knew*. Like they wanted to rub her face in it. Because, seriously, *second-best friend*? Who said that?

Jess Yarsevich for starters.

They'd met during the Adirondack Children's Troupe rehearsals for *Free to Be . . . You and Me.* Jess Yarsevich was fourteen, two years older than Emily. She had recently moved from Tucson with a mother and a prematurely balding older brother, Jared, whom Emily had once mistaken for Jess's father. "Naw, Dad's back in New Mexico. I'm gonna spend the summer with him." Her words twanged. She complained about not having enough winter clothes, though obviously she liked wearing the crap out of her revealing southwestern skirts and tops under the puff of her new upstate New York jacket, always asking if you'd heard of things that she knew you couldn't possibly have ever heard of. Cool Tucson things, people and websites for bands her older brother knew of before they were lame. Jess was membership only. In her club, you were either in or out and you knew immediately, before you'd even had a chance to apply. Most of the kids in the troupe were out. *Free to Be . . . You and Me?* Kind of dorky. But Jess liked Emily; right off the bat they'd made not-too-needy eyeball contact, an eyebrow up, a thing with their lips, and: membership considered. Their eyebrows fit. What are you doing here? Their smiles fit. Then their laughter. Membership accepted!

It was magic.

They'd make demonstrably tortured faces across the room at each other during "It's All Right to Cry." They snuck out to get coffee at the nearby Stewart's gas station. Jess insisted that girls at the University of Arizona in Tucson drank coffee. So they did too and they'd talk about how awesome Tucson was.

Once, afterward, Emily told Jess about her and Peppy's garden. The garden was her favorite thing. The furry, green wholeness of her Route 29 backyard was like a pet or a family member: the flowers waking up in the morning, vines all done up in vegetable ornaments, the berries and the roots, the kind, useless plants that didn't produce food or beauty but existed all the same, and the scent of soil, mulch, and how insects, if you listened right, sang better than birds. They weeded because they had to, to save the others from being strangled to death, but they also had a patch—at Emily's seven-year-old insistence—that they left specifically for weeds, a sanctuary out near the creek. Emily and Peppy working together silently, the only time they were really entirely serious with each other, hour after hour and not a single slip into irony. That was their sacred space, and these were things that she hadn't mentioned to anyone at school—ever. Why? Because plants and grandfathers were uncool? Partly, sure. But were they really *that* uncool? More uncool than time-share Disney World vacations and Jesus? No, it was something else: something like, if she told a girl about her garden, then, naturally, she'd have to tell her all about her grandfather too, about their perfectly contained world and—and then she'd be too close to what happened to her at night. Her sleep problems. And then what would they think? Well, they'd think something like: you are obviously not right in the head, Emily Phane, and you are therefore unworthy of being a friend, best or otherwise. Because, actually, what was Emily even supposed to think? The worlds didn't fit. Emily had to keep things separate, uncontaminated. Later, she'd recognize that some of her let's call them social problems stemmed from this, maybe a lot of them. But on that day, Jess set something off simply by telling Emily how much cooler the trees in Arizona were. The trees in Arizona, she said, were cacti. She said they even grew giant flowers. She said how her brother would go out into the desert with his friends and their uncle's rifle and shoot the shit out of them. To Emily, this was a little burst of light. It was what she'd been waiting for and she couldn't resist, needed to know more, not about massacring cacti necessarily but about how you took care of plants in Arizona, the desert soil—or sand?—and she wanted to know all about the garden that Jess never once mentioned having in Tucson but surely had, secretly had, just like Emily. Emily felt it. Jess loved to garden.

"*Garden?*" Jess said.

"Mine's amazing," Emily whispered.

They were outside waiting to be picked up after troupe rehearsals. It was January, dark, windy; a bone-dry snow hissed around their feet, weightless in the freezing halogen light of the Queens Falls Middle School parking lot.

Jess laughed. "You're hilarious, Emily Phane! Oh my God, I love your sense of humor. I know, right? Who *gardens*?"

Emily balked, recovered, said, "Old people garden." She laughed. "Me and really old people. Obviously."

The ability to crack Jess Yarsevich up overrode any sense of betrayal. Gardens, Jess repeated, wondering why such things existed. Before they moved to Queens Falls, she'd given her brother's friend, Quint Ferris, a blow job, she said, suddenly. "Speaking of gardens—"

Emily felt as if she'd been thrown into a pool. She had never heard anything like this before. She couldn't help staring at Jess's mouth. The same mouth that had just been singing "Parents Are People" and "Don't Dress Your Cat in an Apron." Jess told her how to give Quint Ferris a killer blow job.

"Did it hurt?"

Jess said, "What, why would it hurt?"

Emily thought that it was supposed to hurt a little.

Fourteen wasn't an approaching age so much as a whole new freaking planet, and one that Emily wanted to immigrate to ASAP. Couldn't she just skip thirteen altogether? Maybe, she decided, and maybe this secondhand blow-jobbing was her visa. Because there could only be one thing going on here, don't miss your chance.

"Jess," she blurted. "You're my best friend!"

Sharpened silence, wind. It was like a nightmare where you suddenly can't find your legs. You look and look and: no legs. No nothing. The moment was false. Emily knew it. Jess probably knew it. Best friend? Best crap. It was like the snow around them had suddenly become confetti, had always been confetti, the mountains in the distance nothing but flat Adirondack Children's Troupe scenery. Pretty soon the trees would start singing about gender equality.

The moon hoisted up with ropes. It was so wrong. Emily was so wrong.

"Aw, Em," Jess said in her *Free to Be . . . You and Me* voice. "That is so sweet of you to say. You're like my best friend, too."

Emily hated Jess Yarsevich. "Whatever," she said. Then, "I'm just fucking with you."

Emily had never cussed like that, not once. That wasn't—where did that even come from?

Jess said, "Oh."

Maybe Jess *was* her best friend? Or would be, could be? Maybe Emily had jumped the gun and, wait, could it be that Jess's factious *Free to Be* voice was her true voice? I mean, she was here, wasn't she? She was a terrific singer. She never flaked on a rehearsal or gave less than 110 percent. Emily said, "Well, I mean, I'm sorry, you're like one of my best friends."

They paused, adjusted. They looked at each other and tried to figure out just who they were now, or should be. What had happened and how had it happened so quickly?

"Good, kid, because I was gonna *say*." Jess pretended to laugh.

Emily pretended to laugh.

Kid?

Jess stopped laughing, finally, and offered, "I guess you're my second-best friend." Pause. "In Queens Falls."

They were hardly even tenth or twentieth best friends after that. Maybe Jess *had* begun feeling best friend inclinations and Emily had messed it up. Maybe Jess felt she'd gone too far, that blow-jobbing the twenty-year-old Quint Ferris didn't sit nearly as well with Jess Yarsevich as she'd claimed it had. Jess soon left the Adirondack Children's Troupe—she joined another, bigger theater group in Saratoga. They stopped hanging out. On the rare occasion that they'd run into each other at school they'd mime happiness, say that they'd see each other soon, joke about the old troupe maybe, say they'd call, text, whatever, and then, many call-less and text-less months down the line, stop acknowledging the other altogether. And maybe Jess didn't see Emily. But Emily did see Jess: for a whole year she was acutely aware of Jess's movements through Queens Falls Middle School, where her locker was, her homeroom, what period she had lunch and who she sat with, which friends, at which table. Seeing Jess made Emily feel disgusting—yes, that was really the word—because it reminded her that she was always looking, in a sense, for Jess Yarsevich.

And so it began.

Because then came Lori Freeman in seventh grade. Similar thing. Out of nowhere Lori going, "You're my second-best friend, Emily!" You have got to be kidding me. Emily first thought it was a joke, as if Lori was in collusion with Jess Yarsevich. Then, in eighth grade, the cabal of Stephanie Bouchard and Amber Haviland *and* Jennifer Savona. They all said it. Three second-best friendships. In ninth grade it was Rebecca Hipsh and Desi Acevado and, urgh, Lori bitchface Freeman again. Lori, who, gallingly, actually claimed to have *two* first-best friends at the time, Rebecca Hipsh and Alexi Jones in a mutually beneficial BFF power share, meaning: here was someone who had enough best friendliness to spread over *two* girls in ninth grade but back in seventh grade, back when she'd originally said that Emily was her second-best friend, she didn't. Couldn't. Wouldn't. For reasons Emily would brood herself to death on, Lori Freeman needed to keep her in second place no matter what, a second place that felt, to Emily, exactly like a no place.

Emily attended exactly one sleepover. She was thirteen years old. She'd been invited numerous times before but Peppy had forbidden it. The idea had terrified Emily too. But this time, for whatever reason, she pushed things too far.

"Why can't I go?" Emily knew why. "Everyone's going. Peppy, I want to go."

"You've made that clear enough." He flipped through the TV channels.

"That's all you're going to say?"

"Let's talk about this another time."

"The sleepover's tomorrow."

"Then I propose we talk about it the day after tomorrow."

"That's not funny!" Emily needed to fight this out. For herself, mostly, but also so that she could semi-truthfully tell Alexi Jones that God, it wasn't *her* fault. She was normal. Her grandfather could be such a dick.

"I'm sorry, you're right," he said. "I'm concerned is all. I think that you're not ready." Then, because she made exasperated noises, he said, "Your dreams, Em."

"I am too ready," she said. Then, "Anyway, they're not dreams."

Exactly. Peppy stopped on a sitcom that neither of them enjoyed. "May I talk with this girl's mother?"

"Why do you have to talk to anyone's *mother*? Jesus. You don't trust me? What am I going to do? Drugs? You think I'm going to get pregnant?"

"Hold it, buster."

"You think I'm going to get HIV?"

Peppy turned the TV off. He sighed. No TV plus Peppy's *bemusing* thinky face meant that Emily was actually winning. Emily was not supposed to be winning. "I think that you know why I need to talk to Becky's mother," he said.

"Alexi."

"Excuse me?"

"*Alexi's* mother."

"Alexi," he repeated. Twinkled. "Now, she the one with the ears?"

"That is so mean. Please, I'm being serious!"

They stopped, watched the empty TV. "Anyways." Emily exhaled. "Melissa is the one with ears." You win, you're right. No sleepover. Now let's move on please.

"I suppose they all have ears," Peppy said. "So, then. Which one is Alexi?"

"Alexi's *Alexi*," Emily snapped. She hated Peppy's inability to take her social life seriously, the way he pretended never to remember the names of the unimportant people that Emily pretended were important. Oh she hated that he *knew*.

"Well, I guess it's OK then," he said.

Seriously?

In a reckless, irrational surge, Emily said, "Call her mom then! Fine. What are you going to say? Watch out, my granddaughter's a little bit crazy?" If there was one thing Peppy liked less than talking to other parents, it was talking to anyone, Emily included, about what happened to her at night.

"You're right," he said. "Maybe that won't be necessary." He turned, looked directly at her. "You really want to go to this sleeping over evening?"

No. How dense are you? But she couldn't locate her emotional brakes. "What do you think's going to happen to me? Why not just have me committed," and Emily began to cry. Would you look at how obviously nuts I am? You're going to send this kind of crazy to a sleepover party? With children?

"Sweetheart."

"I'm not crazy!"

Peppy turned the TV back on. He was not good with tears. "I'm sorry," he said. "I know you're not crazy. Like I already said, I won't forbid it. I'm sure it will be OK, and you're old enough to make your own decisions. Maybe it will be good for you. Perhaps I'll throw a little sleepover party of my own here, you never know. House to myself and all. Invite Mr. Jeffries over for some beer pong."

Emily laughed, couldn't help it. "Gross. Jesus, Peppy, what are you talking about?"

Peppy smiled. "Oh, just the latest thing." He loved incorporating and misusing contemporary terminology that he'd heard on TV. It was a routine that always made Emily laugh. He continued, "We'll mosh dance and take some e-mail photographs and we'll AOL them to Becky's party."

"Alexi."

"With the ears."

Emily tried to stop smiling. She needed to put a stop to this and so she made up a brother, an older brother of Alexi's, Keith, and Keith was probably going to be there at the sleepover *the whole time*. Take that, old man. Take *Keith*.

"Suppose Kevin has to be somewhere," Peppy said. "Can't tie him up out back, can they?"

"He'll have his friends over, too. I just remembered. It's like a double sleepover thing?"

"Well," Peppy said, chewing the word. "Well, I trust that none of them will have AIDS."

"But they might," Emily said. There was no hope now. They'd fallen deep into their routine.

"Statistically improbable, but OK."

Not OK.

They were six girls, including Alexi's bossy spit of a sister, Fiona. Fiona spent the first hour or two standing on her head, playing this electronic annoy-o-phone, challenging the big girls to games of Connect Four. She cried when they wouldn't play and she cried when they would and she lost. Sick to her stomach with worry, Emily hadn't slept much the night before. It wasn't only that she was too proud to call it off. She wanted to prove something to Peppy, and herself. She would make her grandfather proud. She was a normal girl. It was the first time she'd ever sleep in a house not on Route 29. Maybe she wouldn't have problems here—maybe, like a ghost, her problems were site specific. She couldn't eat. She was exhausted and she drank as much Pepsi as she could, all day long, can after can, buzzing like a fluorescent light, her head full of flies. The plan was to stay up all night.

Because it was October, Alexi decided that they'd watch R-rated horror movies. She'd borrowed some DVDs from a guy at school. "Let's scare the shit out of each other," she said boldly, presenting the contraband DVDs. Emily had never heard "Future Leaders of

America" Alexi swear before and couldn't help being impressed—and reminded of her truncated second-best friendship with Jess Yarsevich. Is this what sleepovers were like? Shit and horror? Emily had imagined more pink. They were supposed to be gossiping about boys, right? Why weren't they sitting in a soft pink circle gossiping about boys?

They went underground.

The basement was only half done. The half they were in was carpeted, lit, and had a sofa, a TV, and Alexi's father's PlayStation 2. It was his cave, Alexi told them, knowingly. "Man cave," she said, and they all kind of marveled at that, secretly, curiously electrified. Safe inside the cave of a man. This was a place where men went. There were sports posters on the wall, weights, a dusty running machine, and a few golden plastic trophies from the '80s. There was a collection of beer mugs from all over the world, but mostly Milwaukee. These they filled with Diet Sprite. The other half of the basement, behind them, smelled like a concrete dog. It breathed wetly, coldly on their backs and the girls would periodically turn to face it, pretend to see something, scream, and then all of them would flip out and dive laughing, scrabbling under the protective blankets they'd amassed in case the R-rated movies got out of hand.

There were really big cardboard boxes. Anything could be hiding back there in the dark in a cardboard box. Dead babies, partial nudity, spiders, decapitated heads. Emily acted as if she were having an amazing time. She joked throughout the movies, which didn't scare her, only grossed her out. The other girls were happy to have her there, deferring to her expertise. "You're really not scared?" one of them asked. "I can't hardly look."

"It's a movie."

"I know, but I keep thinking something's going to jump out."

"Something will," Emily said. "That's what the movie is about, things jumping out at you. But it's only a movie, and—"

"Fuck!" someone shouted.

Shattering glass, running, butchery. The girls laughed, half hugging one another. Because they were fucking teenagers now, weren't they? More or less officially? They'd bravely repeat the F-word, puffing themselves up, a spell against childhood and fear. "That is so fucked up!" The more they said it, the less frightened they were of the boxes or the bloodbath, the more they giggled like happy little children. Some kind of lesson here? The more you fucked, the less scared you were of fucking, the more childish you invariably became. Emily would recall this later.

Because, otherwise, she was terrified. The fucking spell didn't work on her. One by one, the girls dropped off, leaving only Alexi and Emily. This was nice, and more of what Emily had expected. They whispered in a heavy-lidded, disjointed, overly serious manner. They gossiped, and they talked about the future. Alexi was frightened of high school, the prom, of who would eventually ask her to the prom in three or four years, of not getting into all the Advanced Placement classes, and, she said, eventually not getting into her first choice college because she was white. "They're taking away a lot of our rights, Emily." Emily admitted that she rarely thought about school, or being white. "But you're not one hundred percent white, are you?" Alexi asked. Emily said that she thought that she was. "You could say you weren't though, you know. If you wanted. You're lucky. I would, if I were you." They spoke about which teachers sucked and which of the girls would marry ugly men and which of them would not marry men at all because *lesbians.* "But so who do you think will be the richest? I think I'll be the richest," Alexi yawned. "But maybe we'll both be the richest. You're not tired, Em?"

I am a teenager talking at night with another teenager, Emily thought. "I'm not super tired," Emily said, intent on keeping the increasingly unspooled Alexi awake for protection. "Do you want to watch another movie?"

"Do you? My dad's got some crazy ones upstairs."

"Really?"

"Like unrated crazy."

They slinked upstairs and, in the dark, snatched the first DVDs they found, something called *Band of Brothers*. Alexi was out within minutes. Emily woke her up once, just to see if she could, World War Boring flashing itself over the sleeping girls; Alexi only made a chewy face and turned over, whined. Emily turned the incomprehensible carnage up. Men, she thought, in a voice she'd heard women use on TV. She stood, looked at the trophies. She examined a single blue dumbbell. She turned the trophies around so that the plastic gold jocks faced the wall. Tomorrow, she thought, that would be some chilling and hilarious shit; she'd spook the girls by noticing and not knowing who—or what—did that. How creepy. Tiny plastic gold jocks moving on their own, turning to face the breeze block wall. She got back into her sleeping bag and watched the war. It was 4:00 a.m.

The next thing she was in Peppy's car, dark rushing at her. She was still in her pajamas. Peppy's left hand was on the steering wheel, his right on her shoulder, holding on tight.

"Peppy?"

"Shhh, it's OK, sweetknees. Go back to sleep. Everything is OK now."

"I wasn't asleep."

But then where had she been?

There was a slow road under them. Lights popped here and there, little gasps out in the blackness, the forest, the hills. Shit. Horror. The car's clock said 6:23 a.m. They were on Route 29, Emily knew that much, every turn and buckle and hill ingrained in her body. And then she registered the speed. Not slow. They were fleeing.

"Where are we going?"

"Home." Shoulder squeeze. "We're going home."

"No," Emily pried Peppy's hand off her shoulder. "No no no no." She pushed her head into the window. "I don't want to," she said. *"I don't want to."*

For a month or so, Emily became the girl who'd pretended not to be scared of horror movies and man caves but was, in fact, scared shitless of both and who knew what else. She'd gotten them all in trouble, especially Alexi.

"Well, you sure freaked my mom out," Alexi said. "I dunno, she was actually afraid your granddad was going to sue or something. Like, you were going to have to go to the hospital? I heard her talking to my dad. They were convinced that someone had brought drugs to the party, that we had all done some kind of drugs. They said you had taken acid. They'd seen that kind of thing before. Did you take acid?"

"No."

"Well, my sister can't sleep without the light on now. Least that's what she says. You got her pretty bad, running into her room, screaming and jumping around like that."

"I must have had a nightmare," Emily said. Quietly, "I was jumping?"

"I don't know," Alexi said. "I guess. You were really scared."

Only one other girl had woken up and seen it. Melissa with the ears, of course, and Melissa told people that Emily had *problems*, swear to God, that Emily needed to see an exorcist is what she freaking needed. Samuel Wiener, an inveterate passer of notes and a kind of obvious homosexual who'd pretended to have had a crush on Emily since elementary school, told Emily that Melissa was going around calling Emily a *psycho*. "Oh, and worse. Telling everyone that she never wants to be alone in a room with you again, just in case you snap. Stuff like that. Don't worry, though, she's just jealous because you have normal ears. I think on some level everything she says is about her ears." Emily apologized to everyone. They didn't exactly stop hanging out with her at school, but Emily kept her distance from that clique of girls and they seemed happy to let her. She made jokes when it came up, which wasn't so much after a month or two, and Peppy, of course, never mentioned it again, only once, a week later, saying that Alexi's mother had called and spoken with him. She'd called, initially, to say how sorry she was that Alexi had, unbeknownst to her or her husband, snuck such inappropriately contented DVDs into their house, and that she knew the young man who'd supplied the filth and already had a word with his parents, quite a few words in fact, frankly speaking, and, finally, it was really none of her business but she wanted to say that she knew the name of an excellent child psychologist. If they didn't have one already.

7

—

Emily was six when Peppy first took her to the hospital. Back then, yawning still terrified her. Feeling one coming on, she'd lock up her face, put a hold on her breath. She believed that yawns were how sleep entered you, and if you swallowed too much sleep, yawned too big, too often, you *drowned*. Then they would have you.

There was a barrage—as they say—of tests. Psychological. *She was sane, well-adjusted, intelligent, happy. She sure had an imagination.* Physical. *Tip-top shape.* Secretive, offensively underhanded. *Her grandfather was not abusing her physically, sexually, or emotionally.* Until, finally, she was summoned to the Queens Falls General Hospital sleep lab.

The wires planted into Emily's head connected to a room full of doctors. The doctors attended machines, sinks. You could watch them through a window. The hospital bedroom smelled like a balloon after you rubbed it against your hair and stuck it to the wall, and Emily was not afraid. It was safe to yawn in a hospital. Peppy had prepared her as if she were going to the kind of slumber party that she'd seen on TV—*but with nice doctors.* Plus, new bunny slippers for the occasion. The gunk they used to attach the wires to her scalp was cold at first, and then it tickled, and then it itched. Peppy said it made her look like a dandelion. She fearlessly yawned; she roared. "I'm an *actual* lion, actually, Peppy," she said. The nurses called her Freckles.

Emily had an incident an hour after falling asleep; one doctor and three nurses were there to help secure her arms and legs, keep her, they said, from injuring herself. But they only kept her from not reaching Peppy, who had to stand back, helpless, as Emily screamed, babbled, and then whimpered like a dog with a crunched-on paw. Sometime before midnight, Peppy insisted on taking her home. Enough was enough.

The next day, they returned.

The doctors noted Emily's pretty purple dress and what was her little stuffed monkey's name? William, Emily told them. "I told you yesterday." The nurses kept a distance. Queens Falls, apparently, was still the kind of place where a child could unnerve nurses.

The doctors' eyes landed on Peppy like heavy birds. Like owls. They took him to another room. Emily had been given a coloring book and a single number 2 Ticonderoga pencil.

They told Mr. Phane that what his granddaughter had—in all probability—were called night terrors: a common enough condition, they assured him, deepening their hospital voices. Though, ahem, they said. Shifting a little. Certainly, ahem, little Emily's night terrors were on the more terrifying side of the spectrum. This was something that would disappear in time, they insisted. During puberty, usually, at the very latest. The machines said that her brain was otherwise OK.

"Night terrors, huh," Peppy had said. It had been abundantly clear that his granddaughter was terrified at night.

There was little they could do, but they had pamphlets that they referred to as literature. They cautioned him against any kind of serious medication. Just their two cents, they said. Peppy appreciated this. Had he, however, thought about taking Emily to a therapist? You can never know where these things come from—or what can help.

Back in the car, Emily asked, "Peppy, am I very sick? Do I have to have the medicine now?"

"No," he said. He pulled the car out of the parking lot. "You just have bad dreams."

"They're not dreams." Because she knew, even then. "I already told you, Peppy."

"I understand that," he said. He sighed. "Patience. You'll get better, sweetknees. Doctors said so. You're getting better."

"I'm afraid."

"The doctors said you're shipshape. Good news. They said don't you worry. They'll go away as you get older. Do you want to stop for doughnuts?"

"How older?"

"Dunkin' Donuts just up ahead."

"I want to go *home*," Emily said. Then, "Greg Miller from kindergarten broke his arm on a tree and he got to have a cast on his arm."

"Not the same thing."

"Now we're allowed to draw our names on Greg Miller's arm."

"Emily, nobody is going to put your head in a cast."

"But maybe just at night, Peppy. But maybe not like a *cast*," she said. "Like a *helmet*. Or what if we cut my hair all off?"

Peppy swallowed his smile. "Bad hair doesn't cause bad dreams, and, anyway, your hair is not bad."

"They're not dreams, Peppy."

"Your hair is outstanding."

"But maybe with no hair I could look older, like you, like when they're supposed to go away? You said. When I'm older. They'll think I'm old and they'll go away."

"Who?"

Emily was silent.

"Emily?"

"I don't want to go to sleep without the medicine."

"There is no medicine."

"Then I want a haircut."

"You're fine," Peppy said. Trying to lighten things, "Cutting off all of your hair is not going to make you look old. It will make you look like a goblin."

"Good," Emily said.

"Tell me, how do you think your Peppy got so old? Baldness?"

"Birthdays."

Peppy laughed. "Who loves you?"

"Peppy loves me."

"That's right he does."

The night terrors would occur an hour or so after Emily fell asleep. They were not dreams. There was no narrative, no images, and it was the same thing every single time. It was a concentrated wrongness. It couldn't be explained or described and only made sense from a tongue-tied corner of Emily's consciousness. And it was terrible.

Like this: suddenly, inside sleep, the *wrongness* would thicken and grow until it was all that she was, until it finally broke Emily from sleep, from bed, eyes open, dark rushing in, and she was rushing, too, running through the house blindly toward her grandfather. She would turn on lights, all of them, exploding the house awake. The severe way a room filled with things, herself included, all conjured just like that at a flick of a switch. She needed it but couldn't handle it. Light. What was it? What was any of this? The carpeting and dolls and dumb, sinister pieces of furniture, all the senseless shouts of matter, and all Emily's fault for flicking the stupid switch. Turn them off, make them go away. *Make it stop.* Often, Emily would scream.

Sometimes, in school, she'd get intimations of these night terrors when trying to fix her reality within the concept of outer space, the infinite, or the fact that everything was happening on an ostensibly flat surface on a planet that was actually gigantic and round and rolling at abominable speeds through nothing much whatsoever. Surrounded by what? Light-years of more of the same. Later, the best way Emily found to describe these terrors was that it was like being upside down in her own body.

Peppy would help Emily sip water from a Dixie cup. Guiding her into the bathroom. Here, up up up. Plopping her on the bathroom counter, next to the sink. The homey purr of the tap filling a cup with water. This is how you drink water.

"There, now you, now you, one, two, three . . ."

She'd turn and look with Peppy. The mirror like a guide, a way for Emily to see how it was done while she was apparently in the process of doing it, and Peppy always counting, usually to three, but sometimes higher, numbers stacking, not exactly calming but making more sense than words. The night terrors felt like they would never end, the gaping panic of them, and she felt like there was no escape and that from now on everything was going to be like this because maybe everything was really always like this, or was like this before she was born and would be like this for Emily when she was finally, genuinely dead. Later, as an adult, she would think that she'd been cursed at too young an age with a sideways peek into the exact opposite of life.

Finally, she would hush. Her sobbing would soften and she'd feel herself fitting back into her body. Then, like that, like nothing had just happened, back into sleep.

Generally, mercifully, in the morning Emily wouldn't remember a thing. Not unless she awoke on the living room sofa or in her grandfather's bed, or unless Peppy told her about it or, later, when she was older and more perceptive, by the tense, internal way he went about preparing breakfast. A sleepless hang to his bulk. Cheeriness, tight as a drum.

Waking on the sofa: "Why am I here?"

"You had a bad dream."

She'd remember then. Could still feel the wrongness, the terror of not being real, of not fitting. "But no," she'd say. "No, I didn't. I remember, Peppy. That's not why I'm here."

Sometimes, during those preteen years, she would pray, which owing to her lack of religious instruction was basically a guileless, intuitive form of supernatural haggling. I'll do *this* if you stop *that*. It helped. But going to sleep with CBS TV on the radio helped even more, and moving the bed around the room and never sleeping in the same position twice in a row might have helped as well, hard to say. One evening she'd push her bed to the window, the next she'd lay her head where her feet normally went. The next she'd nudge her bed a few feet to the right or left, or sleep on the floor in her sleeping bag, though Peppy never fully approved of that. Too many crooked old drafts in the house.

"Bad night, Peppy," she'd say.

"Bad night," he'd repeat.

The same way you hoped an actress might break a leg, you never wished Emily good night. What for? She never had them. Bad nighting, as invented by Peppy when Emily was eight, was both accurate and homeopathically hopeful. Mostly, though, it made them both smile. Never failed. Even toward the end, when Emily was twenty-two and Peppy could hardly even talk. "Bad night, Peppy," she'd say, kissing his forehead. His dentureless smile like an attempt to inhale the entire lower half of his face, and a bad night it would be.

But like the doctors predicted, the night terrors gradually lessened as Emily approached puberty, from one a night to one every other night to one a week, then a month, until they ceased altogether around Emily's fifteenth birthday. The damage was done. Sleep had cast its odd, subtle shadow over her life.

Two years of therapy had gone nowhere, or, actually, *everywhere*. Deceased mother this, deceased mother that, and then, of course, the doozy that nobody ever even knew her father. He might be anywhere, anyone, or just as deceased as her deceased mother. Every man was potentially her father. Emily was told that this was how she perceived the world. And those bad dreams that Emily politely insisted weren't dreams? *They were dreams.* She'd have to accept that. She'd have to accept that whenever she saw a man, she thought: Daddy. Better she realized this now, before she entered into more destructive sexual relationships in the future, right? Her bad dreams were probably PTSD-like attempts by her subconscious to attract the attention of a father, who might be anyone, anywhere, et cetera. Or they were sexual in nature, which is why she couldn't properly describe or account for them, or was too embarrassed to. "Tell me again about being *upside down in your own body*, Emily. Where does that mean your head is? Can you point to where your head is on your body when you're upside down in your own body?" Yuck. Gross. Emily walked out on two of her four therapists because they developed a crush on the idea that Peppy was sexually abusing her in the middle of the night while she was sleeping. "But that's not happening," Emily told them. "That's not what I'm here for."

"If I may, isn't it likely that you yourself don't know what you're here for?"

"Like here on earth?"

"Well, you've got a delightful sense of humor. That's established. I appreciate that. For the sake of argument, Emily, let's say that if something like that is happening then you don't know that it is happening. It's not your fault. Only your subconscious knows."

"My subconscious told you to tell me?"

"Couldn't it be that your so-called night terrors are telling everyone?"

Then there was Route 29's near-total isolation. They never got around to having poor Mr. Jeffries nocturnally raping her, but that, Emily assumed, was only because they'd never seen his face.

"Why do you think this Mr. Jeffries keeps his deceased mother in the attic, Emily? Can you tell me a little about his mother?"

"God, I'm just joking!"

"OK, let me ask you a question. Isn't taking nothing seriously the same thing as taking everything seriously?"

Then there was her grandfather's alleged misanthropy: Did Emily feel beholden to it? Enslaved or manipulated or cowed by it? Did she have to feel the same way about the world in order to meet his approval? He was, after all, all she had. Did she think that was normal? Did that frighten her? His age? His mortality? Isolation? Irony? His masculinity? Did his occasional lady friends disturb her? Then, finally, there was her love of plants—now here was a metaphorically fertile subject! Tell us about gardening. How does it make you feel? Tomatoes. Soil. Cucumbers. How do tomatoes make you feel, Emily? How does holding a cucumber make you feel? Because, hm, perhaps gardening was nothing less than Emily's own way of mothering herself and the world around her, a gigantic splurge of overcompensating *nurture* of nature to account for a lack of female role models? She was trying to grow a mother, wasn't she? Or maybe, Emily, you're only trying to grow yourself anew?

Right.

No. Her sleep was not co-opted by dead relatives. Peppy wasn't a deviant. Gardening was a *hobby*. She liked being outdoors: the pebbly sound of the Kayaderosseras, the tall pines and squishy grass beneath her toes. Being curious and terribly sad about not knowing who her father was was different from being emotionally crippled or systematically destroyed, night after night, by an unaccountably rapey lack of father. Or mother. Or anything else she didn't actually need, like the dull sexual insinuations, the how about sketching whatever you feel today sessions, the expensive, torturous logic. She needed a good sleep is what she needed. Maybe she needed a best friend. Mostly, wasn't she a thirteen-year-old girl? Did they have pills for that?

Finally, she said, "They just make me feel smarter than them, Peppy. That's all. I walk in feeling strange and nervous, thinking maybe this time they might help me, and I walk out feeling like they're morons."

Peppy sighed.

"I'm sorry," Emily said. "Dr. Branca's not so bad. It's just annoying."

"I'm sorry, too," he said. "I've got to tell you, Emily, I'm extremely frustrated myself."

If she'd only found one adult person besides her grandfather who could see that the sleep problems were the *cause*, not a symptom. Therapy only convinced Emily that she couldn't open up about these things, her nighttime things, without being misunderstood, manipulated. In trying to cobble together a path toward healing, they'd made her feel more insane, isolated, exasperated. This meant that later, in her teens, when things got unimaginably worse, besides Peppy, there was nobody she could or would talk to about it. If they hadn't believed the night terrors, they'd never believe what came next. Never. Because if the night terrors seemed to exist in an altered place, a wrong and inarticulate region just to the left of sleeping, then what came after the night terrors was like an invasion of that place into Emily's waking, conscious world. It was like as a little girl Emily had crossed over and whatever was there had finally found a way to follow her back.

To make matters worse, at fourteen, Emily crashed into womanhood, alone. Suddenly it was clear that she needed more than the training bra she never had, that her boobs had somehow, over a period of six or seven months, managed to train themselves.

Peppy couldn't know. She worried him enough. She'd have to purchase one herself, like the maxi pads she'd gotten at the Stewart's gas station mini-mart across from school. But since they didn't sell bras at the mini-mart, Emily had begun hiding herself away behind these huge, incontinent sweaters that had once belonged to her grandmother Gillian. One girl asked her why she was wearing a jellyfish to school, but that was about it. Under the sweaters, Emily wore prohibitively tight T-shirts from years ago.

The afternoon she realized it was too late was the first day of spring, though, technically, it was still winter. The sun was white. Everything was melting, dripping, pooling on the pavement. Emily had, without thinking, taken off that day's sea monster sweater and her winter jacket. She stood in the Queens Falls Middle School parking lot, happily watching the birds, waiting for Peppy's car. Her little T-shirt was yellow.

Peppy generally took her to and from school every day.

He said, "Would you look at this afternoon, Em?"

Emily got in the front seat, slammed the door, tossing her bag, jacket, and rolled-up sweater into the backseat. She realized instantly. She might as well be naked. She fastened her seat belt. This made them perk up even more.

"Let's go pick up some food," Peppy said.

Biting her lip, "Sure."

They practiced subsistence shopping. They rarely did big trips, just little sorties he called them, every two, three days. This didn't seem weird or counterintuitive to Emily until later, and then, well, not extraordinarily weird, or no less weird than the massive twenty-four-hour Price Chopper itself. She understood why Peppy didn't want to pilot a shopping cart under those fluorescent lights for any extended period of time, quick in, quick out, like Price Chopper had a limited supply of oxygen.

They pulled into the shallow snow-melt lake of the Price Chopper parking lot. "I'll stay in the car," Emily said.

"What? Just a little piddle puddle. Come off it. You got your boots on."

"But."

"Come on," he continued. "Going to need your moral support, Em."

Maybe he didn't notice. Maybe if she did like normal he wouldn't notice. Grabbing the sweater from the backseat would only draw attention, be weird; it was way too warm for a sweater.

Emily followed him inside, resigned, looking down into the endless parking lot puddle, stepping on the treacherous sun, kicking it a bit, watching it shatter, reform, bobble, follow them regardless. Idiot.

Peppy had wanted rib-eye steaks and Emily, inside Price Chopper and feeling suddenly contrary, amorphously annoyed, embarrassed, as if the boobs were *his* fault, had demanded pizza. She would eat only frozen pizza. She hated steak, actually, she said, thinking that maybe if she argued ridiculously about dinner, he wouldn't notice the untrained breasts. This went on for a while and it was never entirely clear, probably to either of them, how much of a comedic routine the argument was. They got that way sometimes. Finally, Peppy gave in. Emily, recognizing that she'd been being a brat, told him that, OK, no, it didn't really matter. She wanted steak after all. It felt good to be conciliatory. She loved her grandfather and, in a sunny, springtime rush of that, she took hold of his hand. They often held hands in public. Peppy's hand was just where Emily's hand naturally went. "I'm sorry," she said.

She sensed it immediately. Peppy looked to the right, as if he saw someone annoying there, and he yanked his hand from hers. His eyes caught on her yellow T-shirt.

Confusion, hurt, something else: a game. It was a game. Emily snatched her grandfather's hand back. She pulled it back toward her, exaggerating her little-girlhood, squeezing the hand, *mine*.

"Hey now," Peppy's voice rose. They were standing by the ice cream. Swatting her away. "Young lady. Enough. More than enough."

With that, he went looking for food: tall, withery, hunched over the empty wheeled cage of the shopping cart, leaving his grand-daughter among the freezers, on the verge of tears. It was colder here than it was outside. Emily's breasts tightened. She saw her reflection in the window of the frozen food door, a bright yellow woman: pointy, painful, braless nipples. She crossed her arms. She walked out of the Price Chopper, head down, glass doors whoosh-ing open before her—ta-da!—thinking: How stupid. How gross. Oh my God I am gross. She got into the backseat, put on her sweater, then her jacket. Then her seat belt. It was so hot. She was sweating, not crying. That'll show him. She took out a schoolbook. Ten minutes later Peppy returned with frozen pizza.

"You moping?" he said. "Don't mope."

Emily would not lift her head from the book. "Homework," she said.

"Good."

Plus moping.

She never held his hand again, not like that and not until he was too ill to object. You can't be his little girl forever. It wasn't a rejection, more like an animal reaction to an animal development, and it was probably hard for him as well—the obliging of a process that time and her body had already begun. This beginning of that end. But still! If only he'd known how to express his feelings a little better—it didn't have to be such a big deal, the following weeks of thinking Peppy found her body as embarrassing and alien as she did. Was she a second-best granddaughter now? Was there something perverted with her that she still wanted to hold her grandfather's hand? The boobs were obvious, but did she disgust him with the—with her time of the month as well? Sick, illogical, and indulgent thoughts followed sick, illogical, and indulgent thoughts. Could he *smell* her? Horses could. Becky said so. Or was it where Emily found herself putting her hands that her grandfather couldn't deal with? Did he know where she sometimes put her hands, her fingers? How could he, she thought.

How could he not?

8

—

Queens Falls High School did not suck. Like a kitten or a full moon, Emily became effortlessly, inarguably attractive. Particularly during her junior and senior years when she started to make up for all that lost best-friend time with boyfriends.

But it was her absent, troubled next-door neighbor, Harriet Jeffries, whom Emily came to most associate with those high school years, though in a way more akin to a spirit animal than an actual friend. Harriet was a buzzy, cool, evil little hummingbird of a thing. She was something that Emily had always admired from afar, ever since Harriet was little and wouldn't leave her house no matter how much you waved, how many flowers, special pebbles, or dazed toads you left on the front porch for her. Harriet fascinated and thwarted Emily. Since they attended different schools, they rarely saw each other, maybe only once every month, but Harriet loomed large in Emily's conception of herself. Emily was particularly transfixed with the way Harriet's moods sparked and darted. Over the years, they'd had friends of friends in common. They'd even been to the same lame interschool event once or twice, though Harriet never stayed too long. Emily read about Harriet's artistic awards and achievements. But more often, later, Emily would see Harriet walking alone down the side of the road in Queens Falls or Saratoga Springs, or at the dying shopping mall, where they both worked that one summer, giving Emily a chance to stalk Harriet from a distance on a daily basis, or, in the final year before Harriet moved to New York City and Emily moved to Boston, the spate of Harriet sightings in the combination Taco Bell and Long John Silver's parking lot. Her massive canvas, itty-bitty Harriet sitting, legs crossed, on top of her car, painting with what looked like soil. Emily'd spot her there at night, too, furiously slashing at the canvas through the dark. Candles set up all over the hood of her car. Harriet painting outside Walmart, gas stations, the intersection. People honking, giving her the finger. Starbucks coffee cups tossed at her. Harriet Jeffries painting the DMV at dawn. Emily almost never saw Harriet next door.

Emily had always wanted to know what Harriet was up to, feeling connected, like a distant relation, a fantasy BFF. Eventually this grew into something far more private, odd, lightly consuming. Emily thought she *recognized* Harriet Jeffries. It wasn't only Route 29. For some reason Emily was certain that Harriet, of all people, would understand what Emily suffered through, night after night. Perhaps the compulsion behind Harriet's awful paintings spoke to something that Emily wished she didn't understand. They'd speak, sometimes, if they ran into each other, but it never seemed like Harriet wanted to, so Emily wouldn't push it. Instead, she'd ask people about Harriet. Hairless Jeffries? That girl is scary. PMS personified. School massacre waiting to happen. Dyke. Insect weasel bitch. Oh my God, she seriously has the most annoying voice.

But Emily knew different, or thought she did.

For Emily, watching Harriet, even from a distance, was like watching lightning. Harriet berated motorists. This actually appeared to be an important part of her art. Fussing at folks while standing on the roof of her car in the mall parking lot at dusk. She rained curses on the jocks and the phony, insecure bitches. Emily came to believe that Harriet was angry and alive in a way that few people in high school were capable of being. Super intimidating, too, like she alone knew not only why she was so angry but why everyone else wasn't, but totally fucking should be. Emily wished she could be angry instead of frightened, ironic, disengaged. Harriet was more awake than anyone Emily had ever seen. *She was right there.* Even her pouting was loud. Her paintings, of course, were huge. Like her body, Harriet's discontent was small, sharp, dazzling.

In high school, and even later on, Emily daydreamed Harriet Jeffries. True, she didn't even know her, and Emily knew she must have been partially conjuring a Harriet who didn't exist. But still. Harriet, as Emily's spirit animal, appeared to ride her own bucking emotional truths, even wildly contradictory ones. Harriet wasn't strong like a man. Her strength wasn't solid, predictable, dependable—nothing of the sort. She was fierce. Emily thought so, anyway. Harriet could change, she could whip herself in any direction she wanted at any time she wanted and have that direction be entirely hers and, most important, the correct direction. Men, Emily would learn, could not be free spirits. Guys just clunked and lumbered, the sharp elbows of their ideas, beliefs, and egos smashing into everything and often only for the sake of the smash. Call it sport. Not Harriet. Harriet was fooled, sure, because everyone was, but Emily imagined that she also had a level of personal integrity that was off the hook. Her emotional self seemed untethered and therefore true. Five hundred years ago, she'd have been burned as a witch. Two thousand years ago she'd probably have been hailed as a prophet. Then set ablaze.

But who knows.

Emily didn't know anything except that she'd always thought that Harriet Jeffries was cool, especially when she did things like shave off all of her hair or dress like a Glad bag. Ultimately, Emily wished that she could have cared enough about her own identity and presence on earth to go bald or wear emotional clothing.

With boys it was different. Though Emily didn't properly lose her virginity until she was almost out of high school, she developed a reputation. Probably because there was a new guy every month or two and Queens Falls was small. Girls turned on her and boys, amazed, kept trying their luck. Emily was both easy and impossible. She knew how to laugh. Boys gathered around her like villagers around a stone with a sword stuck in it. The fact that Emily never really got crushed out on a boy and that, in spite of that (or maybe because of that), she really did have her pick of them—this infuriated the girls. It ate them alive. She didn't even care! Who the hell was she to not even care? They cared. They'd show her how much they cared. They called Emily a slut. Freak. Fine. Let them be jealous and annoyed. They stopped laughing at her comments in class, frowning, rolling their eyes, sighing and looking away, looking at one another—*give me a break*—whenever Emily said something witty, which was often. She stopped hanging out with girls altogether and she pretended that this did not bother her and that her serial dating was not also a little about revenge.

Boys were a temporary, intoxicating salve. But she just couldn't be consumed. Emily had never felt tortured or ecstatic, anyway, though she had felt rejected and deliciously tongue-tied. Turned on—sure. Emily had fun. But she couldn't feel *serious*. She'd get soooo close, be genuinely into this or that boy, and then: nothing. She'd wake up and feel more alone than ever. She had to keep moving. If she stopped moving she'd see the yawning hole in herself and she'd fall in there and drown.

Later, of course, in Boston, she'd boyfriend up just so she didn't have to sleep alone. This was rarely sordid. Emily could not sleep alone, that was the important thing, and the sex, when it was good, was, as they said, a benefit. Transgression was not attractive to Emily Phane. Mostly she laughed the boys into bed; she had a way of making seduction seem like an accident, a goof. She was in control, always, until she decided, as she occasionally would, that it was safe and OK to be a little out of control, then grrrrr. Watch out.

She needed someone there when she was shaken awake at night—human ears to hear her, hands to remind her that there's this too: other hands. You, me, the whole wide waking world. Normal things obeying normal rules. Proof of a denser reality beyond the one that had begun to leak into her head. Not that she ever told anyone this. What could she say? She said she had nightmares sometimes, that's all. Bad dreams. Now, please, just hold me back to sleep.

Peppy had encouraged her dating. Made him happy, seeing his granddaughter moving forward. He made names for her high school boyfriends, whom he tended to like. They liked him too. Poor Tobin Anderson was the Phase. Isaac Gilmore before him had been, for whatever reason, the Squirm. Pete Harmon was Baby Peacock. Michael Sokol simply Michelle.

He once mentioned, or *seemed* to mention, that her grandmother had been hard on her mother, Nancy.

"Hard like how?"

"Just hard."

"Like with boyfriends?"

"Your grandmother meant well."

Peppy didn't make the same mistake. "I'm too old to kick their cabooses, anyhow." But it wasn't only that. Emily's inability to properly, seriously bond with anyone, male or female, was probably the only way that she had ever failed her grandfather. He wasn't going to live forever, he knew, and she knew that it frightened him. Emily being left all alone. Frightened her too.

As for Peppy, for much of Emily's childhood, he entertained remarriage, he said, in the same way a Shakespeare troupe might entertain a class of toddlers. His occasional lady friends were nice, often intelligent, but, ultimately, they never made more than a lick of sense.

First they came from Peter Phane's past. Gussied up and hungry to mourn, to collaborate. Ready to jump in the time machine his tragedy offered—possible remotherhood!—and a chance to be the useful and appreciated women they could never be with him all those years ago. (Or so Emily assumed when Peppy told her about those days.) They began happening "to be in the neighborhood" shortly after Gillian's funeral, one by one, as if there were a

Fresh Local Widower visitation schedule up at the Olive Garden or YMCA (he said). They just knew. They rarely overlapped. The infant orphan as excuse. They brought with them Tupperwared food, piles of clothing and accessories, Christmas cheer, toys, and a smattering of things they hoped old Pete would file under A Woman's Indispensable Touch. Flowers, Valium, baskets of artificially wood-scented wood shavings, boxes of white zinfandel, VHS tapes, baby-blue bath salts. Ironing. Sweet'N Low. Things got unseemly.

There was Min Sherwood, for example, weeping over episodes of *Quantum Leap*, holding Peppy's hand too hard, so hard he'd feel violent and then alarmed and then simply used, like the safety bar of a roller coaster. He'd joke about this when Emily was older, those early days of widowerhood. The women and their neediness and unnecessary baking, the parenting advice, the parenting magazines—*Mothering; Pregnancy & Newborn; Parents*—the decaffeinated tea. They'd brew pot after pot of the stuff, then forget to drink it. They wouldn't even bother pouring it. Peppy assumed that they felt existentially adrift without something to do in the kitchen every twenty minutes. They enjoyed making cold things hot. "I think sometimes that being a woman warps the brain, Emily."

"Very funny."

"Sure can be."

Peppy said, and may have believed, that he could have genuinely loved one if they'd *merely* been old. If just one had figured out how to do old with any degree of dignity, he said, or goddamn charm. Their clownish abuse of cosmetics. It was as if the primacy of their early feminine physicality, their *looks*, had been so forcibly imprinted on these widows and divorcées that they were now, for all intents and purposes, either batshit with despair or batshittier with delusion. Take your pick, old man. Peppy told Emily that he didn't have the wherewithal. Not at his age he didn't, not after Gillian.

Emily didn't know much about her grandfather's marriage, or her grandmother. Peppy was respectful but unengaged with Gillian's memory. She was a city girl, a rough cookie. That's what he'd say. Here, a photograph. Platitudes like locked doors. Once or twice, Peppy would open up. Emily might catch him after a few glasses of Scotch, and she'd learn that Gillian had thought that Peppy had abandoned her and the marriage when he had abandoned those parts of himself that she'd most adored. The ambitious parts, apparently. The small-town kid making it in New York City parts, the so-called *brilliant* parts that she didn't have enough of either and so where the hell did that leave the two of them? Here? Route 29? Gillian had wanted to see the world with Peter Phane the go-getter. She'd wanted out of Queens, New York. Hadn't they been going somewhere?

Peppy had once written newspaper and magazine articles. He'd traveled. Then he'd stopped, more or less. He'd moved back upstate with a modest inheritance, took an editorial position at the local paper, and settled into his uncle's old hermitage on Route 29, taking his city girl with him because what else was he supposed to do with her? She'd been pregnant with Nancy and intent on dutifully riding out this asinine gentleman farmer phase of his. "I think she started to garden, actually, in order to show me how pointless gardening was." Her ambition played the long game and lost. But he'd been upfront with his wife, he said. He *told* Gillian. Told her that there was nowhere he cared to go. She simply chose not to believe him because, she'd said, she knew him. Peppy said he wished he could have been this person that Gillian knew, the man she thought she'd married, or that, later, she hadn't been so damn intent on punishing the both of them and, eventually, their daughter, and for what? Her own inability to leave? But maybe that was his fault, too.

"I can't imagine you being unhappy."

"Don't suppose I ever was."

He almost certainly had women other than Emily's grandmother throughout the marriage. Emily was not sure how this made her feel. Peppy was so charming, forthright.

He was also all she knew. Growing up, she identified with him, adored him, wanted to be exactly like him, and the truth is, she would probably forgive the incorrigible charismatic anything. She knew that he was good. He never lied to her or attempted to disguise his nature; if Emily asked about one of his women, he would tell her, in detail. But only if she asked, and so she almost never asked. Peppy was discreet. Sometimes, secretly, Emily would even try hating her grandmother like she imagined Peppy possibly did, or had once. Those curdled photographs of Gillian. She saw her like she imagined Peppy saw her. Sour woman. Nag. But Emily was not comfortable with this, and so she didn't ever think too much about Gillian Phane. She did not want to feel complicit.

The gold-rush days of Peter's suitors ended when Emily was about three years old, though there continued to be relapses right up until the end of his life. Every year or two someone would show up, trying to crack the old nut. Winnie Shapiro, whom Peppy was spending time with when Emily was eighteen, wasn't the *batshittiest*, but close enough. Peppy met her at Price Chopper. If you believed him, which maybe you shouldn't, he insisted that Winnie had followed him home from the supermarket in order to check out his new microwave. "I told her, frankly, that it's not new. You're going to be disappointed, I said."

Winnie was a cheery, minuscule woman in her seventies. She had springy grey hair. She emitted heartbreakingly obscene noises in bed. The first time Emily heard it through the wall she thought that Peppy was punching a cat.

Win, as Peppy called her, had the loudest face you'd ever seen. It was her eyes. Her glasses made it seem as if everything she saw was an unalloyed shock. The TV she watched: shocking! The eggplant parm, the peas, this frosty glass of milk. Shocking! Shocking! Shocking! Emily coming home from school. *Winnie Shapiro was shocked.* You never exactly got used to it. She also read ceaselessly, like she was cramming for a test, and, of course, the words on the page shocked her too. The old woman curled kittenishly up on the sofa for entire Sunday afternoons, her two gigantic, stunned eyes pinging back and forth behind *Memoirs of a Geisha. The Poisonwood*

Bible. Snow Falling on Cedars. Peppy, meanwhile, might listen to the game. Cook. Straighten up. He'd tap Winnie's head as he walked by her and, without looking up, she'd make a kiss-kiss noise. Emily had witnessed a number of Peppy's girlfriends, but nothing like this.

"Emily," Peppy said. "Good morning. Win and I would like to speak with you about something."

That morning, Peppy and Winnie had moved their chairs closer together in a way that Emily found distracting. They were eating fruit with spoons. This shouldn't have rankled Emily.

"You want to *speak* with me?" Emily said. "Since when do we announce we want to speak with each other?"

"Manners," Peppy said.

"Emily," Winnie chirped. "We're going to have a baby!"

Peppy laughed; Winnie too. Ha ha ha. Jerks. Winnie had taken over in the house as Peppy's new comic foil. Her laughter yapped. His: like a sonorous, African-American Santa Claus. It was often said that Peppy—Pete to everyone else—resembled a white version of the actor Morgan Freeman.

He was smiling. "Sit yourself down, Em."

Women were particularly susceptible to that voice. Emily used to joke that she could imagine him narrating really slow footage of geologic wonders. Coaxing a wonder along with his voice alone. Peppy, tell me again about limestone. Peppy, make it *erode.*

Emily sat. "You're eating sliced banana with a spoon," she said. "Both of you. Don't think I haven't noticed."

"Strawberries in there too," Winnie said. Her eyes peered comically into the bowl before them. They were sharing a bowl of fruit. One bowl, two spoons. She continued, "Blueberries, raspberries, apple. Oh, there, well what do you know? Some melon. Pear. Let's see. Grapes. Pineapple—did I already say pineapple?"

"Lemon," Peppy said.

"Kiwi," Winnie said. "Beef."

The obscene cataclysm of two very old people laughing like children.

Emily thinking: Please don't say you're getting married. Then: Don't scowl. Be nice. Smile. She'll be gone in a few months. But please don't you say you're getting married.

Because Emily saw why Peppy liked this Winifred Shapiro, and why she probably liked Winnie too.

Winnie said, "Oh, Peter, goodness gracious, show your grand-daughter the letter already!"

Peppy took out an envelope he'd had resting on his lap. "I opened it this morning by mistake," he said. "Well, partly by mistake. I guess we got it a few days ago and it was hiding with some junk or other. Win saw it, actually." His eyes trembled. "Well, OK, here you are—" He passed her the envelope, which also trembled. He said, "I am so proud of you, Emily."

That was how Emily learned that there were people willing to pay her a substantial amount of money to move away from Route 29 and everything she loved. She was officially going to Boston.

The old man didn't believe in college and neither, back then, did Emily, but the unspeakable obviousness of his mortality meant it was time. Playing college made more sense than playing widow. Peppy needed her to leave.

Boston because Emily wanted a city—she saw how her behavior and Queens Falls, or any small town, were an awkward fit, and she didn't think that she was ready to retire from the world like her grandfather; eventually, yes, maybe. Probably. But not yet. He'd had years abroad and then many more in New York City before he'd seen enough, right? What had Emily ever seen but the after-effects of that world? Peter Phane's face wasn't an entirely accurate map.

He agreed. "You'll be wanting to see for yourself. Don't you dare take my word for anything. I'm a malcontent."

New York City as a first port of call was too daunting, *too Peppy*—Emily would suffer her own disillusionment, thank you very much—and nearby Albany, though far bigger than Queens Falls, was a city the same way a scooter is a motorcycle. So it was Boston or Philadelphia. (She had to be nearby, that was a given.) Boston University, in the end, gave her more money.

Could you major in gardening? In granddaughtering? Plants? Not exactly, not at all really, so she decided to major in something like plants, in biology—*the environment.* It didn't matter what. In her scale-tipping application essay she wrote persuasively about how being an orphan made her more in tune to the collapse of the world's ecosystem; how her whole life she'd been searching for a parent, a mother, and found none; and how living in the middle of an authentic verdant nowhere, Mother Earth had been her foster parent, and now look what was happening to her poor mother, herself being abandoned by her rapacious ungrateful children, demolished, unregulated, *et cetera.* Peppy helped. He encouraged the whole orphan thing! He mustered some of his mythical journalistic verve and it had them in total stitches. It was the funniest thing that either of them had ever seen. They laid it on so thick. They even shared a bottle of wine. He called it their please-sir-I-want-some-more essay. It was the most fun they'd had in a long time and mostly, Emily thought, because they'd both been so nervous. They knew what this meant. She was preparing to leave Peppy so that he could die. Peppy was kicking her out so that he could die.

The main reason that Emily did not like thinking about the future was because her grandfather did not live in the future.

Right, but *you do,* he didn't say. You *will.* You have to be somewhere, Emily.

"I don't want to be anywhere else but here," she did say. "I don't want to go."

"Enough," he said. "Now pack your bags."

Thing was, she'd had them packed for weeks.

9

—

The sixteenth floor of Warren Towers was the highest she'd ever been and it was where Emily *lived*. She rode an elevator home. Her window was a TV that you couldn't unplug, and the night-time trance of Commonwealth Avenue traffic muted her. Emily had a horizon. It was ticklish, almost too much, and it turned her on: the thousands of other windows out there, switching on, off, all night long. She'd call Peppy when it snowed. Looking down through the swarming, nearly phosphorescent snow, palm pressed against the cold window. Emily never tired of describing this to Peppy, who never tired of telling her that they had snow in Queens Falls, too. Whoop-dee-do. They also had electricity, dentistry, you name it.

"I miss you, Peppy."

"Yep," he said.

Infuriating. Like a friend you knew was surfing the internet or watching TV while you told of emotionally intricate insights, though, in fact, he wasn't. He had to turn the radio and TV off to hear Emily properly. "Talking on the phone isn't talking," he'd say.

"Would be if you *talked*."

"I love you, my darling," he said. "Now tell me about snow."

In Boston, Emily smoked cigarettes, marijuana, the occasional ironic cigarillo; she drank mojitos and discovered food called cuisine. Cilantro, for example. Falafels and lobster bisque and *negitoro temaki*. She flipped for the plastic Dixie-like cups of melted butter that came with the lobsters that some of the older, parental-charge-card boys she dated bought her from Legal Sea Foods. It became a joke between Emily and one of her first BU friends, Maxine. Emily wondering why they didn't just go and dip everything in plastic cups of melted butter: steak, fingers, cilantro. "See this?" Maxi patting her ass. "*Here's* why."

Emily befriended those who stayed up late. Kids who lived off campus; kids who weren't even technically kids anymore, transitioning from being students to being un- or underemployed. She gravitated toward people who reminded her of Harriet Jeffries. People that Emily thought Harriet Jeffries would, herself, gravitate toward. Emily didn't form many daytime attachments and she soon fell out of love with the gabby high school hotel that Warren Towers revealed itself to be. Though she never got sick of the elevator commute, the height, the CITGO sign, or the canyon-like gash of the Charles at night.

She hated her roommate. Firstly, in theory, just *having* a roommate. Emily was uncomfortable sleeping in the same room with a stranger she couldn't touch or cleave to as she plummeted to sleep. She no longer had night terrors, so no threat of Emily wigging out in the middle of the night, but what happened to her now was worse and left her feeling more exposed, more nuts. Going to sleep, for Emily, wasn't dissimilar from undressing from her own body. That said, Emily would have disliked this roommate under most circumstances. Her name was Erica Baker.

Erica Baker had a shit ton of sisters. This was a conversation that they had maybe three times that first week. Oh my God, Emmylee, you got no *sisters*? The Chinese aborted sisters. Erica Baker talked about this so often that Emily began to wonder at her implications, as if Emily might somehow be complicit in the traditional Sino hobby of sister aborting. Because Erica Baker had three. Five, actually, if you counted her sisters-in-law, which Erica Baker did, *on her fingers*, and every time she mentioned her other, better, biological sisters, which was, seriously, like every fucking chance she got. One, two, three. Then Ryder's wife, *Kelly*. (Sigh. Eye roll.) Four. Then Dylan's wife, Kat. ("Urgh, you have no idea!") Five. A full-fingered hand of sisterhood. It was pathological, if harmless, and Emily would have tried to have figured out which proactively sibling-centric church Erica Baker was involved with but who knew what glassy-eyed planet such a conversation might ultimately crash upon. They weren't pals. Emily would try to nap during the day, which too often collided with Erica Baker's study time or Erica Baker's TV on the laptop time, or her sister time, Erica Baker having nearly identical conversations with each of her sisters, one after another, even (urgh) *Kelly* and Kat, the same mewling litany of Boston's shortcomings. Erica Baker was from Florida and thought, among other things, that the Massachusetts weather was out to get her. Her personally. She was also disapproving and far too inquisitive about the time Emily soon began to spend away from their room at night. She left leaflets on Emily's bed.

The academic side of collegiate life was pretty much exactly what Emily thought it might be, and just as engaging. The professors and the TAs liked Emily, and, mostly, she reciprocated. The cynical, rumpled ones reminded her of Peppy. There were worse ways to spend her time. So for many it was a surprise when the girl who'd appeared so gratifyingly curious and with-it ended up, come evaluation time, right smack in the middle of the giving-a-shit spectrum. Baffled by Emily's exam results or her tentative, weightless essays, professors would, no doubt, think back. The Phane girl hadn't actually asked any piercing questions, had she? She hadn't. Nor had she made any particularly astute points in conversation or, face it, done much at all besides be so heavily present. The absurdist way that Emily looked at things could sometimes be mistaken for a slippery, well-curated intelligence, especially by heterosexual men who'd eventually have to confront the truth. Emily Phane was a perfectly mediocre student.

By the end of her freshman year, she'd moved to a place in Jamaica Plain. She'd happened into a large second-story room—with a porch!—that would have been out of her league if she wasn't room-sitting, more or less, for Tracy de la Cruz, a half Spaniard she'd spent a few nights accidently roaming Somerville with.

Tracy had followed someone to Maine and from there, some-how, to Berlin, Germany, for a week that lasted a month, then more months in Hamburg, if Facebook was to be believed, and just as Emily had stopped paying attention, an e-mail appeared, explain-ing that she wasn't coming back to Boston for a while and, in fact, had decided to "finally put a restraining order" on the MIT phys-ics dissertation that Emily didn't know anything about since they weren't really even friends. Turned out that the story of Emily's Erica Baker horror had made an impression on Tracy and so she got first refusal on her room in the Jamaica Plain house she shared with four other sex-positive women in their thirties. For a Bosto-nian version of next to nothing, too. Just watch her shit, you know? Make sure her plants didn't die of loneliness.

From there on, Emily's life centered on Jamaica Plain. Centre Street, she found, was a good thing to walk beside and toss trou-bles into; she appreciated the trees, hills, the tattoo mothers and the dirty, faded, expensive vegetables. She imagined someday run-ning into Harriet Jeffries here; Harriet seeing Emily and thinking, Whoa, look how cool she turned out! It was possible to get from JP to BU via public transport, but also an amazing pain in the ass and, if anyone asked, it was that which contributed to her low attendance, middling grades, and general ghostliness where BU was concerned. Nobody asked. There was a fine line between doing nothing and waiting. Sometimes she'd sit on her porch, overwhelmed by exile, hating to think of what she was really waiting for. She did enough to ensure there was some kind of excuse for her to be in Boston, and that her scholarship held. Barely. She carpooled to BU with postgrad friends, lesbians particularly. Lesbians loved driving one another around.

Later on, back in Queens Falls, her Boston years felt hypnagogic. This compounded her problem. The dreamy, teasing, pulled-cotton-ball nature of her memories. She'd think back and not be able to see any of her friends as plural entities or place herself as a solid thing among solid things. They were energy fields she'd join, or didn't join but got caught up in for a bit while on her way elsewhere. Nocturnal acquaintances developing and fading; Emily could slot into groups, ride them for weeks, entertain them, be entertained, and then disappear. Poof. No big deal. She was every clique's auxiliary member. She could hang with the eco-polyamorists as well as she could with the middle-class indie girls and their gay besties. Keep moving. People who came to think they knew her best during those years wondered how she'd possibly lived for so long up at Camp Crystal Lake or wherever it was she was supposed to be from. Hick Falls, New York. Smallville. *Deliverance.* Not their sleepless, roving Emily Phane.

"Were you friends with all the creatures of the forest, Em?"

Emily said that she was. "I did a lot of gardening. I've told you guys. Laugh all you want. My grandfather and I were never bored."

They loved this. "Here we go!"

"What is she hiding? Has anyone ever seen a photograph of her cabin? This Pappy character?"

Emily said, *"Peppy."*

"Even better."

"I want to know where the orphan rumor originated. Do orphanages still exist? Has anyone ever seen one?"

Someone passed Emily a joint; she declined. Then, why not, undeclined. Someone got up to go to the kitchen. Someone returned with two Blanchards Wines & Spirits paper bags. "Little of both. But mostly spirits." Sitting down. Bottle, bottle, bottle. Gourmet potato chips. Bottle.

"I'd like to address the persistent Mormon rumors."

Laughter. Something crashing in the kitchen, two girls shouting "Sorry!" in unison.

"Where are the photos? We demand proof. Middle school transcripts at least."

"I thought the Emily Phane birthers were already debunked?"

"I've always considered myself more of a truther. But seriously, has anyone really seen her sleep?"

"Whoa, good point. Ethan? You wanna weigh in here, buddy?"

"Like any day her sister wives are going to show up and drag her into a black van. Back to the compound, Freckles!"

"Pappy don't believe in cameras."

"*Peppy.*"

Emily smiling. "Believe what you want, guys."

During Emily's fourth and final year in Boston, she worked part-time at Les French Flowers in Jamaica Plain. For much of that year she lived there too, sharing a small apartment above the shop with her boyfriend, Ethan Caldwell. Ethan's stepmother, Bo-Ra Caldwell, or Boo, ran Les French. Boo owned the building. Ethan had been five when his father died and he'd never known his biological mother. Boo had raised Ethan as her own. They only spoke Korean at home.

Emily wasn't particularly fond of flowers. To her, Les French was like the vegetable kingdom's version of a charnel house or, better, a kind of whorehouse. Everything just hanging out, all the lurid, stinking, fleshy bits. No romance, no roots, very few leaves. But she liked the work, and Boo became a true friend.

Boo wanted a daughter. It was, perhaps, her defining obsession, and one that Emily came to find endearing. Boo would pine, maternally ogle the little JP babies in fuchsia; the sassy teenagers who needed to cover up their business; the grown-up professional women who needed to "get husband," have some *cake*, buy themselves a nice bouquet, just relax, OK? This was all she'd ever really wanted, she'd tell Emily, *the daughter*. Before Ethan came into the picture, it had been clear that, besides running the register, being mothered was an integral part of Emily's job. You be good. Now mop floor.

Ethan was several years older than Emily and had recently graduated from Yale with an MA in Asian languages and civilization. On occasion, Emily'd heard him and Boo Skyping from the back room, the two of them speaking Korean, and Emily had, of course, assumed that he *was* Korean, or at least half Korean. "My son, Ethan," Boo would say. Never plain old Ethan, and never, ever *step*son. Mysonethan—as if it were one Korean word—mysonethan this, mysonethan that, something she couldn't say without a happy flash of teeth.

He returned on the Wednesday before the Friday when he was scheduled to return. First impression? Ethan looked like a famously handsome actor deep inside the role of a homeless person, like somewhere under his brown homesteader beard and flannel shirt was a noble swell of music and a montage of cinematic redemption: a clean-cut face, dimples, and a standing ovation for the kind of award that remarkably handsome people get in Hollywood movies after they've been bearded and homeless for a little while.

More than that:

There was a certain kind of man that always snagged Emily's gaze. You saw them in supermarkets walking *beside* their shopping carts, never subservient to their shopping. One hand on the cart, just taking the groceries out for a stroll. Sometimes this type even marched ahead, pulling the shopping cart behind them with a single hooked finger. Follow me, food. It was ridiculous and Emily hated that she also found it attractive, if only in the obvious, cavemanly way of motorcycles and push-ups. Anyway, this type, when they bought flowers, wouldn't look at the flowers. They'd march straight into Les French, looking only at Emily. They'd request something *nice*. Emily'd ask more specific questions and they'd act as if she were speaking fart. I don't know, *nice*. Flowers, you know? Roses. Something rosy.

Emily first took Ethan to be this type. The way he strode in. Except, no. Because he was looking at something, actually. He was looking at the door to Les French's back room.

Big mistake, anthropomorphizing *men*. Lizzy, a friend of Emily's was fond of saying this. But still, didn't this man have the most soulful eyes? Dogs can have eyes like this, and terminally ill toddlers: big and sad without the recriminatory self-consciousness of adult sadness. Emily decided that he must be that other, rarer type of customer: the genuinely bereaved. Funeral homes normally bought their own funeral flowers; they had arrangements. You got the occasional internet orders from less-bereaved, out-of-state family members, but that was it. Rarely did walk-ins buy funeral arrangements, but when they had, they'd looked a little like this. Cuddly, almost.

Which is to say, Emily immediately liked him. And she couldn't help wondering whom he'd lost.

"Hello," she said. "Can I help you?"

He was heavyset but tall. Huge, actually. He smiled goofily at Emily and continued walking straight toward Les French's back room. The staff room.

Shit, Emily thought. Drunk homeless guy after all.

"Hey," Emily said. His hand on the doorknob. "Uh, excuse me?"

He put his finger to his lips, shhhh.

"That's the—"

He mouthed, *I know*.

Emily picked up the phone so she could threaten the man with Boston Police Department.

"Oh, God, I'm sorry," he whispered. "She's not back there, is she? I wanted to surprise her."

"Boo?"

"Well, I'd planned on saying it louder."

Emily said, "Mysonethan?"

"Just Ethan." He tossed her a small, effeminate wave. Still whispering: "Thing is, there's a taxi out front holding my stuff for ransom. I didn't have enough cash. They charge extra for boxes."

"Boo's doing deliveries."

"I probably don't need to whisper anymore, do I?"

"It's up to you."

Ethan slipped past Emily and went to the cash register, punched in the code, removed some bills, and strode back out onto Centre Street. Emily opened the register. He'd taken all the twenties. I just let a handsome homeless person take all the twenties.

Ethan's head popped back into the shop, silly little bell ringing above him.

He smiled, again, then a demonstratively woeful glance up at the bell. "Em-ill-ee," he said. "Emily, hey, I'm sorry, but would you mind giving me a hand?"

It didn't occur to her until later that she hadn't told him her name. On the sidewalk were three large suitcases and a few cardboard boxes. Ethan sat on one. Emily stood above him, waiting. His head lightly tilted in the afternoon sun, like he'd been there all day. He had that lipless thing that bearded boys have—where the hair stopped, teeth began. "She didn't tell you I was coming?"

"I thought next week?"

"Yeah," Ethan said. "Me too. Long story."

"I thought you were Korean."

"Like just now?" Ethan said. He laughed. "What changed your mind?"

"No, I mean—" They both laughed.

"I'm joking. I'm sorry. It's been a long day and I'm wrecked. My mother's told me all about you, you know. She thinks that you know how to talk to plants." He stood up. "Thank you for taking such good care of her."

"I don't know how to talk to plants."

"That's what I told her."

"I love your mother."

"Me too."

That was weird. Emily said, "So, um, you want to get this stuff inside?"

Ethan nodded. "If you don't mind, maybe you could help take the two small suitcases up to my apartment? I'll get these boxes."

Forty minutes later the Les French phone rang. Boo had not yet returned; Ethan was upstairs. Emily answered.

"Hello, Emily Phane? Sorry to bother you, but is my other bag, the small green one, still on the sidewalk outside?"

Emily looked out the window. It was. She'd forgotten it. "Well," she said. "I mean, I don't think . . ."

"Shhhhhhh." Ethan was standing behind Emily. She jumped, tensed, turned. He smelled like a shower. He put his stupid phone in his pocket, though Emily remained on hers.

"I'm sorry, Ethan," she said into the phone. "Can I call you back? It's not a good time. I've got to deal with this customer—kind of a jackass, actually."

Ethan turned Emily back around to face the window and the little green suitcase on the sidewalk. "Look," he said. "Beautiful, isn't it? Don't make any sudden moves—we don't want to spook it."

They stood next to each other and watched the suitcase.

"I worry about it, though," Ethan said. "Do you think it'll be OK?"

Emily smiled. "They grow up so quick."

10

———

Eight days later, Boo told Emily that Ethan would be taking her out for dinner. "Guess what?" she'd said. "Something nice for you, Emily!"

Emily hadn't seen much of Ethan since his return. She mostly heard his feet. "I don't know, Boo. I've kind of got plans tonight."

"I make plans."

"Well, I guess." Wait a second. "Wait, does Ethan know?"

Boo said, "I go tell him."

Before Emily could stop her, Boo scooted into the back room and upstairs to Ethan's apartment. She returned shortly with the good news.

For dinner, they got drunk. They went up the street to a bar known for its LGBT softball team. Emily's choice. He was maybe a little too sure of himself—and maybe Emily liked this a little too much. She'd needed to destabilize him, but, in fact, he knew Spud, the trans-man bartender, and even a few of the regulars. Did that explain his pink flip-flops? Ethan was wearing pink flip-flops.

Halfway through their first beer, Emily said, "Ethan, are you gay?"

"Nope."

He was unflappable.

"C'mon," Emily said. "Not even a little?"

"Sure, if you want, Emily. I'm a little gay."

Emily loved how he interacted with Jim Dew, whom she knew from his frequent, fussy visits to Les French Flowers. Jim would bitch, and Ethan, hand on Jim's shoulder, would genuinely listen and sympathize with the exquisite trauma of what it was like being Jimmy Dew all the time, day after disastrous day. Emily watched how people at the bar were drawn to Ethan; it was his wholeness, his slow, large, simple ease with himself. The lesbians most of all. Ethan told Jim to stop being such a queen. Buck up, man. Jim said, "I *know*, right?"

Emily pretended to be immune. Ethan would answer Emily's questions and then suddenly say things like, "Have you ever been to Ipoh?"

"No."

"Really?" Like he was genuinely shocked. "You should go to Ipoh, Emily." He looked intently at her, smiling, and she couldn't tell whether he was making fun of her or having fun. Because why? What or where was *Ipoh*? Why did she strike him as someone who should go to Ipoh? Ethan didn't expand, just kept the questions coming. It took her a while to fall into this rhythm of weird, unexpected revelations. He didn't ask about things he wasn't interested in, and, as yet, he wasn't interested in what she'd planned on him being interested in. He asked Emily if she'd ever dreamt in a foreign language, and, if so, if she thought that English dreams were messier. He asked if she was scared of China. Conceptually speaking, he qualified. Ethan Caldwell was a solid, heavy wooden box that, once opened, revealed buzzing multicolored plastic gears and wheels and clicking levers. Nerdiness, in a way, but a nerdiness that the gravity of his masculinity had warped into something winsome and strange. You never knew what he was going to say.

"I'm supposed to believe this worked on the grad school girls?"

It was kind of working on her and they both knew it.

"Grad school *women*." Ethan smiled like the sun punching through a mass of cloud, Emily thought, but maybe that's because of the beard, and, also, she was a little smashed.

Midway through his fourth or fifth beer, Emily suddenly realized that he was actually listening to her, intently, and, moreover, that she was talking in a way she rarely talked. His eyes seemed alive to intricacies of her voice, as if his eyes were also ears. She was telling him about her garden, of all things, and her theory of plant communication, homologies between neurobiology and phytobiology, about how she understood plants and how she didn't think plants were what everyone thought plants were, and how, OK, she was kind of wasted here, but she really fucking hated Boston University and the stupid things they called plants at Boston fucking University, and then she calmed, and spoke about Peppy, the two of them living way out away from environmental science alone on Route 29. The seasons turning, soft and slow and explicable.

"I like that," he said.

"Well, I'm glad you approve."

"Don't be that way," he said. "Nah. You don't need to be that way."

Emily asked Ethan what he wanted to do now that he was out of school. "Go back to school," he said.

"Like a PhD?"

"That's right."

"What do you want to do after that?"

"I want to be the South Korean ambassador. Ideally. Eventually. I'd like to start off in the diplomatic corps. Or maybe work for the UN. Have you ever been to the UN, Emily?"

He wasn't joking.

He ordered another round of beers.

"Make mine a mojito," Emily said.

"Two mojitos, Spud. Please. Thank you."

Toward what seemed like the end of the night, Ethan asked her, quite simply, if she wouldn't mind coming home with him. Emily said that she would.

"Mind?"

"Come home with you, Ethan."

That out of the way, they continued talking. They talked about North Korean dynastic squabbles. They talked about films that Emily hadn't seen. Ethan wasn't a cat or a dog person—he was a fish person. "We don't get a lot of press, but we're out there." Ethan told Emily about how Korean felt like his native language. They talked about how long it might take for fish to become as domesticated as dogs or cats and it was unbearably sexy. Their eyes locked perfectly. They hadn't even touched hands, brushed elbows, knees, let alone kissed, and Emily began to think she'd misheard this whole coming back home with him thing, or, worse, that he was a psycho as well as a weirdo, and this was some kind of Korean power game, preemptively slut-shaming his mother's new flower girl.

They stepped out into the empty weeknight Jamaica Plain sidewalk. They still hadn't touched. Was this a platonic sleepover, Emily wondered, and would that even be a bad thing?

They whispered through Les French Flowers, as if the flowers were sleeping guard dogs. Into the back room. Upstairs. Into Ethan's apartment. It smelled like musty tea, shampoo, wet paint. Ethan disappeared immediately into the bathroom. The only light came from under the bathroom door and the weak yellow streetlights out on Centre Street.

Emily undressed. It was intuitive, and was easier, somehow, than making the first move and touching him. Power needed to be rebalanced. Ethan returned from the bathroom, leaving that light on and the door open—*Ethan was wearing slippers*—and there Emily was, standing without clothing in the middle of the room.

Lit as he was from behind, Emily could not see Ethan's eyes, and what she saw was drunkenly shifting anyway. She laughed. Ethan laughed, too, but in Korean. Emily was certain that he laughed differently in each language, and here was his intimate, true laugh. Boo's laugh.

Slowly, then, too slowly, Ethan's right hand went to her waist—*they touched*—and Emily shuddered, her heart kicked up, and then his left hand, which couldn't have been larger than his right hand but felt larger, hotter, moved onto her left breast, then up her breast, past her nipple, on up to her neck until he held her there, slightly less gently, then up from her neck and onto her cheek until he was holding the side of her head, gripping her hair, twisting it a little. Then a lot. He looked down at her. Emily had never been this close to this large a man. He was looking right into her eyes with his no eyes, with where she imagined his eyes must be staring directly into hers, and she tried to move forward and turn this off with a kiss already, please, but Ethan wouldn't allow it—until he did—and then it began.

The next morning, getting dressed, Emily said, "What will we tell Boo?"

Ethan lay in bed sipping from a big, manly mug of herbal tea. "What makes you think she doesn't already know?"

"You wearing same as yesterday," Boo noted. And that was that.

Pretty much from that day forward, Emily stayed with Ethan. It was impossible to know what Ethan thought about *them*. She told her friends that she was dating an *unclassifiable* and that it wasn't serious. He thinks he's Korean. He's big but not fat. He's a UN geek. *UN geeks are a thing.* The relationship was open, she'd say, because this was something everyone was saying at the time and they'd never said that it was exactly closed. She even insinuated to some of her girlfriends that she was still seeing other, unspecified men. They'd just smile.

The sex got better. Her friends told her that she'd started talking in clichés, acting all gooey, moony, gross, but they were just jealous because *it was true.* It was like she'd never had sex before Ethan

Caldwell. The way he flipped his own switches. Maybe this had something to do with his upbringing, the losses he experienced, or the way he switched between English and Korean. They'd be out all night and they wouldn't touch, not a hand on a shoulder, nothing, like he was testing her. But he wasn't. Then, back in his room, a switch would flip and everything opened up, rushed in, taking them with it.

Ethan's mother had left when he was a few months old. Her name was Sandra. That's pretty much all he cared to know. Were drugs involved? Probably not; who could say? But you know her name, she's alive, you know California. Did I say California? Well, you *implied* California. What, how, so I have a West Coast tone of voice now? OK, but what about Sandra's family? He must be curious. He didn't need to know, he said, and Emily thought that this had more to do with Boo and a childhood fear of being taken from Boo, probably, than anything else. His love for Boo was fierce. Ethan's father had worked for the State Department and had died in Indonesian traffic. Emily soon started calling her own mother Nancy.

Once in a while, they'd hypothesize about their missing parents. Not Ethan's favorite thing, but he knew it was important to Emily. For her, it wasn't that Peppy didn't like to talk about it—though he didn't—it was that her grandfather really didn't know a single thing about Emily's father or much of what Nancy's life had been like before she returned home to die. Peppy had spent years looking into it, briefly reverting back to his investigative journalistic self that had so charmed the young Gillian, picking up on Nancy's bread crumbs, her unpaid parking tickets and her masterfully diffused unpaid credit card debts. New Mexico, Vermont, California; even London, England, for a few years. Portland, Seattle, Oakland. Denver? Even Denver.

Nancy, when asked, had only assured her parents that Emily's conception had been anything but immaculate. Perhaps Emily's father was part Latino, or Inuit, though a lot of people in Boston assumed Emily's father was somewhat Navajo. Her cheekbones, black hair, something in her disposition too: this wide-plained and inscrutable thing people picked up on. But who knew where her constellation of brown freckles came from—and why *somewhat* Navajo and not a touch Apache or a tad Pueblo or a teeny bit Comanche? No idea. Because Navajo sounded cooler? Admittedly, Ethan kind of thought that it did.

In the past, with friends and lovers, Emily and Ethan had both sometimes acted as if whatever was peculiar about them was down to their orphanhood. Playing the orphan card. *It's not you, it's my dead parents.* Together they called bullshit on all that. Emily hadn't needed anyone but Peppy, and Ethan wasn't tormented by his deadbeat biological *Sandra*, not exactly, and he claimed that the loss of his father, though incalculable, was made bearable by Boo's love. It was both a relief and somewhat disconcerting to admit to each other that their problems, whatever they were, had nothing to do with their parents or lack thereof. They'd both had happy childhoods.

Emily spoke with her grandfather once a day. Usually for only a minute, maybe two. She talked, he listened and hummed, because he was good as gold thank you very much, good as gold. This was one of the prerequisites of her moving to Boston: the ninety-three-year-old would have to suffer these daily check-ins, no ifs, ands, or buts.

Until Ethan, none of Emily's Boston friends, let alone boyfriends, had ever been in the same room with her when she touched base with Route 29. It was too private. But then, one day, there they were: Ethan reading his hieroglyphs and Emily speaking with her grandfather, like no big deal. More than that, she'd just told Peppy a little about Ethan, couldn't help it, nothing really, just some anecdote, so that it didn't seem so weird when at the end of the conversation, just as Emily was wrapping up, saying so long, Ethan looked up from his book and waved at the phone, as in, *Tell your grandfather bye from me.*

"Um, Ethan's waving good-bye," Emily told Peppy. "He's actually being kind of insistent and weird about it."

"He's what? Waving to you?"

"To you."

There was a pause.

Peppy said, "That's not how telephones work."

Emily didn't know how relationships worked. She kept her secrets safe from Ethan. It was, she thought, the only way to keep Ethan as her safe thing.

Surely he picked up on this and, worse, seemed to like this about her. He enabled her. He told her that she felt intrinsically unknowable, and how he couldn't get enough of this.

"Intrinsically, Ethan?"

Foreign, differently sourced, like she was withholding from him her mother tongue. Ethan loved learning new languages and Emily hated how perceptive he fucking was, and what this said about their relationship. Because what would happen when he finally did know her? What if he someday became fluent in Emily Phane? Ethan, she thought, I need to tell you something important about myself.

Imagine what the sun would represent to someone without eyelids. That's where she should have started. *Ethan, I don't know how to sleep.* That people looked forward to sleep, fetishized and ritualized sleep and its accoutrements—what a joke. People doing it *soundly*? For Emily, listening to people talk about sleep was like the way human sexual behavior and mating rituals must seem to the genuinely asexual. *I can't wait to go to sleep.* Like it was a vacation, a safe, incredible destination that everyone knew how to arrive at safely but her. Seriously, where *was* this place? How did you get there from here? Emily's directions sucked, and so night after night she'd get lost and end up someplace else entirely. Someplace bad.

11

The assaults began when Emily was fifteen, shortly after her night terrors ended. They were not the same things. They were to occur nearly every night, occasionally more than once an evening. Lights on didn't help, and Emily had outgrown prayer. Sleeping pills made her more vulnerable, and suicide, the teenage idea of which she'd indulgently flutter around, made even less sense than the prayer. If she died completely they would have her completely. It'd only mean calling it quits on the illusionary waking world. She'd become more herself, not less. Emily, concentrated. The waking world, as intangible and absurd as it was, was the only stuff that stood between herself and hell.

In the very beginning, she couldn't even talk about this with her grandfather. She hadn't wanted to disappoint him or worry him more than she already had. He'd been so proud of her, finally sleeping through the night. Now this? It was too bad to be true.

It starts with a tearing. Not like paper, more like sleep is ripping itself in two, and with it, Emily's head. She hasn't been anywhere, anything, and then she is back. She is no longer asleep.

This is crucial.

She is no less awake now than she is during the day, walking around outside. But she cannot move. She cannot open her eyes. Emily tries, but she is locked in, keys lost. There is no way not to panic. It is exactly like waking up inside a corpse. It is not a dream. It's not even a nightmare.

Imagine a frantic, violent struggle without a single moving part. It is as if the temperature of reality has changed. She can feel herself, every unresponsive part. Her head on a pillow, hair on cheek, blankets bunched up between her knees. Emily feels her knees. Her knees feel like tiny stone islands. Her belly. A shoulder, her lungs. Do not think about the regularity of breathing, which she feels and cannot control and that is beyond horrific: air passing back and forth between her lips like mocking, intrusive spirits. She is breathing, but she is not breathing. Something is breathing her.

Hearts don't beat, they gulp. If you really listen, if you really feel what they do to you inside your chest. The heart is her only moving part and it is a bloated, disgusting thing.

And then they are on her.

Emily's entire head is submerged in screaming. It is a sound that is also a churning, howling physical field. Voices suffocate her, squeezing her. Not her body, not that yet, but the unnamed her at the center of things. Imagine a riot. Imagine the sound of this riot slowed down. Imagine anger as slow sound being poured into your head. The roar and gibbering of madness. Emily feels like she is being eaten alive, from the inside out.

She is wide awake.

She cannot move.

Her eyes will not open.

Emily is just so small here. If you could see her. Trapped inside of who she's supposed to be in a bed in a small room in a house that is small in the middle of nowhere, and she can hear the nighttime pines groan. Tall trees listing in the wind. Through it all, she can hear rain on the roof, the Kayaderosseras fuming, and a truck. The truck sounds like a zipper ripping open the road. There is an outside her house and an outside her body and then there is Emily: a small, trapped, lost nothing. She cannot move. They will not leave her alone. Beyond the storm there is the sky, she thinks. She tries to focus. Surely there's a sky with a moon and it should matter but it doesn't matter because Emily is way too busy being buried alive inside her own body. There is nothing kind or loving watching over her.

If these attacks convince her of anything, it is that evil is a thing like fire is a thing. Evil is real. She tries to open her eyes. Start small, she thinks, tries to think, holding on to small thoughts, a wreckage of words and phrases; the debris of everything she is as the screaming swallows her up. She tries to wiggle her fingers. Toes. Say the word.

Toe.

But her tongue is heavy and dead inside her jaw. She has to remain alert or she'll be nullified, swept up into these sounds forever. They want her; they feed off her fear. They produce it, harvest it. They grow full with it. But she can't not be afraid.

They?

Then there's a drawing back. There always is.

It is just as sudden.

The sounds stop and coagulate outside her into silence. Listen to the room. Because it is inside her room.

Footsteps approach her bed.

Sometimes, here, Emily is lucky and she returns to her physical self. Before the footsteps reach her, she sometimes bursts back alive inside her body again, jolts upright in bed. Hands scrabbling for the light, as if she could physically hold on to light.

This time she is not lucky.

The footsteps stop. It is right there, standing over her. He has stopped. She knows that it is male in the same way that she knows it is evil. Or that it is cold outside, wet. You can feel evil the same way you can feel the wind.

Evil feels nothing like wind.

It waits above her.

It watches.

What does it see? Her body? Her who? What? Emily wants to go home, to be home, to have the keys to her body again. Because then, sometimes, they will be on her.

On her chest, something pushing down so hard that she cannot breathe. Sitting on her chest. Squeezing her chest of air, and her body of herself: trying to push Emily out of herself like toothpaste. Or: it will grab her neck. She will feel hands, actual hands, around her neck. Smearing her head back down into the pillow.

But this time it sits down on the bed beside her. Like: you and me, we need to have a little talk. The weight of it, the way the mattress buckles a bit next to her, shifting her body toward where it is sitting on the bed next to her. It begins to rock. Sitting beside her, back and forth, slowly, then not so slowly. It is trembling. Emily hears the creaking of the bed beneath her—beneath them both—and she hears its breath. It draws closer to her paralyzed face.

I'm sorry, Emily thinks.

Please.

Help me.

Then, like stones thrown sharply into her head, Emily's eyes break open. She springs up. She sobs. And there it is. And it is even worse than she could have imagined: her empty room.

Emily suffered a year of thinking she was insane, possessed, worse, before breaking down one morning and telling her grandfather what was happening to her when he thought that she was finally sleeping soundly. She was sixteen years old.

Standing over her, concerned, hands gripping the back of the chair—when he was most concerned Peppy stood—he directed Emily's "computing." He disliked the internet. "Well, suppose we have to look *in there*, Em. Type in *Google*. Typing it in up there would be best, I think."

"Peppy, I know how to search the internet."

"Sure you do," he said. They stared at the Google home page. "Now ask it a question."

Despite Peppy, they found the term pretty quickly. Sleep paralysis. There was a name for what had been happening to her, and

Emily began to cry. She'd never imagined that what was happening to her could happen to others; it felt too hateful, idiosyncratic. Didn't everyone go insane in her own way?

But here were entire websites, scientific studies, and virtual support networks. Others reported the paralysis, of course, but also, incredibly, the footsteps, voices, the pressure on the chest. That all-pervading sense of an evil presence. Some people even had visual hallucinations—*so-called hallucinations*—the shape of someone standing over the bed, watching, a shadow man moving across the room. Initially, this information had been a relief. She didn't need an exorcist or an institution. It had been named.

The more Emily read, the less sense it made. The anesthetic of it being a *named thing* wore off in increments. Peppy's voice came back to her in relation to the still inexplicable night terrors: "Well, we already know she's terrified at night!" *Emily already knew that she became paralyzed after being asleep.* But not in her sleep, as was insisted. She was awake when it happened. One hundred percent. On this point she had no doubt. "Like this," tapping the table in front of her, telling Peppy, "I'm as awake as you and I are right now. Exactly like this. But I cannot move. It's like being in a coma plus full consciousness. It doesn't feel like it will ever end." The scientists had gotten the so-called symptoms correct and, it turned out, there were many who suffered from this thing. Though none, it would seem, as frequently or as extremely as she did. Emily began to feel as if she were someone suffering from a debilitating migraine, reading about the occasional headache.

The explanations curdled. They wanted Emily to believe it had something to do with *dream leakage*—a lovely way of putting it that meant that she awoke, ostensibly, in the middle of REM sleep, right at that point where your body is paralyzed—because if it wasn't, Emily learned, you'd freakishly act out your dreams, flailing around like a maniac. So there you were: wide awake but still paralyzed, and the dream stuff just started leaking in, drip drip *drop*, and this somehow accounted for everything. It was a glitch of the brain.

But if the dream leakage concept was true, then the type of stuff leaking in would be *limitless*. Wasn't that obvious? Did scientists not dream? The leakage could be anything, sex or Smurfs or musical raccoons. Yet all the people who suffered from SP reported almost identical things. Moreover, she learned that most cultures had traditions encompassing this phenomenon. It was historic, as old as recorded thought. In Newfoundland, Emily learned, they called it the Old Hag. In Newfoundland you could even send the Old Hag to people by reciting the Lord's Prayer backward. (Yes, Emily tried this, and no, there was no way of knowing whether she successfully hagged Lori Freeman.) These things were noted throughout history. It was always a part of us and our conception of sleep. The word *nightmare* itself meant to be ridden by the night mare, as in horse, as in being crushed by whatever these things were, ridden to death. Nightmares, originally, didn't mean bad dreams. Because these weren't dreams. Leaks? Emily wasn't leaking. The more she read about her condition, the more convinced of its reality she became. It was no more a glitch than anything else. Every culture seemingly had a word for it, and a similar supernatural explanation. Incubi and succubi, those rapey demons, of course, but there were so many others. In Mexico it was *subirse el muertro*. The dead person on you. In Fiji, *kana tevoro*. Being eaten by a demon. Emily liked that. In Kashmir it was a *pasikdhar*, which was believed to live in every home and only attacked if God was ignored: punishment for a person who basked in the misfortunes of others. Every single one of these words made more sense than *sleep paralysis*.

Karabasan.

Kaboos.

Haddiela. Jinamizi. They infested humans like lice. Emily wasn't special. She was only cursed. She particularly liked *ogun oru*, which was what some Nigerians called it. *Ogun oru.* Nocturnal warfare.

. . .

Ethan, I don't know what's wrong with me. I'm afraid. I don't know how to sleep. Oh, and Ethan? I've been nocturnally assaulted by demons since I was fifteen years old.

It was impossible.

Because when Ethan slept, *he slept*. Sleep was another of his switches: awake, asleep, he snapped cleanly from state to state. She never woke him, even clinging to him afterward. She was surprised that *they* didn't wake him, actually. That he slept through the roaring, the footsteps approaching their bed. Emily's body being pressed into the mattress.

But of course he must have sensed something.

He allowed Emily a personal space that occasionally bordered on disregard. Did he realize how much she needed that? Maybe. She'd even catch him making sure that she noticed that he wasn't noticing her, giving her space. The way, after a minute of this, he'd look at her, smile.

"Knock it off, Ethan! Your eyes are tickling me!"

He closed his eyes.

"Sometimes you look at me as if I'm made of numbers," she said. This was the night before Emily left Boston for good. She didn't know that she was about to leave Boston for good. She continued, "Like I'm long division you're doing in your head."

"Nah." He thought about it. "But I hate math."

"Should I be concerned?"

He opened his eyes. Nodded yes. Said, "I love you, Emily."

12

———

It was both as improbable and obvious as the sun being a star. Of course he did. Probably Emily even loved him. *Loved him, too.* So why couldn't she say it? Maybe it was only that Emily's sense of motion was deficient, that feeling of falling. Not the end splat of real love, just the vertiginous, romantic drop. Or was that what she'd been experiencing all along? Who did she think she was kidding here?

Jesus.

Emily had just dropped out of Boston University. Speaking of drops. Two weeks ago. She hadn't told anyone yet, least of all Ethan or her grandfather. They'd both wrap the decision around themselves in a way that Emily needed to avoid for as long as possible. Let this one be hers. For now she wanted to savor it, think around it, hold the immensity of it in her head, telling herself: Oh my God you will not believe what you just did.

But here came Ethan with his bulky, destabilizing I love you. Like he knew. Like he was preemptively reaching in and grabbing the hand of her awesome, mysterious future before it had a chance of doing anything truly awesome, like leaving Boston, or him. Neither of which she wanted to do, but still.

She'd imagine moving out of Ethan's apartment. She'd call Maxi or Shumon, or maybe Lizzy or another of her JP lesbian bros. They loved moving women out of the apartments of men who didn't deserve women; she'd call them and they wouldn't ask questions because that would presuppose that they didn't already know. They knew. This was the opposite of what Emily wanted, but she had to constantly, obsessively replay the event in her head to make sure. Breaking up with Ethan. She did this so she could arrive at the point of the fantasy where she realized that she couldn't live without him.

But instead of telling Ethan that she loved him too, she pretended that she hadn't heard him. Then they stopped talking altogether. Then he got up, went to his desk, started tapping things with his pen.

Maybe being truly in love meant elevating her own lusts and emotions to a level of seriousness that Emily just wasn't comfortable with. People need to believe that life is serious. Emily, to stay sane, had always assumed the opposite and behaved likewise. Serious was a slippery slope. Start giving the daytime Ethan stuff its due and you're going to have to listen in close to the night as well. This Emily could not do. But how could Ethan know? She hadn't told him. She couldn't tell him so he didn't know and so it wasn't his fault and, anyway, she really felt like she had bigger things to deal with right now.

Something was wrong in Queens Falls.

She'd called Peppy twice today. Or, more accurately, she'd called nineteen times in two nervy batches: one in the afternoon, one an hour or so before Ethan's I love you. No answer. This was unlike him, though not entirely unprecedented. The TV could be on too loud, that had happened before, or the phone could've been left inside the refrigerator again, under a blanket, upstairs, in the bathroom on top of the toilet. He was ninety-three years old. He'd once taken the phone out to his car by accident, left it in his glove compartment overnight. Phone batteries died sometimes too.

Too? Shut up, Emily.

Peppy could be at Price Chopper! He could be back in the garden doing whatever, the tomatoes, digging around. Though, since his slipped disk, gardening was less likely . . .

He could be dead.

Shut *up.*

"Ethan," Emily said. "Hey, Ethan?"

"Yeah."

"Can we talk?"

Ethan had removed his shirt. Emily didn't know if this had anything to do with her inability to say that she loved him too. He was reading at his desk.

"Just come back to bed," Emily said. "I don't know. Come here. I'm feeling weird, Ethan."

"I'm fine where I am. Honestly. Don't worry about it."

He wouldn't turn around. You couldn't always tell if he was breathing or not, his back was so solid and expressionless. Emily said, "There's something I want to say."

"You don't have to say anything, Emily."

"I dropped out of school."

Ethan's neck tensed.

"I know," he said.

"What? Please turn around."

"Maxi told me," he said, finally facing her. "She was worried. I don't know, Emily. It's not like it's a big shock or anything, your lack of scholarly ambition. I told Maxi to chill, that I trusted you. That you know what you're doing."

"Come to bed, Ethan," Emily said. "I don't know what I'm doing."

"I know, but you know that much. That's more than most people."

"Do you really believe that?"

Ethan shrugged.

Emily said, "You're upset that I didn't talk about it with you, that I kept it a secret."

"I was, I guess." Ethan yawned. It was about 10:00 p.m. Ethan made no move to come to bed. "But what else is new?"

"Ethan?"

"What?"

"I'm worried about my grandfather."

"What do you mean?"

"He's not—" Emily began, and there it was: she crumbled. Suddenly it was real. *I think he's in trouble.*

Seven hours later Emily was in a taxi, alone, heading for South Station. From there she'd take the first Trailways bus to Albany, New York, then another to Queens Falls, and then walk to the hospital that had finally called her around two in the morning, three hours ago.

Her phone began buzzing as soon as she got to South Station. ETHAN CALDWELL. Then again. Three texts she wouldn't open. Then a call from BOO. Then two from MAXI. One from LIZZY. Ethan must have called them all. Then more from ETHAN. She enjoyed feeling the phone vibrate in her hand; it was the closest that she could let Ethan come to her right now. It wasn't close enough, but it was something. Ethan holding her hand like an angry chunk of bees. Finally, she turned it off.

The last hour had not been easy. It had been their first fight, in a sense, but Emily had been adamant, even vicious about the fact that Ethan could not accompany her to Queens Falls.

The sun had come up earlier than it was supposed to. The birds were insane. "What is *wrong* with the birds?" Emily had shouted.

"They're singing," Ethan said.

"They're screaming."

"Emily, it's going to be OK. Please calm down for a moment."

Did she know that she wasn't coming back? She'd packed all three of her suitcases, most of her things. Ethan didn't get it. Emily didn't either. Because she loved the smell of the mornings here, she'd thought, stuffing her suitcases. Loved it all. Despite the motherfucking birds. The smell of the flowers waking up downstairs, the snoring delivery trucks of flowers pulling up each morning beneath Ethan's window . . .

The thought of Mr. Jeffries dialing a telephone made Emily

want to cry. *He had a fully operational human voice.* Harriet Jeffries's recorded voice on Mr. Jeffries's answering machine had been a shock (*"My technophobic dad's not home right now. Or, who knows, actually. He probably is. Either way, leave a message after the—"*) and then the most comforting thing, as if her fantasy BFF was there for her, finally, in her hour of need. Harriet would help. Now, Mr. Jeffries hadn't spoken with Emily, or even gotten the message to Emily that he'd called the ambulance, that her grandfather was alive and on his way to the hospital, which, yes, would have been the fully operational human being thing to do, but what did she expect? The guy was a tree. She'd ruffled his branches enough so that he'd done what needed to be done and that was all she could or would ever ask of him. He had saved her grandfather's life.

Emily on her hands and knees, rooting around under the bed, Ethan's desk, the sofa.

"What are you doing?"

"Nothing."

"I'll help."

"No, it's OK. It's nothing."

Emily did not want him to find the ring. Ethan was the Noticer, something he called himself. Because he noticed things. It was true, of course, and it was maddening and not half as cute as he thought it was because every time he crowed about noticing wasn't he also highlighting the fact that Emily *wasn't*? Emily was the loser. She lost things. She forgot where she placed things. She could ask Ethan anything, where anything was, and he'd know. Where's the purple hair clip? *There.* Hardly lifting his head from his computer, priestly finger pointing. There. And, yes, there it would be. You see my phone charger, Ethan? The nail clippers? My purse? Under that book. In the bathroom, behind the toilet. I think I saw it by the pile of *JoongAng Daily*s. Respectively. It was uncanny and, at first, Emily thought that maybe sometimes he actually hid her stuff just so he could impress her by finding it. But, no, he was simply alive to details like nobody she knew, details he didn't even know he'd retained until she tried calling them up, pulling them out of him. They'd test this. It rarely failed. Ethan liked to think it had something to do with the fact that he saw everything multiple times, in many languages. "Like I've got eight eyes." "More like you're Rain Man," Emily once said. "More like you're the white Korean weirdo in a movie who helps the adorable heroine find stuff."

She was searching for a thin 14-karat gold band. Emily had found it under the living room sofa when she was ten years old. She liked to think that it'd once belonged to her mother, Nancy, and, moreover, maybe it'd been given to Nancy by Emily's father.

For a few childhood years Emily had a ritualistic thing she did. She'd wear the ring and stand before the bathroom mirror, on which she'd taped photographs of her immediate family. Nancy. Peter. Gillian. Then she'd stare at herself, blurring her eyes, staring *behind* her image, as if her face were a Magic Eye picture, finding each one of them—Nancy Peter Gillian—in her own face and then, with some effort, subtracting them. Erasing all the Nancy Peter Gillian she could find. Her father was what remained. High, wide cheekbones. The dark hair, of course, and the freckles. For an electric moment, Emily's father would form, and sometimes he'd go even further and develop his own features. These were stern, unhappy. Masculine lines not suggested in Emily at all, and Emily would hold on to him, desperate. But as soon as he was conjured, he'd collapse back into the Phanes: Nancy Peter Gillian Emily flooding back into the ten-year-old's helpless face.

The ring had almost certainly belonged to one of Peppy's lady friends. She had never worn it in her grandfather's presence. She'd put it on after she got to school and take it off before she got home. She needed it to be what it was. It was one of the few things that they couldn't share, and, because of this, it was the closest thing that Emily had to a piece of her dad.

Ethan stood above her. "Hey," he said. Of course he'd found it.

Emily, on her knees, took the ring and said, "I do," smiled. They both smiled. But not for long.

Then the asshat taxi honking outside with the birds. Ethan helping her suitcases into the trunk. "You really need everything?" he
asked, finally.

She couldn't explain it.

"Emily?"

"I'm sorry, Ethan."

They hugged, did not kiss. Ethan went in for one, but Emily
veered to the side, tilting her head down; then, realizing what she'd
done, tried to kiss Ethan, but no dice. He'd already stepped back.
They looked at each other.

The Trailways bus left South Station at 6:00 a.m.

Boston reeled, turned; it righted itself and was suddenly behind
her. Emily closed her eyes. Ethan could have jumped into the taxi
with her. Wasn't there a last minute where he was supposed to have
opened the door and hopped right in? What had stopped him?

Emily had.

Because this is what would have happened otherwise: Ethan
would have met Peppy. Privately, Emily would have told her grandfather no big deal. *Peppy, I want you to meet Ethan Caldwell. He's
never worked a day in his life. He's secretly Korean. We're not serious.*
Ah-phooey, Peppy'd wave his arm. Bunk. Because he'd see it. Unless
he never opened his eyes again, how could he not see it? She could
almost fool herself, but Peppy? He would see that she loved Ethan
Caldwell and that Ethan was a good, deserving man who loved her
too, and, happily, Peppy would let himself go. That would be that.
They would have murdered him.

13

———

The Queens Falls General Hospital doors shushed open by themselves. Emily stepped inside, a suitcase in each hand. She'd left one on the sidewalk, where the taxi from the bus station had dropped her off. The hospital air smelled of *clean* in the same way that cherry lollipops taste like actual cherries.

Emily didn't know what she was going to do with the other suitcase on the sidewalk. She could barely carry the ones in her hands and where did she expect to put them anyway? She hadn't slept on the bus. She hadn't slept the previous evening. She should have first gone home to Route 29 but what if there wasn't time for home? Hospital light buzzed like a toothache.

Somewhere in this building was her grandfather.

There were people moving and people waiting: the sick and the dazed, and doctors, nurses, janitors. Emily watched two crying women, both fat, pulling dozens of metallic balloons behind them. The balloons bumped, skidded, and scraped the ceiling.

Emily saw someone she recognized.

That frizzy, anxious shrub of hair, the giant eyes. But it couldn't be. But it was. Winnie—Win Shapiro, her grandfather's last great lady friend. Emily watched her from across the room. She was too old. She wore a hospital gown, slippers; she stood next to a relatively young, relatively tall man in a business suit, whose arms she held as he said something that sounded like the snapping of an aggrieved towel. He was way too busy for this shit today.

Emily dropped both of her suitcases. Help me. She waved. Please, help me. But neither Winnie, the man, nor anyone saw her. Next to Winnie and the man: a wheeled hat rack on which a small red balloon had apparently been snagged.

Some weeks before Emily graduated from high school, she'd spent an afternoon with Winnie Shapiro. This was shortly after Emily learned that she was going to Boston and a month or two before Winnie stopped visiting Peppy.

Emily had been ditching study hall, walking along Aviation Road on her way to grab a coffee at Stewart's. The lime-green Renault 16 hatchback pulled up alongside Emily and honked. "Beep beep," Winnie said, from the window. "Emily! Darling! Hello! Would you like me to drive you home?" She looked like a turtle inside a turtle.

"I'm actually supposed to be at school?"

"Would you like me to drive you back to school?"

"God no."

Emily got into the car. Winnie poured about seven white-flavored Tic Tacs into Emily's hand. They looked down at them together. "My mouth tastes like death without these, Emily, I swear," Winnie said, pinching one from Emily's palm. "Yum!"

Emily put the rest into her mouth. "Thanks, Winnie."

"It's a gorgeous day. I was just going for a drive." It was an invitation.

Emily put on her seat belt, tossing her stuff into the backseat. "Sure."

"Will I get in trouble?"

"What, from Peppy?"

"From the police."

"Are you going to molest me?"

Winnie laughed. "Two peas in a pod, you two!"

The car sounded like it had swallowed a mouthful of hornets. They drove into the Adirondack Mountains. Cheonderoga Road, Lake Shore Drive, Trout Lake and Bloody Pond, Wapanak Way, Cat Mountain Road, Wall Street, Finkle Road, Mother Bunch Lane. Winnie announcing the names. They passed an abandoned trailer park that looked like the aftermath of a train derailment and up through Tongue Mountain's frothy tunnel of trees, the sun occasionally smashing through and rolling over the Renault 16 like laughter. "God, I love it up here," Winnie said. "Geologically speaking, neither tongue nor mountain—" Tongue Mountain, Winnie explained, was a range, a series of rolling peaks on the western banks of Lake Jogues.

"I see why my grandfather likes you," Emily said.

Winnie made a face. "Perhaps you'd do good to remind him sometime," she said. They went quiet for a moment.

Tongue Mountain was known for timber rattlesnakes. They parked under an out-of-place sugar maple, a tourist among the spruce and firs. There was a picnic area here, and the entrance to a series of New York State Park–approved hiking trails. The sunlight through the forest was spongy and amorphous. Trees were Emily's least favorite plant.

"My son used to love it here when he was little," Winnie said, distractedly. "Come, come, follow me!"

They went a little ways off a trail to a bright burst of a clearing and then: "Careful now, Emily. If it looks like a rattlesnake, it's probably a rattlesnake. They tan themselves on the rocks around here."

They were standing atop a cliff jutting from the face of the mountain.

"We used to call this the tip of the tongue, my son and I. Because—well, what can one say? Look for the words, Emily. See if you can find the words."

Below them, Lake Jogues. Parasails buzzing by, following their boats like giant predatory jellyfish. Green bubbles of islands, dark blue water. Emily, looking for words, could only say, "Beautiful." Winnie, disappointed, said, "No." Birds flew below them. Tiny chirpers spattering like sideways gusts of hail and large evil ones hanging motionless in the air over the water, flying against the wind. Emily imagined sitting up here on the edge of the cliff, fishing for eagles. They sat. They talked. Or Emily listened while Winnie said things like, "I like to ruminate on Indians!" Emily'd laugh, and Winnie would continue: "That was not a joke! Oh, *you*," but she'd be laughing, too, holding Emily's wrist, elbow, once or twice her knee, always her attention. "Really, you are so like your grandfather! It's more than a little disconcerting."

Emily thought the same about Winnie.

"Well, I'm just fascinated with the Huron-Iroquois. Mmmm. The Algonquins. Look down there, Emily, and imagine how they saw it. The very same water. We aren't supposed to call them Indians anymore though, are we? No matter. But I'm not entirely sure that we know how to see this lake. Don't laugh. Folks today see so differently, don't you think? The older I get, the more I think that I've been dreaming all this time, and, suddenly, finally, I'm getting closer to waking up. Do you see?"

"I think I know what you're talking about."

"Sweetheart, I hope not." Winnie smiled. "I only mean to say that we live up here, we're ostensibly of this place, these mountains, you see. But we're not of them. I do happen to think that even living up here we're still more urban than people who lived in cities, say, only fifty years ago. Certainly one hundred years ago. Can't you feel the distance? How closed off we are to it, especially when we pretend that we're not. Like sitting here. Like hiking, swimming— goodness, if you asked most people what they loved about living up here, they'd say *this*. The lakes. The so-called watersports. Skiing. Have you ever skied? I have never skied. Even if most of the time folks spend outside, and this is a verified truth, Emily, most of the time folks spend actually out of doors is spent pushing or riding a machine that cuts grass. When I first moved here that's all I saw.

Everyone outside mowing lawns. It's militaristic, I thought. It's like giving the earth a GI haircut. Now ask yourself, how would the Indians see this? When I was a young lady I had such interesting ideas."

"Where were you from?"

"Where am I from? These days, the past mostly!" Shaking her head. "Montreal, actually. But I do think we've turned nature into an almost perfectly safe life-sized painting, one that we can enter and leave at will. It's an idea more than a place, Emily. I don't know where we really are half the time, I really don't. Where do we actually live?"

"Winnie," Emily asked, "are you stoned?"

The old woman laughed a bird into the air. "But you simply have the most amazing freckles," she said. "No I am not stoned, young lady! But your *skin*. I'm trying to remember what it was like, you see, being a woman."

"Is being old so different?"

"Old?" Winnie hooted. She squeezed Emily's arm.

"I'm sorry, I mean—"

"*Slack la poulie!* We try our best, your grandfather and I. To be perfectly honest with you. But you hit the nail on the head. It's play-acting at this point. Theater." Winnie sighed. "I wish we'd brought a picnic, don't you? I love picnics. Well. But maybe it always was playacting? Maybe you can try and remind me, Emily. Because, do you know, I feel the same as I did when I was thirty, even if, physically speaking, I'm now something of an entirely different species. I do feel like an imposter."

Emily said, "I sometimes feel the same way."

Winnie nodded seriously. "I should remember that. Thank you. Maybe we always feel this way. Oh, Emily, this costume!" She clapped her little hands. Once, twice, as if trying to wake up. "It's not easy, is it?"

"Wait." Emily made a face.

"Dear?"

"What are we talking about again?"

Winnie said, "You're an interesting young lady. You're not used to conversations, are you? You're so uncomfortable without your jokery. I can tell. But I'm so glad we're having this time. You haven't been exactly welcoming to me, you know. You haven't exactly been Little Miss Congeniality. Will you get in trouble for missing school?"

Emily said, "Probably not." And, "Sorry if I haven't been nice to you, Winnie. Did you really meet my grandfather at Price Chopper?"

"Is that what he told you?" Winnie waved that away. "Dear, I've known that fool of yours since before you were born. Back when he used to be the managing editor of the *Queens Falls Post Star*. He gave me my first job, right out of school. I worked a few years here before graduating to a real paper downstate, then a magazine. I wrote for *Time* magazine for twenty years, you know."

"I didn't know."

"Of course you didn't. It was your grandfather got me in with his old connections. They begged him to come back to work for them. For years. They wanted him back overseas as a correspondent." Emily hadn't known that either.

"Well," Winnie said. Then, "But I tell you, it was like finding a European prince behind the counter of a Long John Silver's. Or maybe just a European? Back when I first worked for your grandfather. It was romantic, I'll be honest, and *mysterious*. What could have driven such a man to such a thing, you understand? To Queens Falls. But that's just bunk, as he would say. In the end it was too disheartening, actually. Worse, it was boring. Someone of his talent wasting away at the *Post Star*." She made a French noise. She flicked her hand. "Tell me, Emily, do you like high school?"

"What?"

Emily wanted to know more about this long lost Pete Phane, but something in Winnie's tone meant she'd turned a corner. Time for other things.

Winnie said, "Is it really like I see it on TV? I have wondered. The drugs and the shootings?"

"Like, has there been a massacre at Queens Falls High lately?"

"I really am so pleased that we're having this chat, Emily!"

Emily was too. "I've never really talked to one of Peppy's girl-friends like this before."

"*Coudonc!*" Winnie said. "Oh, please. That's not who I am."

"I'm sorry."

"Don't mind me," Winnie said, finally, taking Emily's hand in both of hers. "Listen, do you know, when I was your age I was so *concerned* with trying to be just like all the other girls. It was vexing. I even read for the wrong reasons. I approached every book as if it were a self-help book, a Bible, and, you know, the books available to me, and remember this was back in the eighteenth century." Laughing. "These books were not helpful books. It wasn't until I was older that I found reading that reflected anything close to who I was. I was not Laura Ingalls. If I may say, Laura Ingalls, as far as I could make out, did not have a vagina. If only I could have been more like that, you know? What was *wrong* with me?"

"Wait, who is Laura Ingalls?"

"Really? Well, then, apart from the high school massacres, I envy you girls! For you, Emily, a little-known fact: young ladies didn't have vaginas until the late twentieth century. They really didn't come into vogue until the seventies. For six months, *six months*, I believed that mine was the only one that bled. Don't look at me like that! Oh, my poor mother wouldn't dare talk about any of that, you know. Are you kidding me? The other girls, well, what did I know? They *looked* clean."

"You didn't have any close friends?" Emily almost said *best friends*.

"I had brothers. As you've probably guessed, my mother wasn't what you'd call the most liberated woman. Different times. I was raised to wait on my father and my brothers. The way her mother had raised her, I suppose. She didn't know any better. I felt like I was living in a different century from some of my schoolmates. But perhaps this is something that I can only see in hindsight. Back then, I just thought it was because I wasn't pretty enough. What rot! My father was Jewish, a *mopette*, as we say, a little weak, but my mother was Québécois Catholic." Winnie puffed out her cheeks for some reason. Held that pose. Shook her fist. "In their own way, they'd rebelled, just by marrying each other, but then they reverted back to whatever their parents had been, *and with a vengeance.* Try as I might, I couldn't get close to them." She paused. "I had to leave home before I could find myself and make all those tasty, wonderful mistakes you're just on the verge of making for yourself. No offense, dear. If only I had mistakes left to make, Emily! That's when you really know your life is winding down: the wonderful mistakes available to you start drying up and you're left only with the dreary, flatulent mistakes. God knows I'm still trying to make a mess of things, and not doing such a bad job of it if your grandfather is any judge on the matter . . . But perhaps that's my own curse. The way my upbringing equated mistakes with freedom. It doesn't have to be that way. My family, they never really understood me, Emily, but they *forgave* me. Oh, now that was something that I simply couldn't abide back then. How dare they forgive me! Thank you but no thank you. How headstrong I once was. *Tsé veut dire.* You know what I mean. Many years went by before I'd meet them halfway."

"Did you know my mother?"

This took Winnie aback. "No, I didn't, sweetheart. She was just a girl when I worked for your grandfather," Winnie said. She placed a hand on Emily's leg. "Can I be honest with you, Emily? You need to get as far away from here as possible."

Emily was not, generally speaking, a hugger of women. But she tried to hug Winnie Shapiro. She tried to get Winnie Shapiro to hug her back.

The man with the suit shouted, "Hey now!"

Emily stepped back. She said, "It's me, it's Emily."

The old woman made as if she was screaming. But there was not enough of her left to scream—her mouth simply creaked.

The man in the suit cussed, said, "Christ, Ma." He said, "Do you know this girl?"

Winnie Shapiro cowered from Emily, hiding herself around the body of her son as if she were a toddler and he were a leg.

"Ma, stop," he said. "Enough." Then, to Emily, "Do you know my mother?"

"It's OK," Emily apologized. She backed away. "She doesn't recognize me. It's OK. I'm really sorry. My mistake."

"She's not well," the man said, sighing. Raising his voice: "Ma, she just wanted to say hello. Can you say hello?" Then, back to Emily, his eyes slipping from annoyed to *male*. Intrigued, sickeningly flirtatious. "Have I met you before? What's your name?"

"I don't know."

Winnie whimpered.

"I'm sorry," the man said. "What? Where did you say you knew my mother from? Hey." He swatted at Winnie's hand, which tugged at his: *I want to go home take me home.* "Christ's sake. I'm trying to talk to ask this girl here—"

Emily hurried past the beds on wheels. People on wheels. Blood balloons and real balloons and you either had wheels or you had feet and: GET WELL SOON! Emily still had feet. She couldn't look back. Fuck you, she thought. Someone shouted about her suitcases. Fuck suitcases. People said, "Hey, excuse me!" People said, "Ma'am!" People said, "You can't just—!" But Emily did just. She walked into the first tunnel that took her. Then the next. She would get her grandfather out of this building if it was the last thing she fucking did. She would take them both as far away from here as possible.

14

Emily's first three months back in Queens Falls were like trying to hold in your head the color of a brand-new color.

JUNE,

for example, started when the taxi dropped Emily off on Route 29. The first things that struck Emily about being home again were how tall the trees were and then how loud. Their incessant hissing.

She'd had to leave Peppy at the hospital. He'd suffered a massive stroke. *Massive* was their word. He was living entirely by their words now, an actor reading off their asinine script. Emphysema, partial paralysis, medically induced coma. Plus, the script writers noted accusingly, borderline malnutrition, aspiration pneumonia . . .

"Inspiration what?"

"From breathing in vomit, ma'am."

Theirs, Emily assumed.

Her house sitting right there where she'd left it. It was smaller, less yellow than she remembered. On the way, she'd spoken to the taxi driver at length about the best kind of dog. His name was Roy. For a while, until Roy mentioned *flavor*, Emily thought that they'd been talking about actual dogs, like woof woof, and, despite or because of everything, she'd been momentarily happy, watching the middle of nowhere from the window, wondering what Hebrew

Nationals looked like. Did they look Jewish? Could she ask? Was that racist? "Excuse me, this your place, miss?"

"What?"

It was Mr. Jeffries's place, actually, but she'd gotten out, paid Roy, and then, oh my fucking God, accidently hugged him after he removed her suitcases from the trunk and said, "So long." Roy hugged Emily back. He patted her back and told her that everything was going to be OK. What Roy said she needed now was some rest. Drink some fluids, he said.

"It's going to be OK," Emily assured Roy.

"I know it is."

Mr. Jeffries wasn't home. Peppy wasn't home. Trees fucking *everywhere*. Emily managed the rest of the journey on foot.

The bedroom window was open, and Emily listened to Mr. Jeffries's lawn mower. She floated inside the sound of it, eyes closed, waiting for her phone to pick up the song, harmonize, start vibrating along.

The smell of cut lawn, Emily knew from her studies in plant signaling and behavior, was the chemical equivalent of a blood-curdling scream: the grass releasing chemicals into the air to warn other grass, other plants, of the massacre. The smell of the screaming was even louder than the lawn mower. Plants felt pain. Everything that struggles to live must.

Emily closed her window.

Emily's phone would not vibrate.

Emily opened her window again—because maybe the glass? Maybe the glass was hindering the phone's reception?

There was no reception this far out on Route 29, but Emily liked to think that an important enough call might just make it—The Little Call That Could, *I think I can I think I can*—from Ethan, say, in Boston, or one from the hospital with news that Peppy's coma had finally cracked open, hatching him out as good as new. Emily knew that Ethan was calling her. Right this second. Invisible signals shooting from Ethan's phone, from their window in Boston, slicing over suburbs, through the Berkshires, taking a hard right on the Hudson River and hurtling at her, meters above the treetops, then down Route 29 until the call, and Ethan, a mere two miles from Emily's house, were yanked back at the neck like a dog chained to a tree.

Tuesday. Wednesday. Wednesday. Wednesday. Wednesday. Every day felt like Wednesday at the hospital. Emily thought that one of her grandfather's doctors had been flirting with her. The way his eyes bungeed from her eyes to her chest, eyes, chest, eyes. Chest. Every day Emily went in with the intention of flirting back, smiling at least, maybe grabbing a coffee with him, a plastic-wrapped Danish, thinking a good flirt might convince this doctor that her grandfather was not going to die after all.

Better yet, wasn't her grandfather's life worth putting in some overtime for? If not his life, then these tits?

But this guy, my God. He was always more skeevy than she remembered. It was the pubic-like hair on his knuckles. The way his earlobes were more orange than the rest of his face, which itself was more orange, Emily thought, than any human face had a right to be. His breath heaving minty rot all over Emily, saying, "Hum-dee-do, oh, and how are we today, Miss Phane? What up, what *up*?" Like she'd just intercepted him icing a fucking cake. In the ghetto.

"I'm fine, thanks."

"Well, I wish we had better news for you. Please, walk with me."

Emily made a thank-you tray of Rice Krispies Treats for Mr. Jeffries. She'd waited until he was at work before leaving them on his doorstep. She'd never stood so close to his house before. It was family, in a way, a long-lost brother. Mr. Jeffries's house seemed to understand more than anyone what she was going through and she wanted to hug it, like Winnie, like Roy. Peppy once told her how Mr. Jeffries's ex-wife once assaulted them with trays of Rice Krispies Treats. The wife, Harriet's mother, had been unhappy. Toward the end of her stay on Route 29, she'd visit Peppy, secretly, when Harriet was asleep and Mr. Jeffries was at work, and they'd talk into the night. He had given her advice. "She was a good woman," Peppy told Emily. "Married too young is all. I never told her anything she didn't know already. Mostly you can't, you know, with people. Folks just want to hear someone else say it."

"What was she like?"

"Young," Peppy said. "Young people get married to become old, to grow up. Old people, people over fifty, well, they get married to feel young again. There's never a right time."

To everyone's surprise, Peppy broke out of his coma. The stroke had paralyzed the left side of his body. His right side was weird too, but otherwise he was strikingly responsive, even if his face looked like it was melting off his face. Strikingly, they said. Emily liked that. Strikingly! Now that was more like it.

They unplugged him; out came the tubes, wires, everything. He could breathe on his own and he could, they said, even begin learning how to eat again. The aspiration pneumonia got downgraded, no longer aspired to anything. The other stuff took a rain check, leaving Emily to organize the insurance things, money, hospice, medication, equipment, nondenominational evangelical Christian grief counseling and legalities and pinprick specifics that she enjoyed talking about because it was so helpfully and manifestly fucking false. The paperwork existed to help her not smell what she was smelling. Phone calls with bureaucratic offices helped her not dwell too obsessively on things like: How exactly would he shit? He couldn't really walk, could he? How would Emily wash him? Feed him?

But for the first time they were talking to Emily in a way that didn't imply her grandfather was already more or less a stuffed animal. That was enough. He was only dying.

His eyes were all that was really left of the old Peter Phane now, the only two islands of pure Peppy that remained. The deluge and cataclysm of his body had effectively drowned everything else, and even his eyes, Emily saw, were sinking. She would never hear his voice again, not the Morgan Freemany one that could narrate geology, anyway. From there on out, the earth and all its stones would sit unremarked upon and still. He might, Emily was told, soon be able to write a little.

The day before Peppy returned, it stormed. Emily walked out into it for a couple of minutes. It felt like something a woman in her situation might do. But she just got wet and went indoors and watched a sitcom on TV.

Emily had pizzas in the freezer. Diet Dr Pepper. Hebrew National dogs. Little eggs of hope she'd laid all over her house, things she used to like. Reese's Pieces. Cherry Garcia flavored Ben & Jerry's ice cream. She bought a pack of cigarettes because Ethan hated when she smoked. Some white wine because you never know. Carrots. Good soap. The rain sounded like hundreds of thousands of Ping-Pong balls swarming the roof.

Moisturizer and professional natural-extract shampoo. The more expensive the product, the more it smelled of minty soil or Middle Eastern food.

That morning, it'd been sunny. She'd spent the entire previous night cleaning the house. The hospice people would soon be coming by to help Emily prepare. She prepared for them as she would for a job interview. She wasn't above subterfuge. Maybe she could trick them.

The situation comedy convinced her to call Ethan tomorrow before taking her grandfather home. She smoked a cigarette. On TV there'd be a reason, something obvious, as to why she felt like she couldn't talk to Ethan. In the sitcom, Ethan would have already arrived and there'd be applause.

The storm passed and the sun was out again, almost as if it were already tomorrow morning, not eight in the evening. The birds sounded like teeth. Birds reminded Emily how much she currently fucking hated birds. She kept changing the channel, a wasted pianist going up and down scales.

It wasn't until the second Tuesday after Emily arrived in Queens Falls that she was able to communicate with her grandfather. Emily told him that she was going to take him home. His eyes said, No.

She would go back to Boston later, she assured him.

No.

She held his upper arm, she touched the top of his head, fighting her instinct to gather and bunch up the left side of his face, move it back where it belonged, hold it until it stuck. She told him about the sports. She'd memorized the scores for him that morning. No. Emily talked about the world. News. But nothing calmed Peppy's eyes into *maybes* until she talked more firmly about Boston. The awesome life she had waiting for her back in Boston. Don't you worry, she assured him. I'm going back soon.

Did people ever fully recover from a massive stroke plus emphysema plus partial paralysis plus borderline malnutrition plus aspiration pneumonia? Some did. How about from being so unreasonably old? Less.

Emily standing by the open freezer, shoving her face full of ice cream.

She put makeup on each day before the hospice people came to help wash Peppy and whisper to Emily in the kitchen. Low, no-nonsense herbal-tea-warmed voices. Emily smelled cigarettes on one of the women, a comfy staleness that Emily liked. She told this one that it'd be OK if she wanted to smoke in the kitchen.

The looks Emily got from both nurses.

"We don't smoke," the smoker said.

The other nodded.

"Emily, are you holding up all right?"

The TV raging in the other room. It was never off. Emily rarely sleeping. Emily spooning airplanes of food into Peppy's mouth. Spoon after spoon after spoon and Peppy's eyes raging along with the TV, screaming, No.

Emily said, "I'm OK."

"You're doing fine."

"If you need to talk to someone—"

"I'm doing fine."

"Ethan, it's me," Emily said. "I don't know what to say." Pause. "I'm sorry. I'll call later."

Emily sat in her Mazda. She'd pulled off the road, two miles down Route 29. This is where cell reception started again.

She was smoking, but only to finish the pack. Smoking didn't remind her of Ethan. Smoking reminded her how gross smoking was. She could have called from her house, of course, from the home phone, but she didn't want anyone seeing that number, saving it, calling her out of the blue. She was averse to talking to Ethan in the same house as Peppy.

It was the first time she'd called Ethan. He hadn't answered, likely because he was asleep, as Emily knew he would be. It was 4:00 a.m. It would take more than a buzzing Samsung to wake him up.

She came here every day. She'd come here on the way to or from the hospital, but now she sometimes came out here in the middle of the night, or in the early hours before the sun rose. Pulled up on the side of the road, the forest heavy around her car. She'd sit alone in the car and stare at her glowing screen.

This was her internet, too, since she'd spilled tea on her laptop last year. Ethan had let her use his.

Ethan.

Sitting in the car, she'd check her e-mails. She'd only half read them. Then the endless, anxious feed of Facebook updates, and then she'd read and reread the supportive, funny, increasingly hurt daily letters from Ethan. She didn't write back to him.

Please don't give up on me, Ethan.

Emily was weak, exhausted, scared, and she was also, she thought, a terrible person who didn't believe in anything half as much as she was supposed to.

Five days after jokingly asking Emily in an e-mail if he should change his Facebook relationship status—and, of course, not getting a response—Ethan went and changed it to "it's complicated." Emily knew that this was a joke, but he was also right. It was complicated. Then, a few days later, he'd changed it to nothing. Then it went back to being complicated. It was an atypical and therefore heartbreaking admission of confusion, presence, sadness, and Emily couldn't bear it and so, finally, in the most cowardly and comical form of self-destruction there was, Emily deactivated her Facebook account around the first week of

JULY.

Peppy didn't want to eat. He didn't want to communicate using the paper Emily provided. He wanted to watch *Transformers: Revenge of the Fallen.*

She would talk. He would sleep and watch blockbuster movies on TV and not write her messages on the yellow legal pad she'd left on a small table by his right hand, which would not relinquish the remote. His magic wand, his only means of controlling the world around him.

Things got unseemly, as Peppy would have said.

It felt like he wanted to punish Emily with the Disney Channel or *You Don't Mess with the Zohan.* He wouldn't channel surf during the commercials. They watched those too. They watched those *especially.*

It was war. In Peppy's corner: *2 Fast 2 Furious.* In Emily's corner: plants. She started bringing them inside, you know, to spruce the place up. Thinking, perversely, that this would make him remember that there was beauty in the sessile style of life. Plants could be the most implausible and worthy things on earth. Ferns beaming with bouncy self-respect, showing Peppy how it was done. Indoor forestry and aged-grandfather conservation.

It'd been a few years since Emily had been surrounded by that much inhumanity. So much green. Emily felt like a little thing nestling inside a big thing, and she felt loved. She wasn't gardening outside anymore, but she'd go out there a lot, just sort of watching and listening to the bugs, the creek. The occasional deer crashing through the woods behind her house. The distant bovine lowing of summer thunder.

She'd watch Mr. Jeffries inside his house, slowly, inevitably moving from room to room. Living room. Kitchen. Upstairs bathroom. Bedroom. Lights out. Repeat. Having him there was like having a tiny, cold nightlight in the corner of your room—it couldn't really protect you from the monsters but it was, nonetheless, comforting.

She had lost weight. Peppy, of course, had too. His blue dress shirts were now a few sizes too big. Besides that, he wore sweatpants and slippers. His skin was also a few sizes too big for him, especially on his skull, which was strange because it was unlikely that his skull had lost much weight. He could no longer wear his watch. Even though it was summer, he was cold, blanketed. He slept gently, imperceptibly.

Not only did the hospice people help with the obvious and unspeakable but they also regulated the dynamic between grandfather and granddaughter. Pete, in their presence—and they all called him Pete—sparkled. He needed to prove himself worthy of their attention and care, even if their care was the last thing that he wanted. He had the utmost respect for folks doing their jobs. These folks were only doing their job. He was their job and so he made sure not to make their job any harder or more repellent than it had to be. He'd be an exemplary terminally ill patient, a well-behaved prisoner, and in the beginning he wrote to them 100 percent more than he had to Emily, writing THANK YOU and TODAY I AM GOOD THANK

YOU and answering their questions with a neat YES or NO. He even managed to come off all Wild West, lamp-lit and charming, like a leather cactus. This both enraged and comforted Emily. The hospice people also helped adjust Emily to herself; their imminent arrival meant she'd put *outside clothes* on, apply makeup, deodorant, even perfume. She'd clean the parts of the house that Peppy couldn't see. The two of them putting on quite a show, acting as if everything was going JUST GREAT THANK YOU with this dying business, as if both of them weren't, in fact, close to some kind of double suicide. They'd maintain this grotesque pep for an hour or so after the nurses left, holding their respective anguish at bay, poised in case the hospice people should come back. But then Peppy's eyes would grow dim again—and, worse, *disdaining*. Emily would slip back into her sweatpants and, so armored, the battle would begin anew. She would make him come back to life or it would kill her, and she'd make her hostage know this if he knew anything: that he was killing her by not coming back to life. The stubborn old fool had no choice. She wasn't messing around. Shape up or they'd both ship out.

Ethan Caldwell wrote to say that he'd been accepted into his first choice PhD program in New York City. He was going to move to NYC in the autumn. Emily stopped checking her phone. Boston, from Route 29, had all the weight of a dream hours after you've woken up. There was no way that Boston was still happening. She consoled herself that Boston couldn't possibly actually still be happening.

The so-called sleep paralysis attacks, which had been occasional— meaning maybe twice a week—with Ethan in Boston, became acute on her return to Queens Falls. They fell on her with a vengeance.

Three, four times a night or day, depending on when she finally plummeted to sleep.

First, the normal horrors just intensified. Her head in a vise of screaming; footsteps that scrambled rather than walked. The feeling of a hand reaching out and grabbing her neck and then: awake and alone and oh my God no. Her old room. Empty, of course, but vibrating differently, like a screen of a computer about to crash. She'd stumble to the bathroom. The bathroom was the safest room in the house because there was a mirror. Because there she was. Of all things.

She'd fall asleep on the sofa next to Peppy and awaken inside of one of the attacks. She couldn't move, open her eyes, and then she'd feel herself fall deeper. Herself closing around herself for good. This was a new kind of attack. She would almost feel as if she were pregnant with herself, thinking: Was this her future? Some kind of skip in time to a point where Emily would be in a coma but wide awake and surrounded by thick, immovable nothing. She'd feel Peppy near her, not the material Peppy who she could hear breathing but the paralyzed, true Peppy. He was screaming for help. For release. She could smell it. The two of them screaming silently with the plants, stuck listening to the TV, being buried alive. This was her fault. She was maintaining this garden.

"Peppy?" Emily said. She'd finally opened her eyes after an attack. "Peppy?"

It was the middle of July.

He was, of course, in the only place that he ever was now. Emily next to him. But he was staring at her, not the TV. There was something dreadful in his eyes, like the look that Winnie Shapiro had at the hospital. Emily thought, He doesn't see me. He no longer recognizes me.

"Peppy?" she said, and began to cry.

Peppy struck the remote control on his little table. Like a gavel. Like: Stop.

"I'm sorry," Emily said. "Peppy, I'm sorry."

Peppy wrote, IT'S OK.

It was the first thing he'd written to Emily. She couldn't believe it. Don't draw attention to it; she didn't want to spook him back into a blockbuster movie. He suddenly struck her as a little kid who'd been holding his breath until he got what he wanted—which was what? To stop breathing. Had she won? Had he? He was still breathing.

"I had another attack," Emily said.

I KNOW.

Emily needed to change that subject. Something funny. They had to make each other laugh. Could he still laugh? He could snore, so he probably could laugh. She had to pretend this was totally normal. Grasping, she said, "Oh, guess who I ran into the other day?"

WHO?

It was working! "Winnie Shapiro," Emily said. Um. "She was at Price Chopper."

SURPRISED SHE DID NOT FOLLOW YOU HOME . . .

That was more like it. *He wasn't stopping* . . .

DID SHE FOLLOW YOU HOME?

"No, no," Emily said. She laughed. "But she looked good. She asked about you. I told her that you were fine."

THANK YOU.

"Told her you'd married an erotic dancer."

YOU DIDN'T.

"I did indeed."

Peppy hadn't been exactly distraught by the loss of Winnie, but it had shifted him. She was his last. Two years would pass before he talked to Emily about her, and, when he did, on the phone, he admitted that one of the reasons she left him was that he had, actually, asked for her hand in marriage. Her hand, he said. He'd even bought a ring. He wouldn't go into it any more than that.

"Peppy," Emily asked. "Can I ask, why do you think she said no? What happened with her anyway?"

His right hand paused. Hovered over the paper. He wrote, WIN ALREADY MARRIED.

Emily laughed. "No, but really."

REALLY.

"Peppy, c'mon, that's impossible!"

IT IS A FACT.

In other words, Peppy had finally met his match. "That whole time?"

DID NOT KNOW. SEPARATED. GOT BACK TOGETHER. UNSURE. SERVED ME RIGHT.

"Why, Peppy?"

He made a noise. Waved his pen. YOUR GRANDMOTHER, he wrote. He paused. Continued: MADE EACH OTHER UNHAPPY. BUT I HAD BETTER. I HAD LOVES. THEN SHE GONE AND I HAVE YOU. SHE NEVER HAD YOU. SHE NEVER HAD ANYONE EMILY.

Emily felt strange. Peppy's voice would never say something like that; it felt like she was talking to his dream. Unnerved, she said, "I spent an afternoon with Winnie once. I really liked her."

ME TOO.

"She took me up into the mountains for a picnic."

Pause. Then, MAYBE I COULD SEE HER AGAIN?

"Maybe," Emily said. What was she doing?

I MISS HER, Peppy wrote.

Emily looked away. She said, "Do you want to watch TV?"

The TV was already on. Emily reached and got the remote. Put it on Peppy's little table, next to the yellow legal pad on which he was writing, OF COURSE.

That was only the beginning. Somehow Emily had won her grandfather back. His love and his engaging conversation, but especially his humor. Though there was a new sincerity to him that made Emily uncomfortable, most days you couldn't stop his chattering hand, the way his handwriting seemed to chuckle. But it really wasn't until

AUGUST

that the true stakes of the battle of June and July were revealed. By then, Emily was the one hanging on by a thread.

Cleaning out the wastepaper basket next to the sofa, Emily had been feeling choppy, sleep deprived, on edge. She was collecting Peppy's conversations, putting together little piles of them, flattening them out, reading them again. His new voice. The polite handwriting he used for the nurses. The rakish scrawl he used with Emily when he was feeling good.

But there was something else. She discovered unspoken papers at the bottom of the wastebasket that, archaeologically speaking, probably dated back to before he'd begun writing to Emily. They weren't addressed to the hospice nurses. They seemed, in fact, to be for Emily. But the handwriting was all over the place, his new voice's equivalent of a scream or sob.

GO AWAY PLEASE I LOVE YOU GO AWAY LET ME ALONE

Dozens of these, many of them angry, some begging for forgiveness, others for death or, most disturbing to Emily, simply help.

HELP ME EMILY.

HELP.

On August seventh, Emily returned from grocery shopping to find Ethan Caldwell in the kitchen making tea. Holding aloft a teapot. Backlit by sunlight standing at the end of the hallway. Like: You want some, Em? It's fresh.

Then he walked back into the kitchen like no big deal.

He'd found them. The assassin had finally arrived. Emily went to her grandfather, sat next to him. She held his hand. She looked around the room, heart attacking her chest, thankful that Ethan had allowed her this momentary space. Typical, timeless Ethan. He knew her so well. I love you so much. How long had he been here?

How long had she been gone?

What am I wearing?

The sofa already had four or five of Ethan's books. His duffel bag. His phone and laptop. Litter. No, not litter: crumpled-up pieces of yellow paper, entire conversations ripped off and tossed onto the floor around Peppy's feet when, Jesus H. Christ, the wastepaper basket was *right there*. Men.

The TV was off for the first time in a decade.

Her men.

Music playing from Ethan's iPod speaker thing. Gongy wongy Javanese gamelan music; not exactly Peppy's taste, or anyone's taste, but it was sweet if not totally deranged that he'd brought it. The music sounded like cookies baking in the oven.

No, wait. Emily actually smelled cookies.

Ethan.

I will not cry. I will not cry. I will not . . .

"OK, coming—" Ethan said from the kitchen, as if this, too, was the most normal thing. Like everything was OK again. The three of them in this house together. Cookie time.

Peppy's hand was moving.

THE NEW NURSE, he wrote, was still writing, IS A MONSTER.

This pulled Emily up tight. Peppy warned Emily that the monster was in the kitchen. SHHH, he wrote. She began to correct her grandfather, to tell him that Ethan was *Ethan*, when Peppy made a noise. Nugha nugha. Nugha. He was laughing—probably. They both were. Definitely. Then, looking not at the paper but into Emily's eyes, Peppy wrote, HE IS PERFECT.

part three

---

the Community

A route differs from a road not only because it is solely intended for vehicles, but also because it is merely a line that connects one point with another. A route has no meaning in itself; its meaning derives entirely from the two points that it connects.

—Milan Kundera, *Immortality*

15

————

It happened when Howie Jeffries least expected it. It was Tuesday. He had the evening off, but Steve Dube phoned him last minute. Yo, could Howie cover his shift? Steve had, he explained, *dropsy*. "You understand, Jeffries."

Howie did not. He said, "OK."

"OK, champ?"

Howie said, "OK."

"Sorry such short notice." Was Dube laughing? "Owe you one. Hey, by the way, I left my gym bag in the canteen last night. You mind swinging by there first, pick that up for me before lost and found puts it on eBay? You're a pal."

In thirty years, Howie had never seen the lights off in the GE employee canteen. It was a windowless, eternal place, like the Price Chopper or a roadside rest station, like the empty walk-in closet where his wife's clothing used to live. Four tables, two snack-food dispensers, the ever-humming Nescafé machine and a wall-mounted TV for ESPN, Fox News, golf. Everything had disappeared in the darkness. Had Howie missed the memo? He entered. The light switch was not where he imagined the light switch would be.

No matter.

Howie had promised. Blind, he made toward where Steve Dube always held court, planning to root around under the table for a gym bag that had almost certainly fallen into the clutches of lost and found's Mikey Zoschenko. Howie bumped into a chair.

He heard rustling. There was a female giggle, a swallowed breath. Howie stopped where he was, imagining that Tierra from HR and that new guy, Braydon, had come here for none of Howie's business. There'd been talk. But did they have to turn off the Nescafé? Embarrassed, Howie began walking out of the room, backward, quiet as a current.

"Surprise!"

Light, suddenly, and a nightmarish frozen flash of eyes, teeth, T-shirts. Twenty, possibly thirty people, all of them insane. Howie looked behind him, mortified to have stumbled into and possibly ruined someone else's surprise party.

The rest happened quickly. First, the hugs. It'd been years since he'd touched another person who wasn't his daughter, Harri, and here he was, an entire room of hugging people, *including women people*, some snapping his cheek with minnow-like kiss-kisses, everyone wishing him a happy belated fiftieth birthday. Plus, happy thirty years at GE. Howie was paralyzed. It was like going to sleep in Montana and waking up in MTV.

Not since Howie was a boy had anyone thrown him a party, and it was uncomfortable, at first, being happy as a little boy. That they had organized a complex surprise party around the surety of Howie being unoccupied on a Tuesday evening was something, later on, that might have troubled another person. But it pleased him. They knew him. Howie was a pal.

There was a canoe-sized sign on the wall that read HAPPY STONE ANNIVERSARY, JEFFRIES! Next to that, an amusing poster that someone had, no doubt, created on a computer. Mount Rushmore with Howie's Facebook profile face superimposed over the one that wasn't Lincoln, Washington, or Roosevelt. President Jeffries. There was a pile of rocks on a table, too, each wrapped in a colorful ribbon, most with smiling faces painted onto them.

Hugging concluded, Dube gathered everyone's attention. He was stocky, bald; he looked like a hairless, comically suffering cartoon beaver. Little chugging arms. "Having miraculously recovered from dropsy," he began, and everyone laughed. Cheered. Dube continued, said, No, seriously, that this was a very special night. Serious now, folks. Dube taking a drink from his Corona, preemptively moved by his own words, which eventually managed to speak of everyone's appreciation for everyone's pal, Jeffries. If not the life—everyone laughed—then certainly the *soul* of General Electric. Long may Howard Jeffries watch the machines that treat the capital region's wastewater! More party sounds, applause. Now, the stone anniversary, Dube explained, marked ninety years. The stone being the symbol here because, heck, ninety years of marriage or anything would be enough to turn you to stone or make you wish that you were, was he right?

"Depends who you're married to, Steve," Dube's wife, Marcy, shouted.

"Don't I know it," Dube said. "So, we got fifty years of life plus *thirty* years of service at GE—"

"That's eighty, dumbass!" Roger Schulz said.

Dube's best flummoxed face. More hooting from the room as he held his fingers before him, counting. "So it is," he said. "Fine, you got me. But that missing ten years? My guess is that if anyone's hiding an extra ten years somewhere, it's our man Jeffries!" He raised his beverage. Everyone followed suit. "What else is there to say? To ninety more years of Howard Jeffries!"

The room shone with noise. Someone called for a speech, and a vulture of a hush settled on Howie. People began chanting. Speech speech speech. Howie said, "OK."

"Can't hear you!"

Blinkless and burning, Howie stared. This is how deer die. He lifted his right hand—and he put his right hand back down. He put both of his hands into his pockets. OK. About four of the heaviest seconds of Howie's life elapsed before the room erupted into the biggest round of applause yet. Someone said, "Hear hear!" "Jeffries for president!" "Four more years!" The partying began.

Pretty much everyone Howie knew from GE was there, even two of the janitors, old Andy O. and Miguel, and someone, probably Dube, had raided Howie's Facebook friends and invited a few of his fishing buddies. Earl Stolaroff. Mike Ed Walker. Bob. Their wives, too. (Mike Ed Walker's wife could have passed, truth be told, for Mike Ed Walker's brother.) The fisherpeople clustered to one side of the room, sipping quietly; without a rod or a body of water near them they looked exposed, at a loss. Howie wondered if that's how he looked too. The way their eyes scanned the floor, as if scoping out the best spot to cast their lines. Howie made sure not to look at the floor. Besides the jokey pile of stones, Howie received more gifts than all his past fifty birthdays combined. The boys had all pitched in to get him a new rod, an elegant seven-foot six-inch St. Croix LegendXtreme. But that wasn't all. One of the guys, Keith, got him a subscription to *Playboy* magazine "for the nudity"; Benny's wife gave him a wool sweater. "You can't wash it," Benny said. "I told her, what's the point if you can't wash it in a machine? She said quality is the point." Howie got a gift certificate for dinner at Bellaggio's. Lots of fishing-themed curiosities. Two I'D RATHER BE FISHING coffee mugs and a digital alarm clock in the shape of a shark—with working jaw. He got a goldfish in a jar that Stevenson had affixed a small sign to. CATCH ME IF YOU CAN. Howie was so busy being talked to that he couldn't drink his beer. It grew warm in his hand. Simon's wife, Gerty, made a cake in the shape of something Howie didn't have a chance to note. It was gone before he knew it. There were potato chips, pretzels, nachos; someone brought a dish of what Howie could only assume was a taco pie. There was always a group of at least three people around him—it was antagonistic almost, like children poking a turtle with sticks. Except that wasn't it also fun, sometimes? Being poked? Folks care enough to poke, you let them. There was music, even a little dancing. Sloshing left and right, swaying. Tierra and Braydon, in the corner, had slow danced themselves to a standstill. They were basically just hugging now. Howie did not dance. Mostly, he stood in the same place he'd been surprised in, being visited, making sure his smile was under control and wishing, above all, that Harri were here to see how many pals he had. One hour into the party, Howie's ex-wife showed up with her husband, Drew. "Surprise," they said.

They brought two bottles of champagne, one of them already half consumed. She wasn't drunk because she never, ever got drunk, or so she'd claim, loudly, whenever she was particularly drunk. She got *rosy*. She was wearing heels. Drew wore a Christmas red Ralph Lauren sweater with pleated khaki shorts. Black socks, sandals.

Howie was happy to see them both. They brought a gift for Howie the size and shape of a window. It was wrapped in silver paper.

The room, in an attempt to hush itself, momentarily increased its volume with two dozen *Shhhh*s. Like the top of a forest before a storm. Drew said, "Don't even ask how we got that thing in the car." Hand on Howie's shoulder. "It's from Harriett," he said.

Carefully, carefully, thinking it was an actual window, Howie opened it. It was a painting of Lake Jogues. It was a painting so clear and picture-perfect that it might as well have been a window. It was not painted with sludge or soil; it was not a blustery, aggravated abstraction. Harriet had painted him the actual Lake Jogues, and not only that: Howie's favorite spot on Lake Jogues. It was a view of the lake facing the gigantic stone cliff known as Rogers Rock. It was so real that you could hear it. When had she started painting like this again?

Drew pointed something out. There, on the back, Harri had written LAKE JEFFRIES.

Howie wanted to step into the painting, shut the window behind him. It was too intimate. Everyone please turn down your eyes. Turn them off. Howie was smiling too much.

"Don't look so sad!" Dube shouted. "It's a birthday present!"

Because no. Howie wasn't, in fact, smiling. He'd been trying so hard to control his face, to prevent his happiness from cracking it apart, that he'd very likely been glowering.

"That's just how Jeffries *looks*," someone said, shushing the others.

OK.

Well, let's show them how he looked. Howie looked up and fine: he let his face go. It is likely that he smiled because there was more applause, and Howie, finding his voice, said, "Thank you."

He held up *Lake Jeffries* for everyone to see.

"It's from my daughter, Harri." His daughter, the greatest freaking artist in the world. His daughter was happy now, obviously, finally, and she had painted something gorgeous for him. "It's Rogers Rock on Lake Jogues."

Howie's ex-wife said, "Obviously, Howard, your daughter—" Nothing good ever started with *your daughter* or, for that matter, *obviously*. Plus, she had that face. "Your daughter was supposed to be here."

Enough, Drew mouthed.

"Harriet had to get back to the city is all I was going to say, Drew. That's literally all I meant."

"Something she couldn't miss," Drew added.

Howie's ex-wife bitched an eyebrow. (This had been one of Harri's terms for the numerous communication possibilities of her mother's eyebrows.)

Drew continued, "Harriet sends her love. I know she really wishes she could've been here. She made us promise to come. It's my understanding, Howie, that she's been painting that secretly for a long time now. Every time she's come up to visit this year. It's a shocker all right. Unlike anything she's ever done. She really wanted to give it to you in person."

"Thank you for bringing it," Howie said. "Thank you for coming, Drew." Thinking: Harri's been up to visit this year? She never told him. She never visited him. But OK.

Drew said, "Howie, it's our pleasure. I mean that. It's really good to see you, buddy. Wouldn't miss it. Happy belated. Oh, one small request. Harriet asked that we would take some photographs, hope you don't mind."

Howie did not mind. Drew stepped back. Drew held his telephone out before him, turning slowly, a crazy person checking for radiation. Some of the boys came over to appreciate the painting, which one deemed of museum quality. "I've been to the museum," Roger Schulz said. "Jeezum Crow. This could be in the museum."

"I read about this painting sold for forty million. It wasn't even nice like this. You couldn't even tell what it was."

"Could be worth something someday, that's for sure. It is something."

But Howie was listening to his ex-wife, who was standing nearby and speaking into the side of Drew's nodding face. Howie was still tuned into her voice like no other, especially when she was worked up, rosy. She was a poor whisperer.

". . . but seriously, do me a favor and will you stop defending her, please . . . doesn't work, she hasn't worked in years, it's not like . . . his fault anyway, why shouldn't he know, why isn't this the right place, he's bankrolling her and, anyway, you said you'd talk to him. You said, Drew. Why do I have to always be the bad guy I'm sick of it . . . fine, you're right, you're exactly right, this isn't the place I know this isn't the place but then where is the place I'm . . . these people, they blame me for him, oh you know they just do . . . always have, see how they can't even look at me . . . he's not my fault or responsibility, he's not, OK, I'll calm down. I'm calm down. I am calm down, Drew . . ."

The water was blue. The mountains green, and Howie knew what this meant if nobody else did. Harri giving her father the world in accurate colors.

. . .

Two hours later, Howie was driving up the Northway, his ex-wife asleep, laying across the backseat, completely hidden under Lake Jeffries. The painting took up the entire backseat. The ex-wife snored lightly. It didn't sound like waves lapping anything, though Drew, sitting next to Howie up front, had said that it did. "Well, if you listen just right."

They laughed.

Howie had agreed to take them home, both of them way too rosy—she'd said—to drive legally. Predictably, the more his ex-wife bloomed, the nicer things became, and, by the end of the evening, she'd soggily apologized for tending not to like him very much anymore, among other things. "It's your fault, Howard, but I'm so sorry anyway. OK? How's that?"

"That's fine," he'd said. "I'm sorry too."

"I'm so happy you came," she said, possibly forgetting for a moment where she was and whose party she was attending. Maybe it was too much to comprehend: a party all for Howie. But she'd continued, "You look so handsome today, actually. You're not so bad. You are not so bad! We're not doing so bad, are we? Let's face it, Howard, look at us. We didn't turn out bad at all, did we?"

Howie agreed.

"Right?" she said, excitedly. "Right? Tell me about it!"

"You're right," Howie had said. He meant it. He said, "I like Drew very much."

"That means so much, you don't even know. But you know that he likes you too. Too much, I'd say. He's always telling me to lay off, you know?"

Howie nodded. He said, "You don't need to lay off. You say what you have to say to me. It's OK."

"Thank you, Howard!"

"You're welcome."

"It's hard to believe."

"What is?"

"Me, you; everything. But it's good. It's really freaking *good.*" She laughed. She tottered. "Howard, you goofball. I forget how much I like you sometimes. Please try to remind me more often, would you?"

Howie thought that this was a reasonable request. "How?" he asked.

She hugged him. "Just hug me, Howard. For starters? Just freaking hug me."

Drew removed a metal flask from who knows where. He said, "The secret to a happy marriage. Care for some?"

"What is it, Drew?"

"Works for ex-husbands too. Laphroaig single malt whisky. Quarter Cask. It tastes like smoky rope and"—he paused—"burning tires, Pepsi, charcoal, honey wheat, tennis ball, marmalade . . ."

Howie tapped the steering wheel.

"Right, got it," Drew said. "Good man." He took a long pull on the flask.

They headed north.

Interstate 87 was before them. They passed billboards and towns lit up like auto dealerships. Clifton Park. Round Lake. Burnt Hills. Malta. They also passed an actual auto dealership: cold white and yellow lights and still, deep expanses of asphalt carved into the forest. Gigantic flags, lit up and billowing in the night. Yellow signs for jumping deer, ADOPT-A-HIGHWAY PROGRAM NEXT 1.5 MILES, and soon the hills began lumbering up on either side of them, keeping pace. Then the mountains.

Howie said, "You'll pick up your car tomorrow?"

"Mm," Drew said. "What? My cat? Cat's dead. Hey, how about some music, Howard?"

Howie did not know where exactly on the radio one found music that Drew might enjoy. Drew, he knew, was appreciative of culture; he was a retired high school English teacher with a single gold earring, short grey hair. He always recommended books and articles about books on Facebook; he had political convictions and frequently attended Broadway musicals in New York City. Howie found a station that played music.

Drew laughed. "Howard, that is not OK."

"Sorry?"

"What *is* this? Is this what you listen to?"

Howie found another station. "Nope." Then another. Drew shoo-shooed Howie's hand away from the radio. He found what he was looking for. Drew said, "There we go. You into Dire Straits?"

Music was the opposite of fish. Music made Howie uneasy in the same way that people in Walmarts and parades made Howie uneasy. Dire Straits was an affront to the idea of a lake, of ripples and the occasional small, white splash. Howie respected Drew but couldn't understand why Dire Straits existed.

Drew patted Howie's arm. "Harriet, you know, she still tells the story of that concert when she was sixteen. Oh, what was it again?"

Howie said, "Maroon 5."

"Mary mother of God, Howie, you crack me up sometimes! Exactly. Taking your goth daughter to see Maroon 5!"

Fourteen, actually. Howie had planned it for months. He could not help noticing how important music had become to Harri. She was always lost in her headphones, *earbuds* she called them, and so he had asked around at work, wanting to know what exactly they called the kind of music that fourteen-year-old girls listened to with earbuds. Maroon 5, apparently, was what a lot of folks called it. They were age appropriate. They had a song called "This Love" that Dube played for Howie. His own daughter, Tegan, forget about it. Tegan was nuts for those guys. Tegan was a popular and attractive young lady.

Howie purchased two tenth-row tickets to see Maroon 5 at the Saratoga Performing Arts Center. It had been a particular happiness for him, planning their special, cool night out.

But on being presented the birthday Maroon 5 tickets in the Saratoga Performing Arts Center parking lot, Harriet had all but screamed. She had this way of making her entire body a fist. Howie said, "But I thought that you liked music." He floundered. "Your earbuddies."

"My *what*? Jesus, Dad! You can't be serious. What do you think? Who do you think I am?"

"Have you heard the Maroon 5? Maybe you haven't heard the Maroon 5. I've heard them, Harri. I think that they're very cool."

"Oh my God!"

Harri wouldn't budge. She said that Howie didn't know shit about her if he thought she'd want to be here: here with him, first of all, Jesus F-ing Christ, and second of all, Maroon freaking 5—seriously? Seriously? He couldn't be serious! It was so embarrassing and messed up and all he'd have had to do was *ask* her. Talk to her. But no, talking to her would involve talking with her and when did he ever freaking want to do that?

Howie drove them home in silence, hoping that she'd change her mind. They didn't have to miss the concert. He suggested that they swing by and get one of her friends, Bea maybe, Bea could have his ticket. Because perhaps Maroon 5 wasn't the problem. The problem was *him*. Harri was rightfully embarrassed about going to an awesome Maroon 5 concert with her age inappropriate father, and that was OK. That was how it should be. He told her that he would forfeit his ticket.

"Stop stop stop saying Maroon 5!" she screeched. "Are you insane?"

Plus, she'd said, what the hell, she hadn't been friends with Bea in like two years. Three years! Bea'd probably *love* Maroon 5, actually, sure, Harri sneered, and so why didn't he just take Princess Beatrice to see the concert? He and Bea could be lame together. They could boogie.

She said, "You'd like that, wouldn't you?"

"What? No, Harri. I wouldn't like that."

The drive home was desperate, irretrievable.

Harri ran to her room, slammed the door. The sound of that

echoed. Howie stayed up half the night waiting for it to stop, for the silence of Route 29 to be silent again, for his daughter to open her door, come back downstairs, and see the birthday cake. It made no sense. He was sorry. He called in sick. He'd purchased Harri the birthday cake from Price Chopper, a pink cake that said HAPPY FOURTEENTH BIRTHDAY, HARRI!!! The cake person had asked what his daughter liked and Howie, with pride, had told her that his daughter liked music, so they put candy tubas and trumpets and drums on the cake. Howie needed to be in the kitchen with the cake when his daughter reemerged. He would light the candles as soon as he heard her feet on the stairs. He set it all up on the table and he waited. Everyone likes cake.

16

_____

Drew looked back at Harri's painting. He snapped on the overhead light. "It's amazing to think, isn't it?" he asked Howie.

"The French and Indian War?"

Drew guffawed. *"What?"*

Howie had been thinking about the French and Indian War.

"I mean, it's amazing that she's still sleeping under that," Drew said. "But sure, that French and Indian War was something!" Drew looked at his metal flask. "Maybe it's time I had some of what you're having?"

"I thought because the painting—" Howie started.

"Howard, that is not a painting of the French and Indian War," Drew said. "You sure you're under the legal limit there, boss?"

"Yes."

"Well, besides the wife, I can assure you that there are no people in the painting. French, Indian, otherwise."

That was the point, Howie wanted to say. They were hiding. It was likely that Harri herself didn't know the full story of Rogers Rock. Howie, feeling misunderstood, and in an atypically loquacious turn, decided that Drew might appreciate the history. "Do you know about Rogers Rock?" he asked.

In 1758, during the French and Indian War, Robert Rogers was an English officer known for the wily, brutal guerrilla warfare that he deployed against the French and their Indian pals. Howie didn't say pals.

Robert Rogers was more bear than man. The story, which Howie only partially told Drew, and only in the most basic and likely dull fashion, went that Robert Rogers and about 180 of his men, who were rangers and ex–fur trappers, a ragtag group of woodsy, godly, eccentric wanderers conscripted into the English army, made a deep-winter trek from Queens Falls up to the northern end of Lake Jogues toward the French stronghold of Fort Ticonderoga. Howie was not sure why. Usual French and Indian War reasons, he assumed. Famously, Robert Rogers had gone up there before and freed captured English officers, plus had led the occasional provisions raid and Indian massacre. But so this winter became brutal. The snow was deep. The frozen sky a taunting, uncharitable blue. Rogers's men, especially the less hearty ones, began dying off after a week: some were taken by coughing diseases, others by the endless trudging. There were wolves. Toes felt like pebbles stuck in their boots, then fell off. Like teeth. One by one. Fingers and ears fell off. There was little to eat. Then there was nothing to eat. No fires, Rogers insisted, not even little ones, because fires would compromise the whole operation, whatever that operation happened to be. Nobody asked. These were, Howie imagined, silent, staring types, every last one. But he did not tell this to Drew. To Drew, he said, "Many of them died of the cold."

They gnawed on carcasses left by wolves. Some died of that, too. But not Rogers. By the time that they reached what is now known as Rogers Rock, at the northern end of Lake Jogues, he and what remained of his men were finally ambushed, beset by hundreds of murderous Francophile Indians. They'd been hiding. They had obviously been tracking Rogers for miles, waiting until the climate and the lack of provisions had done most of the work for them. This became known as the Battle on Snowshoes because Rogers and his men had been wearing snowshoes.

Howie said, "It is very hard to run with snowshoes." Let alone survive an Indian massacre.

"I like that," Drew said. "The Battle of Snowshoes. It's like sponsorship. This afternoon's battle is brought to you by *snowshoes*."

It was too cold for prisoners. Rogers's men went down by musket, knife, hatchet, and stones hurled from invisible Indians in trees. None was spared.

"Crazy," Drew said. He looked again at the painting. "This place is right up the road and I could tell you far more about the Eastern Front of World War Two, you know, about Stalingrad and the Battle of Kursk, or about the War of the Roses in Tudor fucking England, excuse my English. It's like the forest and the lakes ate our own history. Swallowed it up."

Howie did not understand. He said, "There are a lot of books about the French and Indian War."

Rogers Rock was a massive, sloping cliff, hundreds of feet high. It looked like the crumbling, antagonistic side of a grey, concrete glacier. Few trees grew on it—only some wretched, wiry bushes, a few daring little saplings, ferns, moss. Boulders were always cracking from its side, especially in the frozen winter months.

Drew yawned. He clicked the overhead light off. "So you're saying that this Rogers was killed there?"

"No," Howie said. "Rogers escaped."

Relentlessly pursued. That was the legend. He'd lose the screaming Indians, they'd find him, and they wouldn't stop screaming, the entire forest screaming—the trees screaming—and this hide-and-seek continued for almost an entire day. Finally, Rogers approached the most brutal edge of the cliff and tossed down all of his supplies, even his rifle and his distinctive bear-head hat. He tossed down the already frozen body of a comrade. Then he walked backward from the edge of the cliff, making it look as if two people with snowshoe prints had gone over the edge. Howie thought that this maneuver was called doubling back.

"Something like that," Drew said. "Sure."

"Rogers found another way down to Lake Jogues."

The Indians, catching up with Rogers's trail, looked down at the part of the rock that would come to be called Rogers Slide, and knew that Robert Rogers's game was up. Nobody could survive that fall, slide, whatever. They noted his stupid, distinctive hat, and a British body–like shape, and a bundle of supplies. However, as they were leaving, one Indian saw something unbelievable. There was the hatless figure of Robert Rogers himself, running from the bottom of the cliff, across the frozen lake. It was impossible. Thinking that he'd survived the fall as well as their righteous massacre, the Indians decided that this Rogers was surely protected by the Good Spirit. They let him run.

"The Good Spirit, huh?"

"Yes," Howie said.

"That's what they called it?"

"I believe so."

Howie felt strangely dejected. This wasn't at all what Howie had wanted to tell Drew. But what, then, had he wanted to tell him?

Drew shouted at Rogers Rock in the backseat: "You comfortable back there, honey?" He tapped the side of the painting. "She's comfortable," he told Howie.

"That's good."

"She's sleeping," Drew said. "So maybe, Howard, hey, let's you and I have that talk?"

Howie thought that they had been talking, but OK.

Drew turned the music up a little louder. He said, "You know, she has a point sometimes."

"OK."

"I mean about the money you give to Harriet. Look, I don't mean to pry, she's your daughter, but it has to be said. You know what I'm talking about here."

"The money that I give Harri."

"Well, yeah."

"OK."

Drew sighed, said, "Maybe it's not OK, Howard. Maybe not. Hear me out. Look, you two, you and Harriet, you've got a really special bond, one that, to be honest, you-know-who back there has always been jealous of. The way she comes up here five, six times a year, stops at our house for an afternoon argument at most and then it's off to your house for a week or two."

This was confusing. Howie had not seen Harri in over a year. Perhaps he'd misheard or was Drew more inebriated than he seemed? Howie said, "OK."

Drew said, "It bothers her to no end, Howard. How you can do no wrong in Harriet's eyes. She thinks you inspire her misanthropy, that you set a crummy example. Now, fine, you and I know better. Harriet is and always has been *Harriet*, but there could be a kernel of truth to this, correct?" He stopped. "Hon, you awake back there?" Nothing. "Look, she's a good woman, Howard. She's a good mother. She's a great mother. She tries her best, you know that she does. But Harriet is difficult, to say the least, and those two, I swear, they're like fire and ice, temperamentally so different, and my wife isn't perfect. She'd be the first to admit. She doesn't understand Harriet's art, not like you and I do. Harriet says that she doesn't even try to, but that's not fair. That girl has no idea how much her mother tries. I guess what I'm saying is how long do you think that this can go on?"

"I don't know."

"The point is, New York City. Harriet can't keep living there as if she's some kind of trust fund kid. You're not doing her any favors. She needs to find a real job. Let me ask you something: Harriet says that you've been saving up for a boat?"

Harriet knew about that? How? Howie said, "Yes."

"Well, how is that going?"

Howie said, "Good."

"Really, because the way we see it, and correct me if I'm wrong, you've been giving most of your money to Harriet these last few years."

"Not all of it, Drew."

"Understood. Not all of it. I hate to pry and I'm not saying she's using you, exactly, but, I'm sorry, when do you think this is going to end? When Harriet becomes a rich and famous painter? Do you know how many rich and famous artists there are in New York?"

"No."

"There are three," Drew said.

"There must be more than three."

Drew laughed. "But you know what I mean. It's not only difficult, it's nearly impossible to succeed as an artist in New York these days. Might as well say you plan to make a living playing the Lotto. Be a starving *lottoist*. Can we agree on that?"

"Sure we can, Drew."

"Harriet worries about you," Drew said. He paused. Drank from his flask. "It's why she's up here visiting you so often. Plus, and don't tell our painting back there, but she's always on the phone with me, you know? Not her mother, Howard. Me. Trying to get me to take you out for a drink, check in on you, make sure you're OK. She's got a big heart when she chooses to show it. But she really shouldn't have to worry about you. Is that fair for someone her age? That girl loves you so much."

Howie said, "Drew, I haven't seen Harri in a long time."

"What is that supposed to mean?" Drew grew angry. "You saw her last week, Howard!"

Howie said, "OK."

"OK? Look, I'm sorry, just think about it. I'm sorry. I know that you can't help being the way you are. I get that. I appreciate that. But listen. The question is, man-to-man here, what are we going to do about our daughter?"

Howie was genuinely touched by Drew's *our*. He said, "I don't know, Drew."

Howie no longer loved his ex-wife. He only occasionally missed the idea of her, even if this was an idea that hadn't survived the first few years of their marriage, anyway, and probably wasn't his idea to begin with. Besides the first one, Timmy—just that name, *Timmy*—Howie had never experienced what he'd identify as jealousy. He maintained a certain warmth toward his ex-wife's boyfriends and husbands. They felt familial, like brothers—or, possibly, more successful versions of himself. They were like sports teams that Howie wanted to win.

They'd exited I-87.

They were approaching Howie's ex-wife's house in Saratoga Springs. Howie did not want the drive to end. He and Drew had settled into a comfortable conversation; it was like bantering, almost, something that Howie recognized from TV. Drew told Howie about a book that he was reading. Then they'd watch the road. Drew would joke about politicians whom Howie didn't know; Howie would smile. Drew recommended a movie that Howie might enjoy. Did Howie like a particularly sexy actress? Howie did not know but promised Drew that he would look into it.

Drew told Howie about his ex-wife, a vile woman named Pam. They had a son, also a teacher, who was married to a Baptist and living down in godforsaken Maryland. Drew was a grandfather. He said, "Did you enjoy your party?"

"Well, Drew," Howie said. "I guess they really partied the shit out of me this time."

Drew paused, then laughed so hard that he sprayed whisky onto the dashboard, just like in a movie. Drew couldn't stop laughing. "What the *fuck*?" he said. "I've never—they partied *the what* out of you, Howard?"

"Did they party the shit out of you, too, Drew?"

"Stop, you're killing me!"

This had been an easy, wonderful evening and Howie didn't even care that he was smiling. Who cared? Not the road. Not Drew.

"Yeah, well, the stone anniversary," Drew said, finally. "I gotta say. Those guys, they're good guys, Howard. You're lucky. They're really a good bunch of guys."

"They are."

"But we really should go out for a beer sometime, Howard, you know?" Drew said. "Me and you."

"That would be nice, Drew."

"Nice," Drew repeated. Laughed. "Now, full disclosure time. You haven't told me about that woman. Did I notice something? Don't tell me I didn't."

Howie had no idea what Drew was talking about. "I don't know what you're talking about."

"We don't do coy, you and me, OK? We've been married to the same woman. Why do coy? Do brothers do coy?"

Howie asked if this was part of the joke.

Drew said, "What are you talking about?"

"Well," Howie said. He thought about this. "That we're telling jokes."

"We're not telling jokes!"

But they were. Or, rather, they had been laughing. Howie felt stupid. "OK," he said. Probably he should stop talking now.

"Don't tell me you weren't picking up the same vibes I was from that woman, what's her name? I'm sorry, I forget. She was handsome. Outdoorsy and a little on the, you know, the full-figured side. Really sweet face."

"Marcy?"

"I met Marcy, Howard. She's married. She looks like a mongoose."

Suddenly, Howie knew. Drew was talking about Rhoda Prough. Rho. It was something he'd always kind of known but forgotten; it was obvious, wasn't it?

Was it?

Rho was Darren Prough's ex-wife. By mistake, Howie and Rhoda had always gotten along very well at company picnics, holiday parties, and GE union bowling league nights. Rhoda mistook him for something that he was not. Rhoda, like her ex-husband, enjoyed fishing. There was that. She would get close to Howie and joke, under her breath, about the irritating, dull people around her, his pals, the sheeple she called them, instigating a kind of militant camaraderie of antisocialness. Baaaah, she'd say. Bah. She often tried to impress Howie with how much she didn't like being where she imagined that Howie didn't like being either. But how to tell her that this was only his face? That his face didn't like being anywhere. How to tell her that he never had a problem being where he was, and that most people were nice, if too loud, and that his greatest desire was to be nice to people? That people made him happy.

Rhoda would say, "What are we doing here?"

Howie would say that he didn't know, who knows, and this would make her laugh.

Sometimes she and Howie spoke about lakes.

"This is crap," Rho had said once. "Don't you wish you were up in the mountains? Let's go to the mountains, Jeffries."

"Now?"

Rho barked, "Ready when you are, buddy!"

They never went to the mountains. Howie, also, didn't understand the crapness of not being in the mountains. You were where you were, what can you do?

Darren Prough no longer worked at GE but, apparently, Rho was still friends with some of the other GE wives, or she enjoyed attending their functions in order to tell Howie how crappy they were. It was curious. During the divorce, Darren had referred to Rho as the armadillo. Howie imagined her running through walls, eating pretty flowers. But that was unkind.

Before he left, Rho told Howie that they had to get together soon, go fishing or something. She had said that they should go for a proper drink at a proper bar one of these days and that she knew just the place—up near Fort Ticonderoga. But, Howie knew, that was just the kind of thing that people often said instead of good-bye.

"She was talking to a lot of people," Howie told Drew.

"Who, Howard?" Drew liked that. "So you admit it! Come on, let's have a name."

"Her name is Rho."

Howie dropped his ex-wife and Drew off and they insisted that he get out of the car right this instant so that they could hug him properly. He obliged.

Driving down Route 29, Howie decided that there was no way Robert Rogers had tricked the Indians. Not like that, anyway. Howie knew that rock; there was no safe way down, especially in the winter. No, Howie knew why Rogers alone had survived. He'd stayed there at the bottom the entire time. The Battle on Snowshoes had begun and Rogers had taken off his snowshoes and found a place to hide. Maybe he'd climbed up a tree, or he'd buried himself in snow, or maybe he played dead. Playing dead seemed most likely. Rogers had laid there and listened to his men being slaughtered around him, the soft, safe, grateful sound of their bodies falling in snow, the crack of gunfire and hatchets hitting skin, skulls, bone, backbones, and then, at the last moment, Robert Rogers had gotten up, thrown down his gun, his belongings, everything, and he'd run across the frozen lake, straight toward where Harri had no doubt been when she painted Howie's birthday present. There are no extravagant tricks. No spirits, good, bad, or otherwise. The trick? You keep your head down and hope that nobody notices. Then, at the last moment, you run for your freaking life.

He would promote this version of history the next time he saw Drew, see what he thought, but Howie thought about that, too, and knew that he probably wouldn't see Drew again like this—not for a long while anyway.

Good night, Howie. This had been a good night. He looked at his painting in the rearview mirror, making sure that it was still there. He loved it so much, especially now, without his ex-wife sleeping behind it.

Howie did not realize that anything was wrong until he pulled into his driveway. He smelled it first, stepping from his car. Smoke.

It was sickly, like burning plastic or hair, and his first thought was that his car was on fire, somewhere in the engine, the trunk, and that his car would surely explode before he could get the painting safely out of the backseat. It was almost a relief, then, to find that the smoke was spilling from the open front door of the Phane house. He watched. One second, two. Three. Four. How quiet and unreal, feeling relief harden into horror because there was Emily Phane, on the lawn, lying in the manner of someone who had been on fire and was now dead.

17

———

Emily, asleep on Howie's sofa, looked like a telephone that you expected to start ringing with bad news. Like, at any moment, she would ring and Howie would answer and she would tell him that she was, actually, as a matter of fact, deceased. You were too late.

But she was OK, Howie reminded himself. She breathed; she no longer coughed. The worst was over.

The fire had started in the fireplace. Emily had, of course, started it. Everything would have been fine if she had remembered to open the chimney flue.

Later, Howie saw that it had been started with some pillows, chair pieces, magazines and newspapers, and what looked like a bunch of potted plants. The smoke, with nowhere to go, had stayed home. It had filled the house. The wallpaper around the fireplace had bubbled and charred like a thin sheet of roasted marshmallow. The ceiling was black.

Howie hadn't exactly saved her life, but, he knew, he would have if it had come to that. He had been prepared to do whatever it took, running from his car to Emily. The unexpected thump of his feet had made the earth feel stage-like, hollow. He hadn't used his legs in that manner since high school, and it had thrilled him, the way that he had been able to momentarily outrun his shyness.

So. Freckles and sleep, not soot or ash or death. There were bits of cut grass stuck to the side of Emily's face. She looked otherwise OK. No burning.

He had woken her.

"Mmmph—" Her hands groping for a pillow that wasn't there. "I don't wanna."

Neither did Howie, *but he had.* He did. He was. Howie pulled his neighbor up from the gathering smoke and held her in his arms. He took her to his living room, laid her on the sofa, and found himself back outside, facing the blaze alone. Except it wasn't a blaze exactly, just smoke. Howie noted the green garden hose that snaked from the outside of the house into the front door. He watched water lazily slip out the front door, over the porch, and down the steps to the grass. It sounded like an old fountain at a Chinese restaurant.

The lights were still on inside Emily's house, giving the smoke an eerie theatrical aura. Like a rock 'n' roll person was soon to step from Emily's front door, followed by fireworks, noise. But then, as Howie approached, he heard a loud crack. He jumped. The lights clapped off. Something sizzled. Howie walked through the smoke up to the front door and followed the hose to the fireplace, holding on to it as if he were a mountain climber. The living room was flooded. He stepped on broken pottery, heaps of soggy leaves, mud, clothing, what felt like a squishy wet mattress. He couldn't exactly see. The water must have shorted the electricity, and Howie realized that had he entered the house a minute earlier, he might have been electrocuted. There was no fire now, just smoke. Covering his mouth, Howie stepped back outside. Howie did not call 911.

He coughed. He listened to the pines. They were a community here, he thought. You take care of your own. For ten minutes he waited with Emily's house, as if holding its hand, calming them both down. Gradually, the smoke dissipated. Because you could not be too sure. Never turn your back on smoke.

They'd assess the damage tomorrow.

Howie walked back to his house. He walked down Emily's driveway, turned right on Route 29, and then another right up his own driveway. He approached his living room with considerably more fear than he'd approached Emily's house. She was still asleep. Howie went upstairs, listening to his footsteps, and he found a red, white, and blue afghan in Harri's room, or the guest room, because, despite what his daughter had been telling her mother and Drew, she hadn't been to visit in years. Howie covered Emily with this afghan, tucking her in. Howie went to the kitchen and drank a refreshing glass of milk. Then he went back upstairs.

For some reason, he expected Emily to be awake when he returned, as if she knew he'd brushed his teeth and hair and put on a presentable shirt. Like, for propriety's sake, she'd been waiting for this. She was still asleep. Sleepyhead, he thought.

This sleeping was weird, considering, but she didn't seem to have suffered any visible head trauma besides the bits of lawn that were stuck in her hair like plastic Easter basket grass.

Telling her, in his head, that he'd be right back, don't worry, Howie went to his car and began moving his cache of stone anniversary gifts inside with an emotion he didn't have time to acknowledge as happiness. He left the *Playboy* magazine in the backseat.

Howie sat on a wooden ladder-back chair in the center of his living room on a beige carpet. He observed his neighbor, waited. He practiced hellos in his head. He had never thought about his carpet being beige before. Howie assumed that this was the correct color, in case Emily asked what color it was, specifically, when she awoke, though Howie knew how remote the possibility of such a question was.

Until this moment, he had never thought about how abandoned his living room looked. He'd taken the wooden ladder-back chair from the kitchen. He only had one chair in his kitchen. Slouchless, alert: Howie sat with intense formality. He did not move. He'd brought the chair into the living room because imagine him waiting there for Emily to wake up while sitting casually, intimately, in his ex-wife's tufted Rhapsody chair. That chair was the color of pollen. Even worse, imagine him *standing* above her. His first impulse had been to wait in the bathroom upstairs in the dark. That would not do at all. Even though it was a muggy summer evening, Howie had covered Emily in a red, white, and blue afghan that had once belonged to his mother. Emily was clothed. To Howie's mother, Doris, knitting had been a joyless, patriotic act. She only had red, white, and blue yarn. She didn't follow politics, and she didn't read the paper or necessarily enjoy the company of her fellow man, but ever since her first husband, Nathanial, had died in the Pacific, Doris had dogmatically cleaved to the accoutrements of being a proud American. Toward the end of his life, Guy, Howie's father, in a rare moment of communication, said that Doris, who had passed away several years before, had probably been a more invested widow than wife. Temperamentally, she was just better at it. Basically, she'd felt it was her duty to dress her household in a manner respectful to the country that Nathanial had given his life to protect. *Your father*, she might begin, when speaking of Nathanial to Howie, and then correct herself: "I mean to say, my first husband, Private Nathanial P. Sounes." Howie knew everything about Private Nathanial P. Sounes, certainly more than he knew about his real father, the gentle, ghostly Guy. Howie's father had been 4-F. Something about his heart, and something—like everything—that they never got around to speaking about, though Howie was certain that his father knew exactly what his wife was doing with all her flags and afghans and doilies. Like Howie, Guy Jeffries didn't have a competitive bone in his body. Perhaps that was the real reason for his 4-F. Howie could not imagine his father saying a harsh word to anyone, never mind rousing himself up enough to patriotically kill strangers.

Crickets chirped and stopped, started, stopped; outside, on Route 29, three trucks gusted past, shaking the silence. They left a deeper, darker silence in their wake. Then more crickets and the revving hum of Howie's old refrigerator, the clunking of the clock. It was 2:41 a.m., and time moved reasonably along.

It was 2:42 a.m.

2:43 a.m.

Clunk.

2:44.

The microwave in the kitchen would say it was 5:44 p.m., but the microwave had been insisting, silently, on a different time zone for years. You learn to be tolerant.

He had left Emily with her muddy shoes on so as not to take any liberties with her feet or property. Nobody wants to wake up on a stranger's sofa without her shoes. Mud was only wet dirt. Howie thought about his face and how best to comport it. Sitting in the ladder-back chair, he would try an expression, freeze it for when Emily awoke, which could be any second, then forget which expression it was, erase it, start over, probably make the same exact face again. Who was he kidding? Howie only had one face.

He had never been more afraid of anything in his life than he was of this freckled girl asleep on his sofa. Howie was wearing his muddy shoes indoors, too. Under the circumstances, this seemed like the rectitudinous thing to do. Don't want her thinking that she was the only person wearing muddy shoes indoors, that he had extended deferential treatment to her that might, when she awoke, make her feel self-conscious or in any way uncomfortable. That, and Howie did not want Emily to see his socks.

Harri's painting was behind Howie, the accurate colors of Rogers Rock and his beloved Lake Jogues leaning against the TV. It pretty much covered his entire so-called entertainment center. The painting supported him, rallied him, propped up and straightened his back: he was Robert Rogers, hiding here in plain sight, waiting for Emily to ring.

She looked huge up close, though she was, Howie decided, not so very large. In twenty-five years, he had never been this close to her. In fact, she had lost a tremendous amount of weight. Her dark hair was unwashed. Her brown freckles, if you stared long enough, popped about her face like fleas. Under the Private Nathanial P. Sounes memorial afghan, she wore red shorts and pink socks and a filthy maroon and white Boston University hooded athletic shirt.

Then, and without moving a muscle, she changed. She went from looking like a phone that he was expecting to ring to a phone that was ringing, but internally, ringer on silent.

This did not exactly make sense. The air around her face had changed. The volume of the air was raised, and kept getting louder, louder.

Louder.

Howie stood. He walked across the living room carpet. He paused, steeled his face, and saw the impossible: his hand reaching out and touching his neighbor's shoulder. He shook a shoulder and he snapped open Emily Phane's eyes.

Emily had been awake for what seemed like hours but was probably only minutes or that eternal hell space between seconds. She couldn't place herself inside any kind of immediate, narrative past. Only that she was herself again, stuck inside herself, and she wanted out. She thought she'd found a way out, but nope, she was on her back.

Back was not out.

Emily was back on her back on her fucking living room sofa. She could not open her eyes. She was breathing, and she smelled smoke, but faintly, as if she'd just come back from a Boston party where everyone had been smoking plastic and logs instead of cigarettes, pot. She felt the shoes on her feet.

She couldn't move her feet.

Though she couldn't hear anything but a strangely loud clock, then a strange refrigerator, she knew that her grandfather was in the room with her. There was a caring presence nearby that she hadn't felt in years.

Jiminy crickets, she thought.

Her grandfather breathing.

Buzzing refrigeration.

They were on her.

The sound first, as always, as if her ears were being filled with molten *scream*. She felt herself being pushed down to a small, dark point inside her head. Drowning inside herself. She struggled. She couldn't move. Her eyes, of course, would not open. But something was different this time because when she heard the footsteps approaching her, she didn't sense the evil. Then, a hand on her shoulder, a good hand, Peppy's hand. I'm here. Don't worry.

The carpet was yellowish, old. The walls, too. The fireplace empty and cold, totally clean. It was exactly her living room but all the plants were gone, gone; everything was gone, actually, except for a giant, strange window that reached to the yellow carpet and revealed a view of a cliff, a lake. The air had the bland, white smell of boiling pasta.

For the first time, there was an actual human man standing over her.

His face, which, in her paralysis, she'd anticipated as being made of some kind of pure, grandfatherly goodness, looked angry. Like a chiseled, angry rock. Like tree.

Emily gasped, began coughing.

Mr. Jeffries had finally snapped and abducted her.

His eyes were blue. Emily had never seen her neighbor's eyes. But his face, if you started with these eyes and moved outward, his face wasn't angry at all. It was frightened, resigned, like a courageous little boy preparing himself for a spanking.

He didn't speak or move, as if he'd been possessed by the paralysis that had just held her, and Emily felt immediately, oddly protective.

She stood.

She'd been wrapped in a large, knitted flag. She was dreaming. Not dreaming, walking. She followed Mr. Jeffries down the hall to the kitchen. It was her hall but denuded: no family photographs, nothing but a terrible fish. This was exactly what her house would look like if it were dead.

．　．　．

Even after all that planning, Howie had forgotten to say hello. Emily was trembling; she was coughing, maybe sobbing a little. Then she was still. Except for her eyes, which clicked around the room.

She put up her hood.

Howie took his neighbor to the kitchen. That is, he began walking to the kitchen and hoped that she would follow. Everyone knows that the kitchen is the safest room in a house.

Howie opened a cupboard. He turned and heard himself say, "Do you want a glass of water?"

But he was the only one who heard this, because Emily said, "What?"

She sounded like a woman.

Howie handed Emily a glass. He pointed to the sink—with his face. He watched her grip the faucet as if it were there solely to prevent her from slipping to the floor. She pushed it up, the water came down. Perhaps she was too weak to move the faucet from the hot left to the cold right, or maybe, Howie thought, she just likes her tap water warm. Some folks did.

Howie had moved his computer, toaster, and telephone off the kitchen table. These he had unplugged and planted in a nest of wires on the linoleum in front of the refrigerator. This is why Howie was unable to offer Emily a refreshing glass of milk or ginger ale. On the table, in their place, he'd moved his birthday gifts, including the large pile of stones with faces painted on them.

They stood in the kitchen together. Emily put down her hood.

Put it back up again.

She looked at the stones, and Howie at Emily, and both thought, and not without good reason, that the other was far more gone than they'd previously imagined possible.

18

___

So he was friends with rocks. Probably he had conversations with rocks, had rocks round for lunch. They looked happy at least, Emily thought, and then she noticed an old computer on the floor in front of the refrigerator, plus a toaster, phone, wires. The telephone had been ostentatiously unplugged.

Emily turned her back to the room.

The reflection of the kitchen inside the window above the sink. It was the ghost of her kitchen. She poured herself another glass of water, relaxing, momentarily, inside the comfy, blanket-like sound the water made coming from the faucet. There was a continuum in that sound, one that stretched back to Peppy and childhood safety. The same metal sink, too. The same water.

Mr. Jeffries wore a tucked-in white dress shirt and shapeless L.L.Bean chinos. On his feet, dressy, tasseled JCPenney shoes. Like he was just about to go to work. In 1982. Emily had to use the bathroom. She felt woozy, hypnotized; she coughed. She sipped warm water. Coughed.

The kitchen smelled nice, actually. Like smoke, soil, and . . .

I just burned down my house.

Emily rushed toward the other window. But it gave her nothing but her own reflection, not just her house but everything out there was gone, voided, only the reflection of Mr. Jeffries behind her.

He said, "It's OK."

The voice almost belonged to a teenage boy. It was feathery. It did not fit his face. She saw him put his hand to his mouth, as if in acknowledgment of this fact. It was easier for both of them to talk to each other's reflection in the window.

"My house," Emily said.

"The fire is out. Everything is wet. I'm sorry."

"How did I get here?"

Howie did not want Emily to know that he had touched her. He said, carefully, quietly, "You came to the door."

"I did?"

"You fell asleep on my sofa."

"I don't remember."

"I think your electricity is blown."

"What happened?"

"There was a fire."

"I *know.*"

"OK."

Pause.

"Did you call the fire department, Mr. Jeffries?"

He shook his head. He could not explain it. "The fire was already out. You put it out with a garden hose."

"You put it out with a garden hose?"

"I did not."

"What are you talking about? I need to go. I need to get out of here."

"OK."

Next to the stones on the table was a digital clock the shape of the shark from *Finding Nemo*. There was a goldfish in a jar next to a microwave. The sun would be rising soon; the crickets had become birds.

Emily was trembling. "I think I need to sit down," she said.

"I have a chair," Mr. Jeffries said, sadly. "But it's not here."

In spite of everything, Emily smiled. There were, of course, no kitchen chairs around the kitchen table.

He said, "Would you like some scrambled eggs?"

"*What?*" Like, instead of a chair?

Emily turned and faced Mr. Jeffries, finally. She seriously needed to pee.

Mr. Jeffries winced, looked at his tiny, tasseled feet. He said, "Do you like ginger ale?"

Emily fell asleep in front of the TV. Howie had given her a bowl of Honey Nut Cheerios and a glass of ginger ale, but she hadn't exactly seemed conceptually aware of them, cocooned, as she was, inside the Private Nathanial P. Sounes memorial afghan on Howie's sofa. She had moved the painting and turned the TV on all by herself.

Moments after Howie had brought her the food, Emily had begun blinking her eyes, once, twice, three times, and then they remained closed, almost midblink, one arm jutting from the afghan clutching the spoon.

Emily wore a gold wedding band on her ring finger. It looked, Howie thought, almost exactly like his ex-wife's ring. It was disconcerting. Her hand, too, could have been his ex-wife's hand, but when was the last time he had really examined a woman's hand up close? There were probably more similarities than differences.

Maybe she did not care for ginger ale.

Howie went back to the kitchen for a glass of water, warm, the way she liked it. He left the TV on, the History Channel it looked like, a documentary about Nostradamus and ancient aliens, and then Howie went upstairs. For the first time in years he closed the bedroom door behind him. The house felt muzzled and questioning. Howard, what are you doing?

Good question.

The next morning she was gone. Motionless at the top of the stairs, Howie listened; he was, as they say, all ears. He listened with his skin, feeling for vibrations through his feet and his hand, which gripped the railing as if his house could, at any moment, lurch violently to the left. The silence of his house became a racket, a wreckage of small sounds that Howie found himself parsing through for signs of Emily Phane, awake, asleep, deceased. He thought that he would know what a dead neighbor sounded like if he heard one.

The clock clunked.

The refrigerator brrrrrrrrr'd, and there, another car passing outside on Route 29. In the sky an airplane or a long, slow pull of thunder. A dead neighbor would sound like a clock not clunking.

It was 9:34 a.m. The TV was off. Howie hadn't exactly slept, but Harri's painting had kept him good company.

He descended the stairs.

Howie looked out the living room window. Nothing. He walked to the kitchen and looked out the kitchen window. Emily was in her backyard.

Before leaving she'd moved the bowl of cereal, napkin, and water to the kitchen counter. Howie realized how odd his piles of stones must have looked. Standing safely back from the window, he watched her remove the plants from her house to where her garden used to be. She appeared to be replanting the ones with broken pots; the others she lined up like an audience or army. This was inappropriate. You should not be watching this. Howie had to be at work soon. But that would mean leaving his house, going to his car, and Emily would see him and probably say something. She would have to say something, and so would he.

Howie called in sick.

His manager, Bill Morrow, laughed. It was understood, acceptable. Howie'd sure had the shit partied out of him, hadn't he?

"Oh, yes," Howie said. "Thank you."

"Not a problem, my man. Sleep it off and we'll see you tomorrow. Once every ninety years, right? You earned it."

"OK."

He went upstairs to his spot by the bathroom window and

watched a little longer. Just to make sure. But make sure what? He did not exactly know. The plants seemed threatening. The roof might collapse. Something might leak, explode.

Twenty minutes later, Emily was inside her house. She did not reemerge.

Howie lay down; his room was dusky, cool. Nothing exploded. He'd closed his bedroom door again. The windows in his bedroom were always covered; they'd been blinded for as long as he could remember. He placed *Fishing the Adirondacks* on his chest. It was his alibi for being back in bed and fully clothed before noon. In case folks wondered. He stared upward, allowing himself a momentary seethe against the spider-like magnificence of his ex-wife's dead grandmother's chandelier. He had leaned Harri's painting against the wall. Sometimes he looked at that too, but only once every twenty minutes. He wanted to savor it. He did not want his staring to erode any of the fresh, happy love he felt every time he saw it. Howie imagined where in the painting he would hide if it were winter and Indians were after him, until he really began to feel as if he were hiding inside the painting. Then he fell asleep.

For a long while after napping, Howie thought about going downstairs and plugging the computer back in, seeing if Drew had posted any photographs from the surprise stone anniversary party to Facebook. But Emily might be watching from her window, waiting for him. Howie allowed himself to consider his daughter in the manner that Drew had urged him to consider his daughter. He considered telling Harri that he could no longer give her or New York City any more money, but, then, why couldn't he? Certainly he could. He would. Should. Not only did he not need the majority of his monthly salary—the mortgage of the house was long since paid off, his car, everything—but in his cupboard Howie had his Folgers decaf can with well over ten thousand dollars. Really, what did Drew suppose him to do? Howie didn't prove points. Points either were or they weren't, no need proving them, and his boat savings was not nearly as important to Howie as his daughter's happiness. Worse came to worst, couldn't Howie get Harri to add a boat to her painting? That might suffice. Of course, he wanted to know why she had lied to her mother and Drew, and though the lie wasn't serious, it was strange. Maybe he didn't want to know. Frankly, part of him was pleased that his ex-wife thought that Harri spent so much quality time with him on Route 29. It was almost like it was true. There was a phone next to his bed. He could call Harri and ask her. The least he could do was thank her for the painting. Instead, he went downstairs to make sandwiches, two, both salami, which he brought upstairs and ate in bed.

In this manner, Howie spent nearly the entire day upstairs.

Close to nightfall, he heard something. Someone was knocking on his front door. Then that door opened. "Hello? Mr. Jeffries? Hello?"

Howie held his breath, began paging through *Fishing the Adirondacks*. Then he put that down, got up, and went to his bedroom door. He opened it. He said, "Hello."

"It's me, it's Emily!"

Howie said, "It's Howie."

Fool, he thought.

He heard Emily laugh. "Can I come in?"

Howie walked to the top of the stairs. "OK," he said.

"OK?"

Emily stood at the bottom of the stairs. She smiled; she had changed her clothing. She was holding a tray of what looked like brownies. "I'm sorry," she said. Nervously, she looked behind her. "Well, I made these for you but . . . ," she continued. "You know, like a thank-you. But my oven is electric. No electricity. I thought maybe—?"

"Come in," Howie said. Though Emily was already very obviously inside his house.

She looked behind her again. She laughed. She said, "Plus, the lights don't work. My living room is kind of flooded."

"I'm sorry."

"So these are for you. I know it's weird, but do you mind if I bake them in your oven?"

Howie said, "No."

They stared at each other. Howie knew how ambiguous his no sounded, but he was too paralyzed to do anything but wait and hope that she understood. No, I do not mind if you bake brownies for me in my oven. She did not understand. She said, "Well, all right then." She said, "Good-bye then," waved, and walked back out the front door.

An hour later, Howie stood on Emily's front porch. It was night. He saw through her window.

Halloween had been Howie's least favorite holiday. His parents had forced him to dress up as something frightening, go out, get out, be a normal kid for once. Have a little fun. Little Howie, alone, standing before his neighbors' doors, too terrified to make himself known, waiting sometimes ten, twenty minutes for some other rural monsters to come up behind him, ring the bell, shout, "Trick or treat!" He would silently mouth along, get his treats, go.

"Well, buddy, how'd you make out?" Howie's father, Guy, sitting in front of the TV, in the dark. His father always made to get up when Howie entered the house; he would put his arms on the sofa's cushions, rise slightly, maybe three inches, a show of intent, a full body nod, then he'd let himself plop back down. It was an acknowledgment of Howie's presence, somewhere between a hello and a hug. "Are we good?" he would always ask.

"We're OK," Howie would say, and go to his room, putting his hard-earned treats in the drawer for later.

Howie knocked on Emily Phane's door.

"Mr. Jeffries?" Emily said. But she didn't open the door. She blew out the candles, which was probably the safest thing to do, considering. "Is that you, Mr. Jeffries?"

"Hello," Howie said. He waited.

"Mr. Jeffries?"

"Yes," he said. "I'm right here."

"I know you are. What do you want, Mr. Jeffries?"

"Hello," he said again.

The door opened. Emily's house smelled of smolder, dog, chemical melt. "Hello," she said.

"I think it might be unsafe for you," Howie began.

"What, how?"

"I mean to say," Howie said. "I mean, if you like, you can stay at my house until your house is fixed. The electricity and water damage. You can stay in Harri's room."

Emily, suddenly a little freaked out, said, "Who is Harry?" Oh my God did he think that he lived with someone named Harry?

"My daughter," Howie explained. Then, "She doesn't live with me anymore."

"Yeah, oh," Emily said. She shook her head, almost laughed. She stepped out of her house. "You really don't mind, Mr. Jeffries?"

"I don't."

"Just for a night or two."

"OK."

Emily did not know how much she wanted out of her house until that moment. Her eyes filled with tears. The summer air was perfect.

They walked to his house. Down her driveway, side-by-side, silently, a right on Route 29, and another right up his driveway to his front door, which Howie knocked upon.

"Mr. Jeffries," Emily said. "I don't think that you're home."

Howie covered his face with his hand, trying to push his own smile, laugh, whatever it was, back down inside his mouth. Emily Phane opened the front door and he followed her into his living room.

19

———

Emily took her spot on the sofa. She cuddled in, stretching out into a full body yawn. The entire sofa, apparently, was Emily's spot.

Howie stood in his hallway, lodged halfway between the living room and the kitchen. He said, "Do you want some—?"

The word he gagged on was *supper*. The empty shape of it slid down his throat, taking Howie with it.

Emily said, "What?"

"Eggs," Howie remembered. "Something to eat. Supper."

Emily nodded even though eggs were technically breakfast and gross. But being here was technically insane, so fine, whatever you say. Eggs. She turned on the TV. She needed the television for continuity, balance.

"Good. So I can make you eggs," Howie continued. "While you watch."

Emily turned to the strange man looming in the strange, bone-dry version of her hallway. She said, "You want me to watch you make eggs?"

Howie meant TV. It was like trying to pedal a bicycle with its handlebar. "I also have ginger ale," he said. Harri loved ginger ale. He always kept a few cans of it around in case his daughter visited, even though his daughter never visited. "Bye now," Howie concluded.

"What, wait, where are you going?"

"The kitchen." Howie pointed over his shoulder, behind him. "It's just there."

"Mine too," she said.

Howie covered what felt like another smile with what felt like a clenched fist, and Emily, noting this, smiled too. She said, "Hey, Mr. Jeffries?"

"Yes?"

"Don't worry. This is great. Thank you."

"I'll make fried eggs."

"I'm glad."

Howie sat in his ex-wife's tufted Rhapsody chair. This was his on-special-occasions spot—like when Harri last stayed the night, years ago despite what Drew said, and they'd watched that movie about black and white Europeans, or whenever Howie used to talk to his daughter on the phone, or even with the texting, Howie would sit in the tufted Rhapsody chair while typing a telephone text, and waiting for his Nokia to buzz buzz in response—MISS U 2 DAD—or the morning a couple summers back when his Oldsmobile's cough went terminal and, to be safe, Mike Ed Walker and his doppel-ganger of a spouse, the drowsy, unsettling Shirley "Ed" Walker (as some called her), came over for decaf and ginger ale before taking Howie up Tongue Mountain for a hike to Deer Leap Lake and an afternoon of fishing.

Sitting in the tufted Rhapsody chair made Howie feel like his ex-wife. She felt aggrieved mostly, Howie supposed, like what was she still doing here in this boring freaking chair in this boring freaking house? Howie, when he began to feel like his ex-wife, reassured them both, his ex-wife and himself. Leave anytime you want. Nothing holding you, he thought. Don't be sad.

Emily slept on the sofa. She'd fallen asleep while he was preparing her eggs. He'd eaten the eggs himself, in the kitchen, standing up watching his new fish.

Howie reached over and took the remote from Emily's sofa. He started flipping through the channels. A Red Lobster commercial. Lawmakers say. Sports. Nine out of ten dentists agree . . .

Sports.

Sports.

Come test-drive the all new . . .

Tomorrow, Howie decided. He didn't have a single thing to attach the decision of tomorrow onto, not yet, not even a Thursday or a Friday, and certainly not the all-new Buick Verano. But sitting there in his ex-wife's chair, he had a feeling that tomorrow was a decision as well as a place, and it felt different. Howie's eyes grew heavy. The colors on the TV grew hair.

Enough.

He enjoyed the satisfying gasp the TV made when you killed it.

He listened to the TV-less room, like a beach after a retreating wave or a disappointed wife, standing next to the bed, in the dark, soundlessly putting her pajamas back on. And Howie yawned.

He looked at Emily Phane.

The girl was in trouble. Not just in general, but, he realized, *in there*. Right now. She was ringing again. The person on the other end of the line was having an emergency. She hadn't changed her position or moved, but Howie sensed it.

He became intensely alert to the forest beyond the windows. Pine trees in the warm night wind; deer stopping, ears popped, listening. Howie heard the sound of a thousand pine trees massively waiting, gathering like clouds.

Emily knew the minute she'd reappropriated Mr. Jeffries's sofa that she was going to fall asleep. She had not been afraid. Despite everything, or, rather, despite the tree-faced man with the sad, effeminate voice, Emily had felt safe enough to let go. For once, her hallucinatory exhaustion was not interchangeable with desperation or hopelessness. It felt hazy, good, watched-over. So she'd closed her eyes the second Mr. Jeffries, after apparently torturous deliberation, had, with her encouragement, established a course of action that involved the kitchen behind him and, inexplicably, ginger ale. Mr. Jeffries's discomfort made Emily feel more in control. She listened to the insectoid song of the frying eggs, along with an unaccountably bald woman sobbing into a phone on TV. The woman had a dog that she loved. The woman was on the run from the FBI. She was bald because it was the future. Put the phone down, they're coming to get you. Leave the dog. Run.

Emily fell asleep.

Then she was back, repeating on herself. She hadn't been anywhere, anything, and here was her consciousness gurgling up from wherever, flooding sleep and pinning her down, locking her into herself first, into memory, and then into the impossibly dense stillness of her paralyzed body. Welcome home. She tried to move. She tried to move. She tried to move.

Toes. Fingers. Tongue. Emily tried to locate and flex the muscles in her legs. She could feel everything, the sofa and the scratchy afghan, her chest rising, falling, the air passing through her lips; her heart beating; her tiny tongue inside her open mouth. The tongue was just as important as her two hands—it was one of the primary controls, where her consciousness resided, balanced itself, made her body go. Her tongue was always one of the first places she tried to be.

There was nothing that could help her.

Emily tried to move.

Because why should anything care enough to help her? Emily didn't care if a single cell on her fingertip died, and so what was Emily to the horrific, infinite reality of time and space and matter and . . .

She could not fucking move.

Focus on objects: sofa, afghan, Mr. Jeffries, carpet, TV. Driftwood she could cling to now that her ship had smashed apart on the rocks. But it was meaningless and too late and she couldn't hold on for much longer anyway. Emily screamed inside herself.

She thought about her grandfather, groped for Peppy inside herself again and found nothing, as usual, less than nothing, actually, more like the cold truth that she never knew him either, whatever he'd been. He was just another more insidious part of the absurd illusion of her waking life, and the love that she still felt for him was possibly the most evil part of that reality, love was the unthinking, grasping animal thing, the glue that the waking world used to keep everyone in place, playing along, invested, and not sitting in the corner babbling at the fucking horror of it all.

Because Emily knew.

She knew, she knew. She knew that there was no such thing as death, for starters. She knew that evil existed like fire or the moon. She knew that it wasn't a choice; it was another frequency that was also a thing. She knew that everything was connected, but not in the way that Bob Marley thought. Love was not one. But she knew that she still loved her grandfather, and she knew that she'd loved Ethan even though, in the end, she couldn't actually believe in him either. Poor Ethan Caldwell. She knew that this made her love him even more. She knew that love was animal and dumb and no different from hatred. She knew that being here, stuck and suffering, meant she couldn't believe in anything in the waking world. She couldn't suspend her disbelief. She couldn't enjoy the puppet show after having seen the strings, smelled the booze on the puppeteers' breath, counted the nicks and calluses on their hands. She knew she was only happy now among the plants and she knew that she was killing herself slowly and that this, of course, would solve nothing: that she would still be trapped and that it would be worse, losing this body, these senses, but she knew that she couldn't handle the previews anymore, the anxiety of waiting for them, the nightly, daily, constant sleep visions of being in this hell, with and without a body, stuck with herself forever, and she knew that she'd rather just be here, finally, and dead and in the shit, the Main Event, than living, as she was now, in both worlds. No more of this suspended fear of both worlds. Time to pick a team. She knew that demons

existed. Call them whatever. Ghosts. Spirits. Presences. She knew
that words were as much of an illusion as the other senses her body
came up with: the smelling, seeing, touching. She knew what it was
like to think without words, like a plant, and she knew it was like
seeing the color of a brand-new color. She knew it was total bullshit
but she still wanted to eat delicious Boston food, lobster in melted
butter, tofu burritos, cilantro, freezing cold Riesling, Bukhara's
killer lunch buffet, and she knew she still craved brainless animal
fucking just as she still loved watching stories on TV about attractive people who surmounted hardships. People who made the bad
guys pay for what they'd done. She knew it was a puppet show put
on by the puppets, but she liked a good mystery as much as the next
girl. She knew that they were always around her, the evil spirits,
but she knew that there were good ones, too, probably, somewhere,
but they didn't seem to bother with her, and why should they? She
knew that a lot of religions made a lot of sense but none of them
made enough sense and all of them were too infected by braying
human hatred and money and politics and ignorance and tribal
storybook feel-good crap. She knew that none of what she knew
made much sense in words. She knew that contradiction was at the
heart of everything: that five things both could and couldn't exist in
the same place at the same time. She knew that she couldn't explain
this to anyone and that she didn't want to either, not anymore, that
she didn't give a shit, because she knew that it'd do no good. She
knew that she wasn't crazy. She knew that she was totally fucking
bonkers. Madness was reality without the human brain pretending
to make sense of it. It was slipping outside linguistic understanding. She knew that sometimes she didn't even know all this stuff,
that sometimes she just let herself live and worry about the crashing, comforting mystery of all the people around her, their own
motivating dramas and desires, like Ethan, money, playing games
to win, the nice clothes and how she looked, her hair, boobs, celeb-
rity gossip, the distracting wonders of science and history and sex
and what she wanted to do when she grew up. But she knew that

she had grown up. She'd already grown up and blown it. I'm so sorry, Peppy. She'd left Boston. She'd left science and Ethan. She'd left the internet. She knew that she'd gone too far—but not far enough—and now there was no way back. She knew that Route 29 was as good as any place if you aspired to be a tree. She knew she still had her sense of humor and she knew that this was actually her last line of defense, the only thing keeping her human, alive, on this sofa in this sleepwalking weirdo's house. She knew sleep wasn't what people thought it was. She knew she was doomed, and not just on a human level but on a level that was eternal. She knew what it was like to be upside down in her own body. She knew that she started that fire as a cry for help. Smoke signals. She knew the wedding ring hadn't belonged to her mother. She knew that she would never, ever know her father, who couldn't possibly even give a fucking shit. She knew that there was still some hope, that maybe she wasn't doomed and maybe she was wrong about everything. Everything. And she didn't know why that scared her to death when she knew there was no such thing as death.

They were coming.

But she could still hear the TV. You must hold on to the TV.

The FBI killed the bald woman's dog. Can't say we didn't warn the bitch. Yeah, both of 'em.

Music.

Rueful snorting.

Help me.

Emily heard Mr. Jeffries breathing.

And she felt something new here. Hard to explain, but Mr. Jeffries seemed more real than anyone she'd ever been close to while asleep, paralyzed. He was right there. More than Peppy, Ethan, anyone, like he'd just stepped into it with Emily.

He sat down. He reached over, plucking up the remote, his hand entering the screams that were now enveloping Emily, his hand actually parting the screams, slipping elegantly through them, and Emily, once again, tried to move, to reach up and grab Mr. Jeffries's hand, as if from a lake, as if she really was drowning. Because she really was drowning.

He changed the channels. Sports. Sports. Come test-drive the all-new Buick Verano today.

Help me, please.

The TV snapped off, and into the loud, fresh silence rushed the bad stuff. There wasn't a slow approach this time. They slammed hungrily into Emily, pushing in on her chest. They devoured. They began to feast.

Howie reached in and pulled Emily out. He grabbed her shoulders and lifted her, gathering her up as one would a small child. The impulse he'd acted upon had been as solid and self-contained as a number or a tooth.

Emily's eyes, tongue, hands, toes, and everything opened—were hers again. She didn't scream. She was in Mr. Jeffries's arms. She held Mr. Jeffries until she was able to collect and sustain the illusion around her, the waking world again, until she was the one reassuring Mr. Jeffries. There there, Emily thought. Shhhh.

Emily released Howie from the embrace that she'd appropriated from him as surely as she'd taken his sofa. She sat back down. He did too.

Emily asked Howie if he was OK.

"Yes," Howie said.

Emily turned the TV back on. She made a sound, a deflation, like someone getting into a really hot bath. She said, "You don't mind the TV?"

He did not.

"You look like you mind."

Howie thought about that. "I always look this way," he said.

He expected Emily to smile. She did not. She said, "I'm sorry I slept through your eggs." Then, on second thought, "I don't like eggs."

"It's OK."

"Thank you, Mr. Jeffries. Really."

Howie knew that this was the point where he was supposed to say something else, ask Emily a question about what had just happened, perhaps make a quip, throw out his fishing line and, plop, see what was there. But this he could not do. Normally, at this point in an interaction, Howie would calm his head, close down shop on his face and wait, and wait, and the other person, unless that other person was Rho or drunk—or, God help him, a drunk Rho—got the hint and either nervously chit-chattered through the moment or found a way to leave Howie to Howie. But this person was Emily. Besides that, this person was on Howie's sofa. So, finally, he said, "Can I ask you a question?"

"Sure," Emily frowned. "I guess."

Disaster. Not only because Emily's face had suddenly gummed up with circumspection, but when was the last time that Howie had asked anyone a personal question? It was much worse than ringing a doorbell, this admission that Howie had a specific question he wanted permission to ask. He felt exposed. Trick or treat—or how about please don't even bother opening the door? Howie tightened the mask of his face.

He looked down at the carpet. The carpet. "Is this beige?" he asked.

Emily tilted her head. Um. "The color?"

"The carpet."

"It's yellow."

Howie said, "OK."

"I think it's yellow?"

They looked at the carpet together.

Howie said, "Maybe it used to be beige."

"Mr. Jeffries," Emily smiled. "You are so weird."

They watched TV.

Because the alternative to acting as if this was perfectly normal, both knew, was acting like they'd lived next door for the past twenty-five years and never once said a single word to each other. Confronting that, they'd decided, was kind of impossible given the sofa and the *Frasier*, not to mention the fact that they'd just shared a moment that both of them would have trouble describing as anything less than nuts. They watched a lot of TV.

Howie awoke on the sofa, next to Emily. He stood up. The CNN was on. Emily Phane was, too. Embarrassed, Howie said, "What time is it?"

He generally had little trouble asking questions that concerned numbers. They exposed nothing. He moved into the hallway and its promise of a safe, intermediary state. He stood there.

"It's like five in the morning. You've been asleep for a while. I'm sorry," Emily said. She picked her freckles, rubbed them. They were a mess. "You want me to go home now? I should probably be going."

She looked unwell. The soggy dawn light didn't help, the sky aggressively low, overcast, drizzling all over the house. Emily's eyes were pink. Her arms were too thin, pale, almost dewy. They reminded Howie of something he'd seen on TV about eyeless albino cave salamanders. The air smelled of puddle and musty green. Emily had opened the windows.

Howie respected sleep. He stopped, listened to it—and he knew that he needed maybe three more hours, four tops. There would have been no way that he'd have been able to maintain thirty years of shift work, two weeks of night followed by two weeks of day, without a deferential relationship with sleep. Many of his colleagues were permanently jet-lagged connoisseurs of caffeine, neon energy drinks, worse. Guys who didn't figure out how to manage their sleep shifts quickly got fat, ill-tempered, divorced; early-onset heart disease and alcoholism were well-documented worries. You got to know pretty quick which ones would last. Emily, Howie saw, didn't stand a chance.

"You should stay," he said. "You should sleep."

"Thank you."

"I'm going upstairs now."

Howie wanted to tell Emily about Harri's room but thought it would be too strange, both of them climbing the stairs together. Maybe it was better if she stayed on the sofa.

"Bad night," Emily called out.

Howie, climbing the stairs, paused, then continued without turning around.

"I mean, good night!" Emily said. "Mr. Jeffries?"

He was upstairs. He called down, "Yes?"

"Good night!"

"OK."

Emily couldn't believe that she was still here. She listened to the footsteps above her.

Then nothing.

Then a toilet flushed. Loud. She felt weird about that, but the subsequent and comfortingly domestic rush of the sink, of teeth being brushed, washed that weird away. Emily heard a door close. Slowly, softly, Howie tapping it shut, as if he didn't want to wake himself up. She remembered him knocking on his own front door. Didn't that kind of say it all? Emily liked that so much. She missed him already.

She thought: I won't even start to think about what happened back there with Mr. Jeffries.

Because he was safe. He was as sexually intimidating as a Cheerio.

There was no negativity in the old man, she thought. He wasn't even old. There wasn't any of the crotchety, ossified annoyance that she'd long assumed was his primary motivation for getting out of bed each and every day. If she'd thought of him at all, Emily had thought of him as forever festering here, next door, sitting in his kitchen enjoying a brutal, endless, self-destructive sort of dis-contentment. Like revenge. Life and Mr. Jeffries having an idiotic stare-off, waiting to see who'd flinch first. Like Mr. Jeffries was bearing witness to how bad shit was to prove to everyone just how bad shit really was, and Emily hated that she thought she understood this and, furthermore, if it wasn't true, and it didn't seem the least bit true, then who exactly was Emily describing here?

Fuck.

Because his sleeping face had been revelatory! Everyone looks softer asleep, unguarded, but Mr. Jeffries looked beatific, not like a tree or a stone but like a tree or a stone on which the face of a wise, wondering saint had been carved and, incredibly, was in the process of coming alive to cry blood or something: a miracle! He was more animated asleep, like he suddenly had so much to say if only he wasn't *asleep*. Sleep plied his features with personality and, Emily thought, a sense of communicable history that was unreadable during his waking life. It wasn't just the snoring you couldn't shut up. Emily had felt as if she were getting to know the guy, not the facts of him, but something more essential. And it broke her heart, the way that Mr. Jeffries slept through himself.

Time passed. Emily went to the kitchen. Nobody knows where I am.

She made her yawn full, operatic. She touched the kitchen counter, both palms down, and she could see through the wall.

It was raining.

The drizzle on leaves sounded like distant applause. She poured herself ginger ale. She spilled ginger ale. Shit and fuck and piss poop fuck. Emily cleaned it up.

No.

She did not clean it up at all—Emily stood there thinking about getting a paper towel, watching her intentions wipe ginger ale from the counter as in a dream, and the wall that she could see through wasn't even a wall. It was a window. Emily saw her house. She had never seen her house framed from the window of another house before. It was like looking back in time. Though the distance between the two identical houses could be measured in feet, in walking human feet, Emily thought of the night sky haunted with stars from a million light-years away, many long since imploded. Ghosts come in a lot of different forms.

Peppy had died in Emily's sleep. Right over there in the yellow house. By that point, of course, there hadn't been much difference between Peppy awake and Peppy asleep. He had been *centering*, not dying. Solidifying his states, approaching the balance that would finally pop him out of this existence.

Emily yawned.

Death was such a dumb way of looking at death.

In it for the wrong reasons, Emily thought, remembering. Smiling. IN IT FOR THE WRONG REASONS! had been the final full sentence that Emily's grandfather had written on his yellow legal pad. Meaning, his last words had been a joke, a comment on Andi Hoffmann, a rapacious contestant on the fucking *Bachelor*, the matrimonial game show they both enjoyed. Peppy, weeks before, had referred to Andi as the SHE BEAST.

But from then on out, when he could write, it was a sketchy, whispery, YES or NO or THANK YOU or FINE. He was always feeling either FINE or NO.

He never got to find out which beast the bachelor proposed to on the romantic, fairy-tale island of Saint Lucia.

Emily watched her house.

Mostly, of course, if you asked, Peppy had been feeling NO.

Emily hadn't been dreaming or deeply asleep when it happened. She had been next to him on the sofa, eyes closed, her thinking indistinguishable from the jitter and spew of the TV. It had been like the bottom of her consciousness dropping out. Her eyes opened. She knew. She'd been having one long, seemingly endless near-death experience, almost a year of it, and suddenly death wasn't near anymore, it was gone. This terrible emptying. Emily felt like she was left sitting naked at the bottom of a bathtub, all the water drained out. Her body bristled with sharp, cold goose bumps. Don't look. Do not look. Peppy? She threw up.

Peppy, what have you done?

Hours later, the hospice people found her in the backseat of her Mazda. The seat belt felt good, necessary, and for many minutes she wouldn't let them take it off.

They got Emily inside. They got her stoned. The hospice pills made the hospice people make sounds that Emily could turn into sentences of words or leave as they were, as kind, imbecilic cooing. Bullshit. Bullshit bullshit bullshit. Sitting at the kitchen table, a stupid mug of tea before her, the way the pills made the tea crisp, implausible, and Emily heard herself telling a puffy Hispanic lady about Ethan. Ethan could speak Korean. Ethan had taught her words in Korean.

"*Kkoch* is Korean for flower."

"Pretty."

"You would like Ethan." What the fuck was she talking about? *Stop talking.* "I know you're not Korean," Emily added. "You're from Hispanic?"

Emily's hand was squeezed. "It's going to be OK."

Liar.

Emily was in the kitchen when they removed Peppy from the living room. They had tricked her with the pills and tea and hand-holding and, sweetheart, excuse me, Emily, there really isn't anybody who we can call?

"What?"

"Family or a friend from school? Ethan maybe? You said about an Ethan. Maybe your neighbor?"

"My neighbor?"

"What about your Korean friend, Emily?"

"I want to go home." She was home. She wasn't home. She had lost control. Emily could not stop laughing. She said, "Why am I laughing?"

"You're in shock, Emily. You're crying."

There was no funeral. The legal entity known as Peter Phane had insisted on a cremation, so here was something else Emily couldn't think about: Peppy in an oven. Peppy on fire. Peppy's eyes exploding. She waited in the car. Her Mazda, in the beginning, had been the only space that wasn't charged with emptiness. Emily signed papers. She put *personal effects* into cardboard boxes. Emily chatted with insurance people and bank people and the folksy monsters at the crematorium, and they were all so much more comforting than the hospice nurses. Emily would snap to it, and for the duration of the call she would be the person they required her to be. Insurance Person on the Telephone, please don't go.

"Well, I think that'll be about it, Miss Phane. Everything seems to be in good order on our side. Do you have any further questions?"

She'd run out of questions. She said, "Is there someone else I can talk to?"

"Oh, well, I really don't see—is there a problem? I'm sorry. Maybe I can answer . . ."

"No problem." Coquettishly, "But can I please talk to somebody else?"

Taco Bell, Emily found, was even better than her Mazda. Burger King. Pizza Hut. Long John Silver's. You could sit there as long as you like, just purchase a beverage. Like *personal effects*, Emily appreciated the term. Beverages didn't exist in kitchens or living rooms. Fast-food places felt eternal. Emily felt normal inside a McDonald's. She could be there without being there, and Emily soon began to notice the old people, alone, nursing coffees, milkshakes, giant plastic cups. Fellow travelers on reprieve from the afternoon. It made sense. McDonald's had captured the safe, utilitarian feel of a hospital and placed it beyond the touch of death. There were no surprises at a McDonald's. Better to feel nothing in a place like that than the so-called living room where one had once felt so much. Emily's thoughts slid cleanly off the surface of McDonald's, one after another.

Ethan, for example. She had not seen Ethan in six or seven months.

Peppy's final joke repeated on her. Emily had been in it for the wrong reasons. In what? In everything. Life. Ethan. Boston.

Taco Bell. Sleep. Queens Falls. Love. And suddenly she was in it for no reason whatsoever—right, wrong, or otherwise. Emily was unreasonable.

Hadn't Ethan said that, or something just like that, on the third or fourth day of his Queens Falls visit, before she'd made him leave for good?

The attacks, of course, grew worse. Her sleep, when she slept, crackled with menace. They were everywhere now and she was alone. They swarmed her.

Emily buried Peppy in the backyard. Planting the urn hadn't felt the least bit ceremonial or meaningful. She tried to not draw too much attention to the task. She only did it because she hated having it in the living room like a trophy, and having it in the kitchen felt ghoulish, and she wouldn't put it in her bedroom like a psycho or on the dresser in Peppy's room because she might as well put it on his pillow, night night, and even the *thought* of that was fucking messed up, and no way Emily could put it in the closet or inside the box with Peter Phane's personal effects, so one night she went out back and dug a small hole in the garden and felt productive. There is no closure in gardening.

That year, those years, all of it had happened outside Mr. Jeffries's kitchen window. Emily stared at her yellow house and felt herself suddenly slip into context. She felt something like release.

She turned from the window.

There: a cheery crowd of stones on the kitchen table looking expectantly up at her. Hey, you guys. There was a poster with Mr. Jeffries's face superimposed over Mount Rushmore that Emily didn't want to believe was an actual thing. But it was, she knew, an actual thing. She opened the refrigerator. Ta-da!

20

——

First things first, you've got to learn how to ask questions. Even if you don't want to know the answers. That's normal. In fact, those are usually the kind of questions most people like asking each other," Emily said. "And one more thing, when I'm talking to you, like I'm talking to you right now, you've got to nod or something. It can be creepy otherwise. You're going to have to move your face a little."

Howie said, "I am moving my face."

"Seriously? Exactly what part of your face do you think you're moving?"

Howie did not know. The face part? He held silent.

Emily said, "Your face is not moving."

"OK."

"Try one more time. Try with your head. Nod."

He nodded.

"That was imperceptible. Do you really think that you just nodded?"

He nodded harder.

"Can't hear you."

Howie Jeffries and Emily Phane sat across from each other at a table in the woods. The table was from Emily's kitchen. It wasn't a picnic table but it was where they had picnics so that is what they called it. Emily's idea; they'd moved it out by the banks of the Kayaderosseras behind her house, directly over a stream that fed into the wider, smoother creek. The stream ran under their feet. It was tricky. They'd had to set their chair legs on breeze blocks that Howie dug into the ground, so the chairs wouldn't sink into the wet earth. That they could dip their toes into an icy hurry of water while having lunch or dinner was something they both enjoyed, or Emily enjoyed and Howie pretended to enjoy. He hated removing his shoes in public. His socks? Forget it.

The sun moved messily over the dense pine cover, yellow clouds of light landing here and there across the table, Emily, Howie, everything. But mostly this was a green spot. Bees swung unstable arcs and birds made a highway of the clear strip of sky above the Kayaderosseras, shouting more than singing. Ducks motored aimlessly. It felt like the entire animal kingdom was enjoying a day off, just soaking it in. From where Howie and Emily sat, you couldn't see either of their houses or Route 29. You heard cars occasionally. Howie could see, up the creek a little, where he'd planned on building his family dock and bench. Frogs plopped into the water whenever Emily laughed, which was so much more often these days. Yesterday, at dusk, they saw a deer on the opposite bank of the creek, carefully crunching through the forest like someone chewing a mouthful of glass. Emily enjoyed insisting that it was an elk. It was just a big old deer. She'd started planting things around their table; Howie didn't ask what. Things that didn't need direct sun, he supposed. Moss, probably, maybe mushrooms. She'd moved some shrubs out here too. The rest of the plants, the ones that had survived the smoke and flood, were in his house now. His living room, kitchen. The downstairs bathroom: there was a small potted something on the toilet. Howie sipped his glass of ginger ale. Emily, who disliked ginger ale, now bought Howie ginger ale every time she went shopping. Howie did not have the heart to tell her that he, too, disliked ginger ale. That the ginger ale had been in his refrigerator because once, maybe ten years before, he thought that his daughter said something enthusiastic about ginger ale. It really was a nauseating beverage. Emily sipped milk.

"Now," she said. "The hard part. Lesson one, Howie. I would like you to ask me a question."

They'd been living in the same house for an entire month before Emily called Mr. Jeffries Howie. That was four days ago. He still hadn't once said Emily's name aloud. It was something she was just beginning to notice; thus, this afternoon's conversation lesson.

She waited, watching Howie's face.

"Come on, Howie. Seriously? There must be a million things you want to ask me."

There were not. Howie wanted to ask Emily if he could go back inside and read about fish. He wanted to ask if he could stop talking for a day or two, time off for good behavior. He settled on, "Do you like the Maroon 5?"

Emily gasped and then cracked up. "Oh my God!" She couldn't stop laughing.

Howie really wanted to go inside. "They're cool," he said.

"I cannot believe you just said that!"

Well, Howie thought, I said it.

Sometimes Emily thought that his whole life might be a kind of performance art, that he was putting her on. That he'd been rehearsing and inhabiting this role next door for twenty-five years, getting the character right, tweaking it, and all in preparation for Emily and this big performance. She said, "To answer your almost aggressively insane question, I guess I never really liked music. Not like other kids. People my age, I mean. I like music in movies?"

Howie cast his attention out into the Kayaderosseras.

"Eye contact," Emily said.

Howie pretended Emily's freckles were eyes and said, "My mother cried every time she heard the national anthem. That's my first memory of music. Music made my mother unhappy."

It was also the opposite of fish.

"I like Christmas music," Emily said. Then, "Wait, like tear up patriotically or really, really cry?"

"Really cry," Howie said. "It bothered me." He paused. "My mother also enjoyed Christmas carols."

Softly, "What was her name?"

"Doris."

Howie remembered how his wife and he had once joined a popular Christmas choir; this was either a year before or a year after they married. She had been going through a phase and he had been going through the motions, opening his mouth, pretending; his wife noticed during their second rehearsal and she'd started laughing mid–"Jingle Bell Rock." You, Howard, are the goofiest of balls. Her hand in his. Back then, they had both still believed that his foibles weren't faults, and that they might always be endearing. He wanted to say something about this to Emily. He said, "And my wife, she . . ."

"Name."

Howie blinked. "Doris," he said.

"Your wife's name, dummy."

"Doris also." Then: "But everyone calls her Dori," he said, proudly, as if he were describing someone in the next room. Howie had not said her name aloud or come so close to evoking that next room in years.

"Well, you probably should call her Dori, too, then. Not *wife*. You should say people's names, Howie." Emily wondered whether she was really making this, of all things, a pet peeve? Why?

"Ex-wife," Howie said.

"That's what I said. Doesn't matter. What was Dori like?"

"She was my wife."

"Were you trained by al-Qaeda or something?"

Howie had the locked-jaw look of a politician suppressing a yawn.

"I'm sorry," Emily said. "Why did your mother cry whenever she heard the national anthem?"

"I don't know."

"Really?"

Howie shook his head. Perceptibly.

"But that old flag blanket thing. Is that your mom's, I mean, didn't she make it? Someone made it."

Emily had discovered a box of patriotism in the closet of Harriet's so-called room. (This room was so sad, like some long-abandoned motel room designed for eight-year-old girls.) Emily had been looking for towels. In this box was a folded uniform, a folded flag, and letters that Emily could not open, certain they contained the sort of doomed, high-pitched human sentiment she wasn't yet stable enough to absorb; there were cuff links that, on second look, turned out to be used bullets, as careworn as seashells. There was an exotic pinecone wrapped in a red, white, and blue ribbon. Sweet, silly postcards; a tin of shoeshine. Photographs. Two unused tickets to a theater in Troy, New York. Obviously, Howie's father had been killed during one of the wars.

"Someone made it, that's right," Howie said. "I don't know. Sure, my mother made it. Doris."

Emily backed off a little. "I never knew my mother," she said.

"I know."

Emily played with her food. Howie had prepared this afternoon's picnic. Peanut butter on white bread, cashews, apples and yellow cheese and Pringles. Howie settled back into one of his remarkable stillnesses. Emily mushed bread into little balls, lined them up, and then, one by one, dropped them into the stream beneath the table. She watched the bread balls bob off into the Kayaderosseras, where a few ducks had gathered, waiting. She said, "Did you ever meet my mother?"

"Yes."

It was Emily's turn to say, "OK."

She had not expected this. She did not, in fact, want this.

Howie said, "Nancy."

Nor that. Emily thought, Was Howie actually being an asshole?

Suddenly with this dickish first name thing? She looked questioningly into his eyes, which might as well have been eyelids, seriously, and, against her better judgment, she said, "What was she like?"

Howie did not know how to approach his memory of Nancy Phane with Emily at his side. Mostly, of course, Nancy had unnerved him: her disgruntled clothing, tattoos. She had been older than Howie at the time. She had paced. Everything about Nancy Phane had paced. This was not something that he could or should say to Emily. But Nancy had been sweet under all that: Wasn't that something that Howie's wife had once said, peeping from behind the curtains? Ex-wife, he meant. Dori. Howie said, "She used to spend a lot of time in the front yard."

"What do you mean she used to spend a lot of time in the front yard?"

Howie told her. He told her about the day that Nancy arrived, and what Nancy had looked like, and Nancy standing on the banks of Route 29, as if waiting for a barge to come and take her away. Rarely the backyard. Rarely the house. The fusses with Emily's grandmother. Emily asked questions, Howie answered simply, solidly. Emily wanted to know what her mother looked like. You mean like overweight, really? Impossible. My mother was not overweight, she was *pregnant*, doofus—and what kind of tattoos? Biker bitch? Prison? Celtic punk, Chinese? Spring break sluttoos? Come off it! Emily didn't believe this crap. Her mother sang in Rodgers and Hammerstein musicals. Was Howie certain that they were even tattoos?

"Yes," he said. "What else could they have been?"

"Tights," Emily said. "Leggings." Bruises? Vitiligo? Someone else's limbs entirely?

"Maybe," Howie said. He had realized too late that Emily had not known. That Emily didn't have a single photograph of the Nancy Phane who had given birth to her. "It was a long time ago."

"You sound like you're describing someone else," Emily said. "Maybe you saw someone else. Did you actually meet her?"

"No."

"But you said—but what are you even talking about?"

"I saw her," Howie said. "I didn't know her."

"No, you didn't know her."

"I'm sorry."

"Jesus, please stop already," Emily said, surprising them both. "What else did you see? Must have seen everything, huh? You enjoy the show? Were we entertaining enough for you?"

Howie said nothing.

"Yeah?" Emily continued, as if this was an argument she had to win. She said, for no good reason: "Yeah, and don't think I haven't seen how you keep *Playboy* magazines in your car!"

Howie stood. He walked to the side of the Kayaderosseras. The ducks squabble-flapped, lifted, revealed wretched little feet, and plopped back down, scooting, resettling, la-de-ducky-da.

Howie thought about fishing.

Emily thought about pushing Howie into the fucking creek. "Hey," she called. She knew she sounded like a brat. More than a brat, actually, sure, but that was on him: Howie's geological tranquility. Don't you dare turn your back on me when I'm acting irrational!

Howie thought about which lake he would go to this weekend, and if he would actually ask Rhoda Prough. This time of year, the best options were:

Great Sacandaga Lake.

West Caroga Lake.

Lewy Lake.

Cossayuna Lake.

Or perhaps Schroon Lake? Howie did not necessarily want to go fishing with Rho, but Emily, last night, had told him that he probably had to. Rho had called. Emily had been there, and they watched the phone ring together, as rare as a butterfly flying through the living room. Howie had to answer. Emily overheard. She had been giddy, couldn't believe it. It was a potential date.

Fishing, he had assured her, was not dating.

"My last boyfriend took me on a date to a *taekkyeon* expo. It's Korean foot fighting, like really gay karate."

Howie did not now want to think about Emily Phane or Rhoda Prough or Harri or his wife, ex-wife, *Dori*—or the long-dead Nancy Phane who had started this whole mess. He thought, instead, and more seriously, about which rod he would take. Howie would not take his new, and still unused, seven-foot six-inch St. Croix Legend-Xtreme. He wanted to save that for Lake Jogues, for over by Rogers Rock, even though the fishing there was mediocre to poor. He wanted to show Emily this spot, his spot, reached only by boat. His boat. Next week Howie would purchase a used boat, even if it could not be the 1971 Catalina 27 he had been saving for—because he needed to have the boat before Harri needed any more of his money. Harri could have what she wanted, of course. But only if Howie had it. There had been an e-mail from his daughter with the heading "IMPORTANT INVESTMENT HELP." Howie had not opened it and, anyway, what was that supposed to mean? Investment? Maybe it was ham. It had taken Howie a few months of internet computering to realize that a lot of the e-mails he got were ham. He would find out later what that e-mail was about, after he had bought the boat that, in his mind, he had already painted into his daughter's gift. The boat, himself, his new seven-foot six-inch St. Croix Legend-Xtreme, and Emily Phane floating by Rogers Rock. Though he did not exactly think about it this way, it was a way for all three of them to be together: Howie, Emily, Harri. Howie, with Emily's help, had hung *Lake Jeffries* in the living room, over the sofa. Emily thought it looked pretty there. But it would look pretty anywhere. Sometimes, Howie liked having it there, knowing his daughter and his lake were behind him, supportive, while he watched TV with his neighbor, and sometimes Howie hated that the only time he ever really saw the painting was when he was standing looking at it, which was an odd thing to do. Standing in his living room as if he were in a museum. He had never been inside a painting museum, or any kind of museum that didn't have dinosaurs, but assumed that his daughter's painting would someday hang in one, maybe the big one in Albany. It was that good. It could have been a photograph. Howie had a plan. He had not told Emily yet because he rarely told her anything that she didn't drag from him, but maybe tomorrow he would move the sofa to where the TV now was, under the window, and move the TV to where the sofa was, under the painting. This way they could watch the TV and the painting at the same time.

They, Howie thought.

Well, he could watch both, anyway. Eventually, Emily might return to her own home. This was not something that they had spoken about.

Emily, meanwhile, was going absolutely nowhere until Howie turned the fuck around. She'd sit there all day, night, week. That was about the shape of it.

She wanted to scream. She knew that Howie's ex-wife had been friends with Peppy, for instance, and she could tell him that, see what he thought about *that*. She knew that his ex-wife had gone over there a lot toward the end, and that Peppy had helped her make the decision to leave. Howie wasn't the only one who knew shit.

But here Emily balked. You evil bitch, she thought. What are you thinking?

It wasn't Howie's fault that he had seen her mother and, anyway, she'd asked for it. Thing was, she implicitly trusted Howie's version of Nancy. Hadn't she always known?

She said that she was sorry.

She knew that Howie heard her. But whatever. She sat at the picnic table; he stood. She wished she hadn't said that thing about the *Playboys*.

Emily had stopped wearing her mother's ring around Howie about two weeks ago. She'd begun to notice him looking strangely at it: probably the fact that she wore it on her wedding finger. Emily felt as if she were betraying the only meaningful memory she had of her father by wearing the ring, by potentially exposing the ring to the kind of questions that would destroy the truth of the ring with the truth of the ring. Peppy had known a lot of women. Women wore rings, and complexly married women occasionally took their rings off.

She said, "Hey, you hear me? I'm sorry. Howie, I'm really sorry. Let's go inside. Forget it, OK? We friends?"

Howie calculated the deepest areas of the Kayaderosseras Creek. He moved his mind like a flashlight over the surface of the water; as with Emily's nightmares, it was hard to explain exactly how he found the deeper pockets of water that the best fish called home. Howie could hold his thoughts like other people held their breaths, and he'd watch, wait, forget it, and suddenly know. Friends.

The first week that Emily stayed at Howie's house—or, more accurately, Howie's sofa—had been strange. Things were strange now, actually, if Emily or Howie cared to reflect on their situation, to compare or contrast it to the rest of the non–Route 29 world, but back then? Really strange. For the first four or five days they hardly spoke.

Emily had not been well. She was still not well, obviously, but back then she had been worse, and Howie often wondered if he should call an ambulance or a mental hospital or, at least, his ex-wife or Drew or one of the more dependable and discreet colleagues from work. He was in over his head. However, since he had not done any of that the first night, or the second night, then the third, when any responsible and decent adult should have, and since he had not even called the Queens Falls Fire Department *when the house next door to his house had been on fire,* Howie felt that he had likely squandered any right to expect outside support. That window had closed. Emily Phane was his responsibility. Plus, what would health care professionals or firemen or his ex-wife think when they'd found out that he had kept an emaciated, unwashed, intermittently deranged, and obviously—to others, not Howie— still rather handsome young woman on his sofa? Howie was shy, not naïve. You know exactly what they will think. No, as every day passed, it became clear that this had to be between them and Route 29. Not a secret, necessarily, but something best not talked about. Emily did not seem to care either way. Howie had to make it all better all by himself, and he hoped that he would manage to do so before the police showed up and the news reports began referring to him as a quiet loner. For both of their sakes, Howie had to make sure that Emily Phane did not die.

For starters, he called in sick for that entire week. Since in his thirty years of employment at GE they could count all of Jeffries's sick days on two hands and a toe, various colleagues contacted him, both concerned and, it seemed to Howie, ghoulishly curious. Jeffries out for a full week? You're shitting me. Must be serious. I hope it's not serious. Man, I wonder if it's serious?

Maybe it actually was serious, Howie thought.

Well, sure it was.

He had not been able to settle on a suitable illness. Luckily, a lifetime of studied inarticulation meant he did not need to. But folks called. Drew even texted, and who knew how he'd heard about it—Facebook?

Steve Dube had gotten to Howie first.

"Just heard and thought I'd check in, see how you holding up? You OK, champ?"

"Yes."

"Good for you."

Howie said nothing.

"I mean, you don't sound too hot, if you don't mind me saying," Dube said. Dube went with it: "Not the hot and bothered old Jeffries we know and love, anyways! Ha. No, but seriously, you don't sound too hot at all."

Howie had said no more than two words of, he thought, neutral temperature, but OK. Howie did not enjoy lying. He very nearly could not do it.

"You there, Jeffries?"

"Sure am."

But it was also fun. Like a game: making sure that nothing he said was technically untrue—beyond the initial calling in sick, of course, but even then when his manager had asked what was wrong, Howie been able to say truthfully, "I don't know."

"Doctors, yeah. Tell me about it. Mine gave me six months to live but when I said I couldn't pay the bill he gave me six months more."

"What?"

Clearing his throat, "I mean, it's not serious, is it? Um. They having you in for more tests?"

"No."

On a telephone, Howie disappeared like a foot inside a shoe.

"That was inappropriate. I'm sorry. My doctor didn't give me six months to live," Howie's manager said. "Just to be clear."

"That's good."

"Right. Well then, Jeffries."

But Dube tried to get to the bottom of it: "Don't want to pry, but we were all wondering here, I mean—we're all concerned. One week, huh? You must be pretty sick."

"Mmm." Because mmm wasn't true or untrue.

"I hear you, man. Sure."

Silence.

"Well, look, I guess, you need anything? Mean to say, is there nothing we can't pick up for you? My wife, she's making me ask, says if you need someone to come by, you know, cook you dinner? *Burn* you dinner, actually, between you and me." Dube laughed. "Hey, serious though, maybe we could pick you up some groceries? You got a prescription you need filled?"

"I don't need anything, Steve. Thank you. Thank Marcy for me."

"DVDs, anything, Jeffries. You name it."

"I have to get off the phone now."

"Yeah you do. Just calling to say get better soon, champ. You call whenever you need anything, you hear me?"

The only problem was that Emily needed food. Emily did not like eggs. Howie also needed food, but then: What if someone saw him wheeling a shopping cart when he should have been at home, sick? Now, logically, if he thought about this, because he lived almost an hour from the GE Waste Water Treatment Plant he had only once in the last thirty years run into anyone from work up in Queens Falls—and not at Price Chopper but at the mall— well, this should not have been a genuine worry. He hadn't told anyone *how* he was sick. He could have been mentally sick. He could be sick with something that didn't prevent him from going to Price Chopper to purchase food. Howie saw coughing people at Price Chopper all the time. Howie was not in high school. Nobody was going to call his parents or expel him from GE for grocery shopping. But still. It troubled him. Because, further, what if they saw that he was shopping for two people now—what if they noticed that he was purchasing things that he didn't normally eat? Handsome young lady things like clementines, zucchini, and the pineapple? What if they asked Howie about the pineapple he planned on buying Emily? Howie was unused to operating his life within the confines of an easily identifiable falsehood. He drove nearly seventy miles east, crossing the state line to Vermont. The grocery stores in Vermont were as bountiful as the grocery stores in New York, but navigating them, the ever so slightly offness of them, was exciting, and Vermonters, who resembled upstate New Yorkers crossbred with golden retrievers, made Howie feel elated in an embarrassing way. Lots of tail-wagging strangers. Howdy there! He'd been rattled at first. Maybe, he thought, they had known him from work, or from the internet, perhaps they were friends-of-a-colleague or relatives of friends-of-colleagues who had seen internet computer photographs of his stone anniversary party; who knew nowadays?

Howie soon settled into the fact that this was just how Vermont operated. They said, How you doing? Howie told them that he was doing OK, that he was only looking through boxes of rice and grain. Tell me about it, they'd say. He did. They seemed genuinely engaged. They said, Two for the price of one, might as well get two, see what I'm saying? Sure. Some day we're having.

You said it.

Some drive, too. Howie could have gone and driven another few hours to New Hampshire. Driving down a new road toward a new supermarket in a whole new state, it made Howie feel things he would be mortified to feel on his own road, or at home, or around other people. He thought: Maybe you are not as in over your head as you think. First the successful surprise party—he had been surprised, after all, and everyone appeared to have had a super time—and now this clandestine out-of-state shopping for two.

He could not get over how many new things he saw on the side of a new road. He thought: Wait until I tell Emily.

It would be weeks before he would be able to tell Emily anything of the sort, and even then, Howie, by design, would never be the most chatworthy companion. He did not share experience. Looking back, the first few weeks that Emily spent at Howie's place were an accident of exhausted, nervy, almost stunned half conversations and haunted, nighttime TV marathons. Sofa; kitchen; sofa. TV TV TV TV. Sleep. Nightmare. Sleep. Emily made jokes, once in a while, and Howie got wedged up inside himself and, occasionally, even fought his way out with some of the more endearingly whacked-out statements that Emily had ever heard.

For example. Standing in the hall, out of nowhere, he said: "I don't know where the stones on the kitchen table are supposed to go."

"I was going to ask about those."

"We need room on the kitchen table."

"Uh-huh," she said. Emily had not yet asked what they were doing there in the first place, or why they were smiling. Can of worms. Because you couldn't stop there, could you? They'd man-aged thus far playacting *normal*, and she didn't want to rock the boat or get any closer than she already was. The stones were harm-less, endearing. She said, "We can put them on the counter?"

Howie thought about that. He said, "Would people be upset if I put them outside?"

"Like, the rock people?" Emily asked. "Would the rock people be upset?"

"What?" Howie said.

Pause.

"No, I don't think people will mind," Emily said, carefully.

"OK."

He had not asked for help, but she got up. She helped him carry the stones outside. This was the first thing that they did together besides watching TV, and it was the first time that Emily had been out of Howie's house since she'd come over a few evenings before. She felt more solid than she had in months. She liked the solidity of the rocks in her hands; having a task. They'd brought them back by the creek. They followed an overgrown path behind Howie's house. They made a pile. It was unspeakably odd, Emily thought, watching Mr. Jeffries put the stones down, one by one. He made sure that their smiles faced outward and when, once, Emily put a stone down with its face to the ground, Mr. Jeffries waited until he thought she wasn't looking and, with a subtle twist, adjusted the stone so it faced him: big smile. That was something about him, Emily thought. Every movement. So serious. He didn't waste him-self. She not only liked him, but she realized that she believed in him. "You know what, Mr. Jeffries, we totally should have buried the fish under these stones. You know, like a grave marker?"

"Fish?" Howie said, as if surprised Emily was even there.

"The dead fish you have in the kitchen, yeah."

Pause.

Howie said, "The fish isn't dead."

"I think maybe it is."

Longer pause. Time enough for a breeze and, above them, some kind of altercation between squirrels. Mr. Jeffries said, "Well, it shouldn't be."

"I guess." Then, gently: "When was the last time you looked?"

Howie did not know. How often was he supposed to look? "Yesterday," he supposed.

"Well, today it's dead. But we can check together to make sure. I'm sorry."

"OK." Then, "Do you really think that we should bury the fish here?"

"It probably isn't necessary."

"OK."

They finished piling the stones.

"I can't tell," Emily said. "I'm sorry, but was the fish meaningful? Like a pet?"

"It was a goldfish," Howie said. "It was a gift. Maybe it was sick."

"Probably it was just old."

"It wasn't old."

"You could tell?"

Of course Howie could tell. He was deeply ashamed. He could not bear for Emily to think that he might be bad at taking care of things, that he let things die alone in jars in the kitchen. He said, "Jars are no place for fish."

"Especially all alone. How sad."

"It was a gift."

"I know, I didn't mean that as a criticism." But Emily saw an opening: "Who was it from?" she asked.

Howie bent down, adjusted one last stone that didn't need adjusting. He said, "I don't remember." He really didn't. Lots of folks had been giving him gifts that Tuesday evening. But the shame was now complete. He turned and walked back to the house.

That first week. They were more like refugees who happened to be shuffling in the same vague, unknown direction—*away*—than longtime neighbors or friends or even people who knew the other's name. They sat on the sofa. The sofa was not the past, and, for now, it was safe. The sofa was more movement than either of them had had in years.

They liked each other. Especially after they realized that the other was not the same person they'd lived next door to for twenty-five years but someone else entirely and that, because of this, they didn't really need to draw attention to the fact that they had been neighbors to that other person for so long and never spoken or sat next to him or her on the sofa. Emily thinking: There's only this present moment, anyway, and even that doesn't matter or really exist since everything is an illusion and I am insane. Howie thinking: She needs to eat. I need to go grocery shopping in Vermont.

They kind of had an understanding.

The simplicity of Mr. Jeffries's strangeness was almost ideally suited to Emily's internal and external disconnection. Their paralyses fit. They lived; they didn't assume. Sometimes they even communicated.

Howie helped Emily with her sleeping. Howie made dinner.

"You're like one of those dogs that knows when someone's going to have a seizure," Emily said, several days after she'd moved in. It was the first time she'd really mentioned the issue.

"I don't know," Howie said, uncomfortably. He did not want to speak about this. *Dogs?* Was that what had been happening here? Seizures? Perhaps it made sense.

She asked, "How *do* you know?"

"Know what?"

Emily sighed; scrunched her face. You're right. OK. Moving on.

Howie said, "Do you want to watch TV?"

Technically, they were already watching TV. She'd been talking about their routine, which had begun in earnest on the second night, sometime after Howie had gone up to bed.

There was a knock on his door. Howie had not been sleeping. He had been thinking with the lights off.

That night, Howie had sent Harri a number of texts. Seven. This is what Howie had been thinking about; his phone was still in the pocket of the trousers that he was still wearing, under the covers, for propriety's sake. Maybe his phone would buzz. New York was the city that couldn't sleep. But maybe he had sent the texts wrong.

Howie still had not plugged his internet computer back in because Emily had become agitated at the very idea; just that afternoon Howie had taken it to the living room. He had thought that she might enjoy it. But she had asked him with bossy urgency if he would please, *please* take that thing somewhere else. Emily had, as Harri might say, kind of freaked out, looking at the computer as if it were a window to someplace bad, and so no problem: without another word, Howie had taken the computer up to Harri's empty bedroom. He put it on her bed. Howie looked forward to opening his e-mails and Facebook, seeing the promised stone anniversary photographs, maybe send some to Harri, and, what with Emily Phane recovering on his sofa downstairs, he felt that it might be time to write some of his pals, let them know that nothing out of the ordinary was going on here, everything hunky-dory on Route 29. Mostly, Howie wanted to write his daughter a longer, more accurate thank-you e-mail for the painting. It had been unkind of him to thank her with telephone texts. He thought about writing her another text to apologize for the other texts. Emily continued to knock. Howie continued to think.

The door opened.

"Mr. Jeffries?" Emily whispered.

"I'm in here."

"I know."

"OK."

"Can I come in?"

Howie had not completely removed his clothing since Emily arrived at his house. He had been responsibly prepared for just this sort of thing. "OK," he said.

"There a light?"

Howie turned on his bedside lamp. Light. He felt like something slapped on a grill. Emily was standing in the doorway, maroon BU hoodie up.

She had not yet seen Mr. Jeffries's bedroom. She'd come upstairs because she needed help. How exactly he was going to help her, she didn't know. She'd fallen asleep in front of the TV and, apparently, this time he'd left her there, alone, and so when the paralysis came, so did the footsteps. The attack had been fierce, eternal.

But she already felt better, looking at poor Mr. Jeffries. He appeared to be fully dressed. But that was the least of it.

"Oh my God," she said.

"It's a chandelier."

Too fucking weird: this dowager ice spider hanging above Mr. Jeffries. Emily knew better than to meddle, because, again, questions were a slippery slope at this stage in their cohabitation, but you try and take your eyes off *that*. She said, still whispering, "It's beautiful."

"I hate it."

Dressed and tucked neatly into bed, Howie looked like a cross between an open-casket corpse and a little boy waiting to be read a bedtime story. About fish.

"You hate it?" she said.

"I hate it very much."

For once, speaking felt like the least vulnerable action that Howie could currently take: he couldn't otherwise survive being seen like this, trapped in bed, silent, and so he tried to smile, said, "I think that I keep it there because I hate it so much."

"Why?"

"Because I hate it so much."

Emily nodded rapidly.

"It's the only thing that I hate," Howie said. He hoped that she would leave his bedroom now. Take that and go. Scram. He considered turning the dark back on. What else did she want from him?

"The only thing you hate? Really?"

"Well," he said. How many things could one person hate?

"So what would happen if you got rid of it then?" Emily asked. But she knew: nothing good. The chandelier was homeopathy. It was like one of those strips of poisonous tape you hang from the ceiling in order to collect and kill insects, and, once again, Emily saw the Howie behind the Mr. Jeffries. The guy she'd seen the night before asleep on the sofa. Howie was shy, subtle, and deeply, dreamily weird. There was probably a planet of shit that a guy like Howie could legitimately despise if he'd wanted to.

"Was it your wife's?"

Howie could almost be said to have flinched. "It hasn't worked in almost twenty years." Then, "I still don't know why she put it there. I told her not to. I said put it in storage for when we got a bigger house. Suppose she always knew that we would not get a bigger house. Maybe she put it there to show me."

"Mr. Jeffries," Emily said. "Do you want to come back downstairs and watch TV with me?"

Howie did not. He needed to sleep, but now that her delight concerning his ex-wife's grandmother's chandelier had dissipated, Emily, he saw, was in a very bad way. "You need to sleep," he said. Because she wasn't going away until he said something.

"I know," she said.

Howie understood. She was not going to go away at all. "OK," he said.

This began their arrangement. For the first week it was touch-and-go; it was good that Howie had taken off work. He stayed by Emily's side when she was most tired. He knew when this was, usually, but if not, if he had gone upstairs or outside or to the kitchen, she'd come and say, "You want to watch TV with me?"

He would watch TV with her.

She would close her eyes, and he knew that if she began to have

one of her nightmares, or whatever—seizures, ringing distur-
bances—he would firmly shake her shoulder. Easy as peasy. Eyes
flicking on: white as headlights, then filling with color, relief.

Then sleep again.

Howie usually knew—and, again, they never actually spoke
about how or why. Certainly not what. In fact, he had decided that
he knew not because of the strange, creeping feeling that always
alerted him, but because maybe her breathing changed, or her face
twanged, something imperceptible, a twitch or a catch of her breath
that he picked up on, exactly like with fishing, how if he waited long
enough he usually knew exactly where the fish were. Howie had
no good reason to believe in anything else. Emily's sleep problems
did not, in the end, warrant much reflection. You did things that
needed doing. That was that. He sat. She sat. She slept. He woke
her up if she started ringing, and then she sometimes said something, but more often she did not. She might smile. No biggie.

He gave her space in which to get better without the least bit of
interest in what she happened to be getting better from. None of
your business. She started properly sleeping. She washed herself;
she began eating a little. Then a whole lot. Emily was not well and
did not like the pineapple, but she was not going to die.

By the second week, Howie had gone back to work. He explained
to Emily about his shifts, and exactly when he would need to sleep,
when he would leave for work, and when he would be home, awake,
and able to watch TV with her on the sofa. He knew that she would
not sleep while he was at work. She would wait for him, even though
that first week back was night shifts. The second as well. This was
OK. They would both get less sleep than they needed, true, but it
was only for the time being, until Emily was a little further from a
death that could be legitimately blamed on his inattention. It would
have to work and it did work, for a few days, until the morning that
Emily, apparently exhausted and spooked, came into Howie's bedroom during his four-hour sleep shift. He was wearing his clothing,
as usual, even a belt; he awoke immediately.

"Can I?" Emily asked.

He felt her body indent the mattress next to him.

He could not move.

She asked again, softly, "Mr. Jeffries, do you mind? I know it's weird but—"

"OK."

But OK, he realized, wasn't the same as Mmm, it was more like a word, and, therefore, more like an actual lie. Howie was not OK. This was not OK.

Being asleep was as naked as Howie ever got with Emily, and that took him a few days. Co-sleeping with his neighbor really did a number on him. Colleagues, noticing his moderate decline, thought he must have been a little under the weather still, maybe terminal, nobody knew, so they let him take naps here and there. He hardly slept at home. He caught naps in his car, pulled over on the side of Route 29, or in front of the TV when Emily was cooking or tending her plants. But things soon evened out, and exhaustion helped Howie get used to it. Fine. He would come home from his shift and go upstairs and Emily would be waiting in bed, fully dressed. Emily wrapped in the Private Nathanial P. Sounes memorial afghan, above the covers. They only touched by accident. They touched when Howie had to wake her from one of her ringings, which he seemed to do instinctively here, too, even when he was asleep. He would reach over and shake her and go back to sleep. Soon just sleeping next to Howie helped Emily. She couldn't explain it either.

It was as though the living room flooded with light after that.

Howie's entire house changed, opened up. The TV was on less. Things quickened, felt good. Emily waited for him to get home. The drive to and from work, a drive that used to be exactly the same for Howie in terms of expectation and enjoyment, changed. Leaving the house was a loss. Returning home was something to anticipate. Time began to move differently. For example, the ten days it took Harri to reply to his follow-up thank-you e-mail—after she never replied to his several possibly ill-judged thank-you telephone texts—seemed like a very, very long time. Inexcusably long. Ten days to wait for a reply used to be nothing, but now that Howie shared time, everything had slowed, become richer, more confusing, more alive, every single sound was different knowing that another pair of ears was hearing it, too. What the heck was that? That was an owl. It was a truck. That was the sound of wind moving through trees. You heard it, too? That was only the house. The house was settling. They were synchronizing their senses, deciding together what they saw, agreeing that the carpet was *yellowish*. That they should call the sofa a sofa, not a couch and never a love seat. Two days would feel like a month. Routines melted away, leaving their bones all over the place, jutting here and there, sharp, ungainly, embarrassing, but also leaving Howie with a kind of purity and newness of movement and thought along with the refrigerator full of new foods that Emily had escorted into the house. Fruits that might very well have been nuts. Diet Dr Pepper and cheese so blue it was green; frozen egg rolls, cilantro, Greek yogurt, brown rice, gourmet baloney. Flavors of Pringles that Howie was unused to.

Howie loved the underwater way a room full of plants sounded at night.

They never spoke about Howie's room, or sleeping. Nor did they speak to each other, ever, once inside the bedroom: no good night, good morning, nothing. Speaking in bed would have been beyond the pale, like using the same toilet at the same time.

In fact, the more awake with each other they became, the less they were able even to approach the subject of sleep, and the less they thought that this was odd, or that they needed to. Things were quite normal now thank you very much.

The month passed. They might not talk for a full day or two, but they were together. Emily bought things for the house and things that she thought Mr. Jeffries might like, like a baseball cap. She had wondered what he would look like in a baseball cap. Both of them cooked for each other even if they tended to eat separately. Emily in the living room, always. Howie in his kitchen. The baseball cap made Howie look like an incognito Nazi war criminal on vacation. He wore it around the house, way too high up on his head, until, enough was enough, OK, creepy idea: Emily plucked if off. It was never seen again. They didn't talk much about their past and far less about their future; the present was just kind of there, all over the place, so what could they say? You want to watch TV? Sure do. They never spoke about Peppy. They never spoke about Harriet.

One day Howie followed Emily back to her house so that she could start evacuating the rest of her plants and, she said, get some clothing, some photographs. Howie waited on the porch because Emily had not invited him in.

"It's a mess," Emily said. "Obviously." She stood in the doorway. She was wearing a backpack. She felt a little off to Howie: nervy, aware, like her ears were squinting. She lit a cigarette.

He had never seen Emily do this before.

"Do you mind?"

He did not.

"I found these upstairs." Exhale. "I need to get the smell of the house out of my nose. Everything's smoky and moldy and—I don't know. Something like a raccoon or ferret got in a fight with the couch. Know what? I was thinking that maybe we could move my kitchen table out by the creek."

"Probably not a ferret."

Emily blew smoke rings. "It's refreshing, actually. You ever smoke? It's been a while, so I'm totally buzzed here. Got a nice buzz on."

"Maybe we should get someone over. See about the electricity, the water and fire damage."

"No," Emily said. "But listen, about the table. Wouldn't it be cool if we moved it out back by the creek?"

Howie supposed that he would have to see the table; there were logistics to consider. "Is it weatherproof?"

"Is anything?"

"Yes," Howie said.

"It was just an idea. It doesn't matter."

They watched Route 29. The hanging silence of an empty country road. Emily ashed her cigarette onto her porch. She said, "Mr. Jeffries, why do you have almost ten thousand dollars in a can of Folgers decaf?"

"Depends what kind of wood your table is made of," Howie said, as if he had not heard her. He had heard her. "The kind of lacquer we use," he said. "To protect against the elements." He coughed. "Weather is an element."

"Seriously?"

Howie enjoyed watching Emily tend plants—the way she moved among them, lulling them, somehow, as if plants could possibly be more lulled than they already were. They were everywhere now. The living room, kitchen; even some in the bathroom and the one in the laundry that Emily said was a "little purple-leafed know-it-all thing." There were none in their bedroom. It made Howie feel safe, Emily caring for her plants, like when he was a small boy, in bed, and he would listen to his parents mysteriously tend to the household, moving room to room to recognizable room and some-times, he would imagine, to rooms that did not exist during the day, or that were not available to Howie at all. Howie, in the darkness, could hear his parents walk through rooms that seemed to exist below, above, or just to the left of the actual rooms he knew so well. He loved to fall asleep imagining what was in these rooms, and who, why. Howie's parents were rarely together in the same room after Howie went to bed.

Emily was like a fish and a fisherwoman, Howie thought, sud-denly, and this made sense the same way her sleep ringing made sense. He said, "I am going fishing." This was an invitation.

Emily understood. "I don't know," she said.

"OK."

"I don't think I like fish."

"OK."

"No, but maybe it would be nice?"

"You don't have to like fish to catch them. I think that you would like it."

It was rare that Howie let Emily know what he was thinking. "Really? Why?"

Howie thought about that.

Emily sat down. "Fish kind of freak me out, actually. They don't have eyelids, right? They can't blink."

"I don't kill them."

"Yeah, OK, but *hooks*? You do catch them. I'm sorry, but I don't see the point."

"If you're careful, you can remove them from the hooks without doing serious damage. I can show you how."

"But if you're not going to eat them, why do it? It just sounds mean. Do we have to use hooks?"

"If you want to catch them."

"Let's say I don't."

"Then OK. Then you could use anything."

"I could just throw out free worms?"

"Cast out, sure."

"Like feeding ducks. But wouldn't that undercut your fishing? Wouldn't that be unfair competition?"

"It's not a competition."

"But why get a hook up the jaw when you can get dinner for free?"

Howie sighed. "That is not how fish think."

Howie spoke of fishing. He had been speaking nonstop for about five minutes, Emily thought, when he must have realized, suddenly, that he'd been speaking nonstop for about five minutes. It was like his description of an early-'70s Norwegian tackle innovation woke up, looked around in a daze of fear, and promptly killed itself. Boom—and the heavy, resurgent curtain of Howie's inhibition crashed down over his face. Stupefying as this bait and tackle minutiae had been, Emily wanted it back. She enjoyed hearing him talk with such wakeful enthusiasm. She said, "Howie, OK, c'mon, fess up. What's the money in the jar for?"

It was the first time she'd said his first name. They both knew it. The switch had been flipped.

Mr. Jeffries paused, but not for long, and Howie returned, looked Emily nearly straight in the eye, and said, "Ever since I was a boy I've wanted to live on a sailboat."

*

Emily stood behind Howie on the banks of the Kayaderosseras. "Lesson two," she said.

The sun slashed and slithered down the creek. Howie was never bored. The late afternoon wind picked up. Howie watched the sunlight move like drifts of gold across the surface of the water.

Emily sighed. "I don't have a lesson two, actually." She was standing next to Howie now. "Look, I'm sorry. That was bitchy of me. The *Playboy* stuff. Who cares. You want to go inside now?"

"I have to mow the lawn."

"I'll bet you don't."

Howie shrugged. He thought about what the ducks must look like to the fish.

Back home, finally, Howie and Emily made themselves busy. Howie washed dishes; he put a load of laundry into the dryer. He checked the expiration dates on things in the refrigerator. He stood, for a few seconds, looking at Harri's painting in the living room. He would mow the lawn tomorrow after the TV and the sofa switched places, and then, he thought, I will purchase a goddamn sailboat.

He imagined himself and Emily in a boat, in the painting, feeding the fish around Rogers Rock with free, hookless worms. He would look inside the computer for boats tonight. He sat down next to Emily. She had made them both iced tea, super sweetened; she handed a glass to him, silently. They had not said a word since they'd left the creek. Lemons and sugar; sugar still spinning around the bottom of the glass like river silt. Howie almost expected to find a bottom dweller, a slimy sculpin, say, or an eel, doing circuits. She'd prepared a small plate of cheese and other female foods. Moonlike wedges of apples, a crayon-yellow fruit thing, and crackers seemingly fused together from seeds and sawdust and reddish felt. She had been going a little over the top with the snack plates.

She had just moved a plant from over there to over here. Plus, a drowsy, bored shrub was now sitting on Dori's tufted Rhapsody chair. Howie did not ask.

Emily thought: If only I could see the tattoos. Then I would know.

She turned on the TV. She thought: But know what, exactly? You'd know shit. Indulgently, Emily imagined that the tattoos might be back at her house somewhere, in a drawer, pressed inside of one of Peppy's books, folded in one of his jacket pockets or in a shoe box under his bed. Peppy hadn't exactly lied, he'd never said that Nancy *wasn't* chunky or messed-up or tattooed, but it was obvious that the old journalist had filed a story with her that had been full of holes. Poke a finger in. Put your eye up to one and see: these holes were the bottomless kind. They were fucking pits.

"Do you ever think about who used to live here?" Emily asked.

"Before me?"

"Before us, yeah. But I mean, like a hundred years ago. Back when they built these houses. Like the old mills, when there was a town out here. But in these houses especially. They couldn't imagine us."

It would be like a fish imagining the rest of the duck, Howie thought. The day was hot. He thought of Emily and himself sitting there, staring at the TV, but one hundred years ago. Rogers Rock timelessly behind them. How could they possibly explain themselves? He said nothing.

"They slept here too," Emily said. It was rare for her to speak of sleep. But he had never seen her so unclouded. "Shouldn't be weird, but it is. I imagine them sleeping mostly. The nineteenth-century millworkers or whoever. I used to think of ghosts a lot when I was little. I used to read a lot of books about ghosts and it seemed obvious to me what ghosts were. I think ghosts are the dreams of people a long time ago. Like, if you see one, you're only running into someone else's dream. Like there's some stutter, some skip or momentary flaw in the fabric of consciousness. Or time. Or some-thing," Emily laughed a little. But she didn't stop: "It's why ghosts are so confused, so dreamlike? In the books, anyway. They're not trying to scare you. They're just there, totally in their own zone, stoned almost. They're tripping. They just kind of go through the motions like we do in dreams. The most boring stuff, too. I don't know. Like dreaming of being at work. How they can't be reasoned with and if they really see you that's it, they disappear. They wake up. But somewhere else. I think in some way all that stuff exists right now, like all around us. Like we're all trapped. Those people are here too, somehow, sleeping or whatever. *Paper working*. Doing whatever they did at the mills."

"They invented the flat-folding paper bag at one of them," Howie said.

"Right," Emily said, momentarily derailed. "They did that. But, anyway, I think it's scarier, in a way, than simply running into the spirit of a dead person with a grudge or a secret. Seeing someone trapped in a dream. Because where are we then? We think we're, like, at the forefront of time moving," Emily made a small, cute, diving arrow motion with her hands. Splash! "But there is no for-ward. There is no future. Not like we think. We're not the end point of everything moving onward. Do I sound crazy? I don't think that everything has culminated in us right here, right now. We're just a point on a river that already exists, beginning and end. Everything is a dream."

She wanted to say *nightmare*. She didn't know what she wanted to say. She wanted to tell Howie that there were far worse things than human ghosts, and that these things were real and all around them. That they could see nothing of what really existed. They watched TV.

Howie was confused. He thought about Halloween. "But ghosts aren't real."

"Well, if they were," Emily said. She'd said too much. Shut up. "Do you want to watch this?"

They watched Animal Planet.

But Howie, too, often thought about the temporality of Route 29. Not that he would put it that way. He would find himself daydreaming sometimes that he was living in the past—back before the paper industry had burst up the Kayaderosseras, those half-dozen mills, the old railroad you could still see poking through the mulch of the forest, the veritable boomtown and its workers, German and Polish immigrants mostly, their horses, their stony, sacrificial wives. Coughing babies; snow. Back before the houses were built, abandoned, plundered, and finally retaken by the woods. Every house but his and Emily's. Howie would imagine that the stone walls and foundations you saw in the woods weren't the remnants of a hopeful past but markers toward a future. He would mix the futures up. The paper mills opening and a town sprouting up—horse stables and barns and a Pizza Hut—he and his pregnant wife driving up the route that now had a proper name like any other road. Pine Tree Road. Pretty Street. Evergreen Estates. How happy they were going to be! Both of them getting out of the car, looking up at the house, arms around each other's waists.

Home.

Neighbors everywhere, mowing lawns and returning baking trays with thank-you notes written on purple paper. The sizzle of sprinklers and whatever a nineteenth-century paper mill sounded like. Probably, Howie thought, they sounded like whispers.

"There used to be a lot of houses up here, a hundred or so years ago," Howie said, not turning from the TV.

Emily ate some cheese. She said, "Do you know what, when I was little I thought that you had been there before me. Like, when

I imagined how it used to be, like who lived here before, I'd imagine *you*. I'd imagined that you lived in my house before we did. Isn't that weird? Even though you were way younger than my grandfather. Like you'd always been there."

"My wife and I used to think that about—"

"*Name.*"

"Doris. Dori, my ex-wife, and I used to think that about your grand—" Howie stopped. "Peter and Gillian Phane. That they'd been here forever."

The names stabbed Emily. She did not want to talk about her grandfather, so she said, "What was my grandmother like?"

"I don't remember," Howie said. This untruth came easily, felt true.

"Did you ever speak to her?"

"Maybe once, twice."

But then, why lie about *that*? Howie did not want to lie or tell the truth, he wanted to stand up. He stood. He wanted to go up to Harri's room and look for affordable wooden sailboats on the internet computer. He knew there were unopened e-mails waiting for him as well: one IMPORTANT mail from his daughter and, as of this morning, an ominously subjectless e-mail from Rhoda Prough. Emily usually did not ask Howie where he was going, much less what he was doing when he went there. Their mostly unfeigned lack of curiosity in each other's past or future was one of the things holding them together.

Meaning, normally, Howie could just get up and go, unremarked upon. Not today. "Hey, wait," Emily said. "Howie, where are you going?"

His first name again. Cracks had begun to form.

"Up," Howie said.

"I can see that. Why?"

Why not? "I'm going to go on to the internet computer." Then, why not indeed: "I am going to buy a sailboat."

Emily's mouth popped open. "Like right now?"

"Yes. I'm going to start looking right now, yes." Howie smiled: another crack in the day. Right in the middle of his face. "Yes."

Emily had avoided the computer. There was too much in there that she wasn't ready to see.

Howie said, "Do you want to help me find a sailboat?"

Emily stood, nodded slightly, then eagerly. She turned off the TV with a wizardly zap.

She said, "I've never been in a sailboat before."

"Well," Howie said, "then that would make two of us."

Though there wasn't any precedent, Emily had to assume that this was a joke. She followed him upstairs.

21

———

Howie would no longer throw them back. He wasn't angry at fish, and he could not prepare them in tasty, respectful ways, but Emily was right. He had been doing things halfway for too long and for reasons that he could no longer defend or even fully recollect the impetus behind. Live and let live? Harriet was not a baby. His daughter was no longer helpless and, anyway, she had never looked much like a fish in the first place. Her face had never been a quiet, thoughtless thing. It occurred to him that Harri might have benefited more from a father who obliterated the heads of longnose gar with a hammer, a man capable of letting whitefish perish slowly in buckets full of air. The world does not remember what mercies you show it. Daughters, apparently, less so.

It was not a sport, what Howie did. It was not a competition. In six days he would be picking up the fiberglass twenty-eight-foot O'Day 1983 from its owner in Bolton Landing. The listed price had been, for some reason, $10,995, but because Howie had $10,000 cash, the owner had agreed to lower the price. They found the boat on the internet computer. The boat's name was *Richard*. Its owner's name was also Richard, but everyone called him Dickie. He'd named the boat after himself because, for two years, twenty-three years ago, Dickie had been dying of cancer.

"Won't lie, it was rough. But I didn't want any coffin or a plot of land, you know? I was forty. I wanted to piss off my wife."

Howie had dreamed all of his life of owning an old wooden sailboat. Passing dark mountains and creaking docks and people sleeping in cabins in the middle of the night; peanut-buttering his toast as the sun rose over Tongue Mountain. The wood aspect had been important, but fiberglass would have to do. *Richard* had a bedroom. You could sleep on *Richard*. Emily had brokered the deal. It might have been the first time that she had talked on a telephone in years. She had even joked a little, asking Dickie if he might throw in some sailing lessons.

"For you, doll? Anything."

Howie had not been joking. He had never been on a sailboat. But he had read books and thought a good deal about it. He thought: The fish of Lake Jogues will know my twenty-eight-foot O'Day. He imagined what it would look like to the fish, the reverse shark fin of *Richard*'s keel. How the water would tremble. But, admittedly, Howie had been thinking a whole lot of odd things lately.

He sat by a small pond. His phone buzzed.

"What's that?" Rhoda Prough asked. "What the hell? You plan on catching fish with robots?"

The buzz was coming from Howie's metal tackle box is why she asked.

Howie said, "Cell phone."

He removed it from the tackle box. There was a text that said, "FISHING OR DATING?" The text was from Howie's internet computer. Emily.

"Text," he told Rho.

"Sure," she said. "Important?"

"No," Howie said. He wrote, "DATING," and hit Send.

Because it certainly wasn't fishing.

Emily was on the computer again. She'd finally signed into her e-mail account and, once, for a few minutes, she'd even reactivated her Facebook account; she'd made Howie sit next to her while she did this. "Just, I don't know, just sit there, OK?"

"OK."

Howie continued to stand.

"Well?"

"Sit here?"

"Where else, Howie? Sit. Please. This won't take a minute."

The internet computer was on Harri's bed. Even though they'd been co-sleeping for the better part of a month, it was uncomfortable sitting on Harri's bed next to Emily during the day, awake. It was like Harri could see them. They both had problems thinking about Harriet Jeffries in relation to the direction their lives had taken.

It took hours. Emily had more than two thousand unopened e-mails. Most were crap, junk, she said, delete delete delete delete. It was like excavation, satisfying even for Howie to watch. "E-mail archeology," Emily said. "Let's see what ancient treasures we uncover!" Leaving, unopened, dozens upon dozens of e-mails from old friends, colleagues, professors, Howie didn't really know and Emily wasn't ready to explain or dust them off just yet. She made a file, BONES, and put them all in there. To examine later. Most of these e-mails were from Ethan Caldwell, and most of these had blank subject lines. But some didn't. Some said things like LAST ONE and HELLO FROM NYC or GREETINGS FROM SEOUL. The last one from him was three weeks ago and didn't have a subject line. He appeared to have written at least one a month for more than two years, some with attachments.

"My ex-boyfriend," Emily said.

"I know."

Delete delete delete. Save. Delete.

"Wait, how do you know?"

Howie could have shrugged, said that he just figured; it did seem obvious, so many from this guy. But he said, "Facebook."

"You're so sweet with your Facebook, Howie." Then, "But, wait, you and I weren't even Facebook friends."

"OK."

"I know it's OK, but how did you know about Ethan?"

"I didn't," Howie said. "I don't. Maybe from Harri."

"I wasn't friends with Harriet either. Howie"—Emily laughed—"holy cow, were you *stalking* me?"

"I don't think so."

Emily was looking so much better now. She slept through the night, or the day, or whenever Howie slept. He rarely had to wake her from ringings. She insisted that he give Rho a chance.

"Chance for what?" Howie said. "I fish alone."

"He fishes alone," Emily marveled. "Listen to yourself! Chance for *romance*, my lone-wolf friend. You want to end up like me? Howard Jeffries, you've got your whole life ahead of you."

So here Howie was, sitting beside a small pond in Rhoda Prough's backyard. Rho had tricked him, promising an afternoon of fishing. She'd bring the picnic goodies, she said, *imbibements*. Howie just had to make sure and bring Howie. It had been like she knew, somehow, that Howie had really wanted to bring Emily Phane.

He still wasn't quite certain how any of this had come about. There was that telephone call, of course, then the e-mails that Emily, more girlish than he had ever seen her, had made him reply to. Then a whole bunch of e-mails with increasingly hard to dodge questions. Would Howie like to come over on Saturday? Yes or no? Howie had been poked on Facebook. Even Emily didn't know what that meant.

Rho's pond was about the size of a swimming pool. It was toilet blue, deep. Howie knew right away that no fish could live in it; he smelled sulfur. He sat down. "It's a natural mineral spring," he said.

"Bingo." Rho grinned. "It's the opening of a cave, actually. Like an underground river. No telling how deep it is or even if deep applies. Maybe it's just *long*, know what I mean?"

"You mean we won't be fishing."

"We won't be catching anything, anyway." Rho popped open a

bottle of white wine. "Don't look so glum. How else was I supposed to get you over to my favorite place in the whole wide world?" She looked into Howie's face. "Is there something different about you?"

"Can you drink the water?"

"Well, the coot used to live here sure did. One cup a day. Swore by it. I'd love to say he lived to a hundred and ten, but he didn't even make it to seventy. Plus"—Rho laughed—"it tastes like ass and eggs if you ask me."

They sat on bath towels. Behind them was Rho's small, late-eighteenth-century stone farmhouse. It looked surly, armored in different sizes and colors of rock. Rho called it the armadillo. Howie heard her ex-husband, Darren Prough, in that and realized that she didn't know that he'd called her the armadillo. He felt ashamed for ever having been in the same room with that piece of junk. Two giant oaks covered the house in hot green shade. The windows were open. They sat way up on the top of a hill in eastern New York, near Anaquassacook and the Batten Kill River. You could see the river, squirming like a highway off in the distance. It could have been moving in either direction, or it could have been motionless, like an elongated lake. It had taken Howie an hour to drive here.

He appreciated how the land rolled down from where they sat, and how the sky circled them. It was so different from Route 29. He saw lumps of cow way down there in the yellow haze. Other old farmhouses embedded in little gardens of tree, and a road that only revealed itself as such when a car or truck moved toylike across it. Hawks circled, paused, dived. Far in the distance, the mannered mountains of Vermont.

"I was in Vermont a few weeks ago," Howie said.

"Really?"

"Yes."

She looked at him.

He looked at everything.

"OK." Rho laughed. "That really all you want to tell me about that one? Babe, you're a trip, you know that?"

"I was grocery shopping."

Howie tried to change the subject back to silence.

Rho said, "You know what, when Darren and I were splitting, I used to drive to Vermont for all my shopping and stuff, too. Couldn't bear running into anyone we knew. But, correct me if I'm wrong, Jeffries, you got divorced, what, thirty years ago?"

"Twenty," Howie said. "I like driving."

She looked at him. "Seriously though, you sure I'm not missing something here? Like, you change your hair? Different color contacts? You been working out?"

Howie knew that it was a date because of the candles. Emily had given him a couple of signs to look out for, but they'd been conservative, subtle, and useless in the face of the fact that it was the middle of the afternoon and there was an unlit candelabrum on a bath towel. Obviously, Rho didn't plan on going anywhere. Or, if she planned on going somewhere, she planned on coming back here, with him, when the sun had set. She also had a CD player. European cheese of the sort that Emily was fond of. She took out a small glass pipe that Howie, at first, assumed was some kind of fancy wine opener.

She said, "You want?"

"To hold it?"

It was pot, she explained.

"OK."

"For *smoking*?"

Howie didn't want. Didn't know how. He watched Rho carefully, warily, as if she might change color or rip off her clothing, howl, froth; he hadn't known what. Perhaps she would overdose. He imagined police sirens on the wide, rural wind.

Rho didn't seem the least bit affected by her crime. So why, Howie wondered, did she even do it? She smiled, she talked a blue streak, but what else was new?

Howie felt OK regardless. He sipped wine; it tasted nice. Hint of poultry, chrome, Emily's almond shampoo. He thought that he was supposed to think about what he tasted when he tasted wine but in this case maybe not: Rho didn't pry. Howie would have killed a ton of fish given the chance today, and this thought contented him. He wouldn't have thrown back a single one.

The afternoon was a bath. Howie did not even mind that Rho had teased him until he removed his shoes, then his brown socks. His toes were OK. He moved them, slowly, and compared them to Rho's. Hers were pebbles. Rho had lots to say, but she said it so much better now that they were alone. Suddenly, she didn't seem as bothered by other people, and she did not need Howie to be either. She was a handsome woman. However, having spent the last month or so with Emily, Rho was a thing to get used to. She did not let Howie be Howie like Emily did. She did not coexist. She wanted something different from him, and it took Howie an hour or so to realize what Rho wanted was for Howie to *see her*. Unlike Emily, she wanted badly to be known by Howie, and she wanted to help adjust the manner in which Howie knew her, seeding his perception. She went about this in ways clumsy, crude, and honest, and Howie found himself responding in kind. Not revealing himself, necessarily, because what was there to reveal, but he stopped holding himself so tight.

She was nearly twice Emily's age. She was doubled, in a way: her body, her being, as if two women had joined to create whatever species Rhoda Prough was. Howie liked this species. Had Howie ever heard her giggle before? Not only bark, *giggle*. Her roundness appeared more bloated here under the sun, but bloated in a good, cheerful way, like a steamy bag of popcorn freshly removed from a microwave. Perhaps she had been right. There was something between them. There certainly wasn't a prohibitive, daughterly field around Rho, and this made her femininity exciting, her soft, sun-lazed movements. She was tactile, twangy as an orange. She would pick little bits of grass, twisting them between her fingers. She would smell her fingers. Howie was not only allowed but expected to watch her move. That was special. The way she wasn't wearing a bra; her long, small breasts sleeping on her round belly. Howie could comfortably think about Rho's breasts in the same way that he thought about her elbows, which is not to say that he didn't find Rho's breasts handsome, just not particularly handsome, no more than the rest of Rho, and, if he was honest, they were probably less handsome and beguiling than, for example, Rho's eyes or smile or her blind, puckered toes.

Howie had not been with a woman since he was thirty years old. The last woman he had been with had been thirty years old. Thirty-year-old women have distinct parts on them that demanded a sort of distracting, overattentive fealty. Howie thought himself around that. Thirty-year-old breasts were parasites. Braggy things. Howie let himself smell Rho. It was a muggy afternoon. He had not smelled a woman like this since his wife, and even his wife, Dori, well, not so often. She never really went outside and, if she did, she was slathered in deodorant, OFF! insect repellent, purple-smelling perfume, creams. Rho smelled sharply of herself. Howie remembered sex, suddenly, as you might remember a family member's birthday many months or weeks after it had passed.

Howie worried about Emily.

"So, hey, don't laugh, but I want to play you this music," Rho said. It was something called "Pachelbel's Canon." "It's from before music had words. It can be about whatever you want it to be about."

She showed him the CD cover, shyly opening the case, presenting it to him as if it had the potential to frighten him off. *The Pachelbel Canon and Other Baroque Favorites.*

"I don't really know music," Howie said.

"Well, I'll make an introduction then. Darren, he used to like the hard rock. Winger, White Lion, Ratt, crap like that. Quiet Riot, Judas Priest. Honey, I used to say, Honey, your parents live in *Watervliet.* There's no way they can hear you listening to this Satan rock anymore! Like, you can grow up now, you know? But he loved it. I should have known. You know how he's going to die, don't you?"

"What?"

"Darren. My ex-husband is going to die driving drunk, air-drumming to Def Leppard. I'm serious. Me and the girls went to this psychic in Cape Cod a few years back and she gave me all these details. Freaky as shit. She knew him head to foot, like everything, and that's what she told me would happen. I don't believe that stuff, normally, but how could I argue? Described him down to his shoes. Told me don't waste my time, you know? Different paths. Our paths had crossed and no longer, I don't know, twined? Anyway, we'd gotten what we needed from each other in this life. We'd got all we were able to get from each other and I'm pretty sure I got the bum part of *that* deal," Rho said. "How do you think you'll die?"

The possibility that Rho also knew how Howie would die momentarily alarmed him. Seemed probable. He said, "On a sailboat."

Rho nodded. "I can see that. Yeah."

"OK."

"I think about death a *lot*," Rho said. She finished a glass of wine, poured another. One for Howie too. "I don't want to die alone. Big fear of mine. I told the psychic this and she told me that I *would* die alone. She said, Look, dying alone isn't what you should be worrying about. Dying is nothing. She told me what I should worry about was *living* alone."

"But not drowning," Howie said.

"Excuse me?"

"I want to die on a sailboat, but I don't want to drown." He said this as if it were a request that he wanted to make sure Rho had accurately registered.

Rho said, "Rick Allen, the drummer from Def Leppard, only has one arm. They call him the Thunder God. Darren did anyways. So air-drumming behind the wheel *should* be safer, but what were we talking about again?"

Rho touched Howie for the first time. His knee. Then the part above that, his pre-knee. "You seem different today, Jeffries. I'm a little stoned, what's your excuse? Anyway, I had to babysit my niece, Loleeze, this one time, and my sister-in-law, she had this CD she insisted I play before putting Leezy to bed. *Bach for Babies: Fun and Games for Budding Brains.* Don't laugh."

"OK."

"Thing was, Leezy was already seven years old and stupid as a tub of suds. That's a brain that had long since budded, you hear what I'm saying? But *moms.* They want the best, and I guess she thought: Hey, probably can't hurt! Maybe Bach'd do some good! Anyway, what happened was I fell in love with this *Bach for Babies.* Secretly, you know? I was so embarrassed that I loved it so much because, back then, I'd thought that Bach had made the music *specifically for babies.* Like Bach had made music for babies and music for adults, and I couldn't get enough of the baby music. It made me cry, I'm not even joking. I'm a tough girl but this Bach? So, all right, embarrassed, I took *Bach for Babies* home with me one day. I figured they'd just think freaking Leezy buried it out back or ate it or something. I planned on returning it next time I babysat. But I forgot it, and then next time they had this new one with a freakish cover with like four multiracial babies and this one was called, simply, *Build Your Baby's Brain.* That's where I first heard a song called 'Canon' by Johann Pachelbel. It was the most gorgeous thing I'd ever heard. Long story short, a little while later I discovered, duh, the music wasn't composed specifically for making babies smarter. That was a relief! 'Pachelbel's Canon' is my favorite song. I've got about three or four CD versions of it, but this one is my favorite. It makes me happy and sad at the same time. But here. Shut up, Rho. I'll shut up."

Rho played the song. It was difficult for Howie to follow: it seemed so weak and transparent compared to what he was seeing. The shadow of clouds moving through the fields; the river, the lumps of cow. The music sounded like the ghost of a very pretty gown.

"Nothing?" Rho asked.

Howie shook his head. He shook it hard, as Emily had instructed him. "Maybe I'm too old," he said.

"I said it's also for adults, butthead."

"I don't know how to listen to music."

"Here," Rho reached over and, with both hands, closed Howie's eyes. "One, two." Like a doctor administering to a brand-new corpse.

She played it again, then again. Then again. Howie thought about Emily, what she would do here. She would laugh, surely. He wondered what she was doing now, alone in their house. That was when Howie felt Rho's hand in his own and, for a small second, he thought it was Emily's, that they were in his room, in bed, and suddenly that ghost of a very pretty dress filled with a real body, a woman, and something less like sound and more like emotion. Howie thought: Music is how people pretend that time is human. Music is a way of moving through time unharmed. Music is not a fish, it's a boat.

This made perfect sense; then it did not.

The trick was Rho's hand, holding that. The music sounded like a commercial for diamonds or medication for loved ones losing their minds in the twilight of their years. It was a midrange luxury sedan. The other trick was that all of the emotions people feel when they hear music are already there, inside them, so if Howie was going to feel anything here, he was going to have to feel *something*. It was not going to come from the music. Rho's hand, he supposed, was a start.

Howie opened his eyes.

Rho was looking at him, her face a fleshy plug in the day. She had tears in her eyes.

Howie panicked, pulled the plug, pulled his hand from hers, remembering his mother playing the national anthem and he thought, angrily, suddenly: Why would you listen to something that makes you *sad*?

He caught himself.

No! That was not what was happening here. Rho was not sad exactly. Nobody but Howie's mother had to be sad, and Howie, for once, thought that he had the power to make someone happy. He thought about Emily. Hadn't he helped Emily? Howie could make someone else happy. He reached out and returned Rho's hand to his own.

There.

The day progressed. Rho smoked a lot more, switching from drugs to menthol cigarettes and back again. The white wine, at some point, became red. Then an indigestive pink. Rho had Howie explain his fishing rod. She baited it and fished. She wanted, she said, for Howie to see what she looked like with a rod in her hand. "Joking!" she said. "I'm sorry, oh my God, I am so bad today!"

"You're not bad." But the fish would hear that face from a mile away.

The presence of Rho's house loomed behind them. They were going to be dining in French tonight. Howie tried a menthol cigarette because Emily, he thought, would have. It tasted like coughing and Christmas.

Rho asked Howie questions about his daughter, and he answered as best he could. Emily had never once asked him about his daughter. He did not tell Rho, as he had not told Emily, that Harri's last e-mail had requested from him a loan of more than twelve thousand dollars. This money was an "investment," and to be spent on her art. The number was not a typo. She wrote, "I can break down the costs for you later if you like."

Yes, Howie thought, perhaps that is something I would like.

If she'd have said that the money was for her life, for New York City sustenance, shelter, for a first-class one-way plane ticket home, then Howie would have sent her his entire boat savings, no question, she was his little girl, but that much money for her art had given him pause. He still did not know how to reply. She had never promised to repay him before either. This word: *investment.* Why was that more disturbing? He'd gotten another heated e-mail from his ex-wife, one of her dreaded cap-locked, late-night missives, imploring him to not GIVE THAT GIRL ANOTHER PENNY and, hey, next time Harriet was at his place, which was supposedly NEXT THURSDAY, have her MAYBE STOP BY SO DREW AND I KNOW SHE'S ALIVE FOR A FREAKING CHANGE!!! Howie had no idea what to do with this e-mail either. The only reason he had replied to it was because he was anxious that his ex-wife or Drew might stop by his place looking for Harri and find, instead, Emily.

He wrote, "Thank you for this e-mail, Doris. I will see what I can do."

Normally, he never typed her name if he could help it.

Howie told Rho that Harri had been spending a lot of time at his house lately, painting and whatnot. It did not feel like a lie. Perhaps that was the trick about lying. Several times he thought about telling Rho about Emily, asking Rho for advice about young women and their possibly epileptic nightmares and—but, no, how impossible was the idea of Emily Phane while sitting next to Rhoda Prough? She would not understand. Howie did not understand, not from this distance. Rho lived in the past and the future; Howie's house no longer did, if it ever had. It was like remembering a dream.

He would see what he could do.

Before they went in for dinner, Emily buzzed Howie's phone again.

"u ok?"

Howie figured that he was. He wrote back: "YES I AM OK. ARE YOU OK?"

"i miss you."

Howie and Rho returned to the shore of the pond after a stately, uncooperative dinner. Rho said, "I'm trying too hard here, aren't I?"

"You're trying just fine."

"I remember you said that you liked duck. I'm such an idiot."

It was unlikely that Howie had ever said anything about ducks.

Rho lit the candles. She had stopped talking but could not stop producing noise. She hummed. They listened to the night. Bats slapped the air above them like oars; owls, too, and rabbits or cats or raccoons, crickets, and the occasional insomniac cow in the distance. Trucks. She rested her head on Howie's lap. She breathed. He thought about touching her hair. Rho said, "You know what I hate? I hate stars. I hate the moon and everything up there."

"OK."

"That's just how I feel."

She tossed a cigarette into her pond.

"You can live your whole life alone even if you're married, is what that Cape Cod fortune-teller told me. She said if you know yourself then you'll never be alone. Like, you'll never know anyone if you don't know yourself first. No point even trying. I think about that a lot, but I think I talk too much sometimes. Do you think I talk too much?"

"Sometimes."

"Well, damn." Rho laughed. "Like when?"

"Maybe you have a lot to say."

"That's right, maybe I do. Do you know yourself, Howie?"

Howie knew that he did not appreciate riddles. He thought of many ways to announce that he had to go back home where he lived, though he suspected that he would not be returning to Route 29 tonight. For one thing, he was inebriated. He was worried about Emily.

Rho stood up. "Maybe we should go back to the house," she said, sadly. "Maybe I overplanned this, too."

Inside, after Rho tried and failed to interest Howie in learning how to play poker, then Uno, they sat together in her living room. The floor was unsteady. She put on her *Bach for Babies* CD, flashing him a sloppy, knowing smile. "Our secret?"

Howie said, "I don't know what you're talking about."

Minutes later, Rho ran her finger down Howie's arm.

"I knew it'd be like this," she said. "But not like this, actually. Something like this. I always thought you'd be, I don't know, more *mean*?" She made a serious face. "More of an asshole. I guess I'm glad you're not more mean? You're not mean at all, are you?"

"No."

"I've always had a crush on you, but you know that," Rho said. Her finger stopped on his wrist. "I've kind of looked up to you. My father was the same. You don't suffer fools. You're so *strong*."

Howie could not think of anything to say to this.

"But I get it," Rho said. She pulled back. "I'll stop. You don't want to kiss me. I'll stop. I'm sorry."

Oh, mud, Howie thought.

He closed his eyes. This, he thought, is something that inebriated people are allowed to do: suddenly sleep. He pretended to do that.

But then Howie really was asleep, because the next thing he knew, Rho was pulling him from the sofa and up the creaking, swaying old wooden stairs. They were on a boat. *"Richard,"* Howie said.

"Rho," Rho corrected.

She was naked from the waist down, wearing only a long T-shirt. She'd lit candles in her bedroom. Not a T-shirt, a gown. The bed was white and covered like a wagon.

Howie was unused to being inebriated. Rho undressed him for bed. "Arms up. There we go. Shhhh."

Giggling, she kissed him. They were kissing. It was a sensation like eating and being eaten at the same time. But no rush. It felt like a circle, it felt good, fish mouths silently talking, drowning in air. She nibbled his ear. Howie felt her breasts on his chest, then on his stomach. It felt like she had at least four of them. The word *boobs* popped into his head and he laughed.

"That's more like it," Rho said, also laughing. She took his penis into her mouth.

It occurred to Howie that he was doing this, all of it, for Emily. Or somehow *as* Emily, but that did not make sense because Emily would certainly have opened her eyes here. She hated having them closed.

Everything felt good.

For some reason, whenever he wondered if he would ever have sex again he thought that, if he did—which had been doubtful—he would remember how to do it like people said that you remember how to ride a bicycle. That saying. This was not the case. Howie remembered how to have sex in a similar way to how he remembered extreme, feverish pain: it was a continuum that could only truly be remembered by being powerlessly inside it. It was not casual. It was like a city in a recurring dream that you only remember being in when you're actually dreaming inside it, wandering about, being hunted, ignored, frightened. Being loved. Howie remembered every street. He did not want to open his eyes. He did not want to leave. Why had he ever left? Where the hell have you been?

Hours before, over dinner, Rho had told him that sex was important to her, and she admitted to finding people to have sex with on the internet computer. Men, she'd said. She hoped that this didn't bother Howie. It didn't. It was unusual, he thought, and didn't exactly make sense, but OK. Howie often found new places to fish on the internet computer. He found a boat. Therapy, she'd continued, was like going to school to study yourself—you needed a good professor but you also had to do your homework. Howie had not been sure if homework, in this analogy, was supposed to mean sex with people that Rho met on the internet computer or something else entirely.

Then, in the middle of the night, Howie was awoken with, "By the way, I only met one person online like that and it was a long time ago and it wasn't even good. Howie? I thought you were awake. Howie, sweetie, you awake?"

"Yes."

"Just in case that was freaking you out."

It had not been.

She said, "I don't know why I say the things I say sometimes. You make me feel so safe or nervous or I don't know."

"It's OK."

"Is it?" Rho touched his head as if making sure that it was still there. "I really like you, Howie. That's all. I'm sorry about tonight. If I was a disappointment."

"OK," he said.

He was awake again and not as drunk as he had been. He needed to get home. It was terrible; he hadn't texted or called Emily since before dinner.

"Howie?"

He stood up. "I need to make a phone call," he said.

"What's wrong?"

"Nothing," he said. "I have to call my daughter."

"In New York City? Now? It's four in the morning, Howie . . ." Then Rho laughed. "Do you always call your daughter in the middle of the night after . . . ?"

She turned on the light for him. Howie looked through his pants on the floor of the bedroom. His phone was not in his pocket. Now that was something.

"Oh," Rho said. She explained that she might have taken his phone when he wasn't looking and turned it off because, she said, she'd gotten kind of stoned and, OK, a little paranoid with the way he kept checking it, the constant buzz buzzing text messages he'd been getting, like a high school girl, and she'd really wanted the dinner to be perfect and romantic and she'd been planning it for so long, and she was sorry that it'd all gone to shit, total f-ing shit, but when Howie went to the restroom, and the phone started buzzing again next to his fork and knife, and she was sorry, but who was Emily?

"Shit," Howie said.

"You're mad at me."

He was not. "No," he said. "But Rho, where is my telephone?"

It was in the kitchen. On it were fifteen unopened text messages and more than sixty missed calls, one after another.

Emily would not answer the phone. Howie passed trees that he knew by heart. He searched the radio for Pachelbel's "Canon," thinking that maybe he'd just drive himself to sleep.

He did not want to go home.

He was worried, ashamed, confused. Desire felt like regaining a limb that he hadn't even known he'd been missing. He was also happy.

He could not carry Rho and the past day back home. He did not know how to bring that through the door, and the last month with Emily began to feel like hearsay to Howie: an exaggerated fishing tale. The three-hundred-plus-pound lake sturgeon berserker that got away. Howie saw himself and Emily as Rho might, as anyone would. It was not normal. Then the vision of that splashed once and disappeared beneath the surface. Bloop.

He was exhausted. He was maybe still a little drunk. He had assured Rho that Emily was not a girlfriend. "It's OK if she is," Rho said. "No strings. I get it."

"She is not."

But the idea of bed now, of sleeping next to Emily after all this, after Rho, was unmanageable.

He would try to talk to Emily. He would tell her that they could no longer sleep in the same bed. But, then, wouldn't that be admitting that they had actually been sleeping in the same bed? It was not something he felt like they should talk about.

He had told Rho that he wanted to see her again because she had been so sad there, standing watching him get dressed, handing him a sock, another sock, and also because he did want to see her again. He sure did. But first things first.

· · ·

Howie stood in his living room. Something was missing. The plants stared accusatorily. It was morning. They knew. The TV was on, but muted, CNN types going to town, hurling bricks and bottles, waving flags and swinging burning person-shaped pillows from sticks someplace far away.

There were flayed, thin, silvery junk food wrappers on the floor. Pizza crust parentheses. Two empty bottles of Diet Dr Pepper. Howie remembered what Emily's house had looked like when he'd found Peter Phane half dead on the floor. Emily was the thing that was missing here, obviously, and she was, Howie reassured himself, probably only upstairs in his bedroom. But she was a whole different kind of missing is what Howie also thought. He checked the kitchen.

He opened, closed the refrigerator. From the kitchen window he saw his chandelier in Emily's backyard. It looked as if it had crash-landed from another, more magnificent planet.

Think about that later.

Nor was Emily half dead in the downstairs bathroom. Or the laundry room, and Emily was not in the cupboard with his money, which, Howie saw, was no longer in the cupboard, anyway. Howie went upstairs.

22

Because Emily wouldn't open and read her own e-mail, she read Howie's. Similar to sharing a home and a bed with him, this was an invasion of privacy that she didn't try to rationalize. In a sense, it was all part of the covenant that they'd made. None of this was really happening.

The e-mails she'd read, coupled with Howie's disappearance and his phone going off-line, broke Emily's heart. They made her angry. Most of the e-mails he got, he didn't reply to. His inbox was a fearful container. There was the needy, slangy, admirably indefatigable love of Harriet's e-mails, especially considering Howie's bureaucratic replies (Emily read those, too), and then there were the ones from Dori, Drew, and Howie's pals, most reaching out to Jeffries, as they called him, inviting him to birthday parties, fishing getaways, middle-school graduations, gourmet nights, Little League championships, bowling, or just sincerely inquiring as to how he was doing. Drop us a line, bud.

This may have been behind Emily's decision to remove the chandelier from his room and drag it out into her backyard. She'd meant to take it all the way to the creek, toss it in there, drown it, as if that might wake Howie up, but she'd been far too tired. Now you'll have to find something else to hate, even if it's only your own self-protective and sickening inertia, Emily thought. Even if it's me. Emily sort of wanted it to be her. That would clarify things at least.

Now please come home.

She'd ripped the chandelier and a shoe-sized chunk of the ceiling plaster down around midnight. It was good to have a project. She hadn't slept the night before since it was one of Howie's night shifts, so time had begun to fuzz, waver. Like the good old days.

She called him. She called him. She called him.

His phone was off, but she called him. She texted from the internet.

Sitting, waiting, hoping for Howie to return had begun to feel worse than when she'd been on her own next door, because at least hope hadn't been a part of that equation. This was more like when she'd been waiting for Peppy to die. Like then, she supposed she knew that when Howie returned, if he returned, if he really existed at all, nothing would be the same. It would be like willing yourself back to the exact same dream after being awake for hours.

She'd taken his money and hid it so that Harriet wouldn't get it. Partly, Emily thought that Harriet deserved the money. If that was all the love her father could manage to express, then she should take whatever she could get. But another part of her was jealous. Harriet didn't deserve it; Howie did, Emily did, and the two of them were going to sail away on a boat named *Richard*, because where the fuck was Harriet, anyway?

Clearly that was the mystery. Dori and Drew's e-mails made no sense. Harriet should have been here, right now, in Howie's house. She'd been spending weeks at Howie's house, on and off, apparently. It made Emily's heart race, reading that. It made her dizzy, and she'd had to look over her shoulder. Emily thought often of Howie's iconic daughter—and it had made things here more palatable, less ridiculous. Like, maybe she could become Harriet now, start over as Harriet. The idea of little Harriet held Emily's hand. But what the fuck? Had Harriet come and, if so, where and how had Howie disposed of her body? Or was Harriet hiding? Emily listened to the house. She heard Harriet upstairs when she was downstairs, and vice versa. Emily locked the doors. Closed the curtains. She sensed Harriet's punk eyes out in the dark of the woods. Had Harriet and Emily switched places, or maybe Emily had always been Harriet, and Harriet was insane now, out here with her father, hallucinating herself into the hell of Emily Phane? Emily thought about her past and how unhappened all of it now felt. Boston was a ghost story. Peppy and her childhood wasn't even that, it was a ghost story in a different language. She held her hand before her face; she went to the mirror, said her name. She laughed. Get a fucking grip.

Emily deleted the mail about the money and then deleted the unread (by Howie) follow-up, the one explaining why Harriet needed it so bad, and then she'd put the money under Harriet's bed for safekeeping.

Emily called. She kept angrily calling and then, eventually, she plummeted to sleep.

"You're not even going to ask? Jesus, seriously, what is wrong with you that you haven't even asked?"

Emily was referring to the chandelier. But so what? Why should he ask? Finding out why did not change the fact that the chandelier was in her backyard, that his bedspread was covered with ceiling. Dust, crystal, wire, asbestos. She had used a hammer. What else did he need to know exactly?

"Nothing?" Emily said. "You got nothing for me? If I'd thrown the refrigerator in the creek would you, like, shrug and go buy a new one?"

"Eventually," Howie said.

"I don't know whether to laugh or cry."

"Are you asking me?"

"What?" she said. This tone was new.

"Because if you're asking me, Emily, I would prefer if you laughed."

It took her a moment to realize that he'd finally said her name. The sound of it stunned her. It sounded like a spotlight: like suddenly she was really happening. Found at last.

"Howie?"

Howie said nothing. This wouldn't normally scare her. But it was pouring down now; the living room window like a grey stone.

"It's raining." Howie sighed.

They watched.

Emily said, "Please don't make me go, Mr. Jeffries. I don't have anywhere left to go."

She had been awake for an hour after having slept for nearly five hours, most of those with Howie watching over her. He had found her in a hollow, incoherent state, half sitting, half sleeping amidst the debris on his bed. He had told her that she had to sleep, and told her that she had to not sleep there, in his bed, and she had told him to please not say that. Then begged him to sleep, too, next to her. That it was OK.

It was not OK. They were talking in the bedroom. The spell was broken.

Eventually, he had carried her to Harri's room, where she fell asleep curled up next to the computer. Howie pulled up a chair, sat by the bed. He touched her head as he would have touched the head of his own daughter, when she was young, if she'd ever been the type of girl who needed him to be there, petting her, telling her that everything was OK when it very clearly was not.

Emily would wake every twenty minutes in a state of panic, and she'd ask him why he didn't help her, where he had been. Howie told her that he'd been right there. "I'm right here," he said. But then why'd he let them have her? He told her that he didn't know what she was talking about.

Now they were on the sofa. The TV was off. The plants were, too, somehow, like a movie that had switched from color to black-and-white. It wasn't only the storm. Howie and Emily regarded each other as hungover strangers might after waking in each other's arms. The awkward depth of their intimacy matched only by the fact that everything they'd learned about the other had evaporated with the alcohol. But he'd said her name.

"It's like I'm my own coffin," Emily said. "That's what it's like."

She was explaining. But words weren't much up to it. It was like putting shoes on a headache. She told Howie about her sleep paralysis. She told him about the entities.

Howie said, "I don't understand."

"I mean, what is this?" Emily meant everything. She made an *everything* gesture with her hands.

They listened to the rain.

"I don't know how to help you," Howie said.

"You did."

"OK."

"You helped me before. You knew somehow. I'm not crazy, don't make me feel crazy, Mr. Jeffries. You know what I mean. You helped me." She could not call him Howie anymore.

"I'm sorry."

"These things are everywhere, all around us. They're laughing at us. Because this doesn't feel like it's happening. Being awake. I can't take anything seriously."

Howie said, "I know."

Quietly, "Do you?"

Did he? "I don't know."

Emily said. "Never mind. Look at me."

"OK."

She scooted away from Howie, opening a space between them. They looked into it. Their look greeted each other, acknowledged something, as if they were accomplices who'd just spoken for the first time about a crime they committed together, years before. "Do you think that you're real?" Emily asked.

Howie did not want to think about this crap.

"It's like we're puppets sitting here," Emily said. "OK, I know, enough. I'm so fucked up it isn't funny. Time terrifies me, Mr.

Jeffries. Seriously, I'm so scared of time and being stuck inside it forever. *Consciousness.*" She laughed. "What am I, you know?"

"You're Emily."

"Established. But can I be someone else now, please?"

"I doubt it."

They looked at the window.

Howie said, "It's really coming down."

"You said."

Howie remembered how Rho spoke. The way Rho splurged herself to Howie with such trusting, wanton generosity, chucking her thoughts out of her head like ballast from a sinking balloon—Rho falling around Howie in pieces. She was so unashamedly alive. Howie would speak as she did, as she might. Thinking and talking, it was a communal thing: it was the only thing that made you real among other real things. He had been unreal too long. He said, "I'm very shy."

Emily's eyes widened. "It's more than that."

"OK," he said.

"No, continue. I'm sorry."

Howie said, "I feel like an actor playing a human."

Emily laughed. "You're a terrible actor most of the time!"

"OK."

"I'm not kidding. You're the worst. Totally miscast."

Howie nodded; smiled. Nodded harder.

"Can I say, every time you smile I think you're preparing to bite me. It's going to take a while to get used to," Emily said. She touched Howie's shoulder. "No, listen, but I've never had a best friend. I always used to have a lot of friends, but nobody could get that close, like there was something wrong with me. Turns out, there *was* something wrong with me. Let's face it. The other girls knew. People know. I knew they knew, but I could never figure out what or how. That scared me. I don't think I was being paranoid. Nobody wants to be close with someone who doesn't take seriously what they take seriously. Did you ever have a best friend?"

Howie said, "My wife."

"Doris? Really?"

"Dori. In high school, that's right," he said. "I don't think that we ever should have gotten married."

"Why not?"

"But we used to have so much fun," Howie said, wonderingly.

Emily said, "What kinds of fun things did you do?"

"Well, roller-skating."

Emily gawped her mouth. *"Roller-skating?"*

"For some reason I was better at skating backward than forward; I'd go like this," and Howie stood up, gracefully chugged his arms. Closed his eyes. He laughed, too. Then sat down with the self-contained triumph of someone who had just given a successful speech.

"Oh my God, that's too much! Did you, like, win competitions?"

"It wasn't a competition," Howie said. "It was for fun."

"Mr. Jeffries."

"Well," Howie said. "People always thought that something was wrong with me. But nothing was ever really wrong with me."

"No offense," Emily said, "but I'm pretty sure that something was wrong with you."

Maybe he *was* mean, like Rho supposed. Maybe he'd been hiding in plain sight all this time: someone who hates everything safe behind the immovable mask of someone who hates everything. But it couldn't be that simple, could it? Leaving yourself alone for so long rarely is.

"I wish I'd known you then," Emily said. "Do you think we would have been friends if I was your age?"

"No," Howie said.

Emily nodded. "But I hope we would have said hello to each other once in a while."

"OK."

"More than we did for the last twenty-five years, anyway. Right? It's hard to believe that was us." Emily made a face. "For the record, that was totally your fault."

"I'm sorry I didn't try to help you sooner," Howie said.

"If it's any consolation, you probably haven't helped me. I'm still crazy."

"I don't know," Howie said.

"Me neither." Emily sighed. "I'm sorry. You have helped me, I guess. If keeping me alive is of any value."

"It is, Emily."

Something caught in Emily throat. "Well, thank you."

"What was Ethan like?"

"Wow, really?" Emily wiped a tear from her eye. "Mr. Jeffries with a question!"

She did not want to evoke Ethan Caldwell right now, her half-lived life in Boston, Les French Flowers, Boo. Ethan was a regret, not one of many but the one that could be said, in a way, to contain them all. She told Howie about the last several days that they'd spent together on Route 29.

"I made him go," she said. "I was a monster."

She said that Peppy had loved him too. She told him that she had reacted in a bad way to how much her grandfather loved Ethan and how invisible and secondary she became when Ethan was in the room. MY BOY, Peppy had called him, writing, suddenly, in full, perfectly crafted paragraphs, telling Ethan more about his past than he'd ever told her. Had she really not asked? Was that all it was? The ambitious, lost Pete Phane resurgent, proud, full of a masculine bluster that Emily hadn't even guessed. She felt like a fussy, hysterical little girl and realized that maybe she'd been kidding herself: that she'd always just been that to her grandfather. His trouble girl.

This wasn't true, of course, in fact it was unhinged, but she hadn't been getting a lot of sleep. Did she desperately need Peppy to be what he most wanted not to be: a dying, helpless old man? Had she only wanted to be his protector for once? Maybe. She hated how Ethan disrupted their balanced illusionary household.

She was not nice to Ethan. She would not fuck him; she would not put her arm around him or hold his hand. She wanted to, but she was terrified of that particular longing and where it would lead. She said it was because of Peppy, but it wasn't, and he knew it. It was because she needed him gone. Because, finally, after a few days, Peppy had begun to shut down, as she knew he would. Emily had been passed off to Ethan. Peppy was happy. He could go now.

Peppy had even told Ethan that Emily would be moving with him to New York City soon, and that he'd come and visit. He hadn't been in almost fifty years, he wrote.

SHE LOVES YOU, he wrote.

DON'T LET HER SAY OTHERWISE, he wrote.

BE PATIENT WITH HER, he wrote.

This had made Ethan cry. Emily hadn't told him that she loved him.

PLEASE TAKE CARE OF MY LITTLE GIRL, he wrote. It might have been this that set Emily off.

She made Ethan leave.

Hysterical, as they say. Angry, beyond exhausted, she told Ethan that he had to go home, that this was no place for him, up here in the middle of nowhere. He didn't belong. What did he think he was doing? She told him that she didn't love him. She threatened to call the police unless he got the fuck out, get the fuck out out out, and so he got in a taxi and headed back to the Queens Falls bus station, where, apparently, he stayed for two days, calling Emily, trying to get things to work. "I'm not giving up on you," he'd said. "You need help. I can help you. I love you."

She stopped answering the phone. It was a dream, she told herself. Ethan didn't know her, not really. He would kill Peppy. He couldn't help her. It was too late. She never spoke with him again.

Howie said, "Ethan never came back?"

Emily shook her head no. "Peppy and I never mentioned those days again. He was terrified, I know. How I behaved. But there was nothing he could do. He became worse after that, and so did I," Emily said. "I really don't know what happened after that. *This* happened after that."

"You never told Ethan about your dreams."

"They're not dreams."

"OK."

"I never told him," Emily said. "Everything would have been different if I had been able to tell him. But maybe not. Probably not."

"Your grandfather knew."

"Yeah."

They sat in silence. Howie thought about missed opportunities; he thought about Peter Phane holding baby Emily up for him to see.

"You made him a better person," Howie said, finally.

"What?"

"I saw it."

"What are you talking about?"

"Your grandfather. You made him so happy." Howie realized that he had never been brave enough to take that kind of happiness.

Emily reached out and held Howie's hand. "Thank you." She was crying. "I don't know what to believe. I'm fucking scared, Mr. Jeffries. I'm scared."

Howie said, "I'm sorry I didn't answer the phone last night."

"I'm sorry I killed your chandelier," Emily said. She sniffled, laughed. "So," she said. "The date went well?"

Howie said, "Yes, I think so."

"Is this something we can talk about? I really want to talk about something else. Do you like her?"

"Yes."

"Is she pretty?"

"Well."

Emily laughed. "But you like her."

"She happens to talk a lot."

"Perfect. But you're attracted to her, I hope? Is it serious? She's not married, is she?"

Howie did not know how to situate the reality of Emily inside the reality of Rho. "I have to see," he said.

"I'm happy for you."

"Why?"

"Yeah, that sounds like the sort of thing an ex-girlfriend would say, doesn't it?"

"Does it?"

"Kind of. Maybe I'm not happy for you. Maybe I want you all to myself and I'm terrified of you leaving." Emily felt shiftless suddenly. "Mr. Jeffries, what am I going to do now?"

Howie said, "I don't think you can stay here anymore."

"I know."

They spent the day in conversation. They were saying good-bye and hello at the same time, though neither knew where the other was actually going or, really, had been. Emily didn't go anywhere. She did not go back to her house or to sleep, though she knew that sleep was probably the first destination she'd soon have to set out for alone. Howie still planned on buying *Richard*. Safe on the sofa, they spoke about fishing together, and sailing terminology that made Emily laugh. But *Richard* was less real now; neither could imagine him without the other. Emily told him that the money was under Harriet's bed. She didn't tell him why. He didn't ask. She couldn't tell him about Harriet's e-mails. She wanted to, but that was too much of a violation now. Howie said that maybe Emily should read her e-mails and she agreed. Tomorrow, she said.

Two hours before that night's shift ended, Howie got the phone call. It was an unknown number. Between Rho and Emily, he hadn't had a decent night's sleep in almost two days.

"Dad?" the caller said. "I'm in trouble, Dad. Can you hear me? Can you come and get me, please?"

"Harri?" He almost said *Emily*.

"Please, Dad."

"In New York City?"

"Lake Jogues."

Howie actually removed the phone from his ear and looked at it, quickly, as if there was a mistake. He put it back to his ear. "I'm at work," he said. "It's three a.m."

"I know what time it is."

"Where are you?"

"Lake Jogues, I said. I don't know. The side of the road some-where in the middle of fucking nowhere. You want some land-marks? Trees trees trees trees *rain*." She was crying. "Ring a bell? Fuck it, I'm sorry, wait—" and Harri hung up.

Five minutes later, she called back. The buzz made Howie jump. Harri seemed calmer, almost matter-of-fact, as if she were talking about being picked up after school.

"OK, so I checked the GPS. I've been walking all night, trying to get a signal. I'm on this Padanarum Road. P-A-D-A-N-A-R-U-M. Do you know it? Somewhere between Bolton Landing and, I don't know, *Friday the 13th*."

His daughter was on a mountain in the middle of fucking nowhere.

"I'll be there in an hour and a half," Howie said.

"Don't tell Mom."

23

——

ad, *what* are you doing?"

"What do you mean?"

"When I'm talking. With your head."

Howie had been nodding. Howie had been smiling. He was also going very fast down Tongue Mountain. The rain had stopped and the car windows were open, roaring.

"Jesus, are you on drugs or something? I can't fucking deal with you being on drugs right now, just to be clear. Can we roll up the windows? You haven't started drinking, have you?"

"No," he said. Then he thought about Rho. "Well, maybe once."

"Once?"

"I'm just happy to see you."

"I'm happy to see you too but please enough with the nodding. Keep your eyes on the road. You're freaking me the fuck out. What is up with you? Are you wearing an earring?"

"No."

"Show me your other ear."

Howie turned his head.

Harri said, "Well, something's different."

Padanarum Road became North Bolton Road, then he turned the car off onto Lake Shore Drive. Lake Jogues opened to their left like a trap door into another, darker sky. They passed motels.

Howie said, "Now, tell me about this boy who left my daughter on the side of a mountain road."

"Holy fucking *shit*. Did you just ask me a personal question?" Harri said. Then, looking at her feet, "Oh my God, Dad! Gross! What is that?"

"It is a *Playboy* magazine," Howie said. "Now, tell me what's going on."

"Do I have to?" Harri sat low in the seat, no seat belt; she was soaking wet. "He still has all my stuff. Fucking *everything*. He has all my ideas."

"He has your ideas?"

"My notebooks. My laptop. He has my video equipment, old tapes, shit like that. I mean, he bought them, whatever, but he bought them for *me*. You know? He doesn't use them."

"He leaves you halfway up a mountain?"

"I love you, Dad, but I think I liked it better when you didn't ask questions."

Howie had finally spotted her standing on the side of a mountain road, under a canopy of pines. Harri's littleness still had the power to surprise and move him. Pulling in next to her, she looked like a seven-year-old with breast implants, hips. She was wearing denim shorts, black boots, and a bafflingly gentle, light pink blouse. Pink? His first thought was that she looked like one of those *Toddlers & Tiaras* horrors that he and Emily had watched on the TLC channel. Harri had hair now, too: long, down to her shoulders, and only the high, chopped severity of her bangs harkened back to the time when she used herself as a brutal billboard, telling her father and the world to take a good hard look at what you've wrought—and back the fuck off. She was wearing pretty jewelry. Her face was no longer pierced. She was pretty, he saw this right away: a tiny new woman. Her smile was mysterious and another thing that he had not imagined possible: that smile. Of course, the first thing that she did, before getting in the car, was hurl her telephone into the forest. "Bye bye, fuckface!" she shouted after it.

"Harri?"

"It's *his*," she had said, in explanation. She got into the car. "He has mine."

Then she was hugging him. She smelled of water-reinvigorated perfume, shampoo. It was like he hadn't picked her up from the side of the road but from a shower. Her wet head on his chest. "I'm so sorry," she said. "Thank you thank you thank you."

"It's OK."

She righted herself, and with one of Harri's classic hairpin mood turns, slapped the dashboard. "That motherfucker! I swear to God. Drive, Dad. Please get me out of here. I never want to see a tree again as long as I fucking live, I swear to God. I'm going to kill that piece of shit. Drive, drive, drive—" Howie looked behind them, and into the forest, momentarily concerned that whoever she was talking about was busting through the woods, in pursuit. "Take me home, Dad," Harri said.

"Maybe we should go for breakfast first?"

"What? I'm soaking wet here?"

"Do you want me to take you to your mother's house?"

"No, Dad! I told you. She can't know about this. I'm sorry you had to come get me but, Jesus, can you please not be such a dick about it? I've been hiding from fucking bears all night."

"You saw bears?"

Howie had been calling his house ever since he left work; no answer. It always went to his answering machine, and Howie always hung up. Emily was not supposed to be there, she had promised that she was going back to her own house, but still. Howie was anxious. There would be enough to explain—the fascinatingly stocked refrigerator, the plants, the computer on her bed, the mess of ceiling on his—without Harri coming home to Emily Phane watching TV on the sofa.

They passed through Lake Jogues Village. Howie took his phone out again, discreetly, keeping it in his lap. He tried his house again. He did not know what he would say to Emily if she did answer. How could he warn her with Harri right there?

"Who do you keep calling?"

"What?"

"What is wrong with you? The phone, Dad. You keep calling someone on the phone. Uh, that thing in your hand," Harri said. "Wait, you're not calling Mom, are you? You fucking promised!"

"Oh, my telephone," Howie said. "I'm just looking at it."

"You're just looking at your telephone." Harri grabbed it. "You're calling someone. It's ringing." She put the phone to her ear and made a small scream when she heard her own voice, recorded long ago, telling her to leave a message. "What the fuck?" she said. "That is just about the freakiest thing I've ever heard! You're calling *yourself*? Dad, you're not home, you know."

"I must have hit that by accident." Howie showed Harri his thumb. "My thumb."

"You're a maniac," she said, smiling, relieved that he hadn't been calling her mother.

Howie said, "So who is this boy?"

"Jesus, *Doris*. Did you take parent pills this morning or something? Look, if you have to know, he isn't a boy," Harri said. "But first you have to promise not to tell anyone. Meaning, your ex-wife. Specifically."

"Tell her what?"

"Exactly."

Harri had been seeing an older man for the last year or so, and it had become serious. He was in his midforties. He was a painter and an art professor at Adirondack Community College. ("Which is like being an abortion professor at Brigham Young University, but whatever.") They had, she said, more or less moved in together. She had been spending most of her time in upstate New York, subletting her Brooklyn sublet. She had not visited once. Telling so many lies she didn't know what was real anymore, she said, and she was so sorry. The man had not left her on the side of the road, exactly; he lived up there, had a studio in the mountains. They'd had a fight because, Harri said, he'd fucked one of his students, and not even a pretty one. "This cow. He wasn't even discreet about it. Thought we had an understanding, he said." So she had fled into the night, in the rain. "Like an idiot. I'm an idiot. I'm a fucking idiot. Please, don't be angry. I couldn't tell anyone."

"Why?"

"Why do you think?" Harri said. *"Mom."*

"OK."

Harri sighed. "Thing is, so, like Mom knew this guy a long time ago, I don't know, back when I was little. They had a thing. Well, you know what she was like after you guys split up. I know how this sounds but it's not like that," Harri said. She made a face. "OK, actually it is like that. It's messed up. I know it's messed up. Plus, the guy's a piece of shit. I fucked up. I hate myself enough as it is right now, OK, so please, please don't mom out on me. On top of everything, I've lost my Brooklyn place until December and I have no money, nowhere to go, and I still need funding for my project? I don't know what I'm going to do."

"I don't understand why you haven't visited," Howie said.

"Mom," Harri said. "I already told you. I didn't want her to know."

"I'm not Mom."

"Well, you're certainly doing a good impersonation today."

"Where did you meet this artist?"

"Does it matter? This lame opening in New York and he was—I don't know, Dad. He was old." Harri laughed. "Mostly old. But also different. Refreshingly unhip, like a wise, virile war correspondent type, come down from the mountain? Literally. We started talking and when it turned out that not only was he from around here but he once knew Mom, well, we sort of kept on talking—but I didn't know any of the other stuff, that they'd hooked up or what-ever, Mom and him, not until later and by that point: too fucking late. It should have seemed weird but it didn't, not at the time, and—"

"Name," Howie said.

"What? Oh. Timmy. Timmy Krogerus. I used to joke that it was his juvenile first name that kept him so young, you know, like Dorian Gray's portrait . . . Dad?"

Howie saw chandeliers.

"*Dad?*"

They got out of the car. They had not said much of anything since Timmy.

Harri slammed her door. Like everything, it seemed so much bigger than her. "Thanks for understanding," she said. "Can always count on you, Dad! Knew the nodding concerned parent routine was bullshit, but, hey, thanks for trying!"

Howie did not know what to say. She was right. He had been trying. He wasn't even half finished trying.

Harri went inside.

Howie stood in his driveway. He waited. He felt the rain-cooled sun, listened to the trees drip. Emily's house looked much like it had looked for the past month: empty, yellow. But what, he wondered, would it have looked like if she was actually inside it? Probably the same. The spinning, hateful shock of Timmy had prevented Howie from figuring out a way to forewarn his daughter about his possible houseguest.

He walked purposefully into the living room.

"Worst. Painting. Ever," Harri spat. "If I ever have to see that fucking thing again I'm going to puke."

No way, Howie thought. Not this time. He said, "I like it, Harriet."

Harri flinched. Howie wanted to scoop his daughter up and toss her back into the gigantic painting. That's where she'd come from, where the best parts of her belonged, and behind Rogers Rock, Howie noted the multiple rolling peaks of Tongue Mountain. He imagined her still up there, unseen in the painting, waiting by the side of the road. Because hadn't that always been her dearest wish? To disappear into her work.

"I should have known," she said. Her mood changing from inferno red to blouse pink. "Look at this place. I knew something was different with you. The phone calls, your *questions*. I've never seen so many plants. Dad, look at me."

He looked at her.

"Oh my fucking lord, you have a girlfriend."

Howie thought that he heard something upstairs. Howie thought of Rho. "I don't know," he said. "Not really."

"Holy fucking shit, you *do*," Harri said. Their equilibrium rebalanced. She smiled, yawned. "Look, earth-shattering details later. I need to get out of these clothes, shower, get some sleep, OK? We're probably both tired. Thank you for saving me this morning, I'm sorry for mooding out. Really. Just, hey, take the fucking painting down, would you? I don't care what you do with it just so I don't have to see it when I get up."

"No," Howie said.

"Well—"

"No."

"*But—*"

"No."

It was a start. He was done throwing fish back into the lake. Timmy's last name was *Krogerus*.

"OK," Harri said. She hugged her father. Held on tight. "I love you, Dad. Thank you."

Harri went upstairs. Moments later, Howie heard the scream.

Mr. Jeffries had gone to work, so, for one last time, or a second-to-last time, and for the first time without him there, Emily decided to sleep in his bed. She did not go home, as she'd promised. She figured he would understand. She brushed off the debris. She put the hammer on the bedside table. She got under the covers and flipped through his *Fishing the Adirondacks* book. She'd never opened it before.

This, she wondered, is what he spent so much time looking at?

The fish were ghastly, inhuman. Doll eyes and vicious toothy puckers. She couldn't believe that they were real, that they were everywhere, hovering just under the surface. She understood why people made a hobby of murdering them.

Emily thought that she deserved this last night in the safety of Mr. Jeffries's bed because only minutes after Mr. Jeffries left, Emily had gotten on the computer and written Ethan Caldwell an e-mail.

please call me 518-793-8354

That was it, but it was huge. More than enough. Mr. Jeffries's number. It meant, whatever was going to happen now, she had broken the back of Route 29. She would try. She would go away, wherever that was. She would go to sleep, if she could. She still couldn't bring herself to read any of Ethan's e-mails.

She went to sleep.

Hours later, she awoke, paralyzed. She let herself be buried, and it was terrible. She felt the bed indent next to her. She felt it there, them, and she forced herself to stare blindly into that spot and not be afraid. But she was afraid. This is the world, too, she thought, even if only I know it. The world is many things happening at the same time, in the same place, and I will have to live in all of these worlds. She felt hands on her neck, and she thought: I don't know shit. Kill me. Show me. I'm ready. Now. If you can kill me, kill me. Kill me.

Moments later, the phone rang.

Emily's eyes opened and she began crying. It was Ethan, had to be. But calling at 3:00 a.m.? Yes! He had pulled her out, like he knew. Maybe he'd always known. She did not get up to answer the phone. She wanted to but couldn't, not yet. He called several more times.

One more day, that's all. She needed one more before she could talk to Ethan Caldwell.

Emily read more about fish, learning about where they lived, what they ate, how they spawned. She didn't learn why they lived, why they ate, or why they spawned. Maybe that wasn't important.

She thought about getting out of bed, leaving Mr. Jeffries's house or getting into Harriet's bed, at least, but she couldn't move. She knew that once she left this bed that was it. She did not know what was going to happen to her once she left Mr. Jeffries's room.

Hours later, she heard Mr. Jeffries downstairs, but it was too late. It sounded like he was chatting to the TV and the TV was sassing him back. She could jump out of bed, race across the hallway to Harriet's room. Nah, too silly. She would simply apologize, tell him that she would leave at once. Last time, she'd promise, and maybe now they could even laugh at this, finally, Mr. Jeffries finding her like in the fairy tale, growling, *And someone's been sleeping in my bed.* Emily under a bedspread still covered with a dandruff of ceiling dust, one or two crystals, all manner of junk.

So it happened that the second his footsteps reached the top of the landing, where he could look directly into his room and see her, Emily, trying to make this funny, at least, picked up the hammer by the side of the bed, held it above her head, and shouted, "Surprise!"

24

———

I t had been a deeply peculiar afternoon but things, Emily supposed, were OK now. She sat on the couch in her living room in the dark. Everything smelled of smoky soggy blight. The old house was dead now, mulching itself in the humidity. It was an unredeemable fucking mess and Emily thought about better, more persuasive fires.

It grew darker.

They'd had lunch together, the three of them, six feet dangling over the stream. Harriet was a vegetarian, so they ate vegetables, though Emily tried to bring some fruit and Pringles out too, maybe some cheese, but Howie—Mr. Jeffries—territorial, suddenly, and incapable of looking directly at Emily, had said, "She's a vegetarian."

"I know, but—"

"She eats vegetables."

"Fine."

Harriet had told them about her man, money, and artist troubles—told *them*, as if they were a unit—and they'd done their best to tell her of theirs, or at least Emily had. Mr. Jeffries had hardened. He was a powerful hum, like a refrigerator filled with police. Harriet wouldn't believe that they weren't sleeping together, and the subject was so uncomfortable, so unfathomable in the light of Harriet Jeffries's wakeful presence, that they didn't try too hard to convince her otherwise. Because, uh, *how?*

They had been sleeping in the same bed. Not to mention Emily's clothing, toiletries, plants, and the very un-Howie-like perishables and Diet Dr freaking Peppers. "You got my dad to eat *sprouts*?" Emily was more represented in Howie's house than Howie had ever been.

It was still unclear to Emily, but apparently Harriet's Timmy had been an ex-boyfriend of Harriet's mother, Dori, twenty years ago. This was, understandably, a controversial subject. Mr. Jeffries was not comfortable with it, but his discomfort—or possibly anger— suited him. He was still, alert: like a Secret Service agent or spider. The worst part was that it felt like he was protecting his daughter from Emily.

She failed to explain her so-called sleep paralysis to Harriet.

"Makes sense to me. You have bad dreams," Harriet said. "So you sleep with my dad."

Emily gave up.

Harriet was no longer the teenager dressed as a corpse. She wasn't in costume. Being in love had freed Harriet, obviously, and made her less concerned with disgruntled externalities and, there- fore, even more potently in the moment. The way she used to dress, though at wanton odds with Queens Falls, had actually distorted and stunted Harriet's uniqueness.

"This is so fucked up you have no idea!" she told Emily later, in private. "I guess thank you for taking care of my dad?"

"He took care of me. I know how it must seem, but it's really not like you think, Harriet."

Harriet gave Emily an *it's me you're talking to* look. She said, "Well, to be honest, this sort of lets me off the hook. Talk about freakily fucking fortuitous."

Harriet respected the bizarre. More than respected, she deferred to it. Now that Emily was, improbably, Harriet's father's suspected girlfriend, meaning her prospective stepmother, the two girls finally connected. Emily loved that she fascinated Harriet.

"You can come back with us, you know," Harriet said. She and Emily were walking home through the woods after lunch. Mr. Jeffries had gone ahead.

"No," Emily said. She pointed to the yellow house emerging on their left. "I really do live there, Harriet."

"I'm just saying." Then, quietly, "Can I ask you a question?"

"Sure."

"Did you really set your house on fire?"

They stopped. Emily said, "Kind of."

Harriet nodded, as if she'd finally been given the answer to a mystery she'd always known the answer to. "Awesome." She squeezed Emily's hand. "Fucking awesome."

Emily lit candles. She went to her kitchen. She ate a handful of stale, chewy Honey Nut Cheerios. She opened her refrigerator and was met with a warm death burp of fungus, mold, and what looked like maggots roiling from vegetable-shaped swellings. "Oh! Oh! Oh!" Emily slammed the door, retched. Then she laughed. She imagined Mr. Jeffries standing behind her, sharing the absurdity of a poisonous refrigerator.

She missed him so much.

She lit a cigarette, took two drags, dropped it on the wet linoleum. Fzzzzz. She had no idea why the linoleum was still wet.

And she thought that the honking that she'd been hearing was a car on Route 29. But it wasn't horizontal, it was steady, didn't fade, and so Emily walked through her hallway, into the so-called living room, and looked out the window into the two steaming eyes of Howie's car.

She opened the front door.

"Emily," Mr. Jeffries shouted from the car. It was like hearing a cat bark. "Emily!"

Emily got in, buckled up. Harriet was not in the backseat. "Is everything OK? Mr. Jeffries, what's wrong?"

"I need your help," he said. The car pulled out of the driveway, onto Route 29. It plunged forward.

Emily hadn't bothered blowing out the candles because who fucking cares. Harriet was right. Emily was awesome. She said, "Where we going?"

"We are going to get my daughter's ideas back from Timmy."

They drove north, into the mountains. Emily felt safely shelled. She felt like they were fleeing a disaster that had claimed the entire world but for them. She loved how Howie's headlights stunned the forests around them, freezing trees guiltily, fleetingly, as if they'd been momentarily caught in the act of crossing the road. This was not like sitting next to Mr. Jeffries on the sofa. He was holding the remote now. This was his show.

He handed Emily a piece of paper. He said, "It's a map that Harri made."

Emily clacked on the overhead light. It didn't make any sense. "These are roads?"

"House."

Oh, Emily thought. Duh. Because even in upstate New York, *Bathroom* and *Living Room* and *Painting Studio* weren't typical town names, not to mention the gridlike road system, windows, doors, toilet. This was a detailed floor plan. Harriet had marked in which rooms she had property that they were to take back to Route 29. Two digital video cameras; a hard drive and a laptop; itemized clothing; a cellular phone and books, notebooks, toiletries, *Piece of Shit*. Harriet had placed *Piece of Shit*, clearly labeled, in a town called *Bed*, right beside *Whore Cow*.

Emily asked, "Is this Timmy guy going to be there?"

"Is he on the map?"

Was that a joke? "Mr. Jeffries, are you really OK?" Emily asked.

"Sure am."

"Well, I don't know, can we talk about before? Things feel off between us and I'm sorry. I know I shouldn't have been there. On the positive side, Harriet seemed cool with things. Once she understands that—"

"Timmy is the man my wife left me for," Howie said. He cleared his throat. "My ex-wife, Dori."

Um. "Is this really a good idea?"

"It's a pretty good idea," Howie said. "I'm sorry about this afternoon."

"That's OK."

"I didn't know how to be."

"Well, I guess you did seem different. But not in a bad way exactly. Don't worry about it. You were angry."

"Ever since I was a kid I've been afraid of ringing doorbells. But I want to now." He turned the steering wheel. "I don't think that I'm angry, Emily."

"Maybe you are."

"OK," he said. Then, "But what am I angry at?"

"That's the thing about anger," Emily said. "You're thinking about anger all wrong."

The car accelerated. He said, "Thank you for joining me tonight."

Endearingly formal, as if Emily had agreed to accompany Mr. Jeffries to a polo match and not into the mountains to confront a grown man named Timmy. Emily said, "Where else would I be."

Timmy Krogerus lived deep up inside Tongue Mountain. His house appeared to be homemade. Made, it seemed, quite literally, haphazardly, from square chunks of other homes. It was unlike anything that Howie had ever seen. He imagined that the house had started way at the top of the mountain and tumbled down like a snowball, growing larger, collecting and subsuming other houses along the way. Probably there were entire wings of the structure full of other men's children, wives, pets.

There were windows the size of walls.

There was a trailer jutting out from the side of the structure, as if docking there temporarily.

The lights were on.

The plate glass windows made the place glow like a secret, rustic department store. These were the first lights that they had seen for miles. Timmy's weedy gravel driveway crunched satisfyingly beneath the wheels of Howie's car.

They stopped. The car purred, rattled, ding ding ding ding, and fell still. Howie took the keys out of the ignition. They remained seated. Emily said, "Here we are."

It was pretty dark out there.

Howie realized that he was pretending to collect himself silently so that Emily did not think he was being too cavalier about what he was about to do. The remarkable thing was that Howie did not know what he was about to do. He did not need to collect himself because Howie was, he knew, all there.

Emily was there because he had promised Harri that he would take her along for support. He didn't want Harri to worry either.

"I don't see any cars," Emily said. "Maybe he's not home?"

"Maybe Timmy parks out back?"

"Where is out back?"

She was right. Besides the strip of driveway, there wasn't anything but forest and Timmy's house. There was no real yard, no lawn, just some rooty trails and piles of scrap metal that Howie knew enough about art to know was art. "Look," he pointed. "Some art."

"What?" Emily said. "That's just redneck junk. Do you want me to do the talking?"

"But it's also art," Howie insisted. "What would you like to talk about?"

"Do you want me to talk to Timmy, I mean."

"No," Howie said. "Do you have the map?"

"You think we'll need it?"

"Of course we'll need it."

Emily was being weird. Howie opened the door. The forest

wheezed around him like laughing gas, like gas that was actually laughing, and Howie made what he imagined to be a pleasant noise, very nearly a hoot. Or maybe I'm being weird, Howie thought.

"What's so funny?" Emily asked.

Trees? The pine trees? The scent of them on this improbable lukewarm evening? That his daughter had been hiding up here with the same fellow who'd broken up his marriage almost twenty freaking years ago? Howie listened to the insects, the wind, the hilarious rustle of nighttime critters, and somewhere, over in the dark to their right, water tickled rocks. What *wasn't* funny? Howie said, "Watch your step."

Cautiously, Emily followed.

The entire day had been like a dream where you find yourself doing something very bad and enjoying it. Perhaps I *have* been angry. There'd been a dredging. Howie's past rearing up and laughing, once again, in his face, and it did not frighten him. That was the big surprise. How strong he felt. This is how he should have taken care of Emily all along. They should have been going on dangerous missions from the get-go.

Emily said, "But shouldn't we have a plan?"

"We have a map."

"Please shut up about the map, Mr. Jeffries! You're seriously starting to freak me out."

"OK."

The plan was to retrieve Harri's property. Then they would see what else. There was no doorbell, which was a significant disappointment to Howie, who'd counted on one. He knocked. Emily watched. He knocked hard, harder, now looking at Emily, showing off, like: Would you look at me knocking the shit out of this door?

"That's probably enough," Emily said.

Nobody answered.

Howie said, "Open up, please."

"I think maybe we should come back tomorrow?"

Howie admired his fist, his knuckles. He knocked again. He was not going home without retrieving what Timmy Krogerus had stolen from his family. Howie watched his right hand try the doorknob. "It's open," he said.

He walked inside. Emily, from behind, grabbed his hand, pulling him back. But nope. Howie pulled her into the house, where they then stood, briefly, holding hands like new homeowners.

Emily said, "Shit."

They let go of each other's hands but stood close, neither moving. "Timmy Krogerus," Howie said. He raised his voice. "Hello! Excuse me!"

Emily giggled nervously. She nudged him, whispered, "Tell him about the map."

Good idea. "Timmy!" Howie said. "We have a map!"

The room was both gigantic and cozy, all shipwrecked wood, exposed brick, overlapping Persian rugs; it reminded Howie of an Italian puppet theater that he and Dori had once taken Harri to in New Hampshire. This was the kind of room where inanimate objects became imbued with life, magic, and Howie experienced a sudden wave of happiness. Happiness, of all things. Or was it relief? He looked about him.

The room was robust, too. There were so many healthy objects to snag your eyes on. The room was a community unto itself. Books everywhere, both in breeze-block shelves and in piles, on chairs, under lamps. The brick walls, of which there were two, were painted white; they were empty. The log walls, however, were hung with paintings, elaborate European masks, animal horns, primitive crockery, black-and-white photographs of naked people, and an old Sunoco gas station sign from Howie's childhood. The kitchen, which occupied a corner of the room, was as modern a kitchen as Howie had ever seen. It made him think of astronauts. There was a table made of glass and wood in the center of the room. The safe, motherly smell of well-seasoned food recently prepared, eaten, enjoyed; cigarettes, too, and something that reminded Howie of Rho. Illegal drugs? Probably, yes, illegal drugs. If only Rho could see him now, Howie thought. There were extinguished candles everywhere, poking from wine bottles and rising from giant, colorful melted mounds of wax. There was a record player, which was still on, spinning, record at an end. The speakers played amplified, circular fuzz. Playing cards; sketch pads; lots of interesting hats and things made of leather. Two almost emptied glasses of red wine; three empty bottles. Piles of big city newspapers and art magazines and a gigantic sofa, which looked as soft and welcoming as any that Howie had ever seen. Pillows that somehow managed to look both soft and manly.

Howie did not need a map to know that he was where his wife had wanted to be instead of with him. He was where his daughter had been when she had told everyone that she was with him. He understood now. He wanted to be here too.

"Mr. Jeffries, I think we should go," Emily said.

"Where?" They were finally here.

"He might have a rifle," Emily said. "I'm serious. C'mon, he obviously doesn't want to be—"

Howie said, "Timmy Krogerus?"

The house was empty. Howie knew it. For whatever reason, Timmy Krogerus had gone out, drove off, leaving the lights on because maybe if you lived in a house this wonderful you never wanted to turn it off.

No doubt, Timmy was driving his dinner companion home. He would be back shortly.

"He could be in another room," Emily whispered.

Or, yes, Howie conceded. He could also be waiting in the dark in another room with a rifle.

Howie asked to see the map. Emily took it out. "Look," she said. Emily pointed to things in this room that were on the map. Cell phone on a speaker. Laptop internet computer next to the sofa.

"Good," Howie said. "Could you please get them?"

Emily got them.

Howie looked around. "Is there anything else belonging to my daughter in this room?"

"Mr. Jeffries, please please please. Let's *go*. We can come back for the rest tomorrow, I promise. You're supposed to shoot people who do this sort of thing. Listen to me, I'm not kidding, it would be totally cool for Timmy to shoot us if he wanted to."

Howie told her to go put the laptop internet computer and the cell phone back in the car.

"I'm not leaving you alone," she said.

"Then put them on the porch."

She did as she was told.

Howie walked through Timmy's puppet theater, past the accumulated treasures of a life well lived. There were three doors. He chose the second. "Where does this lead?" he asked.

"Prison? Gunshot wound to the chest?"

"The second door, Emily."

Emily looked at the map. Sighed. "Toward Piece of Shit and Whore Cow," she said. "Apparently."

The bedroom was dark. It smelled of socks, pine sap, cigarettes. Howie could not find the light but did not, in fact, try very hard. He did not wish to see the bed. Emily stumbled forward, rooted out a stack of Harri's clothing, and said, "We're good, let's go."

"Isn't the bathroom attached to the bedroom?"

"Harriet can buy a new toothbrush."

"Shampoo."

"Mr. Jeffries."

"OK." He supposed that she was right. Then Emily was off, down another hall to a new part of the house. She scooped a few small items up. Howie, momentarily disturbed by the bedroom, followed. "Where are we going now?" he asked.

"Most of Harriet's notebooks and cameras and stuff are through here," Emily said. Then, "This is kind of fun, actually. You're right. We should do this more often."

"What do you think of the house?"

"Are you serious? What do I think?" Emily said. "I think fucking creep is what I think. The whole place smells of sleazeball."

"Oh." Howie did not expect that. He had expected that Emily saw what he saw. "I like it here," he said. "This is a really nice house."

"What, like from a design perspective?"

Howie said, "Do you think that it's my fault?"

"No," Emily said. "Jesus, no. What are you even talking about?"

"Nothing," Howie admitted.

"It's not your fault."

"To think that I've always been afraid of this house."

"*This* house?"

Well, all houses. Or was that all people? Or only himself? But why? Howie was having a peculiar freaking day. "I don't know," he said. "But I like this house."

"Well, great, but can we talk about it later?"

"OK."

They both stopped.

Emily whispered, "Did you just—?"

They listened.

They heard wind. Tree. They heard windy trees coagulate into car. Pickup truck. Something. It was difficult to say if the something stopped outside Timmy's house, on the driveway, or if the something had faded down the road, back into Tongue Mountain.

"Mr. Jeffries?"

They did not hear a car door open or close. Listen. They waited. Then, from somewhere in the house, a telephone rang. Emily jumped, grabbing Howie, her nails digging into his arm. Her hand made Howie feel in control. Eventually, an answering machine picked up and they heard Timmy's recorded voice. "Hey, I'm not around, but if you leave a message . . ." Timmy did not sound like a Timmy. He sounded rugged, bemused, comfortable as a leathery old baseball glove. He sounded more like a Billy or a Bruce.

Harri, leaving the message, sounded worried. "Timmy, you motherfucker, pick up. I swear to God. I'm going to call the police. I'm calling the police right fucking now. If anything happens to my dad . . ."

BEEP!

Howie loved that voice so much. He smiled.

Emily said, "You do realize that your daughter's calling the police on us?"

Howie considered this.

Emily said, "For the sake of argument, we have what, fifteen minutes? Twenty minutes? The nearest police station . . ."

"Then hurry up."

Emily shook her head, laughed. Showed him the map. "I think we're almost done. You get the cameras and notebooks in this room, and I'll go through Timmy's so-called Shit Studio, which is right here, and get her electronic stuff. Whatever that means. It's in a cardboard box which is right *there*."

Howie said, "Thank you, Emily."

"I like *your* house, Mr. Jeffries," Emily told him. "For the record. Look at me. You have the best house."

Howie said, "It's not a competition."

Emily found the light switch of Timmy's Shit Studio. On the map, Harriet had written it with dollar signs. *$hit $tudio*

Light revealed dozens of large paintings situated around the room like windows. It was the same painting, in various states of completion.

"Oh, no," Emily said. "Oh my God."

It was the painting of Rogers Rock that Harriet had given to Mr. Jeffries for his fiftieth birthday.

Emily turned to shut the light off, leave the room, tell Mr. Jeffries that the box she sought was missing, elsewhere, mislabeled—*he can never see this*—but she turned and Mr. Jeffries was already there, standing in the doorframe, arms full of Harriet's property, seeing this. Emily watched a smile of pleasure and recognition crack his face. Then she watched it freeze.

"Timmy," he said, as if being introduced. Like Timmy was standing there in the room next to Emily, holding out his hand.

"We don't have much time," Emily said. "Let's get out of here."

Mr. Jeffries walked past her, over to one of Timmy's paintings. This one was less than half done, only the lake really completed, the rock itself sketched in, as if covered by a fog. There were no mountains, no sky. He touched the water, leaving a single fingerprint, like the crest of a wave in the middle of Lake Jogues. "It's really good," he said.

"I guess."

"It's really good to see how it's made." Howie stepped back. Stopped. He turned and walked from the room.

They drove deeper into the mountains, the backseat of Mr. Jeffries's car loaded with newly liberated ideas. Ten minutes ago they'd passed two police cars driving up Tongue Mountain.

Emily felt as if she were on the verge of giggling, weeping, *something*; maybe just bouncing in place a little? She did this. She stopped. The fizz of impossible things happening. Having happened. Though all they'd really done was walk out of Timmy's hippy jam of a house undetected, Emily felt as if she'd scratchlessly escaped an explosion. She felt more alive than she had in years.

Mr. Jeffries turned the radio on, searched around the dials, finally stopping at a classical station. It sounded like they were driving through a swarm of golden, morose insects. Emily couldn't see his face. It was hard to say how he was feeling.

It was past midnight.

"Where are we going?" Emily asked.

Nothing.

"Mr. Jeffries?"

"OK."

"OK isn't a place."

They were not going home. Neither of them, Emily realized, was wearing a seat belt.

Emily needed to talk. "So, you wanna break into some more houses, or what?"

He did not.

Fine. "Do fish sleep?" Emily asked. Because you can't beat fish. Still nothing.

Emily pressed on. "I always wondered. I know they don't have eyelids. I bet they don't sleep."

"They do," Mr. Jeffries said, finally. "But not like us."

Speak for yourself. Emily felt sad, suddenly. She said, "We never got to go fishing."

They drove down from the mountains. They drove into a series of newly built neighborhoods somewhere outside of Lake Jogues Village. Emily noted their names. Evergreen Estates. Bedford Close. Helen Drive. Heinrick Circle. Suburban developments that had lost their way, gotten lodged up here between the mountains; subdivisions from Long Island or New Jersey or TV, stranded, fearful. There was no cover. Few trees surrounded these homes. The streets were smooth, silent. The windows had all been switched off for the night, but the structures glowed like CGI, like 3D, lit by rows of plastic Victorian lamps. Silvery sedans slept in driveways, eyes open. Howie drove slowly, and Emily began to feel dreamy, nice, as though she might fall asleep the way people did in houses like this on TV. Perhaps that was their actual destination. The lawns looked like they were made of Muppet skin. Emily smiled. She still had the map. Maybe here was the way to sleep.

"Seriously, Mr. Jeffries," Emily yawned. "Where we going?"

Howie would know what he was looking for when he found it. But wasn't that a lot of crap? Maybe you need to pretend to have an idea of what you're looking for before you find anything really worthwhile.

They did another circuit through the neighborhoods.

The development had the feel of one of Timmy's unfinished

paintings. Howie imagined opening the front door of one of the houses, stepping inside, creating his own puppet show, animating his own objects. For the first time in more than thirty years Howie realized that he could move house if he wanted to. Howie could freaking *move*.

"You thinking about the painting?" Emily asked.

Not exactly. But he said, "I'm fifty years old."

"I know what you mean."

Did she? Howie said, "It was a birthday present. It was Drew told me that she'd painted it. Probably because he'd asked Harri and what else was she going to say?"

"Uh, *I didn't paint it?*"

"She knew I'd love it."

Emily almost said something. She winced, smiled. Then she closed her eyes.

Howie sped up. He turned right, then left, right, and in an hour they were on Route 29. OK was a place. Howie's daughter was waiting for him—and Emily. Emily beside him sleeping safe and sound.

Emily & the Household Spirit

S he eventually took a bath on the sale of her Route 29 house. The economy, Emily kept hearing. *The economy*, invoked like the name of a good pal who'd been killed doing something stupid, like wrestling alligators. She'd been strongly advised to wait until the market improved, but whatever, Emily needed to improve first and, she knew, getting rid of Route 29 was step one.

Ethan came to call it her *hongza*, or calamity house. Hong Kong, he explained, had a secret database of such places, so why not Queens Falls? *Hongzas* were homes in which remarkably unhinged murders, suicides, or other horrors had occurred. It was a genuine problem, since real estate entered into the *hongza* database lost most of its worth, and depending on the ferociousness of the horror, otherwise innocent floors of Hong Kong high-rises could plummet in value, forever trapping neighboring residents who were suddenly unable to sell. Who wanted to buy a haunted house? Killing yourself in Hong Kong, unless you really wanted to fuck with your neighbors, was an act better accomplished out of doors, off a bridge, in the street. Ethan said he wasn't joking. Emily hadn't been laughing.

She sold her house to a lawyer representing another, richer lawyer from Manhattan. That was nearly five years ago. She invested her Route 29 money—plus the sale of her Mazda and an otherwise aimless hunk of investments Peppy left her—into purchasing a percentage of Les French Flowers. Boo used Emily's money to open Les French Flowers Deux, in Newton. They were partners. Boo managed Newton, Emily the old Jamaica Plain shop, though for the past few years, due to the demands of her PhD, Emily had a tattooed curiosity named Hunter helping out. If all went well, Hunter would soon be taking over Emily's responsibilities. Ethan and Emily were leaving Boston. Probably. Ethan was awaiting word on a junior State Department position in Seoul, South Korea. Emily, meanwhile, had applied for a research grant that would place her at the International Laboratory of Plant Neurobiology at the University of Florence in Italy.

They'd been through far too much bullshit, pain, and spectacular weirdness to let their improbable careers get in the way of their improbable relationship. Emily was already looking into research possibilities in Korea, and Ethan was already poking around Edward Gibbon and a few books about the Medicis. He knew very little about the Old World, and the idea of being the only Korean in Florence excited him, he said, even though he wouldn't be, and, as Emily pointed out, he wasn't. The real worry was that they'd both get exactly what they wanted.

Taking things seriously had changed Emily's relationship with time. It had been the slowest five years of her life. She made mistakes. But her mistakes were now more like the mistakes that someone might make during her first few months navigating a foreign country with a foreign alphabet. Emily didn't set anything inappropriate on fire. She didn't forget to sleep. Everything just felt so real. Had everything always been so real? Had there always been *so much* of everything? So much all the time?

She could barely remember the first few months she spent in New York City, subletting Harriet's Brooklyn sublet. They'd traded. Harriet squatted in Emily's Route 29 house, working on her art, growing closer to her father and getting some distance, then closeness, distance, closeness, and then more distance from *motherfucking Timmy*. Timmy Krogerus repaired Emily's house. He even moved in there for a while with Harriet. From there he helped Mr. Jeffries do all sorts of lovable damage to *his* house, including a log cabin–like extension that didn't seem to serve any purpose whatsoever but, Harriet said, had been fun for the both of them to build. They also constructed an equally useless dock out by the Kayaderosseras. They'd sit there, fish. Sometimes they'd paint. Timmy had started giving Mr. Jeffries lessons. But he might as well have been painting with his fingers, Harriet told Emily; no matter how much Timmy guided him, Mr. Jeffries's landscapes had more in common with Harriet's woeful old rust and pus abstractions than any lake or mountain she'd ever seen. "He's tenacious now is the thing. Dad won't give up on his lake."

But Emily, in NYC, had been far from that. The city was palpable dislocation. It took Professor Ethan Caldwell two weeks before he would even meet her for a quick coffee, a beverage neither of them even liked. He had PhD responsibilities. He had moved on. Memories of Emily would occasionally seize up in Ethan like cramps, he'd tell her, but he never thought that they'd ever have anything more than a haunted friendship. Frankly, he was enraged that this squawky and *monstrously* irresponsible Harriet person—who'd initially contacted Ethan—had actually thought it was a good idea for Emily to come down to New York City in the first place. What had she been thinking? Emily wasn't his responsibility anymore, and he told Harriet this and, also, how did you get my number? Who are you?

Now, of course, Emily and Ethan looked back on the fits and fumbles of their Harriet-enabled time in NYC as *romantic*, but back while it was happening it had been hell. Especially for Emily.

It took time.

Boston, of course, came after that, and then Emily's big idea. Les French had been, in retrospect, about negotiating a controlled crash landing into the idea of a normal life. Ethan knew it was premature, a mistake, but it wasn't, he'd later tell her, the sort of mistake that he thought she'd really come to regret. He knew that she would find another path, but he also clearly saw that she'd require a safe place from which to begin figuring her shit out.

Because all that while, Emily still felt as if she could, at any moment, slip back into the place that Mr. Jeffries had rescued her from. And whether she jumped or she was pushed, she had found the courage to allow her days the same degree of reality as her nights, even if there hadn't yet been any real reconciliation between her two states. The nocturnal assaults continued. They would, like the student loans she took out to pay for her education, torment her for the rest of her life.

Now, waiting to hear from Italy, and several months after her controversial paper on plant signaling and behavior (in relation to *ayahuasqueros* and the shamanic religious practices of the indigenous rain forest tribes of Brazil), Emily would occasionally joke with colleagues that she'd arrived at many of her hypotheses by losing her mind. Her work was undeniably eccentric, but it was never less than rigorously supported. You need otherworldly patience to work with plants in the way that she did, not just slowing yourself down to their speed, but, in a sense, to their dimension. Watching grass grow is easy, Emily would say. *Try watching it speak.* It would take many more years, dozens of papers, and then her popular-science book before the quietly revolutionary extent of her work on so-called plant consciousness would be fully appreciated.

Ethan had been the one to introduce Emily to what he called "the world of crackpot comparative religions." This was shortly before they returned to Boston together. He'd said that some of her unusual states of consciousness were discussed in this or that book, and so she started exploring. Cheondoism, Transcendental Meditation, Nyingma Buddhism, you name it. Real esoteric stuff, too. Chakras. Trance states. Kundalini yoga. For a few months, Emily had been dazzled. It was like suddenly finding ladders and handles and guide ropes all over a world that she'd previously thought of as unmanageable and perilous. Ethan had studied a lot of this stuff and knew it as one might know a dead language. He was proficient.

He was academic. He didn't believe a fucking word. This helped Emily from falling in too deep. Because she did begin, finally, to sleep a little better. Or, rather, *stronger.* This stuff made space for her experiences in a way that hinted at a possible integration of her waking life and her sleeping life.

The propitious end of Emily's new age and, therefore, the start of her scientific journey came swiftly. Her readings had taken her to a book about Siberian shamans. The book's old photographs of the shamans with their high, lonesome faces hypnotized her at first; she couldn't figure out why. Then they spooked the crap out of her, and she realized exactly why. *She'd seen them before.* It was like when she was little and she'd stare into the mirror, subtracting Peppy and Nancy and Gillian from her face. There was that face again, looking back at her from this book. From Siberia, 1906. Too much. Then Emily read exactly how a future shaman was identified. Children with extreme night terrors, exactly like hers had been, would be taken from the village and taught to control their access to the other world. Otherwise, it was said, that access would go bad. Without proper training, it would leak in and destroy them.

No shit, Emily thought.

They were doors. Translators. But mostly they were taught to deal with plants. To commune with plant spirits, so-called. To use the wisdom of the plants to heal and do whatever—to play drums and sit in a tent and diddle around with animal bones, teeth, chunks of bark. Emily told Ethan all about it.

"You want to start playing the drums now?"

"I want to go back to school."

Science would not be a phase. Where once Emily felt estranged from academia and research—from reality, really—suddenly she needed to know more. Emily threw herself into studying the biochemistry of plants, learning about their behavior, their intelligence and signaling, the way they used chemistry to talk. She needed to know how plants communicated and she wanted, she said, to make contact. To talk back. Chemistry was a gorgeous language, and

Emily became proficient. Over the years, she would come to think of herself as a translator as much as a scientist.

Boo, checking through Les French's mail, said, "Something special for you, Emily." She flapped it in the air.

Ethan and Emily stood, expecting it was about Italy, though they both knew that Emily would no doubt be notified via e-mail. Or cell phone. Science, after all.

Boo went snip snip tie snip back to her flowers.

The envelope looked as if it were sent from Victorian England. It contained a heavy card of some sort. It felt and looked like an invitation to a wedding.

"Harriet Jeffries," Emily read the return address. "I don't believe it."

Ethan said, "You don't think—?"

"Timmy's not getting any younger."

Emily opened the envelope.

It was an invitation, but not to a wedding. "Oh my God, it's her opening. New York City. West Chelsea. Solo show. Ethan, it looks pretty serious."

Emily turned the card over. The photograph on the front stopped her cold.

Ethan said, "You all right?"

"What?"

"Did she mention this to you?"

"I haven't really talked with her in a few months . . ."

"What's the matter?"

Emily shook through it. "Nothing," she said. "I mean, I knew she was working on something, the mysterious Route 29 project, that there was a big-time gallerist who was sort of interested?"

"But there was always a big-time gallerist who was sort of interested."

"Exactly."

"Seriously, what's wrong with you? Let me see that." Ethan

looked at the picture on the front of the card. "Whoa, is that what she's doing now? Photographing war criminals?"

"*That's Howie,*" she snapped. Emily snatched the card back. "That's Harriet's father. That's just how his face looks."

"Sorry about before," Ethan said. "I didn't know. I should have known."

Emily was reading a new paper on decision making in plants. Instinct versus behavior. How the trajectory of a root, for example, responds to subtle environmental cues that go well beyond the instinctual. She turned around. Ethan was holding two glasses of red wine.

"Well," Emily said. "It took me twenty-five years to see past that face."

"It's an interesting face."

"Yeah," Emily said. But, to be honest, the face had derailed her. She felt bereft. She often felt like this when she thought about Mr. Jeffries. It was almost as if she didn't know *how* to miss him. "What is it, Ethan, why are you smiling like that?" Then, fully noting the wine, said, "Oh, no, no, no. I've got to work. Later, OK?"

Ethan didn't budge. "You didn't check our voice mail," he said.

"No," she said. "What?"

Then she knew what.

Ethan placed a glass of wine in Emily's hand, softly, here. "It's Italian," he said. "Florentine. Brunello di Montalcino. It's made from *grapes.*" Ethan sipped the wine. "Not quite *soju,* but I'll get used to it."

"Ethan?" Emily was standing.

He shook his head. "I didn't get the job," he said, simply. "I'm so proud of you, Emily."

Seven years later, in Seoul, Emily would learn at a diplomatic dinner party that Ethan hadn't even applied for the job. He'd been offered it cold. It was so romantic, another diplomat's wife said, pulling Emily aside, whispering, sideways glancing at Ethan. That he'd been willing to turn down *that* position, this woman said. It should have killed his career, you know. You guys shouldn't even be here. The woman made a noise then, a Korean noise that meant love can sure make people do idiotic fucking things but isn't that the dream? Isn't it all a dream?

Emily hadn't really spoken to Harriet in a year or so, though they were never too far apart online. Harriet was fond of sudden Google Chat barrages, always irreverent, manic, profane, but never too revealing, and Emily, when she thought about it, would send Harriet updates letting her know that she was thinking about going to Italy, for example, or that she missed her.

For one year, they'd relied on each other, instant BFFs, even if they were rarely in the same place at the same time. When Emily was in Harriet's calamity NYC sublet, Harriet was in Emily's Route 29 calamity house. Total *hongza*-ville. But they talked constantly then, nearly every day, supporting each other through Timmy and Ethan and whatever the hell were they supposed to do now. Sometimes Harriet would come down to NYC and they'd share her small room for a few days or a week, Harriet taking a breather from the middle of nowhere. They'd spend the night watching crap TV, talking through the nature of reality and the rules of beauty, and they'd order Chinese food, sushi, the occasional bottle of vodka. Emily never visited Harriet in Queens Falls.

Then Emily moved to Boston and Harriet moved back to New York City.

The blizzard, which the Weather Channel had given a suitably Old Testament name, had begun shortly after Ethan and Emily left Jamaica Plain for Harriet's gallery in Manhattan. Jebediah was the end of the world disguised as Christmas Eve. The mute, white lack of highway visibility made everything feel deceptively safe and cozy inside Ethan's car, like the whole world was a puffy white airbag. You really couldn't drive more slowly. They listened to a *Learn Ital-*

ian While You Drive set of CDs, Ethan picking it up so quickly that Emily figured he must be cheating.

"How can I be cheating?"

"Your memory is cheating," Emily said. "I don't know. Stop it."

"Grazie per la pizza."

To even the score, Emily told Ethan all about the latest developments in the study of psychotropic biochemistry. Ethan had some new weird facts about Italy, specifically Roman history, which, not atypically, he'd lately become somewhat obsessed with. Did Emily know about Caligula's horse? They talked, loosely, about getting married. It'd make their lives easier abroad. Residency papers, visas, taxes, work permits. Then, following the close call of a truck skidding out in front of them, Ethan pulled the car over and they talked, even more loosely, about having sex. They opted for second base.

They were going to be incredibly late.

They got to Chelsea a little after eleven. The opening was to have started at eight. New York City was muffled white; very few cars on the streets. There were cross-country skiers, though, and adults pulling other adults down the sidewalks on sleds. Buried cars created igloos on the sides of the streets.

Ethan dropped Emily off and went searching for a parking garage. The snow clumped on Emily's face. It went under her sleeves, down her neck. Inside her ears. The gallery was as white as the city outside. It was sparsely crowded, the floor wet, muddy. There didn't seem to be any art whatsoever.

"Phane!" Harriet Jeffries said. "I can't believe it's you, you made it. I mean, *how* did you make it? You come by bobsled? You look incredible, I love your hair. It's so—no longer there!"

Emily's hair was still very much there; it was only shorter. It had been that way for more than a year. But Harriet was off. "You look like a mystical freckled fawn or something. God fucking damn you. So is this mad scientist Emily I've been hearing so much about? I love it. I really can't believe you're here. But where's Ethan?"

"Finding a parking garage?"

"Half the people I know in New York stayed in because of this so-called blizzard, like people who live a few blocks from here, I swear to God. You'd think it was nuclear fallout or something. New Yorkers are grateful for the impeccable excuse. They love natural disasters; it means everyone can stay in and not feel like they're missing out on anything. But *you* make it."

"Well, there's never anything really going on in Boston."

"You drove all the way from Boston?"

"Harriet, we live in Boston!"

"I know, I *know*." Harriet made a frazzled noise. "I'm sorry, this whole week has been—" and Harriet's face did a terrifying impression of this whole week.

Emily placed a calming hand on her friend's shoulder. "I'm so happy for you. This is amazing. You look so great."

She did, too. Harriet was wearing an odd bouquet of clothing and her hair was even longer now, but coiled atop her head. She managed to look both radiant and unsteady, like a tiny porcelain vase balancing on a stick. *But where was the art?*

Harriet said, "Emily, come here, you really have to meet Samir, my gallerist."

"Do I, really?"

Harriet stopped, laughed. "Of course not, what am I fucking talking about! Jesus ladybird Christ. Shoot me. OK, calm down."

Emily bent down and kissed Harriet's forehead.

Harriet beamed. "I thought the Valium would take the edge off." Whispering: "But maybe the coke put it back on? I think it's going well. Let's get some wine. You want some wine?"

"No, thanks."

"Well, pretend you do. You have to hold *something*. Look, there's Vulcan art slut Venetia Cole with the guy from *Artforum*. Come with me, Emily," she said. "I've got to talk with some people. For the next twenty minutes you are not allowed to abandon me or judge me or let me out of your scientific sight."

Emily followed.

Moments later, "People, this is Emily Phane, my sister slash BFF slash woman who kind of made this all possible. Some of you might remember me camping out in her creepy-ass house. Well, Emily here was the one who set that motherfucker *on fire*."

"Where is it?" Emily finally asked. "The art, Harriet?"

"Where is my father, more like."

Her father?

Harriet asked, "Were the roads really bad? He should have been here hours ago. He left around noon. He texted from Albany, what, twelve hours ago? Mom and Drew were like, No way we're driving down in *that* for *art*."

"Your father is coming to New York?"

"Can you believe it? He's the real star here, anyway, you know."

Emily did not know.

Except for on Facebook, Emily had not seen Mr. Jeffries since she left Route 29 for New York City, nearly five years ago. They were friends on Facebook.

The way Emily felt about Howie Jeffries went beyond missing him. She mourned him. She didn't know why.

She kind of knew why.

They had not been able to maintain their friendship after Harriet had arrived; they no longer fit. It passed from them like a dream. They'd both woken up. It had freed Emily from Queens Falls, sent her packing. He had his daughter now. Emily had had nobody.

That time in Emily's life was so difficult to reconcile with her life now, but sometimes she would wake at night, after an attack, say, or after Ethan shifted in bed, and she'd think that Mr. Jeffries was there next to her. Howie, she'd think. She'd remember the sound of his snoring, his protection. His intuitive hand pulling her safely out of hell.

Harriet had quickly realized that Emily and her father had not been romantically involved. But still, she rarely talked about that time either, which was odd for her. Emily, likewise, had minimized her time with Mr. Jeffries when discussing it with Ethan, who still assumed that it was Harriet who had saved Emily. "Harriet's father helped me when I accidentally set my house on fire," she'd told him. "Then Harriet came, as you know, and got me out of there, to New York City, to you, and . . ."

It was one of the few things she hadn't been exactly honest with Ethan about.

Emily didn't feel as if anything had been wrong with her relationship with Mr. Jeffries; just the opposite. It was more that she still didn't know how to think about those few months—or, indeed, the years preceding them—and she didn't want anyone else thinking about that time for her, telling her what happened, what any of it meant. It was hers, whatever it had been, and it was his too. She didn't want anyone's hands messing up her perfect friendship with Howie Jeffries.

OK, so Emily stalked him a little on Facebook. Once every few weeks, just checking it, picking through Howard Jeffries's online trail, and sometimes she even posted things specifically for him to see. There was, for example, an entire article about how beige was the color of the season. She found amusing cartoons about fish. Her way of saying hey. He would, without fail, Like these posts. His way of saying OK.

Because he knew.

Two years ago, Mr. Jeffries sold his house on Route 29 to the same Wall Street lawyer who occupied Emily's house. This happened around the same time that he had changed his Facebook status to "married." It looked like he currently lived somewhere in the eighteenth century, near a pond.

But how happy he looked now in the over-Instagrammed selfies that Rhoda Jeffries constantly posted and tagged him in. Emily had only seen him that relaxed when he'd been asleep. He had a dog named Kevin. He did not have a boat named Richard. He had learned to ski. He'd gained weight. His face hadn't exactly softened, but it was no longer the sort of thing you'd mistake for a cliff.

Harriet told Emily that the only time her father really mentioned anything about Emily was when, while packing up Emily's stuff, he'd asked her if she could please maybe not mention to Rho that Emily had once stayed with him. Emily had been the first secret that Harriet and her father had ever shared. They'd bonded over Emily's nonexistence.

Emily mourned Mr. Jeffries more than her grandfather. Peppy was less gone, in a sense, and Emily understood their time together, knowing that her life and happiness were testament to her grandfather. Her love for Peppy infused everything that she would ever do—and everyone she would ever love, from Ethan to the two children they would have together. Peppy was never far from any of them. Mr. Jeffries's loss was more complex.

"Rho's coming too," Harriet said. "I forget, have you met Rho?"

"No," Emily said.

"Rho is beyond the fucking pale. She's like the upstate New York version of one of those prehistoric Venus figurines."

"What?"

"Let me call him again," Harriet said. She called her father. "Jesus," she said. She wondered at her phone, held it ringing before her. "What the hell, Emily."

"I'm sure he's all right," Emily said. "He's an excellent driver."

"Yeah," Harriet said. "Yeah." But she had clouded. "I'm worried. I'm stoned, actually, a little, but I'm also worried. Does one cancel out the other? Why won't he answer?"

"I'll try Ethan."

"Nothing?" Harriet asked.

Emily shook her head. Stopped calling Ethan. Through the giant plate glass window you could hardly see the other side of the street now. It was the angriest that Emily had ever seen snow. They watched that.

"Maybe the lines are down?" Harriet supposed, quietly. "Do phones still work on lines? Maybe the satellites are down."

Emily called Les French Flowers Deux. Boo, working late, answered; Emily talked to Boo for a short while. Yes, everything was OK, they'd arrived.

"Try someone in New York," Emily suggested.

Harriet put the phone to her ear. On the other side of the room, ringing. "Hey, Asa," Harriet said. "Everything cool over there?"

Asa looked up, saw Harriet and Emily. "You two considering this side of the room?" he asked.

They tried Mr. Jeffries again, and then Ethan, then Mr. Jeffries again. Then they agreed that they wouldn't call for another fifteen minutes. Six minutes later they tried again. Still nothing.

Harriet led Emily into the darkened back room of the gallery. "Here it is," she said. There were ten large screens, ten digital projections. Harriet said that it was called *The Household Spirit*.

"My father finally loaned me the money to finish it," Harriet said. "Obviously. It's about him, anyway. I wanted to keep it kind of a secret from you, so you could see it fresh. I filmed it back when you were in Brooklyn, you know, and I've been editing it, on and off, ever since. Nearly four years? It runs for a day or two, about thirty-eight hours straight." She explained the project. Emily listened.

Harriet said, "But look, I think you're just in time."

"For what?"

They stood looking at the screens.

"He's about to come home."

On each screen a different view of Mr. Jeffries's Route 29 house. It was night. It was autumn. The videos had been slowed down to way less than half speed. Trees dropped leaves in a slow, thick, watery wind. They took forever to reach the ground.

Emily stood alone, surrounded by Mr. Jeffries's house. In front of her, beside her, behind her. She was both inside and outside: walled in by the outside of his house. Spatially, it was disorienting. Where was he? Emily needed to see him.

Emily sat on a cushion on the ground. She placed both of her palms on the ground. Every window in Mr. Jeffries's house was open, lighted. One window per screen. Then there was a screen for the driveway. The roof. The doors. You could see perfectly inside each room, but the colors were off. Brighter than they should be. It took Emily a moment to realize that this wasn't digital trickery—no, the entire house and everything in it and outside it, even the lawn, had been painted the same color as before, just a little bit brighter. The yellowish carpet was more yellowish, the sofa more whatever dull color the sofa was; even Timmy's painting of Rogers Rock popped like a page from a comic book. The microwave. Mr. Jeffries's tackle box and that clickety old "internet computer." It looked like a cartoon of a memory or dream. It felt both empty and inhabited, dead and welcoming. Only the window to Harriet's bedroom was closed, unlit. It was obvious that many of the cameras had been set up from Emily's house, from her windows, roof, from the garden. Peppy's house, she thought. Emily lived somewhere else now. She kept turning her head, looking for Mr. Jeffries.

Three minutes later, his car arrived.

It pulled into the driveway, spectral and slow. He was coming home from a night shift. Harriet had said that she'd asked him to behave for one day exactly as he normally would but to not look at the cameras or turn off any of the lights. The car moved from one screen, disappeared, then came to rest in another screen. The headlights died. It took Mr. Jeffries a minute to open the door, get out.

He stood.

It was like watching a time-lapse video of an assassination. He sleepwalked into his house. Emily felt like she shouldn't be seeing this, it was too intimate, but she couldn't look away. She needed to see his face.

Emily was now completely on his time.

He moved from screen to screen. Emily had time to anticipate which screen the ghost would move into next and she adjusted her position accordingly, scooting herself in a circle around the room, thinking: As long as I can see him, he is safe. I must keep Howie safe. He went to the kitchen. Hovered. Opened the refrigerator and removed a can of ginger ale that Emily knew he hated. Like he was showing the camera, joking almost. He put it back. How he loved his daughter, Emily thought. This, finally, was his sailboat.

It took him twenty minutes to go upstairs. He disappeared for two minutes, probably while climbing the stairs, and Emily felt abandoned. The house became sinister, blaring with menace. She thought that anything could be hiding in there, waiting to hurt him.

Come back please.

He reappeared in the bathroom. He washed his face. He seemed to stare at his face for a long time, but Emily still couldn't quite see it. He was the only thing colored normally, and that, of course, made him look faded, as if he were disappearing. He wouldn't turn to her. Emily badly needed to see his face. Just one last time, she thought.

He brushed his teeth; and he flossed with the meticulousness of someone sewing up a wound. He continued to look at himself in the mirror, and leaves, outside the window, hung suspended in the air.

The bathroom mirror had been painted silver, Emily suddenly realized. There was no face looking back at Mr. Jeffries. But still he stared, as if the video had been paused.

He shut the bathroom lights off.

Emily gasped.

He wasn't supposed to do that, was he? She waited. Perhaps he was going to the toilet, but Emily didn't think so. She watched, for what felt like minutes, holding her breath, and there: she saw him.

Emily could just make him out, and she realized, with a jolt, that he'd been there the whole time. She had been looking right through him all that time. The shape of his head was discernible.

Howard Jeffries standing in the dark of the bathroom at the window, looking out. Did he see in slow motion, too? Emily wondered if his sight had gone ahead, in real time, gazing out into the future while the world around him ground to a halt.

He was looking at Emily.

He knew that she was there, looking at him. They were still keeping each other safe.

Thank you.

Emily began to cry.

Thank you for saving my life.

Suddenly the room that Emily was sitting in ceased to exist. The screens disappeared.

This was not part of *The Household Spirit*.

Emily heard a few cheers from the other room. Shouts of "Blackout!" *Wooooo*s and laughter and calls for looting; a wineglass shattering. Emily was paralyzed. Seconds later, the power returned, but the digital projectors had reset themselves. They showed only blue screens that blinked ERROR.

ERROR behind her. In front of her. To the side.

ERROR.

ERROR.

ERROR.

Harriet burst into the room, looked about. "Well, that's that," she said. "Sorry for abandoning you. Guess there's no point turning this back on now. Ethan's here, by the way. He had to walk twenty blocks and looks like a fucking Sasquatch . . ."

ERROR.

ERROR.

Emily, still sitting, said, "You can't just leave him there, Harriet."

"Wait, what?" Harriet said. "Emily, are you all right?"

ERROR.

Emily laughed; she shook her head no. She wiped the tears from her eyes. She just needed to see the end, she said. Emily needed to see what happened next. Harriet understood. She touched Emily's shoulder, then, without a word, went over and got the projectors working. She said she'd be back shortly. The momentary blackout had reignited the party.

The screens, once again, showed Mr. Jeffries returning home. But Harriet had sloppily synced the videos and now there were two Mr. Jeffries, then three. Four. He brushed his teeth at the same time that he opened the refrigerator for the ginger ale. He got out of his car after a long night of work. Then his car, on another screen, pulled up the driveway. Emily stood. You need to get as far away from here as possible. She was surrounded. She could not move. But then she heard it, like a hand reaching into her panic and waking her up. It sounded as if it was coming from the screens, from deep inside Emily's memory of home: a door opening, a blizzard, and the joy of a little girl shouting, "Daddy!"

Acknowledgments

I am grateful for the patience and invaluable guidance and expertise of my editor, Lexy Bloom, and agent, Sophie Lambert.

The editorial assistance of Shumon Basar, Peter Harmon, and Charly Wilder.

The Akademie Schloss Solitude Fellowship (Studio 33); Joyce and Michael Bala; Neil Castro and Jeffrey Wodicka; the Corporation of Yaddo; Jobcenter Neukölln; Ilke Froyen and the Passa Porta residency; the Hipsh/Wilder clan of Kansas City; twenty-five years of sleep paralysis attacks; Kevin Conroy Scott; Louis Frutel-Wodicka (my favorite person); and Mika Krogerus for the alte Scheiße and neu Home.

About the Author

Tod Wodicka was born in Glens Falls, New York. He is the author of *All Shall Be Well; and All Shall Be Well; and All Manner of Things Shall Be Well.* He lives in Berlin.

A Note on the Type

This book was set in Janson, a typeface long thought to have been made by the Dutchman Anton Janson, who was a practicing typefounder in Leipzig during the years 1668–1687. However, it has been conclusively demonstrated that these types are actually the work of Nicholas Kis (1650–1702), a Hungarian, who most probably learned his trade from the master Dutch typefounder Dirk Voskens.

Typeset by Scribe, Philadelphia, Pennsylvania
Printed and bound by Berryville Graphics, Berryville, Virginia
Designed by Iris Weinstein